About This

By Celia's Arbour by Walter Besant and
1877 in *The Graphic* magazine. Besan
directed his not inconsiderable talent into a tale full of lyrical and precise description of the Portsmouth of his childhood. Rich, vivid and strongly psychological in content, it gives an extraordinarily broad view of Portsmouth society in the mid-19th Century. It places the walled and heavily fortified town at the heart of world events that seem to touch its inhabitants only obliquely, yet they ultimately affect every aspect of their existence. International wars, conspiracies and espionage form the backdrop for the lives of Laddy, Leonard and Celia, whose friendship is explored in this fascinating Victorian novel.

This volume has been completely reset and edited, and includes a preface by Dr Alison Habens, lecturer in Creative Writing at the University of Portsmouth, who gives modern readers a fresh insight into the setting of this beautifully written novel.

Novels by Dr Alison Habens

Dreamhouse
Lifestory
Pencilwood
The True Picture

Books from Life Is Amazing with a Portsmouth theme

Fiction
The Snow Witch - A Portsmouth Novel, by Matt Wingett
Turn The Tides Gently (ebook), by Matt Wingett
The Song of Miss Tolstoy (ebook), by Matt Wingett
Portsmouth Fairy Tales for Grown-Ups - anthology
Dark City - Portsmouth Tales of Haunting and Horror - anthology
Day of the Dead - anthology by Portsmouth Writers' Hub

Non-Fiction
Conan Doyle and the Mysterious World of Light, by Matt Wingett
Ten Years In A Portsmouth Slum, by Robert Dolling
(edited by Matt Wingett)
The History of Portsmouth, by Lake Allen
(edited by Matt Wingett)
Recollections of John Pounds, by Henry Hawkes
(edited by Matt Wingett)

Comedy / Novelty
A Pompey Person's Guide to Everything Great About Southampton
A Southampton Person's Guide to Everything Great About Portsmouth

BY CELIA'S ARBOUR

A TALE OF PORTSMOUTH TOWN

WALTER BESANT
JAMES RICE

Preface by Dr Alison Habens
Edited by Matt Wingett

Life Is Amazing

A Life Is Amazing Paperback

By Celia's Arbour

This New Edition first published 2016 by Life Is Amazing
ISBN: 978-0-9572413-7-4

Cover Art and Design by Matt Wingett
Taken from an original handcoloured engraving,
"Southsea Castle", circa 1830.

Contents

Preface

Like Charles Dickens, Sir Walter Besant was born in Portsmouth but twenty four years later, in 1836. Also like Dickens, ultimately making London his home, Besant documented the lives of the underprivileged in his naturalistic novels, peopled with orphans and women of dubious repute, accountants and criminals and philanthropists. Unlike Dickens, the name of Walter Besant is barely remembered today, though his list of almost fifty publications were best-sellers in his day. So who was Besant? What pleasures await the visitor to his 1878 novel set in the town of Portsmouth? And how has he, a founder member of the Society of Authors, been so long forgotten on the local literary scene?

The son of a Portsea merchant, born in St George's Square, Walter had two brothers, William and Frank, the latter a clergyman who was married to the more famous Annie Besant. She was known for going against the grain, campaigning first for Irish and Indian self-rule, then for women's rights and church reform, finally as a leading proponent of Theosophy. When she and Frank separated, it's possible that the Besant brothers started pronouncing their surname Bes*ant*, with the emphasis on the second not first syllable, to distance themselves from her radical reputation.

Walter Besant lived in the town only until he finished his education at St. Paul's School, which was on the site of the current St Paul's Square; one of the many public and private academies lost in the bombing which wrecked so much of the city in World War Two. St Paul's was not, apparently, an outstanding school, but good enough for Besant to go on and graduate from Christ's College, Cambridge, before teaching mathematics in Lancashire, Leamington and Mauritius. Settling in London in 1867 he is remembered best for his history and topography of the capital in many volumes. Besant never moved back to Portsmouth.

Yet he refers to it, affectionately, as 'the most magnificent harbour in the world' in the opening scene of *By Celia's Arbour*, when the central characters stand on the old city walls, peeping over the parapet towards Portsdown. 'If you looked through the embrasure of the wall, you had a splendid framed picture – water for foreground, old ruined castle in middle distance, blue hill beyond, and above blue sky.' Quite the contrast to Dickens, who said, instead: 'I was born at Portsmouth, principally remarkable for mud, Jews and sailors'!

Besant accompanies his picturesque opening scene with 'evening gun and tintamarre': 'such a firing of muskets, such a beating of drums, playing of fifes, ringing of bells, and sounding of trumpets, that you would have thought the sun was setting once for all...' He brings us back to that place on the city walls he calls Celia's Arbour again at the end of the story, five years later: 'Listen: there is the booming of guns from the Blockhouse Fort; a great ship has come home from a long cruise. Is every salute in future to remind me of Celia?'

The spot where our three characters are standing was demolished in the 1880s. Those original town walls had a view across 'the moat, and beyond the moat a ravelin, and beyond the ravelin the sea-wall; beyond the wall a smooth and placid lake...' The ravelin was a triangle-shaped fortification, found on several places along the old defences, including where the university's Ravelin House now sits, though this could not have been *the* ravelin Besant and Rice mention, since it is nowhere near the sea.

In that setting, an 'eternal triangle' plot. When Besant gave a lecture on The Art of Fiction at the Royal Institution in 1884 he described how, 'the novelist studies men and women; he is concerned with their actions and their thoughts, their errors and their follies, their greatness and their meanness; the forces which act upon them; the passions, prejudices, hopes and fears which pull them this way and that... The very first rule in Fiction is that the human interest must absolutely absorb everything else.'

Testing his new formula for popular fiction, Besant gives us three realistic characters, with a plot which has clear challenges for each to overcome. It was first published in serial form in *The Graphic* and then in three volumes as a novel. There is plenty of human interest in this tale of childhood friends in Portsmouth town: two men and one woman; a 'bromance', a romance, and a melancholy platonic love, with danger from a heartless villain.

For many readers across the nation in the 1870s, following these vibrant characters and their predicaments, the locale of 'the Queen's Bastion' was neither here nor there. For the keen local historian and bibliophile today, though, hoping to find the exact spot the threesome would have stood on the city walls, there are some clues in Besant's text. He describes the site as a pastoral idyll: 'the place where the grass was longest and greenest, the wild convolvulus most abundant, and where the noblest of the great elms which stood upon the ramparts – "to catch the enemy' shells" said Leonard - threw out a gracious arm laden with leafy foliage to give a shade.' As he speaks, he leans against a cannon, an 'old-fashioned 32-pounder', pointing straight up the harbour.

According to old maps, there was no Queen's Bastion; and the old walls that guarded the town were demolished in Queen Victoria's reign as technological advances in weaponry made them redundant. They were replaced by a massive chain of new fortifications around the island's edge and along the top of Portsdown Hill, with four Solent forts: Horse Sand, No Man's Land, Spitbank and St Helen's. No wonder Celia's Arbour is difficult to pinpoint exactly from the novel's descriptions of a north-west facing view through an embrasure, towards Portchester Castle, so fondly remembered by Besant from his childhood.

Some readers in his day must also have been seeking that tranquil spot because, in the Pall Mall Gazette for 6th February 1892, the location is revealed: 'Mr Walter Besant says it is quite right to place Celia's Arbour at the end of the Portsea Walls near the Anchor Gate. The Bastion looked out on the harbour, facing north and west.' Today this places it at the end of Anchor Gate Road, in the the naval dockyard.

(In the course of research for this publication, Matt Wingett and I pinpointed the location variously on the site of Beeston's Bastion, which stood where the modernday Isle Of Wight ferry port stands today, and near the site of Portsmouth University's Lion Gate Building. Though these suppositions were ultimately proved wrong, we've yet to disprove our proposed siting of the Captain's garden at the end of a little cul-de-sac called Sun Street, off St George's Square, which he renamed as St Faith's for the novel.)

The other place key to the storyline is the home of the retired seaman who takes in the two orphan boys and turns their lives around. 'The Captain's house, one of a row, stood separated from the street by the respectability of three feet clear and an iron railing. It looked out upon the Mill-dam, an artificial lake designed, I believe, to flood the moats of the fortifications if necessary. The Mill-dam was not without its charm...' This, of course, is the site of the University of Portsmouth's Milldam Building, where once the sound of mill-wheels and the race of water would have ruled till, as Ladislas relates: 'They have filled up the Mill-dam now; pulled down the King's Mill; destroyed the redoubt; and replaced the bright, sparkling sheet of water with an open field, on which they have made a military hospital.'

Near this same site, the young men were educated, as students of English and History are still, by a course of improving literature and healthy debate. The house probably stood between today's St George's Square and the north edge of the old millpond, in line with Park Road and the railway. And here: 'The only reading Leonard permitted himself lay in books which showed how men have risen from small beginnings to great things. Not greatness in the way of authorship. He had no feeling for literary success. “I would like,” he said, “to have my share in making history, let who will write it. Who would not rather be Hannibal than Livy, or Hector than Homer? If you were to offer me the choice between Sir Philip Sidney and Shakespeare, I would rather be Sidney. All the greatest men have been soldiers and sailors – fighting men.”'

So, what of the non-fighting men who penned this book together? Nothing is known about the writing relationship between Besant and James Rice. Of Besant's forty-plus novels, thirteen were written with Rice. *Ready-Money Mortiboy* made them household names, and they continued with some other staples of Victorian page-turning such as *The Golden Butterfly*, *The Chaplain of the Fleet* and *The Son of Vulcan*. It seems certain that if Rice hadn't died prematurely in 1881 (he was one of the first recorded peanut allergy sufferers) they may have gone on writing together. Rice didn't publish anything (that is on record) without Besant: but as far as literary history remembers Besant, it is almost entirely without ‘and James Rice.’ So it is fascinating to muse on their creative process and wonder how they would have worked on a book like *By Celia's Arbour*.

The novel is tightly plotted, driven by characterisation along the very lines Besant was talking in *The Art of Fiction*. No rambling experiment, the pair could have mapped it chapter by chapter in exact detail, then allocated chapters each to write. It seems likely that Besant wrote the introduction; the effusive scene-setting with nostalgic sights of local interest must surely be his. In several sections we find that same style: slower, more sedate, more visual with less dialogue. The romantic Portsmouth backdrop is probably his, also its sentimental resolution. But in between, we may surmise, are set-pieces penned by Rice; faster paced, with quirky characters, dialogue-based. I imagine the more legal and political aspects were contributed by the lawyer, Rice, and the comic dialects, etc. To call it ‘sub-Dickens’ shouldn't be a dreadful insult; as there are certainly mud, Jews and sailors!

An unexpected feature of the delightfully packed narrative is the appearance of Polish refugees in Portsmouth in the 1850s. In fact, the first group of Polish soldiers arrived by chance when their boat was caught in a storm en route to exile in America, in 1834. (They stayed and built barracks in the town, and have a fine memorial in Kingston Cemetery.) In this story, Ladislas was rescued by his parents' loyal servant Wassielewski when they were murdered by the Russian Tzar, and brought to safety, though disinherited, in Portsmouth. But he says, ‘I was certainly more English than Polish. I could not speak my father's language. I belonged to the English Church, I was educated in the manners of thought common to Englishmen, insular, perhaps, and narrow; when the greatness of England was spoken of, I took that greatness to myself, and was glad. England's victories were mine, England's cause my own, and it was like the loss of half my identity to be reminded that I was not a Briton at all, but a Pole, the son of a long line of Poles, with a duty owed to my country.'

In unravelling the text to see which bits were Besant's and which were written by Rice, I wonder if the 'Polish question' were a shared concern of theirs, discussed at length during the meetings they were certain to have enjoyed at one or other's desks or dining tables. No doubt they discoursed on the liberation of Poland: 'A dream – an idle dream. Poland is no more. The Poles are become Austrians, Prussians, and, above all, Muscovites.' They give this mournful line to 'Laddy' from their own mouths, surely; a fresh topic of the time. And the modern reader could well be surprised to learn that immigrants in Pompey today, Poles in particular, are not such a novelty as some in the city might think.

On Portsmouth's 'literary leyline', where famous 19th century authors lived along leafy avenues through Southsea, Besant has been forgotten; but his impact on those big names was significant. Rudyard Kipling was inspired to become a writer when he read Besant's 1883 book *All in a Garden Fair*. And in a curious story of Conan Doyle's, written after a bout of writer's block, well before he dreamed up Sherlock Holmes, the figure of Walter Besant appears to the hero, Cyprian Overbeck Wells, to help dictate his great work alongside laureates like Sterne and Stephenson and Smollet.

By Celia's Arbour was a rare book, out of print and off the library shelves, in danger of being lost forever, until this new edition in 2016. So now there is a chance to tread the cobbled streets and climb the ramparts of Victorian Portsea again, accompanied by a cast of beguiling characters, in a plot with all the rich pickings of a Dickens.

Dr Alison Habens
alisonhabens.com

By Celia's Arbour

CHAPTER I.
ON THE QUEEN'S BASTION.

TWO boys and a girl, standing together in the north-west corner of the Queen's Bastion on the old town wall.

Leonard, the elder boy, leans on an old-fashioned 32-pounder which points through an embrasure, narrow at the mouth and wide at the end, straight up the harbour.

Should any enemy attempt to cross the lagoon of mud which forms the upper harbour at low tide, that enemy would, as Leonard often explained, be "raked" by the gun. Leonard is a lad between seventeen and eighteen, tall and well-grown. As yet his figure is too slight, but that will fill out; his shoulders are broad enough for the strength a year or two more will give him; he has short brown hair of quite a common colour, but lustrous, and with a natural curl in it; his eyes are hazel, and they are steadfast; when he fought battles at school those eyes looked like winning; his chin is strong and square; his lips are firm. Only to look upon him as he passed, you would say that you had seen a strong man in his youth. People turned their heads after he had gone by to have another look at such a handsome boy.

He leans his back, now, against the gun, his hands resting lightly upon the carriage on either side, as if to be ready for immediate action; his straw hat lies on the grass beside him. And he is looking in the face of the girl.

She is a mere child of thirteen or fourteen, standing before him and gazing into his face with sad and solemn eyes. She, too, is bareheaded, carrying her summer hat by the ribbons. I suppose no girl of fourteen, when girls are bony, angular, and bigfooted, can properly be described as beautiful; but Celia was always beautiful to me. Her face remains the same to me through the changes of many years—always lovely, always sweet and winsome. Her eyes were light blue, and yet not shallow; she had a pair of mutinous little lips which were generally, but not to-night, laughing; her hair hung over her shoulders in the long and unfettered tresses which so well become young maidens; and in her cheek was the prettiest little dimple ever seen. But now she looked sad, and tears were gathered in her eyes.

As for me, I was lying on the parapet of the wall, looking at the other two. Perhaps it will save trouble if I state at once who I was, and what to look upon. In the year 1853 I was sixteen years of age, about two years older than Celia, nearly two years younger than Leonard. I believe I had already arrived at my present tall stature, which is exactly five feet one inch. I am a hunchback. An accident in infancy rounded my shoulders and arched my back, giving me a projection which causes my coats to hang loosely where other men's fit tight, forcing my neck forward so that my head bends back where other people's heads are held straight upon their necks. It was an unfortunate accident, because I should, but for it, have grown into a strong man; my limbs are stout and my arms are muscular. It cost me nothing as a boy to climb up ropes and posts, to clamber hand over hand along a rail, to get up into trees, to do anything where I could get hold for a single hand or for a single foot. I was not—through my unlucky back, the distortion of my neck, and the length of my arm—comely to look upon. All the years of my childhood, and some a good deal later, were spent in the miserable effort to bring home to myself the plain fact that I was *disgracié*. The comeliness of youth and manhood could be no more mine than my father's broad lands; for, besides being a hunchback, I was an exile, a Pole, the son of a Polish rebel, and therefore penniless. My name is Ladislas Pulaski.

We were standing, as I said, in the north-west corner of the Queen's Bastion, the spot where the grass was longest and greenest, the wild convolvulus most abundant, and where the noblest of the great elms which stood upon the ramparts—"to catch the enemy's shells," said Leonard—threw out a gracious arm laden with leafy foliage to give a shade. We called the place Celia's Arbour.

If you looked out over the parapet, you saw before you the whole of the most magnificent harbour in the world; and if you looked through the embrasure of the wall, you had a splendid framed picture—water for foreground, old ruined castle in middle distance, blue hill beyond, and above blue sky.

We were all three silent, because it was Leonard's last evening with us. He was going away, our companion and brother, and we were there to bid him God speed.

It was after eight; suddenly the sun, which a moment before was a great disc of burnished gold, sank below the thin line of land between sky and sea.

Then the evening gun from the Duke of York's bastion proclaimed the death of another day with a loud report, which made the branches in the trees above us to shake and tremble. And from the barracks in the town; from the Harbour Admiral's flagship; from the Port Admiral's flagship; from the flagship of the Admiral in command of the Mediterranean Fleet, then in harbour; from the tower of the old church, there came such a firing of muskets, such a beating of drums, playing of fifes, ringing of bells, and sounding of trumpets, that you would have thought the sun was setting once for all, and receiving his farewell salute from a world he was leaving for ever to roll about in darkness.

The evening gun and the *tintamarre* that followed roused us all three, and we involuntarily turned to look across the parapet. Beyond that was the moat, and beyond the moat was a ravelin, and beyond the ravelin the sea-wall; beyond the wall a smooth and placid lake, for it was high tide, four miles long and a couple of miles wide, in which the splendour of the west was reflected so that it looked like a furnace of molten metal. At low tide it would have been a great flat level of black mud, unlovely even with an evening sky upon it, intersected with creeks and streams which, I suppose, were kept full of water by the drainage of the mud-banks.

At the end of the harbour stood the old ruined castle, on the very margin and verge of the water. The walls were reflected in the calm bosom of the lagoon; the water gate opened out upon wavelets of the lapping tide; behind rose the great donjon, square, grey, and massive; in the tourney-yard stood the old church, and we needed no telling to make us think of the walls behind, four feet broad, rugged and worn by the tooth of Time, thickly blossoming with gillyflowers, clutched and held on all sides by the tight embrace of the ivy. There had been rain in the afternoon, so that the air was clear and transparent, and you could see every stone in the grand old keep, every dentation of the wall.

Behind the castle lay the low curved line of a long hill, green and grassy, which made a background to the harbour and the old fortress. It stretched for six miles, this hill, and might have been monotonous but for the chalk quarries which studded its side with frequent intervals of white. Farther on, to the west, there lay a village, buried in a great clump of trees, so that you could see nothing but the tower of a church and the occasional smoke of a chimney. The village was so far off, that it seemed like some outlying fort, an advance work of civilisation, an outpost such as those which the Roman conquerors have left in the desert. When your eye left the village among the trees and travelled southwards, you could see very little of land on the other side by reason of the ships which intervened—ships of every age, of every class, of every colour, of every build; frigates, three-deckers, brigs, schooners, cutters, launches, gunboats, paddle-wheel steamers, screw steamers, hulks so old as to be almost shapeless—they were lying ranged in line, or they were moored separately; some in the full flood of the waning sunset, some in shadow, one behind the other, making deep blacknesses in the golden water. There was not much life at this late hour in the harbour. Here and there a boat pulled by two or three lads from the town; here and there a great ship's gig, moving heavily through the water, pulled by a crew of sailors, rowing with their slow and measured stroke, and the little middy sitting in the stern; or perhaps a wherry coming down from Fareham Creek. But mostly the harbour was silent, the bustle even at the low end having ceased with the sunset.

"What do you see up the harbour, Leonard?" asked the girl, for all of us were gazing silently at the glorious sight.

"I am looking for my future, Cis, and I cannot make it out."

"Tell us what you think, Leonard."

"Five minutes ago it looked splendid. But the glory is going off the water. See, Cis, the castle has disappeared—there is nothing to be made out there but a low black mass of shade; and the ships are so many black logs lying on grey water that in ten minutes will be black too. Nothing but blackness. Is that my future?"

"I can read you a better fortune out of the sunset than that," I interposed.

"Do, Laddy," said Celia. "Don't let poor Leonard go away with a bad omen."

"If you look above you, Leonard," I went on,"you will see that all the splendours of the earth have gone up into the heavens. Look at the brightness there. Was there ever a more glorious sunset? There is a streak of colour for you!—the one above the belt of salmon —blue, with just a suspicion on the far edge of green. Leonard, if you believed in visions, and wished for the best possible, you could have nothing better than that before you. If your dreams were to get money and rubbish like that"—it will be remembered that I who enunciated this sentiment, and Celia who clapped her hands, and Leonard who nodded gravely, were all three very young—"such rubbish, it would lead you to disappointment, just as the golden water is turning black. But up above the colours are brighter, and they are lasting; they never fade."

"They are fading now, Laddy."

"Nonsense. Sunsets never fade. They are for ever moving westwards round the world. Don't you know that there is always sunset going on somewhere? Gold in evening clouds for us to see, and a golden sunrise for some others. So, Leonard, when your dreams of the future were finished you looked up, and you saw the sky brighter than the harbour. That means that the future will be brighter than you ever dreamed."

Leonard laughed.

"You agree with Laddy, Cis? Of course you do. As if you two ever disagreed yet!"

"I must go home, Leonard; it is nearly nine. And, oh! you are going away to-night, and when—when shall we see you again?"

"I am going away to-night, Cis. I have said good-bye to the Captain, God bless him, and I am going to London by the ten o'clock train to seek my fortune."

"But you will write to us, Leonard, won't you? You will tell us what you are doing, and where you are, and all about yourself."

He shook his head.

"No, Cis, not even that. Listen. I have talked it all over with the Captain. I am going to make my fortune—somehow. I don't know how, nor does he, the dear old man. But I am going to try. Perhaps I shall fail, perhaps I shall succeed. I must succeed." His face grew stern and a little hard."Because everything depends upon it, whether I shall be a gentleman, or what a gutter child ought to expect."

"Don't, Leonard."

"Forgive me, Laddy, but everybody knows that you are a gentleman by birth and descent, and very few know that I am too. Give me five years. In five years' time, if I live, and unless it is absolutely impossible for me to get home, I promise to meet you both again. It will be June the 21st in the year 1858. We will meet at this time—sunset—and on this same spot, by Celia's Arbour."

"In five years. It is half a lifetime. What will have happened to us all in five years? But not a single letter? O Leonard, promise to write one letter, only one, during all the years, to say that you are well. Not leave us all the time without a single word."

He shook his head.

"Not one, Cis, my child. I am not going to write you a single letter. One only thing I have promised the Captain. If I am in danger, sickness, or any trouble, I am to write to him. But if you get no news of me set it down to good news."

"Then, if you will not write, there is nothing to look forward to but the end of the five years. Laddy, don't you feel as if you were a convict beginning a five years' sentence? I do, and perhaps you will forget all about us, Leonard, when you are away over there, in the great world."

"Forget you, Cissy?" He took her hands, and drew the girl to himself. "Forget you? Why, there is nothing else in all the world for me to remember except you, and Laddy, and the Captain. If I could forget the seventeen years of my life, the town, and the port, the ships, and the sailors, the old walls, and the bastions—if I could rid my memory of all that is in it now, why—then, perhaps, I could forget little Cissy. Other men belong to families. I have none. Other men have brothers and sisters. I have none. Laddy is my brother, and you are my sister. Never think, Cis, that I can forget you for one moment."

"No, Leonard, we will try to feel always that you are thinking about us.

The Captain says nothing is better for people than always to remember what others would like them to say, and think, and do. Stay, Leonard." She had made a little bouquet of daisies and the sweet wild convolvulus which spread itself over all the slopes of the walls. Out of this she picked two or three blossoms, tied them up with a tendril, and laid them in a paper. "That is my French exercise for to-morrow. Never mind. There, Leonard, carry that away with you, to remember me by."

"I will take it, Cis, but I want nothing to remember you by."

"And now, Leonard, make your promise over again. Say after me, 'in five years' time'"

"In five years' time"—

"'In rags or in velvet'—be very particular about that, Leonard; you are neither to be too proud to come nor too ashamed, in rags or in velvet."

"In rags or in velvet."

"'In poverty or in riches.'"

"In poverty or in riches."

"'In honour or'—no, there can be no dishonour—'in honour or before the honour has been reached, I will return.'"

"I will return," echoed Leonard.

"And we will meet you here, Laddy and I."

He held her hands while she dictated the words of this solemn promise, looking up at him with earnest and pleading face.

Then the church clock struck nine, and from the Port Admiral's flagship boomed a solitary gun, which rolled in short, sharp echoes along the walls, and then slowly thundered up the shores of the harbour. Then there was a pause. And then the bells began their customary evening hymn. They struck the notes slowly, and as if with effort. But the hymn-tune was soft and sad, and a carillon is always sweet. That finished, there came the curfew bell, which has been rung every night in the old town since the time of the great Norman king. The day was quite done now, and the twilight of the summer night was upon us. Gleams of grey lay in the west reflected in the untroubled sheet of the harbour, the cloudless sky looked almost as blue as in the day, and the stars were faint and pale. Venus alone shone brightly; the trees, in the warm, calm night, looked as if they were sleeping, all but one—a great elm which stood at the end of the wall, where it joined the dockyard. It was shaped in the black profile of the evening, something like the face of a man, so that it stood like a giant sentry looking every night across the harbour.

"I must go," said Celia."Good-bye, Leonard. Goodbye, dear Leonard. Forgive me if I have teased you. We shall look forward—Oh! how eagerly we shall look forward to the end of the five years. Good-bye."

He took her in his arms, and kissed her again and again. She cried and sobbed. Then he let her go, and without a word she fled from us both, flying down the grassy slope across the green. In the twilight we could catch the glimmer of her white dress as she ran home, until she reached her father's garden gate, and was lost.

"Walk with me to the station, Laddy," said Leonard.

We walked away from the quiet walls where there was no one but ourselves, out from the shadow of the big elms, and the breath of dewy grass, and the peacefulness of the broad waters, down into the busy streets. Our way lay through the narrowest and the noisiest. Shops were open, especially places which sold things to eat and to drink. Hundreds of men—chiefly young men—were loafing about, pipes in their mouths, among the women, who were buying in a street market, consisting almost entirely of costers' carts and barrows, and where the principal articles exposed for sale appeared to be hot cooked things of pungent and appetising odour, served and dressed with fried onions. Every night, all the year round, that market went on; every night that incense of fried onions arose to the much-enduring skies; every night the crowd jostled, pushed, and enjoyed their jokes around these barrows, lit by candles stuck in bottles, protected by oiled paper.

"Look at them," said Leonard, indicating a little knot of young fellows laughing together at each other's *gros mots*."Look at them. If it had not been for the Captain I might have been like them."

"So might I, for that matter."

"What a life! No ambition! No hope to get beyond the pipe and beer! If I fail it will be better than never to have tried. Laddy, I mean to make a spoon or spoil a horn, as the Scotch say."

"How, Leonard."

"I do not know quite. Somehow, Laddy. Here we are at the station. You will be good to the old man, won't you? Of course you will, Laddy, a great deal better than I could ever be, because you are so much more considerate. Keep up his spirits, make him spin yarns. And you will look sharp after the little girl, Laddy. She is your great charge. I give her into your keeping. Why, when I come back she will be nineteen, and I shall be four-and-twenty. Think of that. Laddy, before I go I am going to tell you a great secret. Keep it entirely to yourself. Let no one hear a word of it, not even the Captain."

"Not even Cis?"

"Why, that would spoil all. Listen. If I come back in five years' time, a gentleman, a real gentleman by position as I am by birth, I mean to—to ask little Celia to marry me."

I laughed.

"How do you know you will care for her then?"

"I know that very well," he replied. "I shall never care in the same way for any other girl. That is quite certain. But oh, what a slender chance it is! I am to make myself a gentleman in five years. Celia has got to get through these five years without falling in love with anybody else. Of course all the fellows in the place will be after her. And I have got to please her when I do come back. Wish me luck, Laddy, and good-bye, and God bless you all three."

He squeezed my hand, and rushed into a carriage as the engine whistled, the bell rang, and the train moved away. Then I realised that Leonard was really gone, and that we should not see him again for five long years.

CHAPTER II.
THE CAPTAIN.

I WALKED home sadly enough, thinking how dull life for the next five years was going to be. It was half-past ten when I arrived, but the Captain was sitting up beyond his usual hour, waiting to hear the last news of Leonard. He was at the open window overlooking his garden; before him stood his glass of grog, empty, and his evening pipe was finished.

"You saw him off, Laddy?" he asked with a little eagerness, as if Leonard might possibly be lurking in the hall. "You are quite sure he got safely into the train"—five-and-twenty years ago people were not so familiar with railway trains, and they were generally regarded, even by old sailors, as things uncertain about going off, as well as untrustworthy when you were in them. "Poor lad! At Winchester by this time, very nearly. Thirty miles from salt water."

The Captain at this time was about sixty years of age. He was a man of short and sturdy build, with a broad and rosy face like an apple, and perfectly white hair. His whiskers, equally white, were cut to the old-fashioned regulation "mutton-chop," very much like what has now come into fashion again. They advanced into the middle of the cheek, and were then squared off in a line which met the large stiff collar below at an angle of forty-five. Round the collar the Captain wore a white cravat, which put on many folds as the weather grew cold. He never appeared except in some sort of uniform, and paraded his profession habitually, as was the custom among sailors of his standing, by a blue frock with anchor buttons. In winter, he wore loose blue trousers, which, when the warmer days returned, he exchanged for white ducks. Upstairs he kept a uniform of surpassing splendour, with epaulettes, sword-belt, sword, gold lace, and an innumerable number of buttons. But this was reserved for ceremonies, as when a ship was launched, or when the Port Admiral invited the Captain to dinner, or when the Queen visited the Yard. On all other occasions, the blue frock with brass buttons formed the Captain's only wear.

He had great white beetling eyebrows, which would have lent him a ferocious aspect but for the twinkling blue eyes beneath them. There were crows'-feet lying thick about those eyes, which gave them a curiously humorous look, not belied by the mobile lips below.

You might see, by the light of the single pair of candles, that it was a plainly furnished room, having in it little besides a small square table, a horsehair sofa, a wooden armchair, a bookshelf with a hundred volumes or so, most of them boys' school books, and a piano which was mine, given me by Mr. Tyrrell. The walls were decorated with pictures of naval engagements and ships, cut out of illustrated papers, or picked up at second-hand shops, mounted and framed by the Captain himself. Above the mantelshelf was a print of the Battle of Navarino, showing the Asia engaged with two Egyptian and Turkish men-of-war, one on each side of her, the rest of the action being invisible by reason of the smoke. The Captain would contemplate that picture with a satisfaction quite beyond the power of words.

"'Twas in '27," he would say; "I was Lieutenant then: Sir Edward Codrington was Admiral. We sailed into Naverino harbour at 2 P.M. after dinner. Gad! it was a warm afternoon we had, and lucky it was the lads dined before it. Something to remember afterwards. Don't tell me that Turks can't fight. A better fight was never made even by the French in the old days. But their ships, of course, were not handled like ours, and out of eighty odd craft, which made up their fleet, we didn't leave a dozen fit for sea again."

And on the mantelshelf was a model, made by the Captain, of the Asia herself.

The piano, I explained above, was my own. Everything else I had in the world came from the Captain; the clothes I wore were bought by him; it was he who brought me up, educated me, and lifted me out of the mire. I am bankrupt in gratitude to the Captain. I have no words to say what I owe to him. I can never repay, by any words, acts, or prayers, the load of obligation under which I rejoice to be towards that good man.

It began, his incomparable benevolence to Leonard and to me, like a good many other important things, with a crime. Not a very great crime; nor was the criminal a very important person; but, as the Rev. Mr. Pontifex once said of it, it was emphatically a wrong thing, and, like all wrong things, ought to be remembered with repentance. Mr. Pontifex, although he had never had the opportunity of reading a certain great Bishop's Treaties on the Sinfulness of Little Sins, was as uncompromising as that Prelate could wish, and I hope that Leonard, who was the criminal, has long since repented. Certainly it was the infraction of a commandment. Now Mr. Pontifex has repeatedly asserted, and his wife approved, that he who breaks one commandment breaks all. This is what was done.

The Captain's house, one of a row, stood separated from the street by the respectability of three feet clear and an iron railing. It was close to St. Faith's Square, a fashionable and almost aristocratic quarter, inhabited by retired naval officers, a few men who had made fortunes in business and a sprinkling of lawyers. It was a plain square red-brick house, with nothing remarkable about it but the garden at the back. This was not a large garden, and, like others in the old town, was originally intended as a drying ground—all builders in those days were accustomed to consider a house as, in the first instance, a family laundry. The garden was planted with raspberry canes, gooseberry bushes, and currant-trees. Peaches and plums were trained along the walls. There were one or two small pear-trees, and there was a very fine mulberry. In the spaces the Captain cultivated onions, radishes, and lettuce with great success. But the garden was remarkable in having no back wall. It looked out upon the Mill-dam, an artificial lake designed, I believe, to flood the moats of the fortifications if necessary. Projecting iron spikes prevented the neighbours on either hand from invading our territory, and you could sit on the stone-work at the end of the wall with your feet dangling over the water. It was a broad sheet periodically lowered and raised by the tide, which rushed in and ran out by a passage under the roadway, close to which was the King's Mill, worked by the tide. Sitting in the garden you could hear the steady grinding noise of the mill-wheels. The Mill-dam was not without its charm. In the centre stood an island redoubt, set with trees like the walls, and connected with the road which crossed the water by a light iron bridge. There was a single-storied house upon that island, and I remember thinking that it must be the grandest thing in the world to live upon it, all alone, or perhaps with Celia, to have a cask of provisions and absolute liberty to wander round and round the grassy fort, particularly if the iron bridge could be knocked away, and a boat substituted.

They have filled up the Mill-dam now; pulled down the King's Mill; destroyed the redoubt; and replaced the bright, sparkling sheet of water with an open field, on which they have made a military hospital. The garden at the back of the house has got a wall too, now. But I wish they had let the old things remain as they were.

It was in this garden that the Captain was accustomed to sit after dinner, except when the weather was too cold. One day, nine or ten years before my story begins, he repaired thither on a certain sultry day in August at half-past two in the afternoon. He had with him a long pipe and a newspaper. He placed his arm-chair under the shade of the mulberry-tree, then rich with ripe purple fruit, and sat down to read at ease. Whether it was the languor of the day, or the mild influence of the mill hard by, or the effects of the pipe, is not to be rashly decided, but the Captain presently exchanged the wooden chair for the grass under the mulberry-tree, upon which, mindful of his white ducks and the fallen fruit, he spread a rug, and then leaning back against the trunk, which was sloped by Nature for this very purpose, he gazed for a few moments upon the dazzling surface of the Mill-dam, and then fell fast asleep.

Now, at very low tides the water in the Mill-dam would run out so far as to leave a narrow belt of dry shingle under the stone wall, and that happened on this very afternoon. Presently there came creeping along this little beach, all alone, with curious and wondering eyes, which found something to admire in every pebble, a little boy of eight. He was bare-footed and bare-headed, a veritable little gutter boy, clad almost in rags. It was a long way round the lake from the only place where he could have got down, a good quarter of a mile at least, and he stopped at the bottom of the Captain's garden for two excellent reasons: one that he felt tired and thirsty, and the other that the tide was already racing in through the mill like the rapids of Niagara, that it already covered the beach in front and behind, and was advancing with mighty strides over the little strip on which he stood. And it occurred to that lonely little traveller that unless he could get out of the mess, something dreadful in the shape of wet feet and subsequent drowning would happen to him.

He was a little frightened at the prospect, and began to cry gently. But he was not a foolish child, and he reflected immediately that crying was no good. So he looked at the wall behind him. It was a sea wall with a little slope, only about five feet high, and built with rough stones irregularly dressed, so as to afford foot and hand hold for anybody who wished to climb up or down. In two minutes the young mountaineer had climbed the dizzy height and stood upon the stone coping, looking back to the place he had come from. Below him the water was flowing where he had stood just now; and turning round he found himself in a garden with some one, a gentleman in white trousers, white waistcoat, and white hair, with a blue coat, sitting in the shade. His jolly red face was lying sideways, lovingly against the tree, his cap on the grass beside him; his mouth was half open; his eyes were closed; while a soft melodious snore, like the contented hymn of some aesthetic pigling, proclaimed aloud to the young observer that the Captain was asleep.

The boy advanced towards the sleeping stranger in a manner common to one of tender age, that is, on all fours, giving action to his hands and arms in imitation of an imaginary wild beast. He crept thus, first to the right side, then to the left, and then between the wide-spread legs of the Captain, peering into his unconscious face. Then he suddenly became conscious that he was under a mulberry-tree, that the fruit was ripe, that a chair was standing convenient for one who might wish to help himself, and that one branch lower than the rest hung immediately over the chair, so that even a child might reach out his hand and gather the fruit.

This was the Wrong Thing lamented by the Rev. Mr. Pontifex. The unprincipled young robber, after quite realising the position of things—strange garden—gentleman of marine calling sound asleep—ripe fruit—present thirst— overwhelming curiosity to ascertain if this kind of fruit resembled apples—yielded without resistance to temptation, and mounted the chair.

Five minutes later, the Captain lazily opened his eyes.

Boom—boom—boom—the mill was going with redoubled vigour, for the tide had turned since he fell asleep, and was now rushing through the dark subterranean avenues with a mighty roar. But except for the tide and the mill everything was very quiet. Accustomed noises do not keep people awake. Thus in the next garden but one two brothers were fighting, but as this happened every day, and all day, it did not disturb the Captain. One was worsted in the encounter. He ran away and got into some upper chamber, from the window of which he yelled in a hoarse stammer to his victorious brother, who was red-haired, "J—J—Jack—you're a c—c—c—carrotty thief." But invective of this kind, not addressed to himself, only gently tickled the Captain's tympanum. The sun was still very bright, the air was balmy, and I think he would have fallen asleep again but for one thing. A strange sound smote his ears. It was a sound like unto the smacking of tongues and the sucking of lips; or like the pleased champing of gratified teeth; a soft and gurgling sound; with, unless the Captain's ears greatly deceived him, a low breathing of great contentment. He listened lazily, wondering what this sound might mean. While he listened, a mulberry fell upon his nose and bounded off, making four distinct leaps from nose to shirt-front, from shirt-front to white waistcoat, from waistcoat to ducks, and from ducks to the rug. That was nothing remarkable. Mulberries will fall when over-ripe, and the Captain had swept away a basketful that day before dinner. So he did not move, but listened still. The noises were accompanied by a little *frou-frou*, which seemed to betoken something human. But the Captain was still far from being broad awake, and so he continued to wonder lazily. Then another mulberry fell; then half-a-dozen, full on his waistcoat, cannoning in all directions to the utter ruin of his white garments; and a low childish laugh burst forth close to him, and the Captain sprang to his feet.

To his amazement there stood on the chair before him a ragged little boy, barefoot and bareheaded, his face purple with mulberry juice, his mouth crammed with fruit, his fingers stained, his ragged clothes smirched; even his little feet, so dusty and dirty, standing in a pool of mulberry juice.

The Captain was a bachelor and a sailor, and on both grounds fond of children. Now, the face of the child before him, so bonny, so saucy, so full of glee and confidence, went straight to his heart, and he laughed a welcome and patted the boy's cheek.

But the fact itself was remarkable. Where had the child come from? Not through the front door, which was closed; nor over the wall, which was impossible.

"How the dickens " the Captain began."I beg your pardon, my lad, for swearing, which is a bad habit; but how did you get here?"

The boy pointed to the wall and the water.

"Oh!" said the Captain doubtfully. "Swam, did you? Now, that's odd. I've seen them half your size in the Pacific swim like fishes, but I never heard of an English boy doing it before. Where do you live, boy?"

The child looked interrogative.

"Where's daddy? Gone to sea, belike, as a good sailor should?"

But the boy shook his head.

"Daddy's dead, I suppose. Drowned, likely, as many a good sailor is. Where's your mammy?"

The boy looked a little frightened at these questions, to which he could evidently give no satisfactory reply.

"The line's pretty nigh paid out," said the Captain; "but we'll try once more. Who takes care of you, boy—finds you in rations, and serves out the rope's end?"

This time the boy began to understand a little.

Then the Captain put on his hat and led him by the hand to the *quartier* where the sailors' wives did mostly congregate. In this he was guided by the fine instinct of experience, because he *felt*, in spite of the rags, that the boy had been dressed by a sailor's wife. None but such a woman could give a sea-going air to two garments so simple as those which kept the weather from the boy.

He led the child by the hand till presently the child led him, and piloted the Captain safely to a house where a woman—it was Mrs. Jeram—came running out, crying shrilly—

"Lenny! why, wherever have you bin and got to?"

There was another ragged little boy with a round back, five or six years old, sitting on the door-step. When the Captain had finished his talk with Mrs. Jeram, he came out and noticed that other boy, and then he returned and had more talk.

CHAPTER III.
VICTORY ROW.

MRS. JERAM was a weekly tenant in one of a row of small four-roomed houses known as Victory Row, which led out of Nelson Street, and was a broad blind court, bounded on one side and at the end by the Dockyard wall. It was not a dirty and confined court, but quite the reverse, being large, clean, and a very Cathedral close for quietness. The wall, built of a warm red brick, had a broad and sloping top, on which grew wallflowers, long grasses, and stonecrop; overhanging the wall was a row of great elms, in the branches of which there was a rookery, so that all day long you could listen, if you wished, to the talk of the rooks. Now, this is never querulous, angry, or argumentative. The rook does not combat an adversary's opinion: he merely states his own; if the other one does not agree with him he states it again, but without temper. If you watch them and listen, you will come to the conclusion that they are not theorists, like poor humans, but simply investigators of fact. It has a restful sound, the talk of rooks; you listen in the early morning, and they assist your sleeping half-dream without waking you; or in the evening they carry your imagination away to woods and sweet country glades. They have cut down the elms now, and driven the rooks to find another shelter. Very likely, in their desire to sweep away everything that is pretty, they have torn the wallflowers and grasses off the wall as well. And if these are gone, no doubt Victory Row has lost its only charm. If I were to visit it now, I should probably find it squalid and mean. The eating of the tree of knowledge so often makes things that once we loved look squalid.

But to childhood nothing is unlovely in which the imagination can light upon something to feed it. It is the blessed province of all children, high and low, to find themselves at the gates of Paradise; and quite certainly Tom the Piper's son, sitting under a hedge with a raw potato for plaything, is every bit as happy as a little Prince of Wales. The possibilities of the world which opens out before us are infinite; while the glories of the world we have left behind are still clinging to the brain, and shed a supernatural colouring on everything. At six, it is enough to live; to awake in the morning to the joy of another day; to eat, sleep, play, and wonder; to revel in the vanities of childhood; to wanton in make-belief superiority; to admire the deeds of bigger children; to emulate them, like Icarus: and too often, like that greatly daring youth, to fall.

Try to remember, if you can, something of the mental attitude of childhood; recall, if you may, some of the long thoughts of early days. To begin with—God was quite close to you, up among the stars; He was seated somewhere, ready to give you whatever you wanted; everybody was a friend, and everybody was occupied all day long about your personal concerns; you had not yet arrived at the boyishness of forming plans for the future. You were still engaged in imitating, exercising, wondering. Every man was a demigod—you had not yet arrived at the consciousness that you might become yourself a man; the resources of a woman—to whom belong bread, butter, sugar, cake, and jam—were unbounded; everything that you saw was full of strange and mysterious interest. You had not yet learned to sneer, to criticise, to compare, and to down-cry.

Mrs. Jeram's house, therefore, in my eyes, contained everything that heart of man could crave for. The green-painted door opened into a room which was at once reception-room, dining-room, and kitchen; furnished, too, though that I did not know, in anticipation of the present fashion, having plates of blue and white china stuck round the walls. The walls were built of that warm red brick which time covers with a coating of grey-like moss. You find it everywhere among the old houses of the south of England; but I suppose the clay is all used up, because I see none of it in the new houses.

We were quite respectable people in Victory Row; of that I am quite sure, because Mrs. Jeram would have made the place much too lively, by the power and persistence of her tongue, for other than respectable people. We were seafaring folk, of course; and in every house was something strange from foreign parts. To this day I never see anything new in London shops or in museums without a backward rush of associations which lands me once more in Victory Row; for the sailors' wives had all these things long ago, before inland people ever heard of them. There were Japanese cabinets, picked up in Chinese ports, long before Japan was open; there was curious carved wood and ivory work from Canton. These things were got during the Chinese war. And there was a public-house in a street hard by which was decorated, instead of with a red window-blind, like other such establishments, with a splendid picture representing some of the episodes in that struggle: all the Chinese were running away in a disgraceful stampede, while Jack Tar, running after them, caught hold of their pig-tails with the left hand, and deftly cut off their heads with the right, administering at the same time a frolicsome kick. John Chinaman's legs were generally both off the ground together, such was his fear. Then there were carved ostrich eggs; wonderful things from the Brazils in feathers; frail delicacies in coral from the Philippines, known as Venus's flower-baskets; grewsomelooking cases from the West Indies, containing centipedes, scorpions, beetles, and tarantulas; small turtle shells, dried flying fish, which came out in moist exudations during wet weather, and smelt like haddock; shells of all kinds, big and little; clubs, tomahawks, and other queer weapons, carved in wood, from the Pacific; stuffed humming-birds, and birds of Paradise. There were live birds, too — avvadavats, Java sparrows, love-birds, parroquets, and parrots in plenty. There was one parrot, at the corner house, who affected the ways of one suffering from incurable consumption—he was considered intensely comic by children and persons of strong stomach and small imagination. There were parrots who came, stayed a little while, and then were taken away and sold, who spoke foreign tongues with amazing volubility, who swore worse than Gresset's Vert Vert, and who whistled as beautifully as a boatswain—the same airs, too. The specimens which belonged to Art or inanimate Nature were ranged upon a table at the window. They generally stood or were grouped around a large Bible, which it was a point of ceremonial to have in the house. The live birds were hung outside in sunny weather, all except the parrot with the perpetual cold, who walked up and down the court by himself and coughed. The streets surrounding us were, like our own, principally inhabited by mariners and their families, and presented similar characteristics; so that one moved about in a great museum open for general inspection during daylight, and free for all the world. Certain I am that if all the rare and curious things displayed in these windows had been collected and preserved, the town would have had a most characteristic and remarkable museum of its own.

Victory Row is the very earliest place that I remember. How I got there, the dangers to which I was exposed in infancy, the wild tragedy which robbed me of both parents—these things I was to learn later on, because I remembered nothing of them. I was in Mrs. Jeram's house, with three other boys. There was Jem, the oldest. His surname was Hex, and as it was always pronounced without the aspirate, I thought, when I had learned the alphabet, that to be named after one of the letters was a singular distinction, and most enviable. Jem was a big boy, a good-natured, silent lad, who spent his whole time on the beach among the sailors. Moses came next. I never knew Moses' surname. He was a surly and ill-conditioned boy. Leonard Copleston, the third, was my protector and my friend. The day, so far as I can recollect, always began with a fight between Leonard and Moses; later on, towards dinner-time, there would be another fight; and the evening never ended without one or two more fights. From my indistinct recollection of this period, I fancy that whenever Leonard and Moses came within a few yards of each other they as naturally rushed into battle as a Russian and a Turk. And the only good point about Moses was that he was always ready to renew the battle. For he hated Leonard; I suppose because Leonard was as handsome, bright, and clever, as he was ugly lowering, and stupid.

Naturally, at the age of five one does not inquire into antecedents of people. So that it was much later when I learned the circumstances under which we four boys were collected beneath one roof. They were characteristic of the place. The paternal Moses, returning from a three years' cruise in the Mediterranean, discovered that his wife, a lady of fickle disposition, had deserted. In other words, she was gone away, leaving a message for her husband to the effect that little Moses, the pledge of their affections, and his curious collection of china brought from foreign parts, would between them console him for her loss. So he put the boy under the charge of Mrs. Jeram, gave her a sum of money for the child's maintenance until he came back again; smashed the crockery in a rage; wept but little, if at all, for his ruined household gods; went away, and never came back any more.

Jem Hex, on the other hand, was the son of a real widower, also a Royal Navy man, and he was left with Mrs. Jeram to be taken care of under much the same circumstances, except that he was regularly paid for. As for Leonard, you will hear about him presently. In one respect he was worse off than any of us, because we had friends and he had none. There was, for instance, an aunt belonging to Moses who came to see him about once a month. In the course of the interview she always caned him. I do not know why; perhaps because she felt sure he deserved it, as he certainly did, perhaps because she thought it a thing due to her own dignity as the boy's only relative. She wore a dress, the splendour of whose original black colour was marred by patches of brown stuff lying in the creases. She was a stiff and stately dame of forbidding appearance, and manners which were conventional. Thus, she always began the conversation, before she caned Moses, by remarking, even in August, that the weather was "raw." The monthly caning was the only thing, I know now, that she ever contributed towards the maintenance and education of her nephew. Jem Hex had plenty of uncles and other relations. One was a harbour boatman, a jolly old man, who had been in the wars; one was a dockyard foreman, and one was a ship's carpenter. They used to drop into Victory Row for a talk on Sunday afternoons when the weather was warm. I used to envy Jem his superior position in the world and his family connections.

I had friends, too, in plenty, but they were of a different kind. Not rich to begin with—not holders of official rank, and unconnected in any way with the Royal Navy, and, which stamped them at once as objects of pity and contempt, they were unable to speak the English tongue except with difficulty. They were big and bearded men; they had scars on their faces, and went sometimes maim and halt; they were truculent of aspect, but kindly of eye. When they came into our court they took me up gently, carried me about, kissed me, and generally brought me some little simple gift, such as an orange or an apple.

Somehow or other I learned that these friends of mine were Poles, and that they had a great barrack all to themselves, close to the walls, whither I used to be sometimes carried. It was a narrow building, built of black-tarred wood, with windows at both sides, so that you saw the light quite through the house.

It stood just under the walls, almost in the shade of the great elms. Within it were upwards of a hundred Poles, living chiefly on the tenpence a day which the English Government allowed them for their support, with this barn-like structure to house them. They were desperately poor, all of them living mostly on bread and frugal cabbage-soup. Out of their poverty, out of their tenpence a day, some of these poor fellows found means by clubbing together to pay Mrs. Jeram, week by week, for my support. They went hungry that I might eat and thrive; they came every day, some of them, to see that I was well cared for. They took me to their barrack, and made me their pet and plaything; there was nothing they were not ready to do for me, because I was the child of Roman Pulaski and Claudia his wife.

The one who came oftenest, stayed the longest, and seemed in an especial manner to be my guardian, was a man who was grey when I first remember him. He had long hair and a full grey beard. There was a great red gash in his cheek which turned white when he grew excited or was moved. He limped with one foot because some Russian musket-ball had struck him in the heel; and he had singularly deep-set eyes, with heavy eyebrows. I have never seen anything like the sorrowfulness of Wassielewski's eyes. Other Poles had reason for sorrow. They were all exiles together; they were separated from their families without a hope that the terrible Nicolas, who hated a rebel Pole with all the strength of his autocratic hatred, would ever let them return; they were all in poverty; but these men looked happy. Wassielewski alone never smiled, and carried always that low light of melancholy in his eyes, as if not only the past was sad, but the future was charged with more sorrow. On one day in the year he brought me *immortelles*, tied with a black ribbon. He told me they were in memory of my father, Roman Pulaski now dead and in heaven, and of my mother, also dead, and now sitting among the saints and martyrs. I used to wonder at those times to see the eyes which rested on me so tenderly melt and fill with tears.

Three or four days in the week, sometimes every day, Mrs. Jeram went out charing. As she frequently came home bearing with her a scent of soapsuds, and having her hands creased and fingers supernaturally white, it is fair to suppose that she went out washing at eighteenpence a day. Something, indeed, it was necessary to do, with four hungry boys to keep, only two of whom paid anything for their daily bread, and Mrs. Jeram—she was a hard-featured woman, with a resolute face—must have been possessed of more than the usual share of Christian charity to keep Moses in her house at all, even as a paying boarder, much less as one who ate and drank largely, and brought to the house nothing at all but discord and ill-temper. And besides the food to provide, with some kind of clothing, there was always "Tenderart," who called every Monday morning.

He was the owner of the houses in the Row, and he came for his rent. His name was Barnfather, and the appellation of Tenderart, a compound illustrating the law of phonetic decay, derived from the two words *tender heart*, was bestowed upon him by reason of the uncompromising hardness of heart, worse than that of any Pharaoh, with which he encountered, as sometimes happened, any deficiency in the weekly rent. Behind him—the tool of his uncompromising rigour—walked a man with a blanket, a man whose face was wooden. If the rent was not paid that man opened his blanket, and wrapped it round some article of household furniture silently pointed out by Tenderart as an equivalent.

My early childhood, spent among these kindly people, was thus very rich in the things which stimulate the imagination. Strange and rare objects in every house, in every street, something from far-off lands, talk to be heard of foreign ports and bygone battles, the poor Poles in their bare and gaunt barracks, and then the place itself. I have spoken of the rookery beyond the flower-grown Dockyard wall. But beyond the rookery was the Dockyard itself, quiet and orderly, which I could see from the upper window of the house. There was the Long Row, where resided the Heads of Departments; the Short Row, in which lived functionaries of lower rank—I believe the two Rows do not know each other in society; there was the great Reservoir, supported on tall and spidery legs, beneath which stood piles of wood cut and dressed, and stacked for use; there was the Rope Walk, a quarter of a mile long, in which I knew walked incessantly up and down the workmen who turned hanks of yarn into strong cables smelling of fresh tar; there were the buildings where other workmen made blocks, bent beams, shaped all the parts of ships; there were the great places where they made and repaired machinery; there were the sheds themselves where the mighty ships grew slowly day by day, miracles of man's constructive skill, in the dim twilight of their wooden cradles; there was a pool of sea water, in which lay timber to be seasoned, and sometimes I saw boys paddling up and down in it; there was always the busy crowd of officers and sailors going up and down, some of them god-like, with cocked hats, epaulettes, and swords.

And, all day long, never ceasing, the busy sound of the Yard. To strangers and visitors it was just a confused and deafening noise. When you got to know it you distinguished half a dozen distinct sounds which made up that inharmonious and yet not unpleasing whole. There was the chatter of the caulkers' mallets, which never ceased their tap, tap, tap, until you got used to the regular beat, and felt it no more than you feel the beating of your pulse. But it was a main part of the noise which made the life of the Yard. Next to the multitudinous mallets of the caulkers, which were like the never-ceasing hum and whisper of insects on a hot day, came the loud clanging of the hammer from the boiler-makers' shop. That might be likened, by a stretch of fancy, to the crowing of cocks in a farmyard. Then, all by itself, came a heavy thud which made the earth tremble, echoed all round, and silenced for a moment everything else.

It came from the Nasmyth steam hammer; and always, running through all, and yet distinct, the r—r—r—r of the machinery, like the rustling of the leaves in the wind. Of course I say nothing about salutes, because every day a salute of some kind was thundering and rolling about the air as the ships came and went, each as tenacious of her number of guns as an Indian Rajah.

Beyond the Dockyard—you could not see it, but you felt it, and knew that it was there—was the broad blue lake of the harbour, crowded with old ships sacred to the memory of a hundred fights, lying in stately idleness, waiting for the fiat of some ignorant and meddling First Lord ordering them to be broken up. As if it were anything short of wickedness to break up any single ship which has fought the country's battles and won her victories, until the tooth of time, aided by barnacles, shall have rendered it impossible for her to keep afloat any longer.

When the last bell rang at six o'clock, and the workmen went away, all became quiet in the Dockyard. A great stillness began suddenly, and reigned there till the morning, unbroken save by the rooks which cawed in the elms, and the clock which struck the hours. And then one had to fall back on the less imaginative noises of Victory Row, where the parrot coughed, and the grass widows gathered together, talking and disputing in shrill concert, and Leonard fought Moses before going to bed, not without some din of battle.

CHAPTER IV.
THIRTY YEARS AGO.

RECOLLECTIONS of childhood are vague as a whole, but vivid in episodes. The days pass away, and leave no footprints on the sands, one being like another. And then one comes, bringing with it a trivial incident, which somehow catches hold of the childish imagination, and so lives for ever. There are two or three of these in my memory. It is a sunshiny day, and, as the rooks are cawing all day in the elms, it must be spring. Sitting on the doorstep of Mrs. Jeram's, I am only conscious of the harmonious blending of sounds from the Dockyard. Victory Row is quiet, save for the consumptive parrot who walks in the shade of the wall coughing heavily, as if it were one of his worst days, and he had got a bronchial asthma on the top of his other complaints. With me is Leonard, dancing on the pavement to no music at all but the beating of his pulse, enough for him. Jem and Moses are always on the beach. I suppose, but I am not certain, that it is afternoon. And the reason why I suppose so is that the Row is quiet. The morning was more noisy on account of the multifarious house duties which have to be got through. We hear a step which we know well, a heavy and limping step, which comes slowly along the pavement, and presently bears round the corner its owner, Wassielewski. Leonard stops dancing. Wassielewski pats his curly head. I hold up my arms: he catches me up and kisses me, while I bury my face in his big beard. Then he puts me down again, lays aside the violin which he carries in one hand (it is by this instrument that Wassielewski earns a handsome addition to the daily tenpence, and, in fact, pays half my weekly allowance), and seeks in his coat-pocket for an orange. He does all this very gravely, without smiling, only looking depths of care and love almost paternal out of his deep-set eyes. While Leonard holds the orange he places the violin in my hands. Ah! what joy even to draw the bow across the strings, though my arms are not long enough yet to hold the instrument properly. Somehow this rugged old soldier taught me to *feel* music, and the rapture of producing music, before my fingers could handle notes or my hands could hold a bow. He leaves the orange for Leonard and myself, and disappears. Moses returns unexpectedly, and demands a share. There is a fight.

Or it is another visitor, the Captain. He wears his blue frock-coat with brass buttons and white ducks; he carries his hands behind him, and a stick in them, which drags at his heels as he walks. We do not see him till he is with us. We look up, and he beams upon us, smiling all over his rosy face.

"How is the little Pole?" asks the kindly Captain, shaking hands with us. "How is the other young rascal?"

I have a distinct recollection of his eyes wandering in the direction of our boots, which were certainly going, if not altogether gone, both soles and heels. And I remember that he shook his head. Also that in the evening new boots came for both of us. And that Mrs. Jeram said, nodding her head, that *he*—meaning perhaps the Captain—was a good man.

Another recollection.

I am, somehow or other, in the street by myself. How I got there, what I proposed to myself when I set out on my journey, I cannot tell. But I was lost in the streets of the old seaport town. I was walking along the pavement feeling a good deal frightened, and wondering how I was to get back to Victory Row, or even to the Poles' Barrack, when I became aware of a procession. It was a long procession, consisting of sailors marching, every man with a lady on his arm, two and two, along the middle of the street, singing as they went. They wore long curls, these jolly tars, shining with grease, hanging down on either side below, or rather in front of their hats. Curls were the fashion in those days. There were about thirty men in this rollicking train. At their head, limping along very fast, marched my poor old friend Wassielewski, his grave face and melancholy eyes a contrast to the careless and jovial crew who followed him. He was fiddling as he went one of those lively tunes that sailors love, a tune which puts their legs a dancing and pours quicksilver into their feet. Some of them, indeed, were capering along the line, unable to wait till the "crib" was reached. Also down the street I saw another exactly similar procession. How was I to know that the Royal Frederick had been paid off that morning, and that a thousand Jack Tars were altogether chucking away the money in a few days which it had taken them three years to earn? The old Pole would get some share of it, however, for that was the way in which he earned the money which mostly came to me.

He spied me presently standing alone on the kerbstone, and handing the fiddle to one of the men, hurried across the road, and took me in his arms.

"Ladislas!" he said, with his quaint foreign accent. "What are you doing here? Why are you not at home?"

"Bring him over, Fiddler Ben," cried one of the men. "I'll carry the little chap. Lord! what's one boy? I've had a dozen of 'em at home, somewheres. Now then, messmates—Strike up, Fiddler Ben. With a will, my lad."

"It is the son of my old master and lord," began Wassielewski, holding me in his arms helplessly.

"Bring along his lordship, then," said the man. "I'll carry the noble hearl."

The Pole resumed the fiddle with a sigh, and took up his place as band and bandmaster in one.

"Uncommon light in the arms is the noble duke. Many a fo'k'sle kid 'ud weigh more. Poll, our'n 'ud weigh twice as much. Come up, yer Ryal Highness."

I suppose I must have been a very small boy, even for a five years' old child. But the man carried me tenderly, as sailors always do. We came to a public-house; that one with the picture outside it of the Chinese War. There was a long, low sort of hall within it, at the end of which Wassielewski took his place, and began to fiddle again. Dancing then set in, though it was still early in the morning, with great severity. With dancing, drink; with both, songs; with all three, Wassielewski's fiddle. I suppose it was the commencement of a drunken orgie, and the whole thing was disgraceful. Remember, however, that it was more than thirty years ago, when the Navy still retained its old traditions. Foremost among these was the tradition that being ashore meant drink as long as the money lasted. It sometimes lasted a week, or even a fortnight, and was sometimes got through in a day or two. There were harpies and pirates in every house which was open to Jack. Jack, indeed, was cheated wherever he went. Afloat he was robbed by the purser; he was ill-fed and found, the Government paying for good food and good stores; contractors and purveyors combined with the purser to defraud him. Ashore, he was horribly, shamefully cheated and robbed, when he was paid off by a Navy bill, and fell into the hands of the pay agents. He was a rough-hided ruffian who could fight, had seen plenty of fighting, was tolerably inured to every kind of climate, and ready to laugh at any kind of danger, except, perhaps, Yellow Jack. He was also tender-hearted and sentimental. Sometimes he was away for five years at a stretch, and, if his captain chose to make it so, his life was a dog's life. Floggings were frequent; rum was the reward of good conduct; there were no Sailors' Homes, none of the many humanising influences which have made the British sailor the quiet, decorous creature, generally a teetotaler, and often inclined to a Methodist way of thinking in religion, half soldier half sailor, that he is at present.

It was an orgie, I suppose, at which no child should have been present. Fortunately, at half-past twelve, the landlord piped all hands for dinner, and Wassielewski carried me away. He would return after dinner, to play on and on till night fell, and there was no one left to stand upon his legs.

Then Wassielewski would put the fiddle away in its case, and go back to the Barrack, where he sat in silence, and brooded. The other Poles smoked and talked, but this one held himself apart. He was an irreconcilable, and he refused to accept defeat.

One more scene.

The Common Hard, which is still, after all the modern changes, a street with a distinct character of its own. The houses still look out upon the bright and busy harbour, though there is now a railway terminus and an ugly pier; though steam launches run across the water; and though there are telegraph posts, cabs, and omnibuses, all the outward signs of advanced civilisation. But thirty years ago it was a place which seemed to belong to the previous century. There were no great houses and handsome shops, but in their place, a picturesque row of irregular cottages, no two of which were exactly alike, but which resembled each other in certain particulars. They were two-storied houses; the upper storey was very low, the ground-floor was below the level of the street. I do not know why, but the fact remains that in my town the ground-floors of all the old houses were below the level of the pavement. You had to stoop, if you were tall, to get into the doorway, and then, unless you were experienced, you generally fell headlong down a step of a foot or so. Unless the houses were shops, they had only one window below and one above, because the tax on windows obliged people to economise their light. The roofs were of red tiles, high-pitched, and generally broken-backed; stone-crop and house-leek grew upon them. The Hard existed then only for the sailors. There were one or two jewellers, who bought as well as sold; many public-houses; and a plentiful supply of rascally pay-agents. That side had little interest for boys. In old times the high tide had washed right up to the foot of these houses which then stood upon the beach itself. But they built a stone wall, which kept back the water, and allowed a road to be made, protected by an iron railing. An open space gave access to what was called the"beach," being a narrow spit of land, along which were ranged on either side the wherries of the boatmen. A wooden bench was placed along the iron railing near the beach, on which sat every day, and all day long, old sailors, in a row. It was their club, their daily rendezvous, the place where they discussed old battles, smoked pipes, and lamented bygone days. They never seemed to walk about or to care much where they sat. They sat still, and sat steadily, in hot weather and in cold. The oddest thing about this line of veterans was that they all seemed to have wooden legs. There was, or there exists in my memory, which is the same thing, a row of wooden pegs which did duty for the lost legs, sticking out straight in front of the bench when they were on it. The effect of this was very remarkable. Some, of course, had lost other outlying bits of the human frame; a hand, the place supplied by a hook, like that of Cap'en Cuttle, whose acquaintance I formed later on; a whole arm, its absence marked by the empty sleeve sewn to the front of the jersey; and there were scars in plenty. Like my friend's the Poles, these heroes had gained their scars and lost their limbs in action.

Thirty years ago we were only a quarter of a century or so from the long and mighty struggle which lasted for a whole generation, and filled this seaport town with prosperity, self-satisfaction, and happiness. Oh, for the brave old days when week after week French, American, Spanish, and Dutch prizes were towed into harbour by their victors, or sailed in, the Union Jack flying at the peak, the original crew safe under hatches, in command of a middy and half a dozen British sailors told off to take her home. They talked, these old grizzle heads, of fights and convoys, and perilous times afloat. I sat among them, or stood in front of them, and listened. Child as I was, my little heart glowed to hear how, yardarm to yardarm, they lay alongside the Frenchman; how a dozen times over the plucky little French beggars tried to board them; how she sheered off at last, and they followed, raking her fore and aft; how she suddenly broke out into flame, and before you could say "Jack Robinson," blew up with all that was left of a thousand men aboard; with merry yarns of Chinese pigtails, made to be pulled by the British sailor, and niggers of Jamaica, and Dutchmen at the Cape. Also, what stories of slavers, of catching American skippers in the very act of chucking the niggers overboard; of cutting out Arab dhows; of sailing in picturesque waters where the natives swim about in the deep like porpoises; of boat expeditions up silent rivers in search of piratical Malays; of lying frozen for months in Arctic regions, long before they thought of calling men heroes for passing a single winter on the ice with every modern appliance for making things comfortable.

Among these old salts was one—of course he had a wooden leg—with a queer twisted-up sort of face. One eye was an independent revolving light, but the other obeyed his will, and once you knew which eye that was you were pretty safe with him. He had a very profound and melodious bass voice. When I passed he used to growl a greeting which was like the thunder of a distant salute. He never went farther than the greeting, on account of certain family differences, which made us shy of becoming too intimate. I learned the fact from a curious ceremonial which happened regularly every Saturday night. At eight o'clock, or in summer at nine, Mrs. Jeram drew down her white blind, if it was not already drawn, placed one candle on the table, and herself between the candle and the window. The natural effect of this was to exhibit to the world a portrait in profile of herself. She sat bolt upright, and being a thin woman with plenty of bone—though the most kind-hearted of all creatures—the portrait thus presented was angular, stiff, and uncompromising.

Meanwhile in the street outside sat my friend, "timber-toed" Jack—the ancient mariner with the deep voice and the revolving eye. He was perched comfortably on a three-legged stool lent by a friend, his remaining limb tucked away snug and ship-shape among the legs of the tripod, and the peg sticking out as usual at right angles to his body. There he sat and smoked a pipe. From time to time he raised his voice, and in an utterance which shook the windows of every house in the Row, he growled—

"Rachel! Come out and make it up."

There was no answer. Then the neighbours, who always congregated on this occasion, and took an intense interest in the progress of the family jar, murmured a soft chorus of persuasive and honeyed words, meant for Rachel too—who was Mrs. Jeram. But she never moved.

"Rachel! 'Twarn't my fault. 'Twas her as dragged me along in tow. Took prisoner I was."

"Ah! the artful thing"—this was the chorus—"which well we know them; and they'll take in tow the best, at times; and a little in drink as well."

No answer again this time, but an angry toss of the head which conveyed to the silhouette on the blind an expression of incredulity.

After half an hour's enjoyment of the pipe, the old sailor would noisily beat out the ashes. Then we inside the house would hear him once more—

"Then, Rachel, God bless you and good-night; and bless the boys. And, please the Lord, I'll be here again next Saturday. And hoping to find you in a forgivin' mood."

When he was gone Mrs. Jeram would leave her seat and come to her own chair by the fireplace. But her hands always trembled, and sometimes her eyes were wet. For it was her husband, and she could not make up her mind to forgive him the old offence.

That was why, on the Hard, the wooden-legged sailor and I had little or no conversation together.

One day—I was between eight and nine at the time—we were all four on the Logs. The Logs were, to begin with, a forbidden place, and, if only on that account, delightful. But also on other accounts. There was a floating pier there, consisting of two or three square-hewn timbers laid alongside of each other, between posts stuck at intervals in the mud. They had a tendency to turn round beneath the tread of a heavy man, and when that happened, and the heavy man's feet fell in between two logs, it was apt to be bad for those feet. Men-of-war's boats used to land their officers and crew at the end of the Logs; there was a constant running to and fro of sailors, officers, and harbour boatmen. Also, on the left-hand side as you went down this rough pile, there was a space of water some acres in extent, in which lay in orderly rows, one beside the other, a whole forest of timbers, waiting for time, the sun, and salt water together to season them. And if the logs were apt to turn under the tread of a heavy man, these timbers would turn under the foot of a light boy. Judge, therefore, of the joy of running backwards and forwards over their yielding and uncertain ground.

Leonard, who rejoiced beyond measure to run over the Logs himself, would seldom let me come with him even down the pier, and never over the timbers. On this day, however, we had all four gone down to the very end of the Logs; half a dozen ships' boats had touched, landed their men, and gone back again. Jem, the simple and foolish Jem, was gazing in admiration at the sailors, who looked picturesque in their blue shirts, straw hats, and shiny curls. I even caught Jem in the act of feeling whether his own hair behind the ear would not curl if twisted between finger and thumb. Moses was sitting straddle-legged on a projecting log, his boots in his hands, and his bare feet and legs lapped by the water. Leonard and I stood on the pier, watching. Presently there came along a man-o'-war's gig, manned by twelve sailors sitting side by side, rowing their short, deep stroke, without any feathering, but in perfect time. In the stern sat a middy, the very smallest middy I ever saw, no bigger than Leonard, dressed in the most becoming uniform in the world, and calmly conscious of his importance. He landed, gave a brief order, and strode as manfully as his years would allow down the Logs. As he passed on his eye rested on Leonard, and I saw the latter flush.

When the middy was gone I turned to Leonard, and said with the enthusiasm of admiration—

"Lenny, when I grow up I shall be a middy like that."

A small thing to say, and indeed, the grandeur of the boy and his power overwhelmed me for a moment, else I ought to have known, at eight years of age, that children living with charwomen on charity are not the stuff out of which officers of the Royal Navy are generally manufactured.

"Ah! yah!" roared Moses, tossing up his legs.

"What are you laughing at?" cried Leonard in a rage.

"Ah! yah!" he repeated. "Hunchback! Hunchey in a uniform, with a sword at his side."

I declare that up to that moment I had no more consciousness of being deformed than I had of Hebrew. I suppose that in some dim way I knew that I was differently shaped—smaller than Leonard, that my clothes were not such as he could wear, but not a thought, not a rough suspicion that I was, by reason of this peculiarity, separated from my fellows. Then all of a sudden it burst upon me. Not in its full misery. A hunchback has to grow to manhood before he has drunk the whole of the bitter cup; he has to pass through the years of school life, when he cannot play like other boys, nor run, nor jump, nor fight like them; when he is either tolerated or pitied. He has to become a young man among young men, to realise that he is not as they are; to look on envying while they rejoice in the strength and beauty of their youth; to hear their talk of girls and sweet looks and love, while all girls look down upon him, he foolishly thinks, with contempt. I did not feel the whole misery at once. I only realised, all of a sudden that I was *disgracié*, that the grandeurs which I envied were not for me, that I was to be despised for my misfortune—and I sat down in this sudden misery and cried aloud.

A moment afterwards there was a fight. Leonard and Moses. They fought on the narrow log. Leonard was the pluckier, but Moses was the stronger. The sailors in the gig looked on and laughed, and clapped their hands. Through my shameful tears I only saw half the duel. It was terminated by the fall of both into the water, one on either side the Logs. The water was only two or three feet deep, and they came up, face to face, and driving fists at each other across the eighteen-inch plank. It was Jem who stopped the battle, stepping in between the combatants, and ordering in his rough way that both should get out of the water and fight it out on dry land.

"He called me Hunchback, Leonard," I gasped, holding his hand as he ran, wet and dripping, through the streets.

"Yes, Laddy," he replied."Yes, Laddy, he's a cub and a cur, and a thick-headed fool. But I'll let him know to-morrow."

"And you won't let him call me Hunchey, Leonard?"

"Not if I have to fight him all day long, Laddy. So there."

But next day's fight, if it was begun, was never finished, because in the afternoon we both, Leonard and I, walked away with the Captain, each holding one hand of his, Leonard carrying his stick. And when we got to the Captain's it was explained to us that we were to stay there.

CHAPTER V.
THE YOUNG PRINCE.

TEN years of boyhood followed. In taking us both away from Mrs. Jeram the Captain promised her on behalf of Leonard, and Wassielewski on behalf of myself, that we should be brought up, in his old-fashioned way of putting it, in the fear of God and the desire to do our duty. It was an uneventful time, which has left few recollections. I suppose that kind of time—it has been always mine—is the happiest which leaves the fewest memories. Yet its happiness for the want of contrast is not felt. Perhaps it is better not to be happy, and to lead the life of action and peril such as has been granted to Leonard and denied to me. When the time arrives to lie down and go to sleep it must be good to leave behind the memory of bygone great days big with issues dependent on your courage and self-possession. My life has but one episode, and because it is not likely to have another I have sat down to tell it. In the end I am like any rustic on a farm, any secluded dweller on a remote island, inasmuch as one day has followed and will follow another, marked with no other change than from sunshine to rain, from summer to winter.

Of course we were soon sent to school. The fact that I was a Pole, coupled with my deformity, produced in my favour the mingled feeling of respect and curiosity with hardly disguised contempt which boys always feel for a foreigner or a cripple. Of course, too, it immediately became known that we had been living in Victory Row, under the care of a charwoman. Contumely was the first result of the knowledge. Leonard, however, then about eleven, showed himself so handy with his fists—one consequence of his many combats with Moses—with a disregard of superior weight and strength as complete as any one of Nelson's captains might have shown—that any further reference to charwomen or accidents of birth had to be made with bated breath and went out of fashion in the school. New boys, it is true, were instigated, as if it was a joke, to ask Leonard for information as to the price of soap and the interests of washing. The miserable victim introduced the subject generally with a grin of superiority as became a boy who had a father living in the flesh. It was very beautiful, then, to observe how that new boy, after the short fight that followed, became anxious ever after to avoid the subject of charing and charwomen; for however big that boy was Leonard went for him, and however often Leonard was knocked down he arose from Mother Earth bruised and bleeding, but fresh. The bigger the new boy the more prolonged was the fight. The more resolute the new boy the more delightful to spectators was Leonard's bull-dog tenacity. Once or twice the battle was drawn by foreign intervention. Never once was Leonard defeated.

After each battle we walked home proudly certain of receiving the Captain's approbation when he learned the *casus belli*; for he always insisted on hearing the full details, and gloried in the prowess and pluck of the boy.

We led a frugal life, because the Captain had little besides his half-pay and the house we lived in, which was his own, and had been his father's before him. Sunday was the day of the weekly feast. On that day the Captain wore his undress uniform, and we went to church in the morning. After church we walked round the walls, and at half-past one we came home to dinner. It was Leonard's privilege to pipe hands for the meal, which always consisted of roast beef and plum-duff, brought in by the Captain's one servant, while Leonard played on the fife the "Roast Beef of Old England." After dinner there was a glass of port all round, with a double ration for the chief, and fruit for the boys. In the evening we read aloud, the Captain acting as expositor and commenting as we went; we did not go to church, because the Captain said it was ridiculous to suppose there was any necessity for church oftener ashore than afloat. But after I got a piano I used to play and sing hymns till supper, when the Captain told us yarns.

When Leonard was fourteen another change was made.

We left the school, and went, he and I together, to the Rev. Mr. Verney Broughton, as his private pupils. Mr. Broughton, the perpetual curate of St. Faith's, gave us, as I have since learned, these lessons at his own request, and gratuitously, though he was far from being a rich man.

Our tutor was a scholar of the old-fashioned school; he was an ex-fellow of Oriel, and openly held the opinion that nothing new had been written for about eighteen hundred years: he considered science, especially mechanical science, as unworthy the study of a scholar: he looked on Latin and Greek verse as the only safe means of educating the higher faculties: and he regarded the great writers of Rome and Athens as the only safe models of style, thought, and taste.

He was a stout, short man, with a red face, due, perhaps, to his fondness for port, his repugnance to physical exercise, and his habit of spending all the money he could spare on his dinners. A kind-hearted man, and a Christian up to his lights. His method of "working" his parish would hardly find favour in these days of activity, consisting, as it did, in nothing whatever except three services on Sunday and one on Wednesday and Friday evenings. No mothers' meetings, no prayer meetings, no societies, no early celebrations, no guilds. His sermons were learned and scholarly, with a leaning towards morality, and they inculcated the importance of holding Church doctrines. He was a Churchman high and dry, of a kind now nearly extinct. Those who wanted emotional religion went to other places of worship; those who were content with the old paths sat in their square pews every Sunday, and "assisted" in silence at a service which was a comfortable duet between parson and clerk.

We were put through the classical mill by Mr. Broughton. The course made me, in a way, a scholar. It made Leonard a man of action. He read the Homeric battles, and rejoiced to follow the conquering Diomede in the "way of war." He read the tragedies of Euripides, and, like all boys, espoused the cause of Troy the conquered.

He had, however, no inclination in the direction of scholarship, and persisted in looking on books as, on the whole, a rather disagreeable necessity in the training for after-life. For, with the knowledge of his first beginnings ever present in his mind, there grew up in him more and more strongly a resolution that he would make himself a gentleman. Somehow—he did not at all know how—but by some path or other open to lads who are penniless, alone in the world, and almost friendless, he would become a gentleman. Thus, when the Captain proposed that he should enter the navy as a master's assistant, Leonard scornfully refused, on the ground that he could be nothing under the rank of combatant officer. Mr. Broughton suggested that the two Universities are rich with endowments, and that fellowships await those who are strong enough to win them; but Leonard would not hear of the years of study before the prize was reached.

"In the old days, Laddy," he said, "I should have been put into a monastery, I suppose, and made my way by clinging to the skirts of a great ecclesiastical minister, like Richelieu and Mazarin. But I cannot go in for the modern substitute of university and fellowship. Fancy me in a black gown, when I should like to be in a uniform! "

"In the old days," I said, "men sometimes forced their way by joining the Free Companies."

"Ay," he replied, "that was a life worth having. Fancy riding through the country at the head of a thousand lances, gentlemen adventurers every one; a battle every other day, and an adventure the day between. What a pity the time is past for Free Companies. Let us go on the Common and see the soldiers."

That was his favourite resort. The march and movement of troops, the splendour of the array, the regimental bands, the drill of the awkward squad, delighted his soul. And here he would stand contentedly for half a day, watching the soldiers at their exercises.

"If one could only be a soldier, Laddy," he would say; "if there was any chance of rising, as there used to be in the French army! Every drummer boy with a marshal's baton in his pocket."

"And how many were able to take it out of their pocket?"

"One here and there. I should have tried to be that one."

One day, as he was talking in this strain, a soldier's funeral passed us—his comrades carried the coffin. Before it marched the fifes and muffled drums, playing the Dead March; behind it a file of men with arms reversed. We followed. After the short service the men fired a round over the nameless grave, and all marched off at quick step.

"That one has failed, Leonard," I said.

"Ay, he has failed. Poor common soldier! He had but a slender chance. None of them have any real chance."

He was dejected for a few minutes. Then a thought struck him, and he brightened up.

"Perhaps he was only an ignorant, beer-drinking clod. No doubt that was all. Pah! What chance could he have? Such a soldier was not a failure, Laddy. He rose in the world. He became drilled, civilised, and useful. And when he died he was buried with military honours."

At sixteen he gave up his classical work altogether, arriving at the conclusion that it was not by Latin and Greek he would reach his aim. Other things, he discovered, would be of more use to him. Among them was French. He found in the Polish Barrack two or three men who knew French as well as their own language, one of whom undertook, for a very small fee, to teach him. He worked at the new study almost feverishly, learning the language after his own way, by reading French books all day, by talking with his tutor as much as possible, and by learning whole pages of the dictionary. As we had no French books in our little library, we picked up for nothing at a bookstall a packet of old French newspapers and pamphlets dated about the year 1809, which probably once belonged to some French prisoner in the long wars, and these formed Leonard's introduction to the French language. His spare time he devoted to mathematics and to drawing. Here the Poles helped him again, many of the poor fellows being full of accomplishments and knowledge; so that, for the last year of his home life, Leonard was almost wholly in the Polish Barracks. The exiles, to whom this bright and handsome lad was a godsend of sunshine, rejoiced to teach him what they could, if only as a break in the monotony of their idle lives. And while I was welcome among them for my name's sake, Leonard was welcome for his own sake. They taught him, besides French, mathematics and drawing, how to speak Russian, how to ride, with the aid of borrowed steeds, how to fence, and what was the meaning of fortification.

As Leonard approached manhood he assumed a prouder carriage, due partly to the resolution within his heart, and partly to the defiance natural to his position. Mrs. Jeram said he was a prince born. Certainly no one acted the character better. Everything that he did was princely; he spoke as one born to command: with his quick, keen eye, his curly locks, his head flung back, his tall and slender figure, full of grace and activity, he was my hero as well as my leader and protector.

He would not associate with any boys in the town—those boys whose society was open to him—nor would he suffer me to know them. "You are a gentleman of Poland," he said grandly. "You may call yourself a count if that would help you. I am going to make myself a gentleman, whatever my father was. We must not hamper ourselves by early friendships which might afterwards prove annoying."

It was not altogether boyish bounce, nor altogether self-conceit, because, full of sympathy in other things, in this he was inexorable, that nothing whatever should interfere with his determination to lift himself out of the ranks. And almost the only reading he permitted himself lay in any books he could find which showed how men have risen from small beginnings to great things. Not greatness in the way of authorship. He had no feeling for literary success. "I would like," he said, "to have my share in making history, let who will write it. Who would not rather be Hannibal than Livy, or Hector than Homer? If you were to offer me the choice between Sir Philip Sidney and Shakespeare, I would rather be Sidney. All the greatest men have been soldiers and sailors—fighting men."

Then he would dilate on the lives of the French generals, and tell how Murat, Lannes, Kleber, Hoche, Augereau, and Marmont, fought their way valiantly up the ladder from the very lowest round.

How his purpose was to be accomplished, by what means he was to rise, he never explained. Nor did he, I think, ever seriously consider. But we all believed in him. The Captain, Celia, Mrs. Jeram, and I looked forward confidently to the time when Leonard should rise, superior to all disadvantages, a leader of men. If he had told us that he was going to become Archbishop of Canterbury, Lord Chancellor, or even H.R.H. the Field-Marshal Commanding-in-Chief, we should have believed that with the same confidence.

One day—it was Saturday, about Christmas-time—Leonard did not come home to dinner. The Captain waited for no one, and we sat down without him. It was three o'clock when he returned, and it was evident that something had happened, for his face was flushed, and his hands trembled.

"I have been with Mrs. Jeram, sir," he said, in reply to the Captain's look of inquiry. "She has told me about my mother," his voice breaking into a sob—"about my poor mother."

He buried his face in his hands.

"Ay, ay. Poor boy. Natural to ask." The Captain put out his hand and stroked Leonard's curls.

"Mrs. Jeram," Leonard lifted his head and went on, "gave me all she left. Only a wedding-ring. Nothing but a wedding-ring. See; and a message. A strange message. 'Tell my boy,' she said, when she died, 'that if ever he finds his father he must forgive him; but he had better not seek for him. And tell him—but not till he grows up—that his father is a gentleman and his mother was a lady.' That was the message, sir."

"Ay !" said the Captain, clearing his throat. "I knew it long ago, Leonard. Mrs. Jeram told me, when you came here, you and Laddy — you were both alike—gentlemen born"—

"How shall I forgive him?" asked Leonard, springing to his feet, panting and trembling. "How shall I forgive the man who let my mother—his wife—die deserted and alone?"

"The rules are laid down," said the Captain gravely,"clear and distinct: 'Forgive us as we forgive.' Likewise 'Honour thy father.'"

Leonard was silent.

"And as for this wedding-ring," said the Captain, taking it from the boy's hand, "I think if I were you, I would wear it always." He opened a drawer and found a piece of black ribbon. "Uniforms," he went on, without my seeing the connection, at first, "uniforms and badges are useful things. You can't do anything disgraceful in the Queen's uniform. Clergymen wear black to show they are in mourning for the world's sins. Do you wear this ring as a badge only known to yourself, my boy. A wedding-ring—it's a pretty thing," looking at the symbol lying in his hand —"it means purity and faith. If you wear it, boy, in that sense, your mother's memory will be honoured. Purity and faith. Perhaps we've given the ring to the wrong sex."

The Captain turned in his chair, and took up a book. It was his sign that he had no more to say on the subject.

Leonard touched my arm, and we stole out together. Then we took our hats, and went into the street.

"I cannot bear myself, Laddy," he burst out." I am half-mad to think of it. She was deserted; she wandered about, and came here. Mrs. Jeram picked her up, houseless and crying in the street. She had a little money then, but the doctor took it all, because next day, before she could say who she was, or where she came from, I was born, and my mother died. Not a line, not a letter, to say who she was; Mrs. Jeram took me, and promised her whose life—Oh! my mother—was passing swiftly from her—that she would bring me up,"—he stopped here for a moment—"And then she died, and they buried her. ...Do you know where the paupers are buried, Laddy? They buried my mother there."

Yes, I knew. Some of the Poles were buried there. The old parish church, with its broad churchyard, stood a mile and a half from the town. The God's Acre was so crowded with graves that its surface was raised six feet above the level of the road, and the tombstones stood side by side, almost touching each other. But in one corner there was a large open space on which there were no stones, where the grass grew thinly, and where the newly-turned clay, if you looked closely, was full of bits of wood, remains of old coffins. There was no shape to the graves in this corner; only rows of shapeless mounds and irregular unevenness in the ground. This was the paupers' corner, the place where they bestowed those for whose funeral the parish had to pay, so that the contempt of poverty followed after them, and rested on their very graves. I knew the place well, and shuddered when Leonard turned his steps to the road which led to the church. It was nearly four, and the early winter's day was drawing to a close. From a sky almost black poured down great flakes of snow, silently falling and giving an appearance of light after the hidden sun had gone down. As our heels echoed on the iron bridges beyond the Gate, I looked round and saw the ramparts standing up white and smooth, like a great wedding-cake against the gloomy heavens. Down in the moat, the sluggish water lay between two banks of dazzling white, flanked with scarp and counterscarp. Leonard hurried on, and we passed in silence along the streets of the suburb, and so into the fields beyond, till we came to the church standing with its old tower among the dead.

It was growing dark now, in spite of the snow.

The iron gates of the churchyard were open, and the church where the choir were practising for next day's service was partially lighted up. Leonard led the way to the far-off paupers' quarter.

It lay, a quarter of an acre in extent, quiet and peaceful, wrapped in the pall of the soft white snow. About the rest of the crowded churchyard there were paths among the graves, up and down, which were the footsteps in the snow of those who came to visit the dead. Here there were no paths and no footsteps. In the rest of the churchyard there was always some one to be seen—a widow leading her child to see the father's grave, an old man wandering among the monuments of those he had known in their youth, a sister weeping over a brother's grave, a mother over her son—always some one to connect the world of the dead with the world of the living. Here no one came to break the lonely silence of the forgotten graves. Elsewhere there were flowers in spring, cypresses and evergreens in and among the graves. Here there was nothing, not even a straggling briar, and even the grass was so often disturbed that it had not time to grow. For these were the graves, not of the poor, but of the very poor, of those hapless mortals who die in the misery of destitution, and have not even money enough left to buy them a separate resting-place. They lay there, thickly crowded, and every one forgotten. For among their own class Death speedily brings oblivion. Who can remember those that are gone before when from hour to hour one has to think about the next meal? Whether they were buried ten years before, or only yesterday, the hundreds who lay before us in that corner, covered over with a thin layer of mould and the sheet of snow, were everywhere as absolutely forgotten as if they had never even lived. Was it to rescue the dead from this ignoble oblivion that people once worshipped their ancestors?

And amongst them, somewhere, was Leonard's mother.

"Where is she?" he whispered. "Oh! in what spot did they lay her? A lady, born of gentle parents, the wife of a gentleman, to die neglected and be buried like a pauper! And not to know even where she is laid!"

"That does not matter, Leonard," I said weakly. "Her spirit is not in her grave."

He made no answer, but flung his arms above his head.

"My poor dead mother," he prayed, "my poor lost mother! I believe that you can see and hear me, though you cannot come to me. If you can help me where you are, help me. If you can pray for your son, pray for me. If you can lift me upwards, lift me. But how can I forgive my father?"

Within the church, close by, they were practising the responses to the Commandments. And as Leonard concluded they sang—

"Incline our hearts to keep this law! "

He heard the words and applied them, for he turned to me in that quick way of his—

"How can I honour my father, Laddy, when I don't know where he is, or what he is, and when my mother's last words were that I should forgive him?"

But his passion was over, and we walked away from the old churchyard.

CHAPTER VI.
CELIA.

I CAN hardly remember a time when I did not know Celia, but, as my memory of the life with Mrs. Jeram does not include her, our acquaintance must have sprung up some time after we went to the Captain. It was formed, I suspect, upon the walls where we were sent to play, and was allowed, or encouraged by Mrs. Tyrrell, Celia's mother, one of the Captain's friends. Our playground was a quiet place, especially at our end, where the town children, to whom the ramparts elsewhere were the chief place of recreation, seldom resorted. There were earthworks planted with trees and grass, and the meadows beneath were bright with buttercups and daisies. We were privileged children; we might run up and down the slopes or on the ramparts, or through the embrasures, or even clamber about the outer scarp down to the very edge of the Moat without rebuke from the "Johnnies," the official guardians of the walls, who went about all day armed with canes to keep boys from tearing down the earthworks. It was this privilege, as well as the general convenience of the place for children to play in, which took us nearly every day to the Queen's Bastion. There never was a more delightful retreat. In summer the trees afforded shade, and in winter the rampart gave shelter. You were in a solitude almost unbroken, close to a great centre of life and busy work; you looked out upon the world beyond, where there were fields, gardens, and trees; there was our own round corner, with the stately elms above us; the banks of grass, all sorts of grass, as one finds where there is no cultivation, trembling grass, foxtail grass, and that soft, bushy grass for which we had no name; there was the gun mounted on its high carriage, gazing out upon the harbour, a one-eyed Polyphemus longing for human food.

We walked and ran about the walls, we sat, read, and talked in Celia's Arbour. I was the principal reader, because Leonard used to act what I read, and Cis always wanted to do what Leonard did.

My usual seat was on the wheel of the gun-carriage, or in warm weather I would lie extended full length on the grass, while I read, in the high-pitched voice which Nature or my rounded back had given me, the narrative which stole us from ourselves. Why does no one write such books now? We were Don Quixote and Sancho Panza; we were Robinson Crusoe and Man Friday, that is, Leonard was Don Quixote or Robinson, while Celia was Sancho or Man Friday. Up the harbour was a flat little island, a peninsula at low tide, on which was a farmhouse. I daresay it must have been a dismal place to live upon, and by no means free from rats. But to us it was charming, for it was Robinson's Island. To this day I cannot look at the book without seeing the island again, and peopling it once more with the Solitary and his faithful Indian. When we read the "Pilgrim's Progress" Leonard with a stick personated Christian's terrific combat with Apollyon. Or, if we chanced upon the second part, Celia was Mercy, and knocked very prettily at the gate, while Leonard multiplied himself, and became in turns, or at the same time, the Dog, Beelzebub, and the Interpreter.

It was Leonard who called this place Celia's Arbour, after a glee which I found among Mrs. Tyrrell's music. The harmonies of the old four-part song lie in my heart associated with those early days, and with our own retreat. It is a tender glee, whose notes are yearnings and sighs, whose cadences are love's hypocrisies, breathing an almost arrogant confidence, while veiled behind a mask of pretended fear, assumed out of good manners, and certain to deceive no Celia that ever lived. We breathed no sighs, we hung no wreath by our Celia's Arbour, but it was a place where two boys learned to love one girl.

She was at first a wilful and uncertain little maid, her moods like the April sky for fitfulness; her way for the moment the one right way; her will law. She would have been a despot of the fiercest kind, but for one thing which saved her. It was her gift of reading the hearts of those she knew. If by that power of hers she read mine, and so could say with unerring instinct the thing she had to say, always in the way it should be said, then I suppose, she could read others. That wilfulness wore off as she grew up, but the mysterious power remained. She felt, or seemed to feel, what others thought. It is quite certain that this power can belong to those who think little about themselves, and comes from long watchfulness in observing the connection between thought and expression, and learning how to read the lightest flash of the eye. She was an only child, and her father was the very greatest man in all the town. Not that he was greater than the Governor Commandant of the Forces, or than the Port Admiral, but he was the greatest man of the municipality. He held, or had held, all the offices. He was a borough magistrate, ex-Mayor, chairman of everything, churchwarden, Past Master of the Masons' Lodge, and leader in everything. In person he was tall and portly, bearing himself with an upright and solid carriage. When he passed down the street the shopkeepers came to their doors and bowed; mothers pointed him out to their boys as an object of emulation; all the town respected him. He deserved their respect for showing them what Leonard was so anxious to find out for himself, how a man may rise in the world.

He had been errand-boy in a lawyer's office; he worked every evening, and so got learning, and he finally found himself at forty the leading solicitor and the most "prominent citizen" of the town.

He lived, after the fashion of the time, in the same house where he had his offices. It was a large red brick house, the very last in Castle Street before you came to the town wall. It had the door in the middle opening into a broad hall, with a large room on either side. These were the offices, and in addition to them was a certain structure built out at the side devoted to the clerks. The dining-rooms and Mrs. Tyrrell's habitual sitting-room, called the parlour, were at the back, overlooking a garden, large for a town house, planted with standard apples and pears, and standing behind borders in which flourished the common old-fashioned flowers, Virginia stocks, candy-tuft, mouse-ear, London pride, double stocks, wallflowers, gillyflowers, and the rest, including big hollyhocks, round which bees swarmed all the summer, planted in the corners. A gate at the end of the wall was unlocked all day, so that Celia and I could pass in and out without seeing or disturbing the clients. On the first floor was Mrs. Tyrrell's drawing-room, a salon which impressed the visitor with a sense of really aristocratic magnificence, so cold, so prim, and so very comfortless was it. It was never used, except for a dinner-party, that is, once or twice in the year. For lighter entertainments, such as "a few friends to tea," the parlour was thought quite good enough. Celia's piano was in the parlour; there was a grand in the drawing-room; downstairs you found comfort and ease; upstairs splendour and cold.

The daily life of a professional man, thirty years ago, was a good deal simpler, though in many ways more conventional than at present. He lived almost always, like Mr. Tyrrell, in the house where he had his office; he dined at one o'clock, and his dinners were extremely plain. At five he took tea, with bread and butter; at eight he finished work for the day, dismissed his clerks, and sat down at nine with his family to supper, the most cheerful meal of the day, going to bed at half-past ten.

There was no talk in those days of a month on the Continent, of the necessity for change, or an autumnal holiday; a dance for the young people might be looked for, in some quarter or other, three or four times in the year; to dance in the summer was unheard of; garden-parties were never dreamed of; lawn-tennis—even croquet—not yet invented; picnics things to imagine. There was a large garrison in the town, but the officers rarely appeared at the houses of the lawyers, and kept in their own sets; the best available society consisted of the numerous half-pay and retired naval officers, with the clergy and the professional men, and the maidens, who were far more "proper" than are their daughters of rinks and

Badminton, looked on a friendly gathering to tea, with a little music afterwards, or a round game, as the highest dissipation consistent with properly brought up young ladyhood. Yet they were perfectly happy. They did not read so much; they did not know so much as their successors; their taste in Art, Dress, Furniture, and Decoration had not been developed; they had not, like Ulysses, seen many men and many manners; they had no doubts on religion; they had not become strong-minded; they did not sit on School Boards, nor sigh for Female Suffrage; they had never heard of the Subjection of the Sex; they did not envy the wild delights open to rich young persons of their own sex in London, because they did not know them, except in terms too vague to be harmful. Yet they were, I should think, happier than the girl of the present day, because their hearts were set on simpler things. They dressed themselves as prettily as they knew how and could afford. I looked the other day in an old illustrated paper, and saw with a shudder the dresses of the girls whom I knew as a boy; the picture of female beauty adorned in the fashion of the day seemed a horrid caricature; but then the artist had not caught the sweet look of faces which not even a hairdresser can disfigure; and failed in showing the graceful lines which no foolish fashion-copyist can wholly conceal. Pass over the dress. They flirted a little, in their quiet way, after church on Sunday morning, and over the tea-things in the evening. They read novels, of a decorous order, and not in the least like certain romances now in vogue, written "by ladies for ladies." In the course of time, one by one, they got married, and became good wives and good mothers with old-fashioned notions. It was peaceful, this *vie de province*, and would have been virtuous, but for the sin of gossip; it was calm, and might have been happy, but for the misfortune of monotony.

A certain conventionality hung about every act of family life which was, or might be, public. People pretended a great deal. If a visitor called —I speak from information received, and not from my own experience— the work which the young ladies were engaged upon was put aside hastily, and they were presented, on the rising of the curtain, so to speak, reading in graceful attitudes. There was a fiction that callers required refreshment, and the decanters were placed upon the table, with the choice of "red or white." I observed, at an early age, that Mr. Tyrrell, when he took wine, which was not every day, abstained from the decanters reserved for the use of visitors, and opened a fresh bottle for himself. I thought, in those days, that it was disinterested generosity on his part, so as to give his visitors the best, but I know better now. The duration of a visit was inversely proportionate to the rank of the caller. In the case of "carriage company," a quarter of an hour at the outside was granted, so much at least being needed to impress the street. Humbler friends, in whose case the decanters might be speedily put away, and the needlework resumed, could stay a whole afternoon, if they pleased. On Wednesday and Friday evenings, those ladies who could boast of having "experienced" religion, went to church, and gave themselves little airs on account of superior spirituality. No one ever dreamed of inviting himself to any meal whatever, and if anybody was invited, he was made to feel that he was the guest, being pressed to eat of things provided in his honour, and becoming, whether he liked it or not, the centre of conversation. There was, therefore, a good deal of ceremony in our social festivities. The handing of the muffins, the dexterous use of the kettle, the division of the cake at tea, the invitation to hot spirits and water after supper, the request to sing, the management of the album: all these things required grace and deportment; quite young men went through the prescribed duties with manifest anxiety; young ladies were careful not to allow their natural happiness over a little social excitement to interfere with the exigencies of propriety; middle-aged men took a pride in saying and doing exactly the right thing in the right way. Everything in *bourgeois* society of that time had a right way. It is true that this anxiety to keep in the groove prevented originality of conversation; but then we all knew what to expect, were able to criticise the performances, afterwards, of a well-known *rôle*, and to congratulate ourselves on the very proper way in which everybody had behaved.

Pretence is vulgar, but when it is custom it somehow ceases to vulgarise. We have our customs still, but they are not quite so binding on us. There were plenty of vulgar people among us, but we were not necessarily vulgar because we dined at one, supped at nine, gave few parties, never went abroad, and observed little fashions, with little pretences which deceived nobody. So far we were only simple. Celia, at least, who was brought up in the lap of this conventionality, could not be, could never have been, vulgar.

On Sunday we went to St. Faith's Church, which stands in St. Faith's Square. The building belonged to the reign of the Third George, and was, externally, a great barn of red brick, set in a courtyard, surrounded by a red brick wall, and with a roof of red tiles. Inside it was a large white-painted edifice, resting on four pillars. There was a great gallery running all round, and, because the church was crowded, a second gallery higher up at the west end contained the organ and choir. The pulpit, reading-desk, and clerk's desk, forming between them a giant staircase, stood in the middle of the church; all three were broad and roomy; round the altar-rails sat a school of charity children, who pinched each other during the service. In the aisles were placed, between the pew-doors, little triangular brackets, on each of which sat, in evident discomfort, an aged lady, clad in black. They used to rise, curtsey, and open the doors for the gentlefolk when they came and when they went away. I used to wonder why these ancient dames came to church at all, considering the profound misery of those three-cornered brackets. But I believe there was a dole of some kind for them, and once a month they had the satisfaction of finishing the sacramental wine. The arrangement of the pews was irregular, the better sort among them being square. In those you sat upon high narrow seats of rough baize, with your feet on large hassocks, which made your flesh creep to touch. The square pews were a great stumbling-block to children, because they were convenient for making faces at each other, and this often led to subsequent tears. The Tyrrells had a square pew, in which little Celia sat always as demure as a nun. During the Communion Service, while the Epistle and Gospel were read, we all faced to the east out of politeness to the clergyman. Social distinctions were observed in getting up and sitting down. Poor people obeyed the summons of the organ promptly; those who had a position to illustrate, got up in the Grand style, that is, slowly, and with deliberation. They were well on their feet at about the middle of the second line in the hymn, and they held their hymn-books with an air of condescending criticism, as if there might, after all, be something in the words of the poet. At the close of the hymn they sat down as slowly as they had got up, long after the organ had finished, even some moments after the last of the old ladies in the triangular seats had ended her final squawk. And as they sat down they looked about the church as if to see that everybody was behaving properly. The Captain's pew, a long one, was behind Mr. Tyrrell's. Leonard often tried, but never succeeded in making Celia laugh. Not a single glance of her eye did she permit towards the pew where her two friends sat. Not a single smile when, Sunday after Sunday, the Captain lugged a key out of his pocket when the hymn was given out, and audibly instructed Leonard to "get out the tools," meaning the hymn-books. During the sermon, the seats were so high that there was no one to be seen except the preacher and the clerk; the latter was always asleep. And when we came out, we walked away with much solemnity, the elders discussing the sermon.

Time that is long past appears to have been so much longer than any period of the present. In twenty years or so, I suppose, I, for one, shall have finished my earthly career—perhaps, before then. But it does not seem so long to me now, looking forward to the end, as it does looking back on those years of school and early life, on which I have dwelt, perhaps, at too great length. Being a lonely man, without wife, kith, or kin, I like to think of the days when I had a brother and a sister. To be sure, I have them still, unaltered in affection, but they are not here. In the long winter evenings, when I am tired of pupils and melancholy, so tired sometimes that even Mendelssohn cannot bring me comfort, I sit by the fire and see little Celia once more, as she was, wayward and fitful, restless as a sprite, bright as a sunbeam, rosy-fingered as Aurora, dancing in and out among our hours, making them gay as a bright June morning; or standing as Minerva might have done, had that most unfortunate goddess ever known childhood, pensively looking out on the sunlit harbour; or, when she grew older, declaiming with passion against the wrongs she read of and the miseries she saw. For, as in every town where soldiers and sailors congregate, and drink is provided, there were many wrongs and much misery; wicked things which obtruded themselves upon even childish eyes. All evil seems to the young so easy to prevent and cure.

Sitting now by the winter fire, and gazing into the coals, it is always Celia that I see. She runs through my life like a scarlet thread in silk. And for five years—the five years of Leonard's "Wander Time"—we were always together, for I was her tutor.

I forgot to mention that I was a musician. Music is my profession. I am a music-master—"Mr. L. Pulaski" is on the brass door-plate, with underneath, "Lessons in Music and Singing." Music has been my joy and solace, as well as my profession. I believe I could play as soon as I was born; at all events I had no difficulty in learning; and when Mr. Tyrrell heard of my great gift, and generously presented me with a piano, I made myself, almost unassisted, a musician of skill as well as of feeling. For I played at every spare moment, and therefore I learned to play well. It was natural that I should help Cis in her music, and when I left school it was natural also that I should become not only her music-master, but her tutor in other things, and her companion. It was good of Mrs. Tyrrell to trust her to me; it was an education for me to have the charge. No brother and sister could have been drawn more closely together than we two. And I am quite sure that no man could love a girl more than I at all times loved Celia.

CHAPTER VII.
AUGUSTUS IN THE LEGAL.

I HAD one short experience of the way in which other people work for money. It lasted three months, and happened when Mr. Tyrrell, out of pure kindness, proposed that I should enter his office. He said many handsome things about me, in making this offer, especially in reference to his daughter, and pledged himself to give me my articles if I took to the work.

I accepted, on the condition that I kept my afternoons free for Celia, and began the study of the law.

Well, suffice it to say, that after three months the Captain became my ambassador to convey my resignation. And the only good thing I got out of my legal experience was the friendship of the Bramblers.

Augustus Brambler, the head of the family, was one of Mr. Tyrrell's clerks. Not the head clerk, who was a man of consideration, and had an office to himself, but one of half-a-dozen who sat in the room built for them at the side of the house, and drove the quill for very slender wage from nine in the morning to eight at night. Augustus was no longer young when I first met him, being then past forty years of age. And although the other clerks were little more than boys, Augustus sat among them with cheerful countenance and contented heart. He was short of stature, and his face was innocent of whisker and as smooth as any woman's; his features were sketchy, his eyes were large and bright, but his expression, in office hours, was maintained at a high pressure of unrelenting zeal. Nature intended him to be stout, but with that curious disregard for her colleague which Fate often shows, his income prevented the carrying out of Nature's intention. So that he remained thin, and, perhaps, in consequence, preserved his physical activity, which was that of a schoolboy. I was placed under his charge, and received papers to copy, while the chief clerk gave me books to read. I did copy the papers, to my infinite disgust, and I tried to read the books, but here I failed.

Augustus Brambler, I soon discovered, did the least responsible work in the office, enjoying a certain consideration by reason of the enormous enthusiasm which he brought into the service. He magnified his humble office; saw in it something great and splendid; beheld in himself the spring of the whole machine; and identified himself with the success of the House. You would think, to listen to him, that he had achieved the highest ambition of his life in becoming a clerk to Mr. Tyrrell, that his weekly stipend of thirty shillings was a large and magnificent income, and that the Firm was maintained by his own personal exertions.

Certainly these were not wanting. He was in the office first in the morning, and left it the last in the evening. He kept the other clerks to their work, not only by example but by precept, admonishing them by scraps of proverbial philosophy, such as—in the case of one who longed to finish and be gone—

"Hurry and haste are worsen than waste;"

or of one who was prone to scamp the work in order to talk,

"Sure and slow is the way to go; "

while in the case—too common among lawyers' clerks—of one who came too late to office, he had a verse as apt as if it had been a Shakespearian quotation, though I have never seen it in Shakespeare.

"What," he would say, "do we learn from the poet?

"'Get up betimes, and at the dawn of day,
For health and strength to serve your Master pray.
Sharp at clock striking at the point of eight,
Present yourself before the office gate.'

"It should have been nine," he would add, "but for the sake of the rhyme."

His eagerness to work was partly counterbalanced by his inability to do anything. He knew nothing whatever, after years of law work, of the most ordinary legal procedure; he could not even be trusted to copy a document correctly. And yet he was never idle, never wasting his employer's time. Mostly he seemed to be ruling lines laboriously in red ink, and I often wondered what became of the many reams beautified by Augustus with such painful assiduity. At other times he would take down old office books, ledgers, and so forth, and, after dusting them tenderly, would turn over the leaves, brows bent, pencil in hand, as if he were engaged in a research of the most vital importance. At all events, he did not allow the juniors to waste their time, and, as I afterwards found out, was only continued in the service of Mr. Tyrrell because he earned his weekly stipend by keeping thE youngsters at their work, carrying with him wherever he went an atmosphere of zeal.

He had not been always in the present profession.

"I have been," he would say grandly, "in the Clerical, in the Scholastic, and in the Legal. Noble professions all three. I began in the Clerical—was a clerk at Grant and Gumption's, where we had—ah!—a Royal business, and turned over our cool Thousands. Thought nothing of Thousands in that wholesale house. Mr. Gumption, the junior partner—he was an affable and kind-spoken man—once took me aside, after I had been there two years or so, and spoke to me confidentially. 'Brambler,' he said, 'the fact is this work is not good enough for you. That's where it is; you're too good for the work we give you. I should say you ought to change it for something superior—say in the Commercial Academy line, where your abilities would have full scope—full scope.' I thought that advice was very kindly meant, and I took it, though it really was a blow to give up sharing in those Enormous profits. However, he seemed to know best what was to my advantage, and so I retired from Grant and Gumption's with the best of recommendations, and joined Mr. Hezekiah Ryler, B.A., in his Select Academy for Young Gentlemen. Perhaps the salary was not so good as might have been desired, but the work—there was the great advantage—the work was splendid. There you are, you know, that's what it is, in that line—there you are. Dozens of possible Shakespeares learning their Latin grammar under your direction; posterity safe to read about you. 'This great man,' the biographer will say, 'was educated at the Select Academy of Mr. Hezekiah Ryler, B.A., one of whose assistants was the zealous Augustus Brambler.' That thought was enough to reconcile me to much that was disagreeable, for there are things about the work of an ush—I mean the assistant of a Commercial Academy, which some men might not like. I was with Mr. Ryler, B.A., for a year, I think, when he suggested—his manner was kindness itself—that perhaps I should find a more congenial sphere for my talents. I gave up the Scholastic, and tried some other line. He was so good as to suggest the Legal, and so I tried it. That was twenty years ago. Since then I've been going backwards and forwards between the Scholastic, the Legal, and the Clerical. It's a very remarkable thing, if you come to think of it, to be born with a genius fit for all three professions."

He firmly believed himself endowed by Nature with exceptional qualities, which fitted him equally for the positions of commercial clerk, legal clerk, or schoolmaster, and regarded the numerous dismissals which rewarded his labours as so many compliments to his energy and worth. In the sense I have already explained he was invaluable; his honesty and enthusiasm were contagious, and he never, I am sure, understood that, owing to some strange fogging of his enthusiastic brain, he could do nothing at all in the way in which it ought to have been done. When he was in the employment of a merchant his figures always came out wrong; when he was a teacher the boys never learned anything; and when he was a lawyer's clerk he could only be trusted to rule lines in red ink, copy letters in the press, serve a writ, and make a show, with a pile of paper, of doing important work. Yet, because the man was well known in the town for his breezy enthusiasm, for his integrity, and for the honesty which characterised all he did, Augustus Brambler had never been long without a place. He was now, however, a fixture at Mr. Tyrrell's.

One evening, after I had been a month or so in the office, he invited me, in the finest manner, to take supper at his house. Had he bidden me to a lordly banquet the invitation could not have been conveyed more grandly. I accepted, and walked home with him, presently finding myself in a back parlour lighted by a single candle, multiplied by two on our arrival. The cloth was laid for supper, and half-a-dozen children, from ten or twelve downwards, crowded round the bread-winner, and noisily welcomed him home. They were all absurdly like their father, their eyes were as twinkling, their faces as full of eager enthusiasm; their figures as stout. And there was exactly the same regularity of diminution in their size that may be remarked in a set of Pandean pipes.

The mother, on the other hand, was thin and anxious-looking. It was easy to see that this poor wan-cheeked and careworn creature shared none of her husband's golden joy in the present.

We sat down at once to the meal, Augustus Brambler saying grace in an impressive manner. It was a rich, and even an unctuous grace, such a grace as might be pronounced before a City dinner, thanking the Lord for the many and various good things He had provided for His creatures. And then, the hearts of all attuned to the solemnity of the occasion, he seized the knife, and looked round him with the air of one who is about to commence an important work.

"Bread, my children, bread and cheese. Your mother will carve the cheese. Mr. Pulaski—I should say, perhaps, Count Pulaski? No. My dear, Mr. Pulaski takes supper with us incognito, like a foreign prince. It is not often that we receive a nobleman at our simple table. Pray assist Mr. Pulaski from the green corner, which is more tasty. Crust, Mr. Pulaski? Forty-seven, your elbows are on the table. Forty-six, calm your impatience. That boy, Mr. Pulaski, will carry through life the effects of the fatal year in which he was born."

While he talked, he went on distributing crust and crumb with the same vigour with which he was wont to rule the red ink lines.

I ventured to ask if the children had no Christian names.

"It is only their father's way," said the mother. "They have names like any other Christians, but I don't think they know them themselves."

Augustus—the children being now all helped—sat back in his chair, and waved his hand with importance.

"My own theory," he explained, "formed even before I married, while I was in the Clerical. Matured while in the Scholastic, where I had access to works of philosophy, including the first book of Euclid, and to works of biography, including Cornelius Nepos. Published, if I may use the expression, while in the Legal. It is this, Mr. Pulaski. Childhood catches measles and whooping-cough, and shakes them off; but a child never shakes off the influences—Forty-eight, if you do not obey your sister you shall go to bed—of the year in which it was born. My eldest," he said, pointing to the tallest of his family, a girl, "was born in '44. She is therefore predisposed to poetry."

I did not ask why, but the girl, a pretty child of twelve, blushed and looked pleased.

"Her brother, Forty-five," Augustus continued, "is restless and discontented. That is easily explained if you think of the events of that year. A tendency, my boy, which you will have to combat during life. Like Asthma."

"When we come to Forty-six," he went on, "what can we expect? The Famine Year. The appetite of that boy would strain the finances of a Rothschild."

Forty-six, who was a healthy, rosy-cheeked boy, with no outward marks of the great Famine upon his fat little figure, was working his way diligently through a great crust of bread and cheese. He looked up, laughed, and went on eating.

"Forty-seven,"—pointing to a little girl,—"the year of calm. The calm before the storm. The next boy is Forty-eight. Ah! the year of rebellion. He is a boy who questions authority. If that boy does not take care to struggle with his tendency, I should not be surprised, when he grows up to find him throwing doubt upon the Thirty-nine Articles "

"O Augustus!" cried his wife.

"I should not, indeed, my dear. Forty-nine is gone to bed. So is Fifty. So is Fifty-two."

I was afraid to ask after Fifty-one, for fear there had been a loss, but I suppose the question showed in my face, because the family faces instantly clouded over.

"We never had a Fifty-one," said Augustus sorrowfully.

His wife sighed, and the little girls put their handkerchiefs to their eyes. Forty-six took advantage of the general emotion to help himself to another piece of bread.

"No Fifty-one," Augustus sighed."It was our unlucky fate. What a boy that Fifty-one would have been! All the wealth and genius of the world came to the front that year. I even wish, sometimes, that he had been twins."

We were all deeply touched, nor did it occur to me till afterwards that we were lamenting over a mere solution in the chain of annual continuity.

"But talking is dry work," resumed Augustus,—taking up a brown jug, one of those jolly old jugs, with a hunt upon them in relief, that are only now to be seen in the National Club—and bestowing an Anacreontic smile upon his family. "What have we here, boys and girls, eh? What have we?"—as if there were an infinite choice of drinks in that house. He poured out a glass, holding it up to the light, turning it about, and critically catching the colour at the proper angle. "Clear as a bell—sparkling as champagne. Let us taste it.—Toast and water, my children—aha! Toast and water—and—the—very—best—I ever tasted."

We had glasses round, and all smacked our lips over the nasty concoction, and he went on in his enthusiastic strain.

"It is a splendid business, the Legal. We are making —not to betray the confidence of the house, only we are here all friends—we are actually making more than two hundred pounds a month; think of that, children, Two—Hundred—Pounds—a month. Fifty pounds a week—eight pounds six shillings and eightpence every working day. Nearly fifteen shillings an hour—threepence a minute! "

All the children gave a great gasp. At the moment they firmly believed their father to be personally in receipt of this fine income. Poor little shabby boys and girls, with their darned and patched clothes, their bread and cheese banquets, and their toast and water. It was, indeed, a splendid income that their father enjoyed.

Supper ended, the children went off to bed. Then we put out the candles, not to waste light, and sat round the open window for half an hour, for it was a warm night, talking.

At least Augustus Brambler talked. And I began to see what an atmosphere of imaginary ease the man lived and moved. His social position was, in his own eyes, an enviable one; his abilities were recognised; his future was one of steady advance; his children were well fed, well dressed, and well educated; his poor wife as happy as himself.

From time to time I heard a footstep overhead.

"It is Herr Räumer. We allow him to occupy our first floor," Augustus explained grandly. He was not by any means anxious to hide the fact, that he had a lodger who paid the whole of the rent, but it was his way of putting it.

I knew Herr Räumer by sight, because he came a good deal to Mr. Tyrrell's office. He was a German—a very big man, tall and stout, with a white moustache—a great mass of perfectly white hair, of the creamy whiteness which does not convey the impression of age or decay, and had a tread like a cat for lightness. He walked as upright as a soldier, wore blue spectacles out of doors, and had a curious voice, very deep with a rasp in it. But as yet I had never spoken to him.

"He is our lodger," said Mrs. Brambler. "And he gives us a deal of trouble with his veal cutlets."

"Eats them with prunes," said Augustus.

"And complains of his tea. But he pays his bill every week, and what we should do without him I am sure I do not know. He is a very regular man. He has dinner at six, and smokes his pipe till half-past ten. Then he goes to bed. Where is Ferdinand, my dear?"

"At work in his room. But it is almost his time." As he spoke the door opened, and Ferdinand Brambler came in. It was almost too dark to see him, but I knew his face, having seen it about the streets as long as I could remember. He was very much like his brother, being short, smooth cheeked, and inclined to be stout, but he had not the same look of eager zeal. That was replaced by an expression of the most profound wisdom. And he had a habit of throwing his head backwards, and gazing into the sky, which I understood later on.

I rose to go because it was past ten. As Augustus led me out of the room I heard Mrs. Brambler ask anxiously—"What have you done to-day, Ferdinand?"

"A leg of mutton," he replied in a sepulchral voice. "And I think heeling and soling for one of the children's boots besides."

CHAPTER VIII.
THE UNFORTUNATE YOUNG NOBLEMAN.

I CONTINUED my acquaintance with Augustus Brambler after I left Mr. Tyrrell's office. The atmosphere of that place very soon, as I have explained, became unbearable to me. The tips of my fingers began to feel as if they were made of parchment, which, as Cis confessed, would be bad for playing. In those days, too, clerks always stuck their pens behind their ears, a practice to which I could never reconcile myself. The association of that beautiful and delicate organisation the ear, the only avenue of the sixth sense, the appreciation of music, with quills and legal forms, was revolting. Then what harmonies can be got out of the scraping of pens upon paper? The wind in the trees one can understand; and the waves by the shore; and the purling of a brook; but the scratching of steel, which you hardly perceive at first, but which makes itself heard with a strident noise which after a time becomes out of all proportion to the size of the instrument, who is to become reconciled to that? As an instrument of torture, I can conceive nothing worse than a room full of pens all at work together.

Old Wassielewski, who after nearly effacing himself during the schooldays was beginning to take a new interest in my proceedings, approved of my giving up the law. That a Pulaski should be a clerk in a lawyer's office was a blot upon the scutcheon; that he should become an actual practising lawyer was an abandonment of everything. When my destiny came to me in the shape of music-lessons, he was good enough to signify approval, on the ground that it would do for the short time I should want to work for money. I paid small attention to his parenthetical way of looking at life—all the Poles lived in this kind of parenthesis, waiting for the downfall of Russia, carrying on their little occupations, which lasted them till death allowed their souls to return to Poland, under the belief that it was only for a time. The Captain, however, deserved more respectful attention. He had small admiration for writing in any form; was accustomed to confound the highest works of genius with the commonest quill-driving; quoted an old acquaintance of the ward-room who once wrote a novel, and never held his head up afterwards; "Sad business, Laddy. Half-pay at forty."

As for giving music-lessons, the Captain was perplexed. To play on any instrument whatever seemed to him a waste of a man—at the same time there was no doubt in his own mind that I was only half a man. And when he clearly understood that I did not propose to lead a procession of drunken sailors like poor old Wassielewski, or to play the fiddle at a soldiers' free-and-easy, he gave in.

"Have your own way, Laddy. Jingle the keys and make other people jingle. There's sense in a song like 'The Death of Nelson' or 'Wapping Old Stairs'—and those you never care to play. But have your own way."

Gradually, the Captain came to see some of the advantages of the profession."You give your lesson, take your money, and go. So much work and so much pay. No obligation on either side. And your time to yourself."

It was evident to me, as soon as I began to give lessons, that I was engaging myself for the rest of my life to become a music master. I became a music master, because there was really nothing else for me at which I could earn my bread. Teaching of any other kind would have been intolerable, if only for the fact of my unlucky figure. Æsop, himself the most philosophical of hunchbacks, would have trembled at the thought of facing a class of boys—that age which La Fontaine says is without pity. But to sit for an hour beside a girl playing exercises while the mild-eyed governess played propriety was different. So I gave up everything except the piano and the organ, and started in practice as a teacher of the pianoforte. As Nature had given me a reasonably good pipe, I engaged myself at the same time to teach singing.

I was eighteen then, perhaps too young to take upon myself the responsibility of teaching. But pupils came to me, and in a few months I was happily beyond the want of any further help from the Captain. People invited me to give lessons from different motives; some because they thought that a Pole would take their girls at half the price of ordinary professors—in the same way, after the Commune of 1871, the friends of the exiles got them pupils on the ground that they would teach French for a shilling an hour; some came to me because I was young, and they wanted to boast that they were encouraging rising genius; a few, no doubt, because they really thought I could play well and teach their daughters. One lady who had a select boarding and day school—she dressed in black cotton velvet, and bound her brows with a black ribbon, as if to compress and control the gigantic intellect beneath—engaged my services, as I afterwards learned, in order that she might announce on her cards that music was taught at Cape St. Vincent House (established 1780) by the "young, unfortunate, and talented Polish nobleman, Count Ladislas Pulaski." But as there is no possible romance about a lad of five feet nothing, with long arms, crooked back, and round shoulders, parents who came from a distance, allured by the "unfortunate foreign nobleman," were not allowed to see me. I found out the thing after a time, and was foolish enough, being then quite young, to throw up the engagement in a rage quite befitting my illustrious descent. Afterwards I learnt to behave with patience when I was received, as always happened, with a certain deference; but I really think that English people did not grovel before a title so abjectly twenty years ago as they do now—and I grew accustomed to overhear the familiar whisper:

"A Count, my dear, in his own country, and here too, if he chooses to enjoy the title, of most distinguished Polish family."

"Enjoy the title." What a wonderful expression! Does a Duke awake in the morning and begin to smack his lips when a valet says"Your Grace"? Does he stand before his title as before a picture, catching it in different lights? Does he turn the name about as a jewel of many facets, pleasing his eye with the lustre? I have tried to imagine all the sensual delights possible to be got out of an acknowledged Countship, were one independent enough to bear it openly, and I have always failed.

My lessons were given in the morning, so that I had the more time for Celia. Long before this I had become a son of the house at the Tyrrells'. I came and went unnoticed; it was not thought necessary to improve the family tea or supper on my account; no cakes and muffins were provided, and the decanters were not produced in my honour. That was very pleasant. Also it was an understood thing that I was Celia's companion, guardian, duenna, watch-dog—anything. "It is a great comfort," said her mother, "to feel that she is with Ladislas. He is so steady."

In those days there were no choral societies, madrigal unions, or part-singing in our town. Girls sang duets, but young men seldom took any trouble to cultivate their voices, and unless sometimes when, under pressure, they attempted ambitious things set for high tenor voices, like "Good-bye, Sweetheart," or "Ever of Thee," wreaking a wicked will upon time and tune, they never sang at all. Musical young men, as they were called, were looked upon with a little disfavour as likely to turn out badly. Therefore it was a novelty in our small circle when Celia and I sang duets.

She learned to play, not brilliantly—perhaps from some defect in my teaching power—but softly and delicately, as if she loved what she played. She had the power of bringing out fresh sweetnesses, such as I had never felt in my own playing of the same piece. It is so always in the highest music. Play it a hundred times, exhaust, as you think, every chord of passion, yearning, faith, prayer, and hope, teach yourself to believe that it is a landscape which you have studied under a thousand effects of light and shade until you know its every possible aspect. Another plays it. Lo! on every side you discern hitherto undiscovered glades of sweet greenery arched by great cathedral aisles in which birds sing endless songs of praise; and clear before you, erewhile so dark and doubtful, lies the path which leads to the higher world, a sunny lane planted by loving hands with flowers, bordered with honeysuckle and meadowsweet, stretching broad and bright to the Gates of Emerald. The best thing about being a musician is that you can understand the music of others.

I encouraged Celia to play only from the best composers, because, while we have the best music to teach us, and the best poetry to speak our thoughts for us, it seems so great a sin to waste ourselves upon lower and ignoble things.

In course of time I began to essay little things of my own: feeble flights, imitations, echoes of the masters. Celia played them, praised them, and then went back to the masters. This showed me what a mere apprentice I was. For that matter I am not yet out of my articles.

Sometimes, after playing one of my own studies, it would please us to see Mrs. Tyrrell waking up out of the doze in which she spent most of her afternoons, and nod her head placidly—

"That is a very pretty piece of Mozart, Celia. I always liked that movement."

Or : "That has always been my favourite in Mendelssohn."

Why is it that people should take shame to themselves for not understanding music, and cover themselves with ignominy by the pretence? No one is ashamed to say that he does not know Hebrew or mathematics. And yet, unless one goes through the regular mill, how can music be known any more than mathematics?

Mrs. Tyrrell reminded me of those fakeers, or yogis, who attain to Heaven by perpetually gazing upon a particular toe. She spent her afternoons in a motionless contemplation of the work which she held in her hands. From time to time her eyes closed, but only for a few moments, when the lazy eyelid lifted, and the limpid eyes, which were like the eyes of fallow-deer for absence of care, rested again upon the work. A gentle, easy, motionless woman, who could not understand her bright and eager daughter. A good woman, too, and a kind mother, always careful that her Celia had the best.

We were at that age when the soul is charged with uncertain longings. Youth is the time when poetry has the greatest power over us. There are so many things we have to say; our thoughts fly here and there like a young bird in early summer, not aimlessly, but without control; the brain has not been forced into a single groove, and hardened by long continuance in that groove; the ways of the world are all open. There is no relief in speech, because, for such thoughts, the tongue is powerless. Therefore one falls back upon poetry. It makes me sad now to think of the days when our minds, saturated with the winged words of Keats, Byron, or Wordsworth, were as full of clouded visions, sunlit, mist-coloured, crossed with gleam of glory, as any picture by Turner. Where are they gone, the dreams of youth? "Où. est la neige d'autan?" For if, in the after years, one such vision comes, evoked for a few moments by the breath of some mighty music, it is but a passing gleam. The fierce noontide light of midday soon disperses the clouds,, and gathers up the mists. Perhaps, when evening falls upon us, they will come again, those glimpses of the better world.

We wandered hand-in-hand, a pair of dreaming children, or sat in Celia's Arbour, gazing out upon the broad bosom of the harbour. From the moat below us, which was the practice-ground of young buglers, trumpeters, and drummers, there came blown about by the breeze, the reveille, the call to retreat, the charge, and the eager rub-dub of the drum, which somehow acts so strongly upon the fighting nerves of the soldier. And every day in that busy port there was the firing of salutes, the solemn Dead March for a regimental funeral, with the quick rattle of muskets over his grave, the band of a regiment marching through the streets, and the booming of artillery practice, sounds to remind us of the world outside, to which we did not belong, but which fired our imagination.

And many kinds of life. At the end of the grassy meadow before our feet was a gate leading into the upper end of the Dockyard. Through the gate streamed the Liberty men, like schoolboys at play. And after them, going along as slowly as they possibly could, would be sometimes driven a file of wretched convicts, spade in hand, to dig and entrench in some of the Government works. There was a horrible fascination in looking at the convicts. What crimes had they committed? Why were they unhappy above other men who had sinned and not been found out? What miserable mothers and sisters mourned somewhere their degradation? How could they bear the grey uniform of disgrace, the horrible companionship of criminals, the wretched life on the hulks? Which were the men whose time was almost up, and how would they meet their release, and the return to a world which for ever afterwards would scorn them?

Sentiment all this, perhaps; it is the unhappy thing about us all when we pass into the work time, and youth's brief holiday is over, that we have no more sentiment, which is often but another name for sympathy. Men try to crystallise themselves into critics, and therefore put themselves as much as they can outside the emotions. That is what makes poets, novelists, and painters hate and detest the *métier* of critic.

Meantime, no news of Leonard. We knew that there could be none, and yet we hoped. Leonard, of course, would keep his word. He would not write for five years; but yet, perhaps, in some indirect way, there might come news about him.

"I wonder in what way, Laddy? Of course he will be successful. Sometimes I think he is in London, writing poetry. Suppose he is already a great poet, everybody buying his wonderful verses?"

This was an extreme view to take, but then we were quite ignorant of publishing, and thought, perhaps, that a poet sprang ready-made into existence and popularity. However, on cooler thoughts, the idea of Leonard taking to poetry did not commend itself to me.

"He may have gone to the Bar, Laddy, and be a great advocate."

It certainly did occur to me that advocates are seldom great at one or two and twenty.

"Or perhaps he may have become a merchant prince. Not a small trader, you know, but a great man, with fleets of ships and armies of clerks."

We breathed faster, and looked at each other with flushed cheeks. What success was too great for our hero?

"Laddy," Celia went on, sagely, "we must not choose, because we might be disappointed. Then Leonard would see the disappointment in our faces, and that would hurt him. We must wait—and hope. Patience, Laddy."

"Patience, Cis."

It was some proof of the strength of Leonard's character that everybody believed in his success. This young hero had gone forth to conquer the world. There would be no difficulties for him. Celia and I naturally looked upon him, our elder playfellow, with the respect of those who had been children with him, and younger than himself. This kind of feeling never dies out. The opinions of childhood throw out roots which spread all through the after years, and cling round the heart of eighty as much as round the heart of ten. And to this day I regard Leonard, just as I used to, as a being quite superior to myself.

The Captain openly spoke of him as one who had gone into the world to show what a man might do in it. Mr. Tyrrell, who was not naturally an enthusiastic man, would congratulate the Captain on the success of the boy. And Mrs. Tyrrell—how that good lady managed to be infected by the general enthusiasm I do not know—quoted Leonard as an example, when she felt inclined to moralise, of what religion and industry will effect for young people. What she thought they had done for Leonard I do not know. Perhaps she pictured him in a Bishop's apron. As for Mrs. Jeram, who also fell into the popular delusion, she openly thanked Providence for bringing such a boy into the world. She always knew, she said, by those infallible signs which only experienced persons can detect, that the baby—meaning Leonard—was going to be a great man.

There were others, too. The Rev. Mr. Broughton, when he met the Captain or myself, would invite us to go home with him and drink Leonard's health in a glass of curious brown sherry, adding that he always knew that boy would get on. And Mrs. Pontifex once warned us solemnly against the pride that comes of worldly success.

All this was very delightful, and helped to keep us in a glow of pride and pleasure which made the long five years pass away quickly. There was only one discordant voice. It came from Herr Räumer, who lodged with the Bramblers, whose acquaintance I had now made.

"You think," he said, in his German accent, "that this— what do you call him?—this boy has become a great man. What do you know about it? Nothing. What can a boy do without money and without friends? Nothing. He is some poor clerk in a merchant's office; he is a shopman behind a counter; he is an usher in a school; he has gone to Australia, and is a wretched shepherd. What else can a poor boy become? Great man! Bah! you are all fools together, Ladislas Pulaski. But go on, go on, if it will make you happy; go on till you find out the truth."

CHAPTER IX.
HOPES AND FEARS.

IN the year 1854 began the Russian war. To me, because in those days I read few papers and took small interest in politics, the first signs of the impending struggle came from the Polish Barrack. Here, from the autumn of 1853, there reigned an unwonted animation. Letters and foreign newspapers were received daily; secret information was whispered about; strangers came down from London; the men gathered themselves into little knots and whispered. The most eager of them all was Wassielewski. He was transformed; he bore himself erect, with head thrown back; those deep-set eyes of his lost their look of expectant melancholy, and were bright with hope; he even seemed to have lost his limp. It was easy for me to understand that all this preliminary joy meant another rising in Poland. The weakness of Russia was to be the opportunity of my compatriots. In this quiet retreat they were plotting and conspiring. I came and went among them as I pleased, known to every one. They did not tell me their plans, but I observed that as they talked their eyes from time to time turned to me, and I discerned that they were discussing whether I should be made a conspirator with the rest and a sharer in their visions. I understood—it was only part of the general humiliation of a hunchback—that they were undecided whether one so useless physically could not be of use in the way of his name; whether, in fact, it was worth while to sacrifice my life, as well as their own, because I was Ladislas Pulaski. For the first time I felt a Pole indeed, in the strange thought that perhaps, after all, I, too, might be called upon to strike my blow, such as it was, for Polish freedom.

I had been kept strangely ignorant up to this time, and even later, of my own family history and of the circumstances under which I was brought to England. I knew that I was the son of a Polish noble; that my father perished in one of the obscure and hopeless village risings which took place some years after the great insurrection of 1831, and were too local to be recorded in contemporary history; also, that it was old Wassielewski who brought me, a mere infant, in his own arms, safely to England. When I asked the Captain for further information, he put off the question. When, as a boy, I asked Wassielewski, he patted my head kindly and bade me wait. I understood, therefore, very early, that there was more to be told in somebody's good time.

I believe that it was by the Captain's wish that I was kept from the knowledge of things which might have maddened my boyish brain; because I can hardly give Wassielewski credit for an act of forbearance towards the Romanoff name which lasted twenty years.

In the spring of 1854, when it became quite certain that Russia would have to face the strongest combination of allies ever formed, the day of deliverance seemed to be dawning for Poland. It was a delusive hope, as we know, because Prussia and Austria, *participes criminis*, could not look on in silence while the Russian part of the divided land freed itself and set a bad example to their own Poles. I have sometimes dreamed an impossible thing—that Germany, which pretends to be the most advanced outpost of civilisation, and Austria, which boasts of her easy rule, might some day join together and restore their share in the unholy partition to Liberty. What madness possessed them ever to dismember that ancient kingdom of independent Slavs, which could never threaten Germany, and stood as a bulwark against the barbaric Muscovite? But it was a foolish dream. Nations never voluntarily make reparation. Unto the fourth and even the fifth generation they pay for crimes in their children's blood; but they do not make atonement for the sin.

While the hopes of the exiles were highest, Wassielewski began to tell me tales of Polish daring and Russian cruelty.

"You are a Pole," he used to finish his narrative; "remember always that you are a Pole. You owe yourself to your country. It may be your duty, as well as mine, to die in her cause. The day is coming when you will have to act."

But as yet, nothing of my father.

In those days, too, Herr Räumer first began to talk to me. I met him at Mr. Tyrrell's office, and he invited me to visit him at his lodgings, which were, as I have explained, the first floor of Augustus Brambler's house.

Here he received me with great cordiality. Indoors he removed the blue spectacles, which he habitually wore in the streets, and showed a pair of keen bright eyes which certainly did not look as if they required any shelter from the light. His room was furnished with great simplicity, like the quarters of an officer on active service—a table, a sideboard, one or two chairs—his own being a wooden armchair—a slip of carpet before the fire—a pianoforte—constituted all that his simple wants required. On the wall hung one or two weapons, a pair of rapiers crossed, a rifle, and a brace of pistols. On the mantelshelf were two or three pipes, and a cigar-case. In the open sideboard I observed a goodly row of bottles, which I rightly judged from their shape and colour of the glass to contain German wine. Herr Räumer drank every day a bottle of this for dinner and another bottle before going to bed. He had one of those heads which are never the worse for wine, however much they swallow.

I felt very small sitting opposite this big man with the keen eyes which looked straight through me, his great head crowned with a mass of grey hair, his face, which looked like the face of one who commanded men habitually, adorned with the heavy white moustache and the long white eyebrows, the strong and resolute chin, the upright pose, the very strength in the man's figure—all this impressed me.

He saw that I was impressed, and I think it pleased him.

He began to talk at once about Poland. He had long, he said, felt deeply for the sorrows and sufferings of my unfortunate country. Unhappily, as I knew, he was a German, and in Germany there were some sympathies which were not to be openly expressed. If a German gentleman, he said, desired liberty of the Press, freedom of discussion, elevation of the masses, liberal institutions, the restoration of Poland, or any kindred thing, it behoved him to be silent and possess his soul in patience. Here in England, and the doors closed, alone with a Polish gentleman, he could speak his mind. The fact was, the condition of things not only in Russia, but also in Austria and Prussia, was deplorable. He saw before him one who had suffered in the cause—I thought afterwards that my own exertions in the cause as a year-old baby hardly entitled me to speak as a martyr—he could tell me cases of Russian cruelty which would make my blood boil.

"There is," he said, "thank Heaven! left to mankind the sacred duty of rebellion. The Czar knows of this, and trembles on his throne. From generation to generation the duty is handed down. Even now," his voice sank to a whisper,"even at this very moment, it is whispered that the Poles are meditating another insurrection. Russia's weakness is Poland's opportunity. While her energies are all bent upon the war, the Poles will rise again, and proclaim the Republic of Warsaw. But of course your friends in the Polish Barrack tell you all that is going on."

"Indeed they do not," I replied, with a jealous feeling that if they did I should hardly be justified in retailing their information to one who, however much he might sympathise with the cause, was certainly not a Pole.

"I imagine," he said, "but of course I know nothing, that an attempt will be made this very year. It seems a favourable moment. The Polish exiles will return to join in the movement. It is devoutly to be hoped that they might succeed. And so Wassielewski tells you nothing. It seems hardly fair."

"Nothing."

It did not strike me till afterwards that it was strange that Herr Räumer should know anything of Wassielewski.

"Ah! he thinks the time has not yet come. And yet you are seventeen, you are strong, and can handle a gun. It is not well of Wassielewski. Courage, my boy. I prophecy that many a Russian shall fall by your hand yet."

He always spoke on the assumption that another outbreak was to come, that I was to take part in it, and that the Poles were keeping the knowledge of my own past from me. The prospect had its charm, even to me, the peaceful musician. I do believe that, hunchback as I was, I should have played the part of a man had Fate willed that I was to revisit my native country.

He changed the subject and presently began talking about music. Then he sat at the pianoforte and began to run his fingers up and down the keys. He could not play, but he possessed—many men do—an almost instinctive power of picking out melodies, and filling them with simple chords. He asked me if I knew the German national airs, and then he began to sing them. We all know them now, these simple lieder with the tears in every bar—but twenty years ago they were not so well known. He sang them sentimentally, and if it had not been for that strange rasp in the voice, musically. The tears came into his eyes as he sang.

"The sorrows," he said, "of other people are so very sad—at a distance. Seen close, they annoy."

But the weeks passed on, and nothing was done. As hope changed to doubt the faces of the Poles grew despondent, Wassielewski left off telling his stories of Polish valour; he lost his look of eager expectation, and he hung his head, as before, with dejected air and mournful deep-set eyes.

"It is all over," said Herr Räumer one evening. "Your life is safe, friend Ladislas. For so much you ought to be thankful. And the Russians need not fear your rifle for another year or two. No doubt," he added with a gentle sneer, "they are thankful, too."

"Why is it all over?"

"Because Austria and Prussia will not permit revolt. Have they not got Poles of their own?"

I began to declaim about the wickedness of Governments and statesmen.

Herr Räumer heard me politely.

Then he filled another pipe, leaving the old one to cool, drank two glasses of hock, and replied slowly —

"Quite true, Ladislas Pulaski. No doubt at your age I should have thought, and perhaps said, the same thing. The wickedness of diplomatists is a reproach to modern civilisation. Yet, if you consider the matter, you will acknowledge that without their wickedness, there would be really very little in life worth having. No indignation, no sermons, no speakers at meetings, no societies. What a loss to Great Britain!"

"We could do without societies," I said.

"A great deal more would go if political and other wickedness are to go. There would be no armies, no officers, no lawyers, no doctors, no clergymen. The newspapers would have nothing to say, because the course of the world could be safely predicted by any one. All your learned professions would be gone at a blow."

I laughed.

"Music and painting would remain."

"But what would the painters do for subjects? You can't create any interest in the picture of a fat and happy family. There would be no materials for pathos. No one would die under a hundred; and, as he would be a good man, there would be no doubt about his after fate. No one would be ill. All alike would be virtuous, contented, happy—and dull."

"Why dull?"

"Why dull? Because there would be nothing left to fight, to fear, to guard against. Dull?" he took his pipe from his mouth, and yawned. "Dull? The human brain cannot conceive of a more appalling, of a more sleepy dullness than that of the world gone good."

"At least, the rulers of the world are supposed to be always trying to bring that end about."

"Supposed, my young friend? Yes, by you, and enthusiastic young gentlemen like yourself. Dull? Why if you think of it, you would not even have your virtues left, because there would be no need for them. Bravery, self-denial, patience, resignation, patriotism, thrift—-these would all vanish, because there would be no longer any occasion for them. No, Ladislas Pulaski, the wickedness of diplomatists keeps the world alive. There are always plenty of fools to shout, fling up their caps, believe everything they are told, and go away to get killed. The world go good? Much as I deplore the wickedness of wicked man, I trust that general goodness may not happen in my time."

Herr Räumer was right. There was no Polish rising. But our little colony was broken up and thinned by the departure of many of the exiles. Some went out on secret service; some fought in the Turkish lines; a few volunteered in the English and French armies; some joined the German Legion. But Wassielewski stayed on, sadder, more hollow-eyed than ever.

***

One day, about the beginning of the war, I was saluted in the street—it was on the Hard—by a tall and good-looking young sailor, in his naval rig, the handiest ever invented.

"Hope you're well, sir."

It was Jem Hex.

I shook hands with him. He told me that he was going aboard the

Impérieuse for the Baltic Sea Fleet, and that they hoped to have a lively time.

The Baltic Fleet! The war was a real thing, then. And good-natured Jem was going to have the honour of fighting for his country.

He seemed to take it very easily; and he had all the old sea-dog's confidence in thrashing the enemy.

I asked him after Moses.

"Moses," he replied, in a hesitating way. "Moses—well —Mr. Pulaski—if I were you, sir—I don't think I'd ask about Moses. He hasn't turned out —not what you might call a credit."

One figure I missed, among others, from the row of wooden-legged veterans on the beach.

It was that of Mrs. Jeram's erring husband. The old man fell off his stool one night, outside his wife's house, in a fit. She took him in and nursed him till he died. So they were reconciled. And then Mrs. Jeram came to be housekeeper to the Captain.

CHAPTER X.
WAR.

WAR! I was eighteen at the close of the "long, long canker of Peace," as Tennyson called it—why does every poet try to be a Tyrtæus? And why should holy Peace be called cankerous? The country put on its rusty armour, sharpened its swords, and sent out aged generals brought up in old traditions of Peninsular times. When news came of the first Turkish successes at Oltenitza, and we read of the gallant defence of Silistria, one began to realise that we were actually in the piping times of war. For my own part, I was pleased and excited, independently of my private, and Polish, reasons for excitement. It seemed to my foolish understanding that the forty years since Waterloo, those years in which the world had done so much in a quiet and peaceful way to make wars more bloody, had been quite wasted and thrown away. The making of railways, the construction of steamers, the growth of great armaments, were things done slowly and without dramatic tableaux. Now what the world likes, in contemplating the never-ending human comedy, is that from time to time the curtain should fall for a few moments on a thrilling and novel situation. This we were going to have.

"It is splendid, Cis," I cried, with the latest war news in my hand. "Splendid. Now we are going to live in history. We too shall hear hymns to the God of battles; we shall understand the meaning of the war fever; we shall know how men feel who live in a time of battles, sieges, and victories."

Celia did not respond as I expected to this newly-born martial enthusiasm.

"And the soldiers will be killed," she said sadly. "The poor soldiers. What does war mean to them but death and wounds?"

"And glory, Cis. They die for their country."

"I would rather they lived for their country. Laddy, if the new history that we are going to live in is to be like the old, I wish it was over and done with. For the old is nothing but the murdering of soldiers. I am sick of reading how the world can get no justice without fighting for it."

Looked at from Celia's point of view, I have sometimes thought that there is something in her statement. So many kings; so many battles; so many soldiers fallen on the field of honour. Blow the trumpets; beat the drums; bring along the car of Victory; have a solemn *Te Deum*; and then sit down and make all things ready for the next campaign.

"What good," this foolish young person went on, "does the glory of a nameless soldier shot in a field, and buried in a trench, do to his mourning people? I know, Laddy, needs must that war come, but let him who appeals to the sword die by the sword."

When General Février laid low the author of the world's disturbance, and the Poles lamented because their enemy was gone before they had had time to throw one more defiance in his teeth, I thought of Celia's words, and they seemed prophetic.

"Why do the Russians fight the Turks?" she went on. "What harm have the Turks done to the Russians, or Russians to Turks?"

I suggested outraged and oppressed Christians.

"Then let the Christians rise and free themselves," she went on, "and let us help them. But not in the Czar's way. And as for the soldiers, would they not all be far happier at home?"

Nor could any argument of mine alter her opinion on this point; a heresy which strikes at the very root of all wars.

To be sure, if we read history all through—say the history of Gibbon, the most bloodthirsty historian I know—it would be difficult to find a single one out of his wars that was chosen by the people. "Now then, you drilled men," says King or Kaiser, "get up and kill each other." The *Official Gazette* proclaims the popular enthusiasm, shouting of war-cries, and tossing of caps—the value of which we know in this critical age. But the people do not get up of their own accord. There is a good deal of fighting again in the Chronicles of old Froissart, but I remember no mention anywhere of popular joy over it. The historian is too honest to pretend such nonsense. In fact, it never occurred to him that people could like it. They were told to put on their iron hats, grasp their pikes, and make the best of things. They obeyed with resignation; their fathers had done the same thing; they had been taught that war was one of the sad necessities of life—that, and pestilence, and the tyranny of priests, and the uncertainty of justice; you had to fight just as you had to work, or to be born, or to die; the pike was an emblem of fate. For wise and mysterious purposes it was ordained by Providence that you were to be cuffed and beaten by your officers before being poked through the body by the iron point of the enemy's pike. It has been, hitherto, impossible for mankind to get out of this mediæval way of thinking; some Continental nations, who believe they are quite the advance-guard of civilisation, even go so far as to preserve the cuffing to this day as part of their Heaven-sent institutions. It is taught in the schools as belonging to the Divine Order, and therefore to be taken with resignation. At the same time, we need not go so far as to expect actual love for cuffing—with desire for more cuffing

—from modern Prussians, any more than from mediæval French or English.

Not one single common soldier, among all the millions who make up the rank and file of modern armies, wants to go fighting. And yet what a lot of fighting there is!

Suppose, some day, when the glorious army on either side was ordered to advance, the brave fellows were to sit down instead with a cheerful grin, leaving the kings to fight out the quarrel in a duel.

Now and then, things getting really intolerable, the people wake up and have a Jacquerie, a Revolution, or a Reformation. But that is civil war, the only kind of war which the unpatriotic mob really cares about.

"All the world," said foolish Cis, "praying daily for peace. And praying for peace since ever they began to pray at all. And what has come of it?"

"I do not see much good," said the Captain, who took the mediæval view about war, "in praying for what you must help yourself to. If all the world agreed on peace, there would be peace. And then it would be no good having a bigger fleet than your neighbour."

I try to put my obvious point in a new and striking light: that nations who will not sit still, but get up quarrels with other nations, ought to have all their arms taken from them. Fancy Russia without an army or a fleet, obliged to live peacefully and develop herself! Why, in ten years she would be civilised; and then we should see strange things. But my point, however cleverly put, will not convince the Captain, whose opinions on the necessity of war are based upon the advantages of a superior fleet.

After all, it is a great thing to be the adopted son of a land like this isle of England, which can never again, we hope, be made to serve the ambition of kings and priests; never more drive her sons by the thousand to the slaughterhouse, or her daughters to lamentations and tears, for aggrandisement. The only country in Europe of which such a boast may be made.

When will it cease? When will men be strong enough to say, "Enough; we will have no more of your military caste; we will have no more of your great armies; we will never fight again, except to defend ourselves?"

And Russia to set herself up as the protector of Christians! Russia to be the advocate of humanity! Russia the champion of civilisation! Ask the opinions of Poland on these points; go seek those of Turkestan; of Circassia; of Khiva; of Siberia. Call on the Czar and the Court to tell their secret history which everybody knows; on the nobles to lay bare the story of their lives; on the officers to confess their barbaric licence; on the judges and officials to confess their corruption; on the priests to explain how they set the example of a Christian life. Call on police, secret agents, spies, ministers, governors, and soldiers to speak of Russia's Christian virtues in brutal beatings, torture of mind as well as body, infamous delations, universal bribery, filthy prisons, and inhuman punishments. That done, wish the arms of Russia success, and pray that all the world may become Cossack, and the kings of the world imitators of the Czar.

But I am a Pole, and may be supposed consequently to hate Russia. That is a popular error. The Poles do not hate Russians. Their qualities, their characteristics, are ours, because we are all of one common stock; as for their vices, they are encouraged by the governing class, because without the degradation of ignorance and drink they could not be depended on, these poor mujiks, to obey orders. We only hate the Romanoffs, who are Germans. But we like the Russians. And the English people will find out, on that day when the great unwieldy empire drops to pieces, and the spectre of the Romanoff terror is laid for ever, what good qualities there are in Russian, Muscovite, or Pole, and how by the aid of the Devil, who invented autocratic rule, the good has been perverted into evil.

But what had the English and the Russian soldier done to each other, that they should be made to fight?

A most foolish and jealous girl's question. And yet—and yet.

And yet—it was pitiful to see our brave fellows, full of fire and enthusiasm, go down the narrow streets of the town to the Dockyard Gates on their way to the East. They marched in loose order, headed by the Colonel, the bands playing "The Girl I left behind me." The streets were lined with the townspeople; the women crying, some of them even kissing the soldiers; the men waving hats and shouting; the children laughing and running for joy at so splendid a spectacle. Among the honest faces of the rough and rude soldiers—far rougher, far ruder then than now—you could see none that were not lifted proudly, flushed with hope. Drill the Muscovite and send him out to fight; he will go, and he will fight as he has been taught, a dogged, obedient creature. He asks for no reason, he neither questions nor criticises. When he begins to question, the end of the Romanoffs will not be far distant. Drill a Frenchman and order him into the field. He goes with a yell and a rush like a tiger. And he is as dangerous as a man-eater. The German, who, more than all men, hates soldiering, goes unwilling, patient, sad. He is among other men the least pleased to fight. But the Englishman goes willingly, quietly, and without shouting. He likes fighting. And if he begins he means to go on.

When the Dockyard Gates closed upon the Adjutant and the Doctor, who rode last, men and women alike turned away with choking throats and swelling hearts, ashamed to shed the tears that stood in their eyes.

The men were going to fight for their country. Could there be a nobler thing than to fight, and for that sacred cause to die?

And yet Celia asked, what had Russians and Englishmen done to each other that they should fight?

Some day, perhaps even in my own time, the pale figure of Revolution, red-capped, gaunt, and strong, will stalk into the Summer Palace, and bring out the Romanoffs, disturbers of the world's peace, one by one. "See," she will say to the onlookers, "they are but men, these Czars, two-forked radishes, like yourselves. They are not stronger, bigger-brained, or longer-lived than you. They are troubled by exactly the same passions; they have no better education than the best of you. But they must have war to delude ignorant people, and keep them from asking questions. As for you eighty millions, you want peace, with the chance of growing crops, and enjoying sweet love of wife and children. Once get this family with all their friends across the frontier, with strict orders that they are not to come back any more, and you shall have all that you reasonably want."

That is what the eager-faced woman with the Phrygian cap said, eighty years ago, to the French, who believed her, and proceeded to act in the courage of their convictions. They made a mess of it because they expected too much. But they set an example, and we have not yet seen the end of that example.

Day after day the tramp of soldiers down the streets, infantry, cavalry, artillery, all alike light-hearted, all starting on the journey of death as if it were a picnic.

When the news came of the first fighting we grew less tender-hearted, and sent out fresh squadrons with the same enthusiasm but fewer tears. The war fever was upon us, pulses beat fiercely, we had less thought for the individual men and more for the army. We were bound to win somehow, and the soldiers went out to win for us. If they fell—but we did not think too much, then, about falling. Individual life is only valuable in time of peace. In times of war it has a commercial value of its own—life for life, and perhaps one life for ten if we are lucky.

"I daresay," said the Captain one day, "that there is a Russian way of looking at things, though hang me if I can see it. But, mark me, Laddy, unless a man sticks tight as wax to his own side, shuts his ears to the other side, won't hear of an argument, that man can't fight happy. There's no comfort in a battle unless you feel you're on the Lord's side. Wherefore hang all sea lawyers, and let every man, now, hate a Russian as if he were the Devil."

To do our red-jackets justice, that is about what they did.

Besides the long lines of soldiers embarking every week in the huge transports, there were the preparation and the despatch of the great and splendid Black Sea and Baltic Fleets.

It is something to have lived in a time when such ships were to be seen. It is a memory which binds one to the past to think of that day, in March 1854, when the Baltic Fleet set sail amid the prayers of the nation. Never was so gallant a fleet sent forth from any shore, never were shores more crowded with those who came to criticise and stayed to cheer. We had already—Cis and I among the number—cheered old Charley Napier when he walked down the pier to embark on his ship, pounding the timbers with his sturdy little legs as if they had been so many Russians. To-day he was on board the *Duke of Wellington*, the biggest ship in the world, a great floating fortress mounting a hundred and thirty-one guns, built to sail when wind was fair, with a crew of a thousand men, and an admiral who meant fighting. No one who ever saw that day will forget the departure of the Fleet. It was a fresh and breezy day in March; the sun came out in occasional gleams, and shot long arrows of light athwart the clouds. The sea was dark with multitudes of boats, yachts, steamers, and craft of all kinds; the shore was black with the thousands who sat there watching for the signal to be given. And riding at anchor lay the ships on which the fortunes of England depended. There was the *St. Jean d'Acre*, of a hundred guns; the *Royal George*, of a hundred and twenty— she floated over the place where lay the bones of her namesake, the flag-ship of Admiral Kempenfeldt, when he went down with "twice four hundred men," and almost as many women; the *Princess Royal*, of ninety-one guns; the *Impérieuse* and the *Arrogant*—I was launched on board the *Arrogant*, and remembered her well—there were, all told, in that Baltic Fleet, though all were not gathered together, between fifty and sixty ships. Presently we saw the Queen's steamer, the *Fairy* —the pretty little yacht, with her three sloping masts—threading her graceful way swiftly in and out of the ships, while the Jack Tars manned the yardarm, and cheered till the shore took it up with echoes and the counter-cheering of the spectators. When the old men with Nehemiah saw the diminished glories of the Second Temple, they lifted up their voices and wept. When the old men on our shore saw the magnified glories of the Victorian fleet, they lifted up their voices and wept, thinking of the days that were no more, the breezy battle with a foe who dared to fight, the long chase of a flying enemy, the cutting-out, the harvest of a score of prizes. This time, with better ships, better crews, we were going on a fool's quest, because all the good we did was to keep the Russians within their port. Well, our trade was safe. That was a great thing. The ships would go up and down the broad ocean without fear of the Russians, because these were all skulking behind Cronstadt towers. I am not a Muscov, but a Pole, yet I was ashamed for the Russian sailors, who were not allowed to strike a blow for their country, while the soldiers were dying in thousands, dogged, silent, long-suffering, in obedience to the Czar whom they ignorantly worship.

They sailed, the Queen leading the way. Out flew the white canvas, fluttering for a moment in the windy sunshine, and then, with set purpose, bellying full before the breeze, and marshalling each brave ship to her place in the grand procession.

The Armada passed out of sight, and we all went home. The Captain was moved to the extent of a double ration that night; also, he sang a song. And at prayers, he invented a new petition of his own for the honour and safety of the Fleet. There were occasions, he said, when if a man did not feel religious he didn't deserve to be kept on the ship's books any longer. And he told us—Cis was staying with us that day—for a thousandth time the story of Navarino.

When the fleets were gone, and the soldiers nearly all sent off, we began to look for news. For a long time there came little. Charley Napier told his men to sharpen their cutlasses; that was just what the old fellow would do, because, if he got a chance of fighting, he meant fighting. But he did not get that chance. Within the fortress of Cronstadt, in ignoble safety, lay the Russian fleet, afraid to come out. There was a little bombardment of Sweaborg, Helsingfors, and Bomarsund; we made as much as we could of it at the time, but it was not like the fighting which the old men remembered. And only a few prizes here and there. One was brought in, I remember, by the *Argus*, at sight of which we all turned out to cheer. The Captain sorrowfully said that in the good, old days when he entered the Navy, about the year 1805, he might have been in command of a dozen such prizes every year.

CHAPTER XI.
THE WAR, AND AFTER.

THAT summer of 1854 was a long and dreary time. We were waiting for something to be done, and nothing was done. Good Heavens! Were our generals stupid or incapable, or were they dreaming away the time? Who does not remember the cholera at Varna, after the long and unnecessary delay, the sickness of the troops before a blow had been struck, and at last the embarkation for the Crimea? So great and terrible was the spectre of Russian greatness, that even the three great Powers of France, Turkey, and England hesitated before attacking this monstrous Frankenstein in his den. They went at last, greatly daring, and their reward was—Alma.

And then followed the splendid months of barren victory—Inkermann, the soldier's battle, the foolish braggadocio of the Light Cavalry charge, followed by the cruel winter and the unmerited sufferings of the troops, for which a dozen commissariat officers ought to have been shot.

About this time I saw my compatriots, the Russians, for the first time. Some prisoners were brought to us; they wore flat caps and long coats; they had good-natured faces, not at all foolish; they had wide noses, like Tartars, and they made themselves quite happy and comfortable with us, carving all sorts of toys, and showing a power of laughter and humour quite incompatible with the devilry which we had been accustomed to attach to the Muscovite character. They were only devils, I suppose, by the order of the Czar, and in the ranks. Outside the ranks as peaceable, docile, and quiet a set of fellows as ever wanted to grow an honest crop in peace.

But how we received the news in those days! With cheers, with illuminations, with feastings, with receptions of captains, generals, and admirals. Still the exodus of our *juventus* went on. The *juvenes* were younger, smaller, and more rustic in appearance. They all, however, had the same gallant bearing, these brave country lads, fresh from the plough and the stable, redolent of Mother Earth. A few weeks before, and they were leaning against posts in the village street, feeding pigs, driving calves, striding with a sideward lurch after cows, sitting almost mute on a bench in the village alehouse. Now they were well set up, drilled, inspired with warlike ardour, filled with new ideas of duty, responsibility, and a career; ready to do—and to die. Let us confess that the readiness to die is always qualified by that belief which every soldier has, that he, if no one else, will be the one person to escape. If it were not for that saving clause, I fear that even in the times of greatest danger to the country service in the ranks would not be popular. Men did not volunteer for those charming fights in the arena before Nero, when all had to die on the ground. Quite the contrary; they disliked that kind of fight, and I have often thought how greatly the vivacity and ardour of the combat would have been increased if the combatants had been told beforehand that one —say the bravest—would have his life spared, with a pension of a shilling a day ever afterwards. *Vos morituri salutant* might have been said by those fresh-cheeked young English lads on their way to club muskets at Inkermann, and to fall in the storming of the Redan.

And after a while they began to send the wounded home.

To receive them, a hospital was built in one of the meadows under the Ramparts, and a portion of the wall was railed off for the convalescents to walk upon. This made our own end at the Queen's Bastion still more quiet and secluded.

In 1856, the sick and wounded were brought home by every ship that arrived from the East, and week by week, sometimes daily, might be seen filing up the long and narrow street, a long and dismal procession. It consisted of sailors carrying stretchers, four to every stretcher. There was no band now, nor would be any more for most of the poor men upon the stretchers, till the muffled drums and the fifes went before the coffin and played the "Dead March." The townsfolk who had turned out to wave their handkerchiefs when the soldiers left came out now to greet them back. But what a greeting! and what a return! Some, sitting half-upright, waved feeble hands in response to those who lined the way and cheered their return. Their faces were pale and worn with suffering; sometimes a sheet covered the lower limbs, which were mutilated and crushed; some, a little stronger than their comrades, sat up, laughed, and nodded. Some, worn out by the rolling of the ship, the pain of their wounds, and the long sufferings of the campaign, lay back with closed eyes, patient, and sad to see, and made no sign.

And here and there one was borne along ghastly, the pallor of death upon his cheeks, life done for him; not even vitality enough left to think about the future world; his eyes half open, with a fixed glare which observed nothing. This, with the row of tombs in the Crimea and at Scutari, was the end of all that pride and pomp of war. What was it Tennyson said:

"The long, long canker of Peace is over and done."

We were to wake to nobler aims, leave the sordid and base, give up cheating and strike home, were it but with the cheating yard-measure.

Well. The war came, ran its course, and ended. What nobler ends followed? How much was abolished of the old cheating, the sordid aims, and the general baseness of a world at peace? How much less wicked and selfish were we, when all the fighting was finished, and the soldiers come back to us?

And after all, we return to Celia's question, "What had they done to each other, the Russians and the English, that they should stand face to face and fight?"

"Take me away, Laddy," Celia said one day, after seeing one of the gloomy processions of the wounded partly file past. "Take me away. I cannot bear to see any more. Oh! the poor soldiers—the poor soldiers——. What punishment can be great enough for the men who have brought all this misery upon the earth?"

What, indeed? But Nicolas was dead. General Février killed him. Perhaps, after all, he was not the guiltiest. But he gave the word. It is to be hoped, for their own sakes, that autocrats do not know what war means, else surely the word never would be given even to save the throne, and every nation would manage its own affairs in quietness.

And yet England had to fight. It seems most true that the war could not be avoided. All that blood, all that suffering, the moans of so many thousands of wounded, the tears of so many thousands of women and children, the awakening of so many evil passions, the letting loose of so many devils, must fall upon the head of Russia. First to excite revolt among the Christian subjects of the Turk: then to make difficulties for the Turks in putting down the miserable victims of the Russian plot; then to call on Europe to mark how Turkey treated her subjects; then to proclaim herself the protector of Christians; this was Russia's game in 1828, in 1853, and lastly, in 1876. And the glory of the poor soldiers? They died for their country, and have such glory as belongs to one of a nameless fifty thousand fallen on the field.

The fight was just and the victory righteous. We pay the penalty now of not having carried the war to its legitimate end. We should have restored Poland, driven Russia back to the Caucasus and the Caspian, giving Finland again to Sweden, and taken away her southern ports. All this we could have done; it was possible to England and France twenty years ago. Will the chance ever come again?

Through the whole of the war there was no man in the town who took a keener interest in it, who was oftener in the streets, who hung more about the harbour, or talked more with soldiers and sailors, than Herr Räumer.

The war, in any case, did good to our own people at the Dockyard town. There had never been such times since the good old long war, when a man who had a shop near the Hard had but to open it and stand all day taking the sailors' money as fast as they poured it out over the counter. Every ship that came home brought her sailors to be paid off, the money to be all spent in the town; every ship that sailed for the East carried away stores for the soldiers, chiefly bought in the town. Those who were in the way of all this money-making made fortunes out of it, and retired to suburban villas, with gardens, for the rest of their lives. I do not think that the green coffee berries, the putrid preserved meat, the mouldy compressed hay, or the biscuits that walked about animated by a multitudinous hive of lively creatures, were supplied by any of our people. We were too patriotic; we had friends on board the ships if not in the regiments—could we send them out rotten provisions or brown paper boots? Then there was the revelry.

Out of all the millions spent in the Crimean War, think how many went in the drink-shops and the dancing-kens. The fiddle of old Wassielewski, I know, was in constant request; often and often I heard the well-known sound—I knew his style, which was distinct from that of any other of the sailors' musicians—from behind the red curtains of a sailors' public-house, behind which Jack and Jill were dancing, drinking, and singing. The China War, by the way, was long since played out, and the picture had given way to another, in which Russians were playing an ignominious but dramatic part. A side picture represented French sailors and soldiers, very tight of waist, mustachioed, and black of hair, fraternising merrily with our own men—with drink, hand-shaking, and song, they were celebrating the *entente cordiale*. Listen! It is the sailors' hornpipe, within is one who, grave of face and agile of foot, treads that mazy measure alone, while around are grouped the crowd of sympathetic rivals, who drink, applaud, and presently emulate. The dancer is facing old Wassielewski, who sits with outstretched left leg, his deep-set eyes fixed on the opposite wall, his thoughts far away in the dreadful past or the revengeful future, while the fingers, obedient to his will, play the tune that he orders but does not listen to. It is, I know—because I do not look in, but feel all this—a low room, and it is redolent of a thousand compound smells, ancient, fish-like, capable of knocking a stranger down and stunning him with a single blow. The windows have never been open for twenty or thirty years; of course, once in a way, a pane was broken; and there were occasions when some young mariner, ashore after three years' cruise, was fain, out of the plethora of his joy, to find relief in smashing them all. But the smell of that room was venerable by age and respectable by association, though more awful than it is permitted to me to describe. Jack and Jill did not mind it; they liked it. There was rum in it, plenty of beer, a very large quantity of tobacco, onions, beef-steaks, mutton-chops, boiled pork and cabbage, pea-soup, more tobacco, more rum, more beer. That smell, my friends, is gone; the public-house is gone, Jill is almost gone, Jack is an earnest Methodist by religion, and he spends his time ashore at the Sailors' Home.

And there then was the Dockyard, with all its extra hands, and the work going on day and night, so that the solemn silence of the darkness was unknown. Victory Row must have lost one of its chief charms. For the whole twenty-four hours there was the incessant tap-tap of the caulkers, the heavy thud of the steam-hammer, the melodious banging of the rivets, followed by countless echoes from the many-cornered yard, and the r—r—r—r of the machinery. No rest at all, except on Sunday. That emergency must be great indeed when the British Government would ask its workmen to give up their Sabbath rest.

As for the sailors, there seemed no diminution in their numbers, or in the number of the ships which crowded the harbour, and were perpetually coming and going with their thunder of salutes. Jack only had two stages: he was either just paid off, and therefore ostentatiously happy with his friends around him, his fiddlers, and his public-house, or he was just embarking again on a newly-commissioned ship, going off for another cruise with empty pockets, coppers terribly hot, and perhaps, if he was Jack in his youth, with his faint and dimly seen ghost of a possible repentance somewhere lurking about his brain, a spectral umbra pointing heavenward which faded as the shore receded, and vanished about six bells in the morning.

For soldiers, we fell back upon the militia. We have never yet grasped the truth that England may have to defend what she has got; that she is not only the admiration, but also the envy, of all other nations; that Russia would like Constantinople and India; Germany, Australia—good Heavens, think of the shame and ignominy of letting any un-English-speaking country have Australia; the States, Canada; France, Egypt and Syria; Italy, Cyprus; Greece, Crete, and so on. When these facts have become convictions, when we fairly understand how great is our position in the world; what a tremendous stake we have in it; how much of unselfish humanity depends on the maintenance of English hegemony; then will England arm every man between fifteen and fifty, and make all from twenty to thirty liable to foreign service. Patriotism sleeps, but it may be awakened. If it continues to sleep, farewell to England's greatness. A century of ignoble wealth, a generation or two of commerce diverted, trade ruined, industries forgotten, and the brave old country would become worse than Holland, because the English are more sensitive than the Dutch, and the memories of old glory combined with present degradation would madden the people and drive them to—the usual British remedy, drink.

In 1855 we—I do not speak as a Pole—were rather better off in the matter of regiments and recruits than we should be in 1877, were the occasion to arise. In all these years, we have learned nothing, taken to heart nothing, done nothing, prepared for nothing. We have no larger army, we have no better organisation, we have no more intelligent system, we have not made our officers more responsible. Twenty years ago, we threw away twenty thousand men—with a light heart sent out twenty thousand men to die because we had no system of control, transport, and commissariat. All these poor lads died of preventible disease. What have we done since to make that impossible again? Nothing. Talk. At the very Autumn Manoeuvres, when we have weeks to prepare and a paltry ten thousand men to provide for, we break down. Continental nations see it, and laugh at us. What have we done to make our children learn that they must fight *pro patria*, if occasion arise? Nothing. Board schools teach the Kings of Israel; the very atmosphere of the country teaches desire of success and the good things which success brings with it: no school teaches, as the Germans teach, that every man is owed to his country. That may come: if it does not come soon, farewell to England's greatness. Again: that the Empire was created and grew great, not by truckling to the pretensions of modern diplomatists, but by saying: "Thus far, and no farther." "Do this wrong or that, and you will have to fight England." That the most glorious country that the world has ever seen, the finest, the richest, the most splendid, the most religious, the least priest-ridden and king-ridden, was made what it is by its children being willing and able to fight—all these things were not taught in 1855, and are not yet taught in 1877. Good heavens! I am a Pole, and yet more than half an Englishman: and it makes me sick and sorry to feel how great is the parsimony of an Englishman; how noble are his annals; how profound a gap would be made in the world by the collapse of England; and how little English people seem to understand their greatness. I have been waiting for twenty years to see the fruits of the Crimean War—and, behold, they are dust and ashes in the mouth.

Revenons à nos moutons. Our garrison then consisted of a couple of militia regiments. They came to us, raw country lads, like the recruits whom we sent to the East; but, being without the presence of the veterans to control and influence them, they took longer to improve. And yet it is wonderful to notice how an English lad takes to his drill and tackles his gun from the very first, with an intelligence that is almost instinct. He is, to be sure, almost too fond of fighting. There is no other country besides England, except France, where the recruits can be taught to march, to skirmish, and the rest of it, without the aid of Sergeant Stick, so largely employed in the Russian, German, and Austrian services. These young fellows come up to barracks, with their country lurch upon them, their good-natured country grin, and their insatiable thirst for beer. They retained the last, but in a very short time got rid of the first. One whole regiment volunteered for foreign service—I forget what it was—and went to Corfu, the island which a late Prime Minister, more careful of a theory than of a country's prestige, tossed contemptuously to Greece, so that all the world sneered, and even the gods wondered. Well, these rustics of militiamen, I declare, after a few weeks were as well set up, pipe-clayed, and drilled as any regiment of the line, and as trustworthy in case their services should be required.

In one thing, one must needs confess, they were inferior to the regulars. It was not in perpendicularity, which they easily acquired. We were still in the pipe-clay days, when the white belt and the cross shoulder-straps were daily stiffened by that abominable stuff; the white trousers of summer had also to be kept in a whited sepulchre semblance of purity by the same means; a man who is pipe-clayed cannot stoop; the black leather collar kept the head at an unbending line with the body; and the yellow tufts on the shoulder, with the swallow-tails of the absurd regimental coat and the tiny ball of red stuff on the regimental hat, all combined to necessitate a carriage ten times stiffer and more rigidly upright than in these degenerate days. The most lopsided and lurcher-like of rustics was bound to become perpendicular. But their failing was in the way they took their beer. The old regular got drunk as often as the militiaman, but the drunker he got the stiffer he grew, so that when he was quite helpless he fell like a lamp-post, with uncompromising legs. And we, who knew by experience how a soldier should fall, remarked with sorrow rather than anger that the militiaman fell in a heap like a ploughboy, and so betrayed his customary pursuits.

CHAPTER XII.
THE BRAMBLER FAMILY.

THIS was an especially good time for Ferdinand Brambler, the journalist, and consequently for the children. Such years of fatness had never before been known to them. Not, it is true, that Fortune befriended Augustus. Quite the contrary. War might be made and peace signed without affecting his position in the slightest. Nothing ever happened to better his position. On one occasion even—I think it was in 1856—he received an intimation from Mr. Tyrrell's head clerk, who had vainly trusted him with some real work, that his resignation would be accepted if he sent it in. Therefore, with the enthusiasm ever equal to the occasion, he hastened to desert the Legal, and once more returned to the Scholastic, taking the post of writing and arithmetic master in a Select Commercial Academy.

"After all," he said to me, "the Scholastic is my real vocation. I feel it most when I go back to it. To teach the rising generation—what can be nobler? I influence one mind, we will say. Through him I influence his six children; through them their thirty-six children; through them again their two hundred and sixteen—there is no end to the influence of the schoolmaster. I shall be remembered, Mr. Pulaski, I shall be remembered by a grateful posterity."

Perhaps he will be remembered, but his chances of exercising permanent influence were scanty on this occasion, because, although he taught with extraordinary zeal and activity, the Principal actually complained, after three months, that his boys were learning nothing, and gave him notice in the friendliest and kindest manner.

Some secret influence was probably brought to bear upon Mr. Tyrrell at this juncture, when the Brambler household threatened to lose the income derived from the labour of its chief, because Augustus went back to his old office and his old pay, sitting once more cheerfully among the boys, mending the pens with enthusiastic alacrity, serving writs with zeal, copying out bills of cost with ardour, and actively inspecting old books in an eager search for nothing.

"I do think," he said in a burst of enthusiasm, "that there is nothing after all like the Legal. When you have deserted it for a time, and go back to it, you feel it most. Law brings out the argumentative side—the intellectual side—of a man. It makes him critical. Law keeps his brain on the stretch. Often on Saturday night I wonder how I have managed to worry through the work of the week. But you see they could not get on without me."

Perhaps not, but yet if Augustus had known by whose fair pleading he was received back to become a permanent incubus on the weekly expenses of that office

In the Scholastic, in the Clerical, or in the Legal, Augustus Brambler never changed, never lost heart, never failed in zeal, never ceased to take the same lively and personal interest in the well-being of the House. He had his punctual habits and his maxims. He was a model among *employés*. Fortune, when she gave Augustus a sanguine temperament and a lively imagination, thought she had done enough for the man, and handed him over to the Three Sisters as sufficiently endowed to meet any fate. And they condemned him to the unceasing and contented exercise of illusion and imagination, so that he never saw things as they really were, or understood their proportion.

But during the years of war the children, in spite of their helpless father, waxed fat and strong, and even little Forty-six looked satisfied and well-fed.

It was through the exertions of their Uncle Ferdinand.

I had long observed that whenever anything was going on—and something in these days was constantly going on—Ferdinand, besides Herr Räumer, was always on the spot. Whatever the nature of the ceremony, whether it was the embarkation of a regiment, or the arrival of the invalided, or a military funeral, or an inspection of troops upon the Common, or a launch, Ferdinand was in attendance, and to the front, wearing a face of indescribable importance, and carrying a notebook. This in hand, he surveyed the crowd on arrival, and made a note; cast a weather eye upwards to the sky, and made a note; drew out his watch, and made a note; then as soon as the Function began he continued steadily making notes until the end. I did not at first, being innocent of literary matters, connect these notes with certain descriptions of events which regularly appeared on the following Saturday in the local Mercury. They were written with fidelity and vigour; they did justice to the subject; they were poetical in feeling and flowery in expression. A fine day was rendered as "a bright and balmy atmosphere warmed by the beams of benevolent Sol;" a crowded gathering gave an opportunity for the admirer of beauty to congratulate his fellow-townsmen on the comeliness and tasteful dress of their daughters; when a ship was launched she was made by a bold and strikingly original figure to float swan-like on the bosom of the ocean; when a public dinner was held, the tables groaned under the viands provided by mine eminent host of the George; the choicest wines sparkled in the goblet; animation and enthusiasm reigned in every heart; and each successive flow of oratory was an occasion for a greater and more enthusiastic outburst of cheering. The writer was not critical, he was descriptive. That is the more popular form of journalism. Froissart was the inventor of the uncritical historian. And Ferdinand was born either too early or too late.

For all these beautiful and gushing columns, invaluable to some antiquary of the future, were due to the pen of Ferdinand Brambler, and it was by the frequency of the occasions on which his powers were called for that the prosperity of the Bramblers depended. And Ferdinand, an excellent brother, and the most self-denying creature in the world, worked cheerfully for his nephews and nieces. Beneath that solemn exterior, and behind those pretensions to genius, there beat the most simple and unselfish of hearts.

Ferdinand did not report; first because he could not write shorthand, and secondly, because he thought it—and said so —beneath the dignity of genius to become the "mere copying clerk of Vestry twaddle." He lived on his *communiqués*, for which, as he was the only man in the place who wrote them, and therefore had the field all to himself, he received fairly good pay. During the Crimean War he had a never-ending succession of subjects for his pen, which was as facile as it was commonplace. It was the history of the regiment; it was a note on the next roster; it was the service roll of a ship; it was the biography of a general; nothing came amiss to the encyclopaedic Ferdinand; and whatever he treated, it must be owned, was treated with the same hackneyed similes, the same well-worn metaphors, and the same pleasantries; for, while Augustus looked on life through the rosy glasses of a sanguine imagination, Ferdinand regarded things from the standpoint of genius. He wrote for a provincial weekly paper; nothing higher would take his papers; he was not the editor; he was not even on the regular salaried staff; he was a mere outsider, sending in articles on such topics as occurred to him; but in his own imagination he wrote for posterity. Like Augustus, he believed in himself. And just as Augustus assumed in the family circle the air of one who unbends after hard intellectual labour, so Ferdinand when he emerged from the ground-floor front, which was his study, and contained his library, moved and spoke with the solemnity of one with whom his genius was always present.

From 1853 to 1857 the family flourished and grew fat. For after the Russian War was finished, and the Treaty signed—to be broken as soon as the semi-barbaric Muscovite thought himself strong enough—there arose in the far East another cloud. I have often wondered whether the Indian Mutiny, like the late Bulgarian insurrections, was got up by Russian agents, and if so, I have reflected with joy upon the maddening disappointment to the Tartar that it did not happen just two years before.

We had achieved peace, not a very glorious peace, because we ought to have driven Russia back to the Caucasus as a frontier before any peace was thought of, but still peace, and with the memory of those three years upon us, the sufferings of our troops, the unpreparedness of England, the rascality of contractors, and the inefficiency of our officers, we were glad to sit down and rest. How have we profited by the lesson of twenty years ago? What security have we that on the next occasion, when our men are ordered out again, the same things will not happen again—the green coffee, the putrid preserved meat, the shoddy coats, the brown-paper boots, the very powder adulterated?

Peace! Well we had fought two or three gallant battles, been jealous of our gallant allies, killed an immense number—say, altogether, with those who died on the march, and those who died of disease, and those who died in the field, about half a million of Russians, fifty thousand Englishmen, double the number of French, and the same number of Turks; we had put a sudden end to Tennyson's "long canker of peace;" and made it war—first for righteous reasons, and then for the lust of blood and battle, the red-sheeted spectre which rises when the trumpet sounds and fires the blood of peaceful men. As for the morality at home, as I asked in the last chapter, were we the better?

Then came the Indian Mutiny. For a while it seemed as if the very foundations of the Indian Empire were shaken. And at no time were the hearts of Englishmen more stirred in the whole of England's history than by the tales of massacre and murder which came by every ship from the East. The troops which had enjoyed a brief year of rest were hastily re-embarked: the flags which bore the names of Alma, Inkermann, and Balaclava were carried out again to get the names of Lucknow and Delhi; but the men who marched out in '54 with the sturdy look of men who mean to fight because they must, went out now with the face of those who go to take revenge because they can. It was a war of revenge. And, whatever the provocation, it was a full and even a cruel measure of revenge that the British soldiers took. We were growing sick of "history," Cis and I. We waited and watched while the red coats went and came; wanted to go on without excitement with our music and our reading, and we longed for peace.

"The Lord," said the Captain, "gives us peace, and the Devil gives us war. Until the nature of men is changed, there will be peace and war in alternate slices like a sandwich. In good times the sandwich is meaty. Meanwhile, let us keep up the Fleet."

We came to the spring of 1858. Mr. Tyrrell was Mayor for the second time. It was the year when Leonard should return—five years on June the twenty-first. Celia looked at me sometimes, and I at her. But we said nothing, because we understood what was meant. And one day I surprised the Captain in Leonard's room. He was opening drawers, arranging chairs, and trying window blinds. "All shipshape, Laddy, and in good order. Don't let the boy think the vessel has got out of trim after all these years."

The Mutiny was over, the punishment had been inflicted, and our town was now comparatively quiet. No more hurried preparations of armaments and despatch of ships. Things became flat; the people who had not already made fortunes out of the war saw with sorrow that their opportunity was past; the extra hands at the Dockyard were discharged; and the town became quiet again. It was bad for all who had to earn their bread—even I felt the change in a falling-off of pupils—and it was especially bad for poor Ferdinand Brambler.

I met him one day walking solemnly away from the Yard, notebook in hand. I stopped to shake hands with him, and noticed that his clothes were shabby, his boots worn at the heel, his hat ancient, and his general get-up indicating either the neglect of outward appearance peculiar to genius, or a period of financial depression. While I accosted him, his brother Augustus passed by. He, too, was in like pitiable guise. And he looked pinched in the cheeks, albeit smiling and cheerful as ever.

"What will it run to, Ferdinand?"he asked anxiously.

"I should say," said Ferdinand with hesitation, "unless I am disappointed, mind, which I may be, I should say it will be a pound of tea, the greengrocer's bill, and something to Forty-seven's new shoes."

"The wife did say," replied Augustus, "that the children's breakings-out are for want of meat. But if we can't have meat we can't. Awfully busy at the office, Ferdinand. Money pouring in. Nothing like the Legal."

Poor Ferdinand, who by long struggling with the family wolf had got to look on everything he wrote as representing payment in kind, was right in being proud of his profession, because he had nothing else to be proud of. It was not in quiet times a lucrative one, and I should think, taking one year with another, that this poor genius, who really loved literature for its own sake, and with better education and better chances might have made something of a name, received from his profession about as much as his brother in the Legal, and that was sixty pounds a year.

I repeated this conversation to the Captain at dinner. He became silent, and after our simple meal proposed that we should go for a walk. By the merest chance we passed the Bramblers' house.

"Dear me," said the Captain, "the very people we were speaking of. Suppose we pay our respects to Mrs. Brambler."

The poor mother was up to her eyes in work, her endless children round her. But the little Bramblers did not look happy. They wore a pinched and starved look, and there was no disguising the fact that they were breaking out.

Forty-eight scowled at us with rebellious looks; Forty-six was wolfish in hungry gaze, and even the mild-eyed Forty-four looked sad.

Mrs. Brambler read the pity in the Captain's eyes, and sat down, bursting into tears, and throwing her apron over her face. The elder girls stole to the window and sobbed behind the curtain—the younger children sat down every one upon what came handiest, and all cried together. They were a very emotional family.

"So—so," said the Captain, "we were passing—Laddy and I—and we thought we would drop in—thought—we—would—drop—in. Come here, Forty-six—Does this boy, do you think, Mrs. Brambler, have enough nourishment?"

"Augustus does all he can, Captain, and so does Ferdinand, I'm sure. But there was the rent, and we behind with everybody—and—and—sometimes it's 'most too much for me."

"We dropped in," repeated the mendacious Captain, "to invite the children to tea and supper to-night—"

"Hooray!" cried Forty-six, dancing about, and the faces of all lighted up with a sunshine like their father's.

"It's only your kindness, Captain. You don't really want them."

"Not want them? Where is Forty-four? Come and kiss me, my dear. Where is your colour gone? Not want them? Nonsense. Nothing but shrimps and periwinkles, and watercress, perhaps, for tea; but for supper —ah!—eh! Laddy, what can we do in the way of supper? What's in the larder?"

"A leg of mutton, a beefsteak, and a pair of chickens," I replied. "I think that is all."

The larder was in fact empty, but this was not a time to parade the vacuum.

"You see, Mrs. Brambler; much more, very much more, than we can possibly eat. Friends in the country. And we did think that the steak for supper—"

"Ah! " cried Forty-six irrepressibly.

"With the leg of mutton for yourself, and the pair of chickens—"

Mrs. Brambler laughed through her tears.

"There—go along, Captain," she said. "We know.—But if it wouldn't trouble you, the children shall go and welcome."

"Very lucky, Laddy," said the Captain in the street, "that the larder is so full. Let us call at the butcher's as we go home."

I ventured to mention to Herr Räumer the distressed condition of the family with whom he lodged.

"I know it," he said, helping himself to a glass of hock. "I have seen for some time that the children were not properly fed. It is a pity. A good many children about the world are in the same plight."

"Help them," I said sententiously, "when you can."

He shrugged his shoulders and laughed.

"I am past sixty. I have seen so much distress in the world that I have long since resolved to help nobody. The weakest goes to the wall in this best of all possible worlds. If it is not the best it is not my fault, because I did not make it. Every man for himself, as you will say at sixty if you are honest. This is a comfortable chair, this is good Hock, this is excellent tobacco. Why should I trouble myself because people are starving in the room below us any more than because they are starving in China, which is a good many miles off? Pity and charity are excellent things in the abstract. Applied to individuals actually before you, they are disquieting. *Allans, cher Ladislas, soyons philosophes*."

He was a man of infinite pity in the abstract, wept over any amount of woe served up in the yellow paper covers of a French novel, but in the presence of actual suffering he was callous. "Every man for himself." Since I have grown older I have learned to distrust many a philanthropist whose sympathies grow deeper the farther they reach from home.

"And now," he went on, changing the position of his legs,"let us be cheerful, and talk of Celia. Pretty, delicate, little Celia. Tall and *gracieuse* Celia. Choice and delicious Celia. She is a credit to you, Ladislas Pulaski. Her husband will thank you. I drink her health. Ah! The English girls. . . After all, we must grant these islanders some superiority. They are stupid, ignorant, and prejudiced. They call Continental diplomacy bad names, and are going to ruin themselves because they will not have secret service money. But their girls—their girls are charming. And the most charming of them all is Celia."

CHAPTER XIII.
A FLOWER OF LOVE.

IT was very early in that year, or at the end of 1857, that I made a discovery about myself. Regarded from the point of view which the climbing of so many following years have enabled me to reach, the discovery seems a thing which might have been expected—quite natural, and belonging to daily experience. At the time, I remember, it was most surprising.

I suppose no one would believe that a young man could come to the age of one-and-twenty, and remain so little of a man, as I did. But I was deformed. I was morbidly sensitive of ridicule. I was extremely poor. I had some pride of birth; I could not possibly associate with the professional men, the drawing, dancing, and music masters of the town, who might have formed my set. Their thoughts were not mine; their ways were not my ways. Not that I claimed any superiority. Quite the contrary. Men who could ride, hunt, shoot, play billiards, and do all the other things which belong to skill of hand and eye, seemed, and still seem to me, vastly superior to a being who can do nothing except interpret the thoughts of the great masters. In a country town, unless you belong to the young men of the place, and take part in the things which interest them, you fall back upon such resources as you have in yourself. There was nothing for me but my piano and my books for the evening, and Celia in the afternoon.

It was partly on account of my deformity that we were so much together. When Leonard went away I had hardly an acquaintance of my own age in the town—certainly not a friend; and I was at the age when the imagination is strongest, and the need for close companionship is felt the most. In adolescence the heart opens out spontaneously to all who are within its reach. The friends of youth are close and confidential friends; there is no distrust, no reserve. I think it is rare for such a friendship as that between Celia and myself to exist between two persons who are not of the same sex, neither brother and sister, nor lovers. Yet it existed up to a certain time, and then, without a break on her part, but after a struggle on mine, it was resumed, and has been since continued. There was no shadow of restraint between us, but only a perfect and beautiful confidence, when Celia was a girl and I was a boy. Like me, but for different reasons, she lived apart from other girls: she had no schoolgirl friendships; she never went to school, and had no masters, except myself. I taught her all I knew, which was not much, in a desultory and methodless fashion, and the girl poured out to my ear alone—it was a harvest sixty and a hundredfold—the thoughts that sprang up as clear and bright as a spring of Lebanon in her pure young heart. The thoughts of youth are sacred things; mostly because young people lack power of expression, they are imperfectly conveyed in the words of the poets, who belong especially to the young. Great utterances by the men of old sink deep into the hearts of those who are yet on the threshold of life. They fertilise the soil, and cause it to blossom in a thousand sweet flowers. There is nothing to me, a teacher, and always among the young, more beautiful than the enthusiasms and illusions of youth, their contempt of compromise, their impatience of diplomatic evasions, their fancied impartiality, and their eager partisanship. And I am sometimes of opinion that the government of the world—its laws—its justice—its preaching—its decisions on war and peace—its expenditure —should all be under the control of youth. Before five-and-twenty all but the hardest men are open to higher influences and nobler aims. The lower levels are reached, step by step, through long years of struggle for luxury and position. Let the world be ruled by the adolescent, and let the wisdom of the *senes*, who have too probably become cynical, disappointed, or selfish, be used for administration alone. Above all, no man should be Autocrat, King, President, or Prime Minister after his five-and-twentieth year. As yet, however, I have made no converts to my opinions, and I fear I shall not live to see this admirable reform.

I have had many pupils, and won some friendship among them, bat Celia was my first and best. No one was ever like her in my eyes, so zealous for righteousness, so pitiful for wrong-doers, so sweet in thought. Perhaps we loved her so much—the Captain and I—that we saw in her more virtues than she possessed. It is the way of those who love. What would this world be worth without that power of illusion which clothes our dear ones, while yet in life, with the white robes of Heaven?

"Has she wings somewhere, do you think, Laddy?" said the Captain one evening. Turning over the pages of the Bible, he lighted on a chapter which, he announced to me, bore upon the subject, and he would read it. "Celia's price," he read, commenting as he went along, "is far above rubies. That is perfectly true. The heart of her husband—she shall have a good one—shall safely trust in her. If he can't trust in her, he won't be fit to be her husband. She shall rejoice—there is prophecy for us. Laddy—in time to come. Many daughters—listen to this—have done virtuously, but Celia excels them all. The woman that feareth the Lord she shall be praised. Now, if that does not bear upon the girl, what does?"

It was not possible that our boy-and-girl confidences should remain permanently unchanged, but the change was gradual. I noticed, first of all, that Celia's talk grew less personal and more general. As I followed her lead, we ceased in a measure to refer everything that we read or played to our own thoughts. So that we grew more reserved to each other. An invisible barrier was rising between us, that we knew nothing of. It was caused by the passage of the girl into womanhood, imperceptible as the rising of the tide, which you do not notice until you compare your landmarks, and see how the water has gained. It was the transformation of the child, open as the day, candid and unreserved, into the woman—the true emblem of her is this figure of the Veiled Nymph — who hides, nourishes, and guards her secrets, gathering them up in the rich garner of her heart till she can show them all to her husband, and then keep them for her son. A woman without the mystical veil is no woman, but a creature androgynous, amorphous, loathsome. So that Celia would never be again—I see it so well now—what she had been to me. Her face was the same as it had been, set grave at one moment with its fine delicate lines and ethereal look, and at the next bright and laughing like a mountain stream, but always sweet with the same kindness when she looked at me. Only it seemed at times as if I were groping about in the dark for the soul of Celia, and that I found it not.

"Cis," I said, one afternoon—we were in our old place, and she was leaning against the gun looking thoughtfully across the harbour. The tide was out, and instead of the broad lagoon was a boundless stretch of green and black mud, intersected by a stream of sea water, up and down which boats could make their way at all tides. "Cis, do you know that we are changed to each other?"

Almost as I said it, I perceived that if Celia was changed to me, I was no less changed towards her.

"What is it, Laddy?" she asked, turning gently and resting her eyes on mine. They were so soft and clear that I could hardly bear to look into them—a little troubled, too, with wonder, as if she could not understand what I meant. "What is it, Laddy? How are we changed?"

"I don't know. I think, Cis, it is because—because you are growing a woman."

She sat down beside me on the grass. She was so much taller than I that it was nothing for her to lay her hand upon my shoulder. We often walked so. Sometimes I took her arm. But now the gesture humiliated me. I felt angry and hurt. Was I then of such small account that she should change in thought, and yet retain the old familiar fashion, as if it mattered nothing what she said or did to me? It was a shameful and an unworthy feeling.

"Because I am grown a woman?" she repeated quietly. "Yes I believe I am a woman now."

She was, indeed, a stately, lovely woman, with the tall and graceful figure of Helen, and the pure face of Antigone, elastic in her tread, free in the movements of her shapely limbs, brave in the carriage of her head, full of strength, youth, and activity. Her face was long and oval; but her lips, which is not usual in oval faces, were as full and as mobile as the leaf upon the tree. Her features were straight and delicate. All about her was delicate alike, from the tiny coral ears to the dainty fingers and little feet, which, like mice, went in and out. A maiden formed for love, altogether and wholly lovable; sweet as the new-mown hay, inexhaustible in loveliness—like the Shulamite, fair as the moon, clear as the sun, lovely as Tirzah, a spring of living waters, but as yet a spring shut up, a fountain sealed. And as I looked up at her my heart sank down within me.

"But why should that make a difference between us, Laddy?"

I put her hand from my shoulder roughly, and sprang to my feet, because suddenly my heart overflowed, and words came bubbling to my lips which had to be repressed. I walked to the parapet, and looked across the arbour, battling with myself for a few moments. Then I turned. The girl was looking at me with wonder.

"Why should that make any difference, Laddy?" she repeated.

I was master of myself by this time, and could answer with a smile and lightly.

"Because yon have put away the thoughts of a child, Celia. You no longer think or speak as you used to. Not any sudden change, Cis. Do not think that I complain. I was thinking of what we were a couple of years ago, and what we are now. You cannot help it. You show your womanhood in your new armour of reserve. Very bright and beautiful armour it is."

"I meant no reserve, dear Laddy. We always talked together since we were children, have we not? and told each other everything."

"Not lately, Cis; have we?"

She hesitated, and blushed a little. Then she evaded my question.

"Why, who could be more to me than you, Laddy? My companion, my tutor, my brother. What have I to hide from you? Nothing, Laddy, nothing."

"Not that you know of, Cis. But there is a change. I think that we do not talk so freely of our thoughts as we did. Do we?"

She pondered for a moment.

"I thought we did, Laddy. At least I have not thought anything about it. There is no change indeed, dear Laddy. What if I am grown up, as you say, into a woman?"

"What, indeed, stately Cis? Only girls are so—they wrap themselves up in their own thoughts and become enigmas."

She laughed now.

"What do you know about girls, pray? We have so few thoughts worthy the name that we can hardly be said to wrap ourselves in them. And why should girls be enigmas any more than your own sex, sir."

"I don't know. Perhaps because we want to find out more than they care to tell us about themselves."

"Perhaps because men always think and talk of women as a class. Why can't they give us individuality? You see, Laddy, we are different from men chiefly because we have no ambition for ourselves. I suppose it is in our nature—so far we are a class—that we desire peace and obscurity for ourselves, and greatness only for those men we care about. I have no hopes for myself in the future, Laddy. But I want to see Leonard famous, and you a great composer of beautiful music, and the dear old Captain happy in your success, and my father to grow in honour and reputation. That is all my prayer for myself and my friends. And I like to think of good men and women working all over the world to make us all better and happier. Perhaps it may come in my way some day to do something quietly for the love of God."

"You do something quietly already, Cis," I said, "because you live as you do live."

"Ah, Laddy, I have so many people who love me. Life is very easy when one is surrounded by the affection of so many. Suppose one had been born in the courts, where the voices are rough and men swear. Look at that troop of miserable men." She pointed to a gang of convicts passing through Liberty Gate. "What have been their temptations? How could they have lived the Christian life?"

"Their standard is lower than yours, Cis. Do you remember the statue of Christ, which was always higher than the tallest man? The higher one's thoughts carry one, the more wonderful, the more unattainable, seems the Christ-like life. But our talk has led us into strange paths, Cis. All this because I said you were grown a woman."

"No, sir, you called me names. You said I was an enigma. See now, Laddy, I must never be an enigma to you. I promise this. If ever you think that I am hiding any thought from you, ask me what it is, and I will confess it unless it is an unworthy thought, and then I should be ashamed."

"You could not have unworthy thoughts, Cis."

She shook her head.

"Foolish and frivolous thoughts. Vain and selfish thoughts," she said.

"Never mind them now. Let us only continue as we always have been—my brother, my kind and sweet-faced brother."

Mine, indeed; but that she did not know. She took my hands in hers, laid her sweet fair cheek to mine, and kissed me on the lips and forehead. I think I feel her kisses still, I did not dare—I could not—return them. For when that ruby-red rose blossom of her lips met mine I trembled in all my limbs.

Think. I was small, mean of appearance, and deformed, but I was past twenty-one years of age. I was a man. And I loved the girl with an unbrotherly love, and with a passion which might even have belonged to a man whose back was straight.

If I trembled when she touched me, just as I rejoiced when I saw her, or heard the rustle of her dress, the kisses which she gave me struck my heart with a coldness as of death. Of course I knew it all along, but there is always a reserve power of illusion in youth, and I may have deceived myself. But now it came home to me with clearness as of crystal that Celia could never, never, by any chance, care for me—in that way.

I realised this in a moment, and pulled myself together with an effort, returning the gentle pressure of her soft warm hand just as if my heart was as calm as her own. Then I answered in commonplace and at random.

"Thank you, Cis. Some day, perhaps, I shall take you at your word, and make you confess all sorts of hidden things. Tutor and pupil is all very well, so is elder brother and younger sister. But you are six inches taller than I already."

I have always thought that this simple speech was just the wisest I ever made in my life, because I was so very near saying what I should have repented ever after. Had I said what was in my heart, and almost on my lips, I might have destroyed the sweet friendship which existed then, as it still exists, pure and strong as the current of a great river. I thank God solemnly that I refrained my lips. "Whoso," says the wise man, "keepeth his tongue keepeth his soul from trouble." I loved her, that is most true; in those days when I was yet struggling with the impulses of a passionate love, there were moments when the blood ran tingling and coursing through the veins, and when to beat down the words running riot in my brain, was almost beyond my strength. We were so much together, and she was so unconscious. She could not understand how her voice fell upon my soul like the rain upon a thirsty soil. Even when we were apart there was no moment when Celia was not present in my thoughts. All the morning the music of my pupils, even the very scales, sang, "Celia, Celia, Celia," in accents which varied with my moods, now wild and passionate, now soft and pleading, now hopeful, and now despairing.

There was one time—I do not know how long it lasted—a week or a dozen weeks—when I was fain to pretend illness because the misery of crushing this hopeless love was too great for me, and I craved for solitude.

CHAPTER XIV.
ON THE SEA-SHORE.

IN those days the new suburb, which is now a large town, had hardly yet begun; there was no sea-wall along the beach outside the harbour, and half a mile beyond the rampart you might reach a place perfectly lonely and deserted. There was a common, a strip of waste land where the troops drilled and exercised, and beyond the common an old castle, a square and rather ugly pile built by Henry VIII., when he set up the fortresses of Sandown, Walmer, and Deal. It was surrounded by a star fort, and stood on the very edge of the sea, with a sloping face of stone which ran down to the edge of the water at low tide, and into the waves at high, protecting the moat which surrounded the town. As a boy I regarded this fortress with reverence. There had been a siege there at the time of the Civil War. It was held for the King, but the governor, after a little fighting with his Roundhead besiegers, surrendered the castle, and then the town itself capitulated. One pictured the townsmen on the wall, looking out to see the fortunes of the battle, the men for Church and King side by side with their sour-faced brethren who were for God and country, the discomfiture of the former when the Royal Standard was hauled down, and the joy of the Puritans when their party marched in at the town gates. Of course in my young imagination I supposed that the town walls were just the same then as now, with their bastions, curtains, ravelins, and glacis. It was a lonely place in those days, fit for a dreamy boy, or a moody man. Beyond the castle the beach stretched far, far away under a low cliff of red earth, curving round in a graceful line; behind the beach was a narrow strip of ground covered with patches of furze, whose yellow and sickly sweet blossoms seemed to flourish independently of all seasons; on its scanty edge grew sea poppies; and here, amid the marshy ground which lay about, we used to hunt as boys for vipers, adders, and the little evvet, the alligator of Great Britain, who is as long as a finger and as venomous as a lamb. Sometimes, too, we would find gipsy encampments planted among the furze, with their gaudily-painted carts, their black tents—every real Rommany has a black tent like the modern Bedawi or the ancient dweller in the tents of Kedar. While we looked at the bright-eyed children and the marvellous old women crouching over the fire of sticks and the great black pot, there would come out of the tents one or two girls with olive skins and almond eyes—not the almond eyes of Syria, but bolder, darker, and brighter. They would come smiling in Leonard's face, asking him to cross his hand with silver. When he said he had no silver they would tell his fortune for nothing, reading the lines of his palm with a glibness which showed their knowledge of the art. But it was always a beautiful fortune, with love, fighting, wife, and children in it.

Behind this acre or two of furze stood, all by itself, a mill, and there was a story about this mill, because its centre pillar, on which the vanes revolved, had once been part of the mainmast of a French frigate taken in action. And higher up the beach again—because this was a place full of historic associations—stood two old earthwork forts at intervals of half a mile. The ramparts were green with turf, the grass all blown inland, and lying on the days of summer in long swathes upon the slopes, beaten down by the sea breeze; the moats were dry, and these, too, were grown over with grass; there was an open place at the back where once had been a gate and a drawbridge; there was a stonework well in the open part of the enclosure, only some inclined to the belief that it was only a sham well and masked, *prœtexto sub nomine*, a subterranean passage to the castle; the fronts of those forts were all destroyed and dragged down by the advancing tide. No ruined city in Central America, no temple of the Upper Nile, no tell of Kouyounjik could be more desolate, more lonely, more full of imaginative associations than these forts standing upon the unpeopled beach in a solitude broken only by the footstep of the Coastguard. Before Leonard went away, and when we were boys together, this place was to us as the uttermost part of the world, a retreat accessible on a holiday morning, where one could sit under the cliff or on the grassy slopes of the fort; where I, at least, could dream away the hours. Before us the waves ran along the shingle with a murmurous sh—sh—sh, or, if the day was rough, rolled up their hollow threatening crests like the upper teeth of a hungry monster's jaw, and then dashed in rage upon the stones, dragging them down with a crash and a roar which rolled unceasingly along the beach. In the summer months it was Leonard's delight at such times to strip and plunge, to swim over and through the great waves, riding to meet them, battling and wrestling till he grew tired, and came out red all over, and glowing with the exercise. After a storm the beach was strewn with odds and ends; there were dead cuttlefish—Victor Hugo's *pieuvre*—their long and ugly arms powerless for mischief on the shingle; their backbone was good for rubbing out ink, and we had stores enough to rub out all the ink of the Alexandrian Library. There were ropes of sea-weed thicker than the stoutest cable; if you untwisted the coils you found in them strange creatures dead and alive—the sea-mouse, with its iridescent tufts of hair; little crabs with soft shells killed by the rolling of the pebbles; shells inhabited by scaly intruders, cuckoos among crabs, which poked out hard, spiky legs, and were ready to do battle for their stolen house; starfish, ugly and poisonous, sea-nettles, and all kinds of sea-beetles. And lying outside the weed were bits of things from ships; candles, always plenty of tallow candles; broken biscuits, which like so many of Robinson Crusoe's stores were spoiled by the sea-water; empty bottles, bits of wood, and once we came upon a dead man rolling up and down. Leonard rushed into the water, and we pulled him up between two waves. He was dressed in sailor's clothing, and wore great sea-boots, his face was bruised by the stones, and his black hair was cut short. Also he wore a moustache, so that he could not possibly be an English sailor. When we had got him beyond the reach of the waves, we ran to tell the Coastguard, who was on the cliff half a mile away, telescope in hand.

First he swore at us personally and individually for troubling him at all with the matter. Then, because Leonard "up and spake" in answer, he changed the object of his swearing, and began to swear at large, addressing the much-enduring ocean, which made no reply, but went on with its business of rolling along the beach. Then he swore at himself for being a Coastguardsman. This took altogether some quarter of an hour of good hard swearing, the excellent Solitary finding greater freedom as he went on. And he would have continued swearing, I believe, for many weeks if necessary, only that a thought struck him suddenly, like unto a fist going home in the wind, and he pulled up and gasped—

"Did you, did you," he asked, "look in that dead man's pockets?"

We said "No."

Then he became thoughtful, and swore quite to himself between the teeth, as if he was firing volleys of oaths down his own throat.

"Now, lads," he said at last, "what you've got to do is this. You've got to go straight away to the parish," which I suppose he took for a police office, "and tell the parish to come here and look after that man. I am not stationed here to look after dead men. I'm for live smugglers, I am. You tell the parish that. Not but what its proper for you to tell the Coastguard everything that goes on along the coast. And next time you fish up a drownded man you come straight to me first. No manner o' use to look in their pockets because they've never got nothing in 'em. Them nasty fishes, you see, they gets into the pockets and pulls out the purses."

His belief in the emptiness of drowned men's pockets did not prevent him from testing its correctness. At least we looked back, and observed him searching diligently. But I suppose he was right, because the"parish" certainly found nothing in the pockets.

It was to this place that I came, as to a wilderness, to struggle with myself. Here I was free to think, to brood, and to bring railing accusations against Providence because I could not marry Celia. Sitting on the lonely beach I could find a gloomy satisfaction in piling up my grievances against high Heaven. Who was I that I should be singled out for special and signal misfortune? Had I been as other men, tall, straight, and comely, Celia might have loved me. Had I come to her gallant and strong, rich and noble, one born in high station, the son of a brave and successful father, I might have had a chance.

Day after day I wandered here brooding over my own wrongs, with bitter and accusing soul. The voice of the sea echoed the sorrow of my heart; the long roll from left to right of the ebbing or the rising wave was the setting of a song whose words were all of despair; the dancing of the sunlit waves brought no joy; my heart was dead to the blue sky, flecked with the white wing of seagull, and dotted along the distant horizon with the far-off sails of passing ships. It pleased me to lie there, with my chin upon my hand, thinking of what ought to have been. During this time I was with Celia as little as possible, and at home not at all. Both she and the Captain, I remember now, were considerate, and left me alone, to worry through with the trouble, whatever it was. It was not all hopeless; it was partly that for the first time in my life I thoroughly understood what I was, what my prospects were, and what I might have been. I said at the beginning that it takes a long time for a hunchback entirely to realise what his affliction means; how it cuts him off from other men's pursuits; and how it isolates him from his youth upwards. I saw before me, as plainly as I see it now, a solitary life; I thought that the mediocrity of my abilities would never allow me to become a composer of eminence, or anything better than the organist of a church and the teacher of music in a country town; I should always be poor; I should never have the love of woman; I should always be a kind of servant; I should live in obscurity and die in oblivion. Most of us live some such lives; at least they can be reduced, in hard terms, to some such colourless, dreary wastes of weary years; but we forget the compensations. My dream was true of myself; I have actually lived the life of a mediocre musician; I have few friends, and yet I have been perfectly happy. I did not marry Celia; that I may premise at once; and yet I have been happy without her. For I retained her love, the pure and calm affection of a sister, which is with me still, making much of me, petting and spoiling me almost while I write, as it did twenty years ago. Surely there was never any woman before so good as Celia. The vision of my life was prophetic; it looked intolerable, and it has been more than pleasant. Say to yourself, you have thirty years to live; you will rise every morning to drudgery; you will live poorly, and will make no money; you will have no social consideration; you will make few friends; you will fail to achieve any reputation in your profession; you will be a lonely man—is that a prospect to charm any one? Add to this that your life will be contented, that you will not dislike your work, that you will not live for yourself alone, that your days will be cheered by the steady sunshine of affection; and the prospect changes. Everything in the world is of magic. To some this old town of ours has seemed dirty, crowded, mean; to me it is picturesque, full of human interest, rich in association. To some my routine would be maddening; to me it is graceful and pleasant. To some—to most—a career which has no prizes has no joys. To me it is full of joys. We are what we think ourselves; we see everything through the haze of imagination; why—I am told that there is no such thing as colour in nature, but that it is an effect of light—so long as the effect is produced I do not care; let me only thank the Creator for this bunch of sweet peas in a glass before me, with their soft and delicate tints more beautiful than ever human pencil drew. We see what we think we see; people are what we think they are; events are what they seem to us; the man who least enjoys the world is the man who has the faculty of stripping things of their "effects;" who takes the colour from the flower, or the disinterestedness from love. That is common sense, and I would rather be without it.

One evening—it was after dusk and rather cold—I was still sitting in the enjoyment of a profound misery, when I became aware of a Voice addressing me. The Voice was inside my head and there was no sound, but I heard it plainly. I do not pretend that there was anything supernatural about the fact, nor do I pretend to understand how it happened. It sprang from the moody and half-distracted condition of my mind: it was the return of the overstretched spring: it was the echo of my accustomed thoughts, for the last fortnight pent up and confined in narrow cells to make room for the unaccustomed thoughts. This is exactly what the Voice said to me—

"You were a poor Polish boy, living in exile, and Heaven sent you the Captain to educate you, give you the means of living, and make you a Christian gentleman, when you might have grown up among the companions of profligate sailors. You are an orphan, with neither mother, brother, nor sister. You have no relations to care for you at all. Heaven sent you Leonard to be your brother, and Celia to be your sister. From your earliest infancy you have been wrapped in the love of these two. You are deformed, it is true; you cannot do the things that some men delight in. Heaven has sent you the great gift of Music: it is another sense by which you are lifted above the ordinary run of men. Every hour in the day it is your privilege as a musician to soar above the earth, and lose yourself in divine harmonies. You have all this— and you complain.

"Ungrateful! With these favours you sit here crying because you cannot have one thing more. You would have Celia love you, and marry you. Are you worthy of such a girl?

"Rouse yourself. Go back to your work. Show a brave and cheerful face to the good old man your benefactor. Let Celia cease to wonder whether she has pained you, and to search her heart for words she has never spoken; work for her and with her again; let her never know that you have hungered after the impossible even to sickness.

"And one more thing. Remember Leonard's parting words. Are you blind or are you stupid? With what face could you meet him when he comes home, and say, ' Leonard, you left me to take care of Celia; you trusted to my keeping the secret of your own love. I have betrayed your confidence, and stolen away her heart.' Think of that."

The Voice ceased, and I arose and walked home changed.

The Captain looked up as I entered the room, in a wistful, sad way.

"Forgive me, sir," I said. "I have been worrying myself—never mind what about, but it is over now, and I am sorry to have given you trouble."

"You have fought it down then, Laddy?" he asked, pulling off his spectacles.

I started. Did he, then, read my soul? Was my secret known to all the world?

Only to him, I think.

"When I was a young fellow," he went on, walking up and down the room with his hands behind him, "I fell in love—with a young lady. I believed that young lady to be an angel, and I daresay she was. But I found that she couldn't be my angel, so I went to sea, which was a very good way of getting through that trouble. I had a spell on the West Coast —caught yellow fever—chased the slavers—forgot it."

I laughed.

"Do you recommend me to go out slave-chasing, sir?"

"You might do worse, boy. She is a beautiful creature, Laddy, she is a pearl among maidens. I have always loved her. I have watched her with you, Laddy, and all the love is on your side. I have seen the passion grow in you; you have been restless and fidgety. I remembered my own case, and I waited. No, my boy, it can't be: I wish it could; she does not look on you in that light."

After supper he spoke allegorically.

"I've known men—good men, too—grumble at their posts in an action. What does it matter, Laddy, when the enemy has struck, where any one man has to do his duty? The thing is to do it."

This parable had its personal application, like most of the Captain's admonitions.

"You have been unlike yourself, Laddy, lately," said Celia.

"Yes, Cis, I have been ill, I think."

"Not fretting, Laddy, over things."

I shook my head.

"It seems hard, poor boy, sometimes, does it not? But your life will not be wasted, though you spend it all in teaching music."

She thought I had been brooding over my deformity and poverty. Well, so I had, in a sense.

Enough of my fit. The passion disappeared at length, the love remained. Side by side with such a girl as Celia, one must have been lower than human not to love her. Such a love is an education. I know little of grown women, because I spend my time among girls, and have had no opportunity of studying woman's nature, except that of Celia. But I can understand what is meant when I read that the love of woman may raise a man to Heaven or drag him down to Hell. Out of this earthly love which we share in common with the lowest, there spring for all of us, we know, flowers of rare and wondrous beauty. And those who profit most by these blossoms sometimes express their nature to the world in music and in verse.

CHAPTER XV.
LA VIE DE PROVINCE.

THE twenty-fourth of May was not only the Queen's birthday, and therefore kept a holiday in the port, with infinite official rejoicings and expenditure of powder, but also Celia's as well. On that account it was set apart for one of the Tyrrells' four annual dinner-parties, and was treated as a Church festival or fast day. This was the period of early Christianity, when any ecclesiastical day, whether of sorrowful or joyful commemoration, were marked by a better dinner than usual, and the presence of wine. On Ash Wednesday and Good Friday we had salt fish, followed, at the Tyrrells', by a sumptuous repast, graced by the presence of a few guests, and illustrated, so to speak, by a generous flow of port, of which every respectable Briton then kept a cellar, carefully labelled and laid down years before. The *novus homo* in a provincial town might parade his plate, his dinner service, his champagne—then reckoned a very ostentatious wine. He might affect singularity by preferring claret to port, and he might even invite his guests to drink of strange and unknown wines, such as Sauterne, Bucellas, Lisbon, or even Hock. But one thing he could not do: he could not boast of his old cellar, because everybody would know that he had bought it. Mr. Tyrrell was conscious of this, and being himself a *novus homo*, he evaded the difficulty by referring his wine to the cellar of Mr. Pontifex, the husband of Mrs. Tyrrell's aunt. Now Mr. Pontifex was a man of good county family, and his port, laid down by his father before him, was not to be gainsaid by the most severe critic. Criticism, in our town, neglecting Literature and the Fine Arts, confined itself to port, in the first instance, municipal affairs in the second, and politics in the third. As the two latter subjects ran in well-known grooves, it is obvious that the only scope for original thought lay in the direction of port. Round this subject were grouped the choicest anecdotes, the sweetest flowers of fancy, the deepest yearnings of the Over-soul. A few houses were rivals in the matter of port. The Rev. Mr. Broughton, our old tutor, was acknowledged to have some '34 beyond all praise, but as he gave few dinner-parties, on the score of poverty, there were not many who could boast of having tasted it. Little Dr. Roy had a small cellar brought from Newfoundland or New Brunswick, whither, as everybody knows, the Portugal trade carries yearly a small quantity of finer wine than ever comes to the London market. The Rev. John Pontifex inherited, as I have already said, a cellar by which Mr. Tyrrell was the principal gainer.

There were two or three retired officers who had made good use of their opportunities on the Rock and elsewhere. And the rest were nowhere. As Mr. Broughton said, after an evening out of the "best" set, that is, the set who had cellars worth considering, the fluid was lamentable. Good or bad, the allowance for every guest at dinner was liberal, amounting to about a bottle and a half a head, though seasoned topers might take more. It was port, with rum and water, which produced those extraordinary noses which I remember in my childhood. There was the nose garnished like Bardolph's with red blossoms; there was the large nose, swollen in all its length; there was the nose with the great red protuberance, waggling as the wearer walked, or agitated by the summer breeze; and there was the nose which paled while it grew, carrying its general appearance, not a full-voiced song and pæan of rum, like its brothers of the ruddy blossom and the ruby blob, but a gentle suspicion of long evening drinks and morning drams. Some men run to weight as they grow old; some dry up. It is a matter of temperament. So some of those old topers ran to red and swollen nose, rubicund of colour and bright with many a blossom; while some ran to a pallid hue and shrunken dimensions. It is true that these were old stagers—the scanty remnant of a generation most of whom were long since tucked up in bed and fallen sound asleep. The younger men—of George Tyrrell's stamp—were more moderate. A simple bottle of port after dinner generally sufficed for their modest wants; and they did not drink rum at all. The Captain, for his part, took his rations regularly: a glass of port-every day, and two on Sunday; a tumbler of grog every night and two on Sunday. To Sundays, as a good Churchman, he added, of course, the feasts and festivals of the Church.

Let us return to these occasions.

On Good Friday, it was—it is still, I believe— *de rigueur* to make yourself ill by eating Hot Cross Buns, which were sold in the streets to the tune of a simple ditty, sung by the vendors. On Whit Sunday, who so poor as not to have gooseberry-pie, unless the season was very backward? Lamb came in with Easter, and added its attractions to heighten the spiritual joy of the season. Easter eggs were not yet invented; but everybody put on something new for the day. The asceticism of Lent had no terrors for those who, like ourselves, began it with more than the customary feasting, conducted it without any additional services, broke its gloom by Mothering Sunday, and ended it by two feasts, separated by one day only. The hungriest Christian faced its terrors with cheek unblanched and his lips firm; he came out of it no thinner than he went in; as for the spiritual use he made of that season, it was a matter for his conscience to determine, not for me to resolve. We marked its presence in Church by draping the pulpit, reading desk, and clerk's desk with black velvet, instead of red. The Rev. Mr. Broughton always explained the bearings of Lent according to the ordinances of the Church, and explained very carefully that fasting, in our climate, and in the northern latitude, was to be taken in a spiritual, not a carnal sense. It was never meant, he said, that Heaven's gifts were to be neglected, whatever the season might be. Nor was it intended by Providence, in the great Christian scheme, that we were to endanger the health of the body by excessive abstinence. This good shepherd preached what he practised, and practised what he preached. During Lent the hymns, until I became organist, were taken more slowly than at other seasons, so that it was a great time for the old ladies on the triangular brackets. The Captain, who had an undeveloped ear for music, said that caterwauling was not singing praises, but it was only fair to let every one have his watch, turn and turn about, and that if the commanding officer—meaning Mr. Broughton—allowed it, we had to put up with it. But he gave out the "tools" with an air of pitiful resignation. On Trinity Sunday, Mr. Broughton, in a discourse of twenty minutes, confronted the Unbeliever, and talked him down with such an array of argument that when the benediction came there was nothing left of him. It is curious that whenever I, which is once a year, read that splendid encounter between Greatheart and Apollyon, I always think of Mr. Broughton and Trinity Sunday. When Apollyon was quite worsted and we were dismissed, we went home to a sort of Great Grand Day dinner, a Gaudy, a City Feast, a Commemoration Banquet, to which all other Christian festivals, except Christmas, were mere trifles. For on Trinity Sunday, except when east winds were more protracted than usual, there were salmon, lamb, peas, duckling, early gooseberries, and asparagus.

From Trinity Sunday to Advent was a long stretch, unmarked by any occasion of feasting. I used to wonder why the Church had invented nothing to fill up that space, and I commiserated the hard lot of Dissenters, to whom their religion gave no times for feasting.

The influence of custom hedged round the whole of life for us. It even regulated the amount of our hospitalities. Things were expected of people in a certain position. The Tyrrells, for instance, could hardly do less than give four dinner-parties in the year. Others not in so good a position might maintain their social rank with two. Retired officers were not expected to show any hospitality at all. To be sure this concession was necessary unless the poor fellows, who generally had large and hungry families, were allowed to entertain, after the manner of Augustus Brambler, on bread and cheese. Mrs. Pontifex again, who had very decided Christian views, but was of good country family, admitted her responsibilities by offering one annual banquet of the more severe order.

A bachelor, like Mr. Verney Broughton, was exempt from this social tax. He gave very few dinners. To make up for this, he would ask one man at a time, and set before him such a reminiscence of Oriel in a solid dinner, with a bottle of crusted port after it, as to make that guest dissatisfied with his wife's catering for a month to come.

The guests were divided into sets, with no regard for their special fitness or individual likings, but simply in accordance with recognised social status. The advantage of this arrangement was that you knew beforehand whom you would meet, and what would be talked about. I knew all the sets, because at most of their entertainments I was a guest, and at some a mere umbra, invited as *ami defamille*, who would play and sing after dinner. On these occasions my profession was supposed to be merged in the more creditable fact of my illustrious birth. When strangers came I never failed to overhear the whisper, after the introduction,"Count Pulaski in Poland, but refuses to bear the title in England. Of very high. Polish family." One gets used to most things in time. Mr. Tyrrell divided his dinner-guests into four sets. In October we had lawyers, one or two doctors, perhaps a clergyman, and their wives. At the summer feast (which was the most important, and was fixed with reference to the full moon for convenience of driving home) there were the important clients, who came in great state, in their own carriages. In February we entertained a humbler class of townspeople, who were also clients. And in December we generally entertained the Mayor and officers of the borough, a thing due to Mr. Tyrrell's connection with the Municipality. The May banquet was wholly of a domestic character. The dinners were solid and heavy, beginning early and lasting an immense time. After dinner the men sat for an hour or two consuming large quantities of port.

"If this," Celia used to say, "is society, I think, Laddy, that I prefer solitude."

She and I used to sing and play duets together, after dinner, occasionally giving way to any young lady who expected to be asked to sing. The songs of the day were not bad, but they lasted too long. It is more than possible to tire, in the course of years, of such a melody as "Isle of Beauty" or "Love Not" (a very exasperating piece of long-drawn music), or "My Pretty Page," a sentimentally beautiful thing. The men, some of whom had red faces after the port, mostly hung about the doors together, while the ladies affected great delight in turning over old albums and well-known portfolios of prints. Photographs began to appear in some provincial drawing-rooms in the early fifties, but they were not yet well-established. It was a transition period. Keepsakes and Books of Beauty were hardly yet out of fashion, while portrait albums were only just beginning. Daguerreotypes, things which, regarded from all but one point of view, showed a pair of spectral eyes and nothing else, lay on the table in red leather cases. Mural decoration was an art yet in its infancy, and there must have been, now one comes to think of it, truly awful things to be witnessed in the shape of vases, jars, and ornamented mantel-shelves; the curtains, the carpets, the chairs, and the sofas were in colours not to be reconciled on any principle of Art. And I doubt very much whether we should like now the fashion in which young ladies wore their hair, dressed their sleeves, and arranged their skirts. Fashion is the most wonderful of all human vanities; and the most remarkable thing about it is, that whether a pretty girl disguises herself in Queen Anne's hoops, Elizabethan petticoats, immense Pompadour coiffure, Victorian crinoline, or Republican scantiness, whether she puts patches and paint on her cheek, whether she runs great rings through her nose, whether she wears a coalscuttle for a bonnet, as thirty years ago, or an umbrella for a hat, as last year, whether she displays her figure as this year, or hides it altogether as fifteen years ago, whether she walks as Nature meant her to walk or affects a stoop, whether she pretends in the matter of hair and waist, or whether she is content with what the gods have given her—she cannot, she may not, succeed in destroying her beauty. Under every disguise the face and figure of a lovely woman are as charming, as bewitching, as captivating, as under any other. When it comes to young women who are not pretty—but, perhaps, as the large-hearted Frenchman said, *il n'y en a pas*—there are no young women who are not pretty.

We were, then, ignorant of Art in my young days. Art in provincial towns as commonly understood did not exist at all. To be sure, we had an Art speciality of which we might have been proud. There was no place in the world which could or did turn out more splendid ships' figure-heads. There was one old gentleman in particular, a genius in figure-head carving, who had his studio in the Dockyard, and furnished her Majesty's Navy with bows, decorated in so magnificent a style, that one, who, like me, remembers them, is fain to weep in only looking at the figure-headless ironclads of the present degenerate days.

As for conversation after dinner, there was not much between the younger men and the ladies, because really there was hardly anything to talk about except one's neighbours. In London, probably, people talked as much as they do now, but in a country town, as yet unexplored by Mudie or Smith, there could be very few topics of common interest between a young man and a girl. The Great Exhibition of 1851 did one great service for country people; it taught them how easy it is to get to London, and what a mine of wealth, especially for after memory and purposes of conversation, exists in that big place. But remember that five and twenty years ago, in the family circle of a country town, there were no periodical visits to the town, no holidays on the Continent, no new books, no monthly magazines; even illustrated newspapers were rarely seen: there was no love of Art or talk of artistic principles, or Art schools; there were no choral societies, no musical services: no croquet, or Badminton, or lawn tennis. And yet people were happy. Celia's social circle was too limited to make her feel the want of topics of conversation with young men. No young man except myself was ever invited to the house, and of course I hardly counted.

When the formal dinner-parties were held, the guests at these banquets were principally old and middle-aged people. At our birthday dinner only the very intimate friends and relations were invited. Mr. Tyrrell had no relations; or at least we never heard of them, but his wife was well connected; the Pontifexes are known to be a good old county family, and Mrs. Pontifex, Mrs. Tyrrell's aunt, often asserted the claims of her own ancestry, who were Toplingtons, to be of equal rank with her husband's better known line.

Of course, the Pontifexes always came to the dinners.

Mrs. Pontifex—Aunt Jane—was fifteen years older than her husband, and at this time, I suppose, about sixty-five years of age. She was small in person, but upright and gaunt beyond her inches. It is a mistake to suppose—I learned this from considering Mrs. Pontifex as a Leading Case —that gauntness necessarily implies a tall stature. Not at all. "If," I said to Cis one day, "if you were to wear, as Aunt Jane wears, a cap of severely Puritanic aspect, decorated with a few flowers which might have grown in a cemetery; if you were to arrange your hair, as she arranges it, in a double row, stiff curls, set horizontally on each side of her face; if you were to sit bolt upright, with your elbows square, as if you were always in a pew; if you were to keep the corners of your lips down—as Aunt Jane does—so—Cis—why even you would be gaunt. John of Gaunt, so called because he resembled Aunt Jane, was, I believe, a man under the middle height."

She married the Rev. John Pontifex, or rather they married each other, chiefly for money. They both had excellent incomes which united made a large income; they were both desperately careful and saving people; they held similar views on religious matters (they were severe views), and I suppose that Aunt Jane had long learned to rule John Pontifex when she invited him—even Cis used to agree that he would never have invited her—to become her husband.

Mr. Pontifex was a man of lofty but not commanding stature. Another mistake of novelists and people who write. You have not necessarily a commanding stature because you are tall. No one could have seen anything commanding in Mr. John Pontifex. He was six feet two in height, and, although by nature austere, he looked as meek as if he had been only five feet; the poor man, indeed, never had the chance of looking anything but meek; he had a pale face and smooth cheeks, with thin brown hair, a little grey and "gone off" at the temples. His features were made remarkable by a very long upper lip, which gave him a mutton-like expression as of great meekness coupled with some obstinacy. In fact, she who drove John Pontifex had at times to study the art of humouring her victim. Since his marriage he had retired from active pastoral work, and now passed his time in the critical observation of other men at work in his own field. He held views of the most Evangelical type, and when he preached at St. Faith's we received without any compromise the exact truth as regards future prospects. He spoke very slowly, bringing out his nouns in capitals, as it were, and involved his sentences with parentheses! But in the presence of his wife he spoke seldom, because she always interrupted him. He was fond of me, and for some reason of his own, always called me Johnny.

In strong contrast with his clerical brother was the Perpetual Curate of St. Faith's, my old tutor, Mr. Verney Broughton. The latter was as plump, as rosy, as jolly as the former was thin, tall, and austere. Calvin could not have looked on the world's follies with a more unforgiving countenance than the Rev. John Pontifex; Friar John could hardly have regarded the worldliness of the world with more benignity than Rev. Verney Broughton. He was a kind-hearted man, and loved the world, with the men, women, and children upon it; he was a scholar and student, consequently he loved the good things that had been written, said, and sung upon it; he was a gourmand, and he liked to enjoy the fruits of the earth in due season. Perhaps he loved the world too much for a Christian minister; at all events, he enjoyed it as much as he could; never disguised his enjoyment, and inculcated both in life and preaching a perfect trust in the goodness of God, deep thankfulness for the gifts of eating and drinking, and reliance on the ordinances of the Church. Mr. Pontifex amused him; they were close companions, which added to the pleasures of life; and he entertained, I shall say, dislike for no man in the world except Herr Räumer, whom he could not be brought to admire.

"He is a cynic," he would say. "That school has never attracted my admiration. He delights in the *double entendre*, and is never so much pleased as when he conveys a hidden sneer. I do not like that kind of conversation. Give me honest enthusiasm, admiration, and faith. And I prefer Englishmen, Ladislas, my boy, though you are only an Englishman by adoption."

CHAPTER XVI.
A DINNER-PARTY.

THERE were several other people who entertained similar views with regard to Herr Räumer. Mrs. Pontifex disliked him excessively for one. Everybody began with distrust of this man; then they grew to tolerate him; some went on to like him; all ended with cordial hatred—it would be hard to say why. His eyes, without the blue spectacles, which he put off indoors, were singularly bright, though rather small. He had a way of turning their light full on to a speaker without speaking, which was as embarrassing a commentary on what you had just said as you can imagine. It conveyed to yourself and to everybody else, which was even more humiliating, the idea that you were really, to this gentleman's surprise, even a greater fool than you looked. Perhaps that was one reason why he was so much disliked.

You noticed, too, after a time, that he saw everything, heard everything, and remembered everything. When he spoke about his personal reminiscences, he showed an astonishing recollection of detail as if he preserved photographs of places and persons in his mind.

He was always about Mr. Tyrrell's office, and kept there a fireproof safe, with his name painted on it in white letters. He carried the key in his own pocket. Of course I knew nothing of the nature of his business, but it was generally understood that he was a German who had money, that he chose to live in our town for his own pleasure and convenience, and that he invested his funds by Mr. Tyrrell's help and advice in local securities.

The Captain and little Dr. Roy always made up the party. Everybody liked the little doctor, who stood five feet nothing in his boots, a neat and well-proportioned abridgment of humanity, with a humorous face and a twinkling eye. He was an Irishman; he had been in America; and it was currently reported that if he ventured his foot on Canadian soil he would infallibly be hanged for the part he took in the rebellion of eighteen hundred and forty something. In certain circles he had the reputation of being an Atheist—he was in reality as good a Roman Catholic as ever touched holy water—because he was constantly crying out about bad drainage, and taunting people with the hundreds of lives wantonly thrown away, he said, every year, and struck down by preventible diseases. "As if," the people said piously, "the issues of life and death were in man's hand." So typhus fever went on, and the town was not drained.

The birthday dinners were all alike, with the same guests. The year went on, and we met on the anniversary to drink Celia's health and talk the same talk. Let me take one of these dinners, the last at which this company met together for this purpose.

The Rev. Mr. Broughton took in Mrs. Tyrrell, so that Celia fell to Mr. Pontifex; Mrs. Pontifex, of course, took Mr. Tyrrell's arm. The grace was "pronounced" by Mr. Broughton. He was less unctuous over the petition than poor Augustus Brambler, but he threw considerable feeling into the well-known words, and had a rich, melodious voice, a fitting prelude to the banquet. Grace said, the benevolent divine surveyed the guests and the table with the eyes of satisfaction, as if he wished it was always feast time.

There were no *menus* laid on the table in those days, and you did not know what was coming as you do now. But there was the smell of roast meats which, if you remember what things belong to the season, was almost as good as a *menu*. And the things were put on the table. There were no dinners *à la Russe*. You saw your food before you. The host carved, too, and very laborious work it was. But it was still reckoned part of a gentleman's education to carve with discretion and skill. I should like to have seen Mr. Broughton's face if he had been compelled to sit in silence during the mangling of a hare. Perhaps, however, he was too much of a martinet, and the exquisite finish with which he distributed a pheasant among half-a-dozen guests, however admirable as a work of Art, pointed to an amount of thought in the direction of dinner beyond what is now expected of the clergy.

Mr. Pontifex, on the other hand, was a wretched carver.

"I am now more at ease," he would say, "in the Pulpit than in the Place of the Carver, though, in my youth, when I was at Oxford, when, alas! the pleasures of the—ahem— the Table, were in my day placed above the pleasures of the Soul—I was considered expert in the Art of Carving. There was one occasion, I remember—with sorrow—when a Goose was placed upon the board—"

"I wish, Mrs. Tyrrell," interrupted Mr. Broughton—and indeed we had all heard the goose story before—"I wish I could persuade my landlady to give the same thoughtfulness to things as your cook. It is so difficult to make some women understand the vital importance of dinner. I can order the raw materials, but I cannot, unfortunately, cook them."

Mrs. Pontifex, I saw, sat opposite her husband, who took his dinner under her superintendence. I sat next to that divine, and felt pity for him as a warning or prohibition came across the table, and he had to shake his head in sorrowful refusal.

In his rich, mellow voice, Mr. Broughton, on receiving his fish, remarked—

"The third time this year, and only the 24th of May, that I have partaken of salmon. The Lord is very good—"

"No, John Pontifex," said that clergyman's wife loudly, "no salmon for you."

"My dear," he ventured to expostulate feebly, because he was particularly fond of salmon.

"Ladislas Pulaski, who is young, may make himself ill with salmon and cucumber if he likes," said Aunt Jane, "but not you, John Pontifex. Remember the last time."

He sighed, and I took the portion intended for him.

"The Lord is very good," resumed Mr. Broughton, "to nearly all His creatures," as if Pontifex was an exception.

Dr. Roy began to talk of salmon-fishing in the Saguenay River, and we were all interested except poor Mr. Pontifex, whose face was set in so deep a gloom that I thought he would have rebelled.

He picked up a little when an *entrée* of pigeons was allowed to stop at his elbow. But the undisguised enjoyment with which he drank his first glass of champagne brought his wife, who was at that moment talking of a new and very powerful tract, down upon him. in a moment.

"No more champagne, John Pontifex," she ordered promptly.

"Another glass for me," cried Mr. Broughton, nodding his head. "A glass of wine with you, Mrs. Pontifex. I am a bachelor, you know, and can do as I like."

It was not manners to refuse, and Aunt Jane raised her glass to her lips icily, while Mr. Broughton drained his with an audible smack. In 1858 we had already in provincial towns passed out of the custom of taking wine with each other, but it was still observed by elderly people who liked the friendly fashion of their youth.

I thought this assertion of independence rather cruel to Mr. Pontifex, but it was not for me, belonging, with Celia, to the class of "young people," to say anything at a party unless previously spoken to or questioned. Then Aunt Jane began a talk with Herr Räumer, chiefly about the sins of people. As you came to know this German well, you discovered that, whenever he did talk about people, he had something bad to say of them; also when he spoke of any action, however insignificant, it was to find an unworthy motive for it. Perhaps, however, I am now in that fourth and bad stage mentioned above.

Mr. Tyrrell was silent during the dinner, perhaps because he had to carve industriously and dexterously; he drank wine freely; but he said nothing. Celia noticed her father's taciturnity, and I saw her watching him with anxiety. No one else observed it, and when the first stiffness of ceremony wore off, there began the genial flow of conversation which ought to rejoice the heart of a hostess, because it shows that every one is feeding in content. Mr. Tyrrell, a florid, high-coloured man, who usually talked fast and rather noisily, was looking pale; the nerves of his cheek twitched, and his hand trembled.

When the cloth was removed—I am not certain that the old fashion of wine and dessert on the polished dark mahogany was not better than the present—we all drank Celia's health.

"In bumpers," cried Mr. Broughton, filling up Mrs. Tyrrell's glass and his own to the brim with port. "In bumpers all. And I wish I was a young man again to toast Celia Tyrrell as she should be toasted. Don't you, Brother Pontifex? Here is to your *beaux, yeux*, my dear. Some day I will preach a sermon on thankfulness for beauty."

"God bless you, Celia, my child," said her father, with a little emotion in his voice. "Many happy returns of the day, and every one better than the last."

"The best thing," continued Mr. Broughton, "for young girls is a young husband—eh, Mrs. Tyrrell? What do you think?"

"Vanity," said Aunt Jane. "Let them wait and look round them. I was thirty-five when I married my first."

"When I was at Oxford," Mr. Pontifex began, glancing anxiously at his wife—"When I was at Brazenose, Oxford (where I was known, I am ashamed to say, as—as—as Co-rin-thian Pon-ti-fex, on account of the extraordinary levity, even in that assemblage of reckless youths, of my disposition), there were some among us commonly designated as—as—as Three—Bottle—Men!!!" He said this with an air of astonishment, as if it was difficult to credit, and a thing which ought, if printed, to be followed by several notes of admiration. "Three—Bottle—Men! The rule among us was—I regret to say—No—ahem—no Heeltaps."

"John Pontifex!" interposed his wife severely. "Recollect yourself. 'No Heeltaps,' indeed!"

"My dear, I was about to conclude this sad Reminiscence by remarking that it was a Truly Shocking State of Things."

He spoke in capitals, so to speak, and with impressive slowness.

"When young people are present," said Aunt Jane, "it is well to consider the religious tendency of anecdotes before they are related."

Mr. Pontifex said no more.

"I will tell you, by-and-bye, Pontifex," said the jolly old parson, whose face was a good deal redder than at the commencement of dinner, "I will tell you, when the ladies have left us, some of our experiences in Common

Room. Don't be afraid, Mrs. Pontifex, we shall not emulate the deeds of those giants."

"In my house," said Aunt Jane to her niece reproachfully, "it is one of our Christian privileges not to sit over wine after dinner; we all rise together."

"From a lady's point of view," observed Herr Räumer, "doubtless an admirable practice."

"Not at all admirable," cried the Captain, who had been quiet during dinner. "Why shouldn't we have half-an-hour to ourselves to talk politics and tell yarns, while the ladies talk dress?"

"In my house," said Aunt Jane, "the ladies do not talk dress. We exchange our experiences. It is a Christian privilege."

Dr. Roy uttered a hollow groan, doubtless from sympathy with Mr. Pontifex.

Just then Mrs. Tyrrell sat bolt upright, which was her signal, and the ladies left us.

"Aha!" cried Mr. Broughton, "confess Brother Pontifex, that you do not appreciate all the Christian privileges of your house."

He shook his head solemnly, but he did not smile. "Three bottle men, were you?" said Dr. Roy. "Gad, sir, I remember at old Trinity, in Dublin, some of us were six bottle men. Not I, though. Nature intended me for a one pint man."

"It is only the German student," said Herr Räumer, "who can hold an indefinite quantity."

"I sincerely hope," said Mr. Pontifex, as he finished his glass, "that things have greatly changed since that time. I remember that the door was generally locked; the key was frequently thrown out of the window, and the—the—Orgy commenced. As I said before, the word was 'No Heeltaps.' It is awful to reflect upon. Thank you, Dr. Roy, I will take another glass of Port. There were times, too, when, in the wantonness of youth, we permitted ourselves the most reckless language over our feasts. On one occasion I did so, myself. The most reckless language. I positively swore. My thoughtless companions, I regret to say, only laughed. They actually laughed. The cause of this—this Iniquity arose over a Goose. It is a truly Dreadful Event to look back upon."

"We used at Oriel," said Mr. Broughton, again interrupting the Goose story without compunction, "to drink about a bottle and a half a head; and we used to talk about Scholarship, Literature, and Art. And some of the men talked well. I wish I could drink a bottle and a half every night now; and I wish I had the Common Room to drink it in. It is a Beautiful Time for me to look back upon."

It was as if he tried in everything to be a contrast to his brother in Orders.

"The rising generation," said Dr. Roy, "who work harder, ride less, smoke more tobacco, and live faster, will have to give up Port and take Claret. After all, it was the favourite Irish wine for a couple of hundred years."

"Ugh!" from Mr. Broughton.

"The longer the Englishmen drinks Port," said Herr Räumer, "Port and Beer, the longer he will continue to be—what he is."

As this was said very smoothly and sweetly, with the rasp peculiar to the voice, giving an unpleasant point at the end, I concluded at once that the German meant more than was immediately apparent.

"Thank you, Herr Räumer," said Mr. Broughton sharply; "I hope we shall continue to remain what we are. The appreciation of your countrymen is always generous. As for Port, I look on that wine as the most perfect of all Heaven's gifts to us poor creatures. This is very fine, Tyrrell. From Pontifex's cellar? Brother Pontifex, you don't ask me to dinner half often enough. Forty-seven? I thought so. Agreeable,"—he held the glass up to the candles: we had wax candles for the dining-room —"with little body, but quite enough. Rather dry," he tasted it again."How superb it will be in twenty years, when some of us shall not be alive to drink it! The taste for Port comes to us by Nature—it is not acquired like that for Claret and Rhine wines—pass me the olives, Roy, my dear fellow. It is born with some of us, and is a sacred gift. It brightens youth, adorns manhood, and comforts age. May those of us who are blessed by Providence with a palate use it aright, and may we never drink a worse glass of wine than the present. I remember," he went on sentimentally wagging his head, which was by this time nearly purple all over, "I remember the very first glass of Port I ever tasted. My grandfather, the Bishop of Sheffield, gave it to me when I was three years old. 'Learn to like it, boy,' said his lordship, who had the most cultivated palate in the diocese. I did like it from that hour, though, unless my memory fails me, the Bishop's butler had brought up too fruity a wine."

The more Port Mr. Broughton consumed the more purple the jolly fat face and bald head became. But no quantity affected his tongue or clouded his brain, so that when we joined the ladies he was as perfectly sober, although coloured like his favourite wine, as Mrs. Pontifex herself, who was making tea.

Mrs. Tyrrell was asleep when we came upstairs, but roused herself to talk with Dr. Roy, who had certainly taken more than the pint for which, as he said, Nature intended his capacity.

Celia was playing, and I joined her, and we played a duet. When we finished I went to ask for a cup of tea.

By the table was standing Mr. Pontifex, a cup in his hand, and a look of almost ghastly discomposure on his face, while his wife was forcing an immense slice of muffin upon his unwilling hands.

"Muffin, John Pontifex," she said.

"My dear," he remonstrated with more firmness than one might have expected; "My dear, I—I do not wish for any muffin—ahem."

"It is helped, John Pontifex," said his wife, and leaving the unhappy man to eat it, she turned to me, thanked me sweetly for the duet, and gave me a cup of tea.

Mr. Pontifex retreated behind his wife's chair. As no one was looking I stole a plate from the table, and with great swiftness transferred the muffin from his plate to mine. He looked boundless gratitude, but was afraid to speak, and after a due interval returned the empty plate to the table, even descending so far in deception as to brush away imaginary crumbs from his coat. His wife looked suspiciously at him, but the muffin was gone, and it was impossible to identify that particular piece with one left in another plate. In the course of the evening he seized the opportunity of being near me, and stooped to whisper sorrowfully—

"I do not like muffin, Johnny. I loathe muffin."

The party broke up at eleven, and by a quarter past we were all gone. As I put my hat on in the hall I heard the voice of Herr Räumer in Mr. Tyrrell's office.

"This is the day, Tyrrell. After she was eighteen, remember."

"Have pity on me, Räumer; I cannot do it. Give me another year."

"Pity? Rubbish. Not another week. I am not going to kill the girl. Is the man mad? Is he a fool?"

I hastened away, unwilling to overhear things not intended for me, but the words struck a chill to my heart.

Who was "she"? Could it be Celia? "After she was eighteen"—and this Celia's eighteenth birthday. It was disquieting, and Mr. Tyrrell asking that white-haired man with the perpetual sneer and the rasp in his voice for pity. Little as I knew of the world, it was clear to me that there would be small chance of pity in that quarter. Herr Räumer and Celia! Why he was sixty years of age, and more; older than Mr. Tyrrell, who was a good deal under fifty. What could he want with a girl of nineteen? It was with a sad heart that I got home that night, and I was sorely tempted to take counsel of the Captain. But I forbore. I would wait and see.

I met Mr. Pontifex next morning. He was going with a basket to execute a few small commissions at the greengrocer's. He acted, indeed, as footman or errand boy, saving the house large sums in wages.

He stopped and shook hands without speaking, as if the memory of the muffin was too much for him. Then he looked as if he had a thing to say which ought to be said, but which he was afraid to say. Finally, he glanced hurriedly up and down the street to see if there was any one within earshot. As there was no one, he laid two fingers on my shoulder, and said in agitated tones, and with more than his usual impressiveness—

"I am particularly partial to salmon, which is, I suppose, the reason why I was allowed none last night. When I married, however, I totally—ahem—surrendered—I regret to say—my independence. Oh; Johnny, Johnny!"

CHAPTER XVII.
AN OLD PROMISE.

AFTER a disquiet and uneasy night, haunted with Cassandra-like visions of coming trouble, I arose, anxious and nervous. "Am I going to kill the girl? Wait till she was eighteen?" What could these words mean except one thing? To connect Celia, even in thought, with this smooth and cynical old German was worse than any union of May and December. Innocence and trust: belief in high aims and pure motives on the one hand—on the other that perfect knowledge of evil which casteth out faith. A maiden whose chief charm, next to her beauty, to the adept of sixty, was her strange and unwonted ignorance of the world and its wickedness. And yet—and yet—we were in this nineteenth century, and we were in England, where men do not give away or sell their daughters, unless in novels: how could it be possible that a man of the world, a successful man, like Mr. Tyrrell, should contemplate, even for a moment, the sacrifice of his only child on such an altar?

As our misfortunes always fall together, I received, the next morning, on my way home from giving my last lesson, a second blow, from an equally unexpected quarter. This time it was from Wassielewski. The old man, who had been dejected and resigned since the failure of his schemes in 1854, was walking along upright, swinging his arms, with an elated air. When he saw me he threw up his long arms, and waved them like the sails of a windmill.

"It is coming," he cried. "It is coming once more. This time it will be no failure, And you shall take your part. Only wait a week, Ladislas Pulaski, and you shall know all. Silence, until you are admitted into our plans."

He shook my hand with a pressure which meant more than his words, and left me, with his head thrown back, his long white hair streaming in the wind, tossing his arms, and gesticulating.

I had almost forgotten that I was a Pole, and the reminder came upon me with a disagreeable shock. It was like being told of some responsibility you would willingly let sleep— some duty you would devolve upon others. And to take my part? Strange transformation of a cripple and a music-master into a conspirator and a rebel.

For a week nothing was said by Mr. Tyrrell, and I was forgetting my anxiety on that score when, one afternoon, I went as usual to see Celia. There were, as I have said, two entrances, that of the front door, which was also the office door, and that at the end of the garden, which was used by Celia and myself. This afternoon, by some accident of choice, I went to the front door. To the right was Mr. Tyrrell's private office; as I passed I saw that the door was open—that he was sitting at his table, his head upon his hand in a dejected position, and that beside him, his back to the empty fireplace, stood, tall, commanding, as if the place belonged to him, Herr Räumer.

He saw me, and beckoned me to enter the office.

"Here is Celia's private tutor, adviser, and most confidential friend," he said, in his mocking tones."Here is Ladislas Pulaski. Why not confide the task to him? Let him speak to Celia first, if you will not."

What task?

Mr. Tyrrell raised his face, and looked at me. I think I have never seen a more sorrowful face than his at that moment—more sorrowful or more humiliated. I had always known him bold, confident, self-reliant, of a proud and independent bearing. All that was gone, and in a single night. He looked crushed. Now, it was as if another spirit possessed the well-known features, for they were transformed. What had this man done to him—what power over him did he possess that could work this great and sorrowful transformation?

Herr Räumer had taken off his blue spectacles, and his sharp keen eyes were glittering like steel. If the man was cynical, he was also resolute. Years of self-indulgence had not softened the determination with which he carried out a purpose.

"Ladislas Pulaski," he went on, seeing that Mr. Tyrrell did not speak, "knows Celia better than you, even—her father—or than myself, her future husband."

"Her what!" I cried, as he announced the thing in a calm judicial way, like the voice of Fate.

"Her future husband," he repeated." The words are intelligible, are they not? Celia will become my wife. Why do you look from Mr. Tyrrell to me in that extraordinary manner? Is there, then, something monstrous in the fact?"

"Yes," I replied boldly. " Celia is eighteen, and you are sixty."

"I am sixy-two," he said." I shall live, I dare say, another eight or ten years. Celia will make these ten years happy. She will then be at liberty to marry anybody else."

"What you hear, Ladislas," said Mr. Tyrrell, speaking with an effort, and shading his eyes as if he did not venture to look me in the face; "what you hear from Herr Räumer is quite true. Celia does not know yet—we were considering when you arrived how to tell her—does not know—yet. Our friend here insists upon her being told at once. The fact is, my dear

Ladislas," he went on, trying to speak at his ease, and as if it were quite an ordinary transaction, "some years since—"

"Ten years," said Herr Räumer.

"Ten years since, our friend here did me a service of some importance."

"Of *some* importance only, my dear Tyrrell?"

"Of very great importance—of vital importance. Never mind of what nature."

"That does not matter, at *present*," said Herr Räumer. "Proceed, my father-in-law."

"As an acknowledgment of that favour—as I then believed—yes, Räumer, it is the truth, and you know it—as I then believed, in a sort of joke—"

"I never joke," said the German.

"I promised that he should marry Celia."

"That promise I have never since alluded to until last night," Herr Räumer explained. "It was a verbal promise, but I knew that it would be kept. There were no papers or agreements between us; but they were unnecessary. As friends we gave a pledge to each other. 'My dear Tyrrell,' I said, 'you are much younger than I am; almost young enough to be my son. You have a daughter. If I am still in this town when she is eighteen years of age, you must let me marry her, if I am then of the same mind.' My friend here laughed, and acceded."

"But I did not think—I did not understand—"

"That is beside the mark. It was a promise. Celia was a pretty child then, and has grown into a beautiful woman. I shall be proud of my wife. Because, Tyrrell"—his brow contracted—"I am quite certain that the promise will be kept."

"The promise did not, and could not, amount to more than an engagement to use my influence with Celia."

"Much more," said the other. "Very much more. I find myself, against my anticipations, still in this quiet town of yours. I find the girl grown up. I find myself getting old. I say to myself—'That was a lucky service you rendered Mr. Tyrrell.' And it was of a nature which would make the most grateful man wish silence to be kept about it. And the promise was most providential. Now will my declining-years be rich in comfort."

"Providential or not," said Celia's father, plucking up his courage; "if Celia will not accept you, the thing is ended."

"Not ended," said Herr Räumer softly. "Just beginning."

"Then God help us," burst out the poor man, with a groan.

"Certainly," responded his persecutor. "By all means, for you will want all the help that is to be got. Mr. Pulaski, who is entirely *ami de famille*, is now in a position to understand the main facts. There are two contracting parties. One breaks his part of the contract—the other, not by way of revenge, but in pursuance of a just policy, breaks his. The consequences fall on the first man's head. Now, Tyrrell, let us have no more foolish scruples. I will make a better husband for your girl than any young fellow. She shall have her own way; she shall do what she likes, and dress —and—all the rest of it, just as she chooses. What on earth do women want more."

I felt sick and dizzy. Poor Celia.

Herr Räumer placed his hand upon the bell.

"I am going to send for her," he said. "If you do not speak to her yourself I will do so. As Ladislas Pulaski is here to give us moral support"—the man could not speak without a sneer—" it will be quite a *conseil de famille*, and we shall not have to trouble Mrs. Tyrrell at all. You can tell her this evening, if necessary."

He rang. Augustus Brambler, as the junior clerk, answered the bell. I noticed that his eyes looked from one to the other of us, as he took the message from the German, in a mild wonder. Augustus ran messages of all sorts with equal alacrity, provided they were connected with the office. He would have blacked boots had he been told to do so, and considered it all part of the majesty of the law.

When Celia came, Herr Räumer made her a very profound and polite bow, and placed a chair for her.

She looked at her father, who sat still with his head on his hand, and then at me.

"What is it, papa? What is it, Laddy?" she asked.

"Your father has a communication to make to you of the very greatest importance," said Herr Räumer softly and gently. "Of so great importance that it concerns the happiness of two lives."

I hardly knew the man. He was soft, he was winning, he was even young, as he murmured these words with another bow of greater profundity than would have become an Englishman.

Then Mr. Tyrrell rose to the occasion. Any man, unless he is an abject coward, can rise to the occasion, if necessary, and act a part becomingly, if not nobly. You never hear of a man having to be carried to the gallows, for instance, though the short walk there must have a thousand pangs for every footfall. Mr. Tyrrell rose, and tried to smile through the black clouds of shame and humiliation.

"Celia, my dear child," he said, " Herr Räumer to-day has asked my consent to his becoming, if you consent, my son-in-law."

"Your son-in-law, papa?"

"My son-in-law, Celia," he replied firmly; the plunge once made, the rest of the work appeared easier. "I am quite aware that there are many objections to be advanced at the outset. Herr Räumer, you will permit me, my friend, to allude once and for all to—"

"To the disparity of age?" No wooer of five-and-twenty could have been more airily bland, as if the matter were not worth mentioning seriously. "The disparity of age? Certainly. I have the great misfortune to be forty years older than Miss Tyrrell. Let us face the fact."

"Quite so. Once stated, it is faced," said Mr. Tyrrell, gaining courage every moment. "The objection is met by the fact that our friend is no weak old man to want a nurse, but strong and vigorous, still in the prime of life."

"The prime of life," echoed the suitor, smiling.

"He is, it may also be objected," said Mr. Tyrrell, as if anxious to get at the worst aspect of the case at once; "he is a foreigner—a German. What then? If there is a nation with which we have a national sympathy, it is the German nation. And as regards other things, he has the honour of—"

"Say of an Englishman, my friend. Say of an English lawyer and gentleman."

Mr. Tyrrell winced for a moment.

"He is honourable and upright, of an excellent disposition, gentle in his instincts, sympathetic and thoughtful for others—"

"My dear friend," the Herr interposed, "is not that too much? Miss Tyrrell will not believe that one man can have all those perfections."

"Celia will find out for herself," said her father, laughing.

"And now, my child, that you know so much, and that we have considered all possible objections, there remains something more to be said. It is ten years since this project was first talked over between us."

"Ten years!" cried Celia.

"As a project only, because it was impossible to tell where we might be after so long a time. It was first spoken of between us after an affair, a matter of business, with which I will only so far trouble you as to say that it laid me under the most lively obligations to Herr Räumer. Remember, my dear, that the gratitude you owe to this gentleman is beyond all that any act of yours can repay. But we do not wish you to accept Herr Räumer from gratitude. I want you to feel that you have here a chance of happiness such as seldom falls to any girl."

"In my country, Miss Tyrrell," said Herr Räumer gravely, "it is considered right for the suitor to seek first the approbation of the parents. I am aware that in England the young lady is often addressed before the parents know anything of—of—of the attachment. If I have behaved after the manner of my people, you will, I doubt not, forgive me."

I ventured to look at Celia. She sat in the chair which Herr Räumer had given her at the foot of the table, upright and motionless. Her cheeks had a touch of angry red in them, and her eyes sought her father's, as if trying to read the truth in them.

"You should know, dear Celia," Mr. Tyrrell went on, "not only from my friend's wish, but also mine, I—I—I think, that we can hardly expect an answer yet."

"Not yet," he murmured; "Miss Tyrrell will give me another opportunity, alone, of pleading my own cause. It is enough to-day that she knows what her father's hopes are, and what are mine. I would ask only to say a few words, if Miss Tyrrell will allow me."

He bowed again.

"Ten years ago, when this project—call it the fancy of a man for a child as yet unformed—came into my brain, I began to watch your progress and your education. I saw with pleasure that you were not sent to those schools where girls' minds are easily imbued with worldly ideas." Good heavens! was Herr Räumer about to put on the garb of religion? "Later on I saw with greater pleasure that your chief companion and principal tutor was Mr. Ladislas Pulaski, a gentleman whose birth alone should inspire with noble thoughts. Under his care I watched you, Miss Tyrrell, growing gradually from infancy into womanhood. I saw that your natural genius was developed; that you were becoming a musician of high order, and that by the sweetness of your natural disposition you were possessing yourself of a manner which I, who have known courts, must be allowed to pronounce perfect. It is not too much to say that I have asked a gift which any man, of whatever exalted rank, would be proud to have; that there is no position however lofty which Miss Tyrrell would not grace; and that I am deeply conscious of my own demerits. At the same time I yield to no one in the resolution to make that home happy which it is in Miss Tyrrell's power to give me. The slightest wish shall be gratified; the most trifling want shall be anticipated. If we may, for once, claim a little superiority over the English, it is in that power of divining beforehand, of guessing from a look or a gesture, the wishes of those we love, which belongs to us Germans."

It was the first and the last time I had ever heard this mysterious power spoken of. No doubt, as Herr Räumer claimed it for his countrymen, they do possess it. Most Germans I have ever seen have struck me as being singularly cold persons, far behind the French in that subtle sympathy which makes a man divine in the manner spoken of by Herr Räumer.

The speech was lengthy and wordy; it was delivered in the softest voice, and with a certain impressiveness. Somehow— so far at least, as I was concerned, it failed to produce a favourable effect. There was not the true ring about it. Celia made a slight acknowledgment, and looked again at her father.

Then Herr Räumer turned effusively to me.

"I have no words," he said, "to express the very great thanks which I—which we—owe to you for the watchful and brotherly care which you have given to Miss Tyrrell. It is not in the power of money—"

"There has never been any question of money," said Mr. Tyrrell quickly, "between Ladislas and us."

"I know. There are disinterested people in the world, after all," Herr Räumer said with a smile. "You are one of them, Mr. Pulaski. At the same time," he added airily, "you cannot escape our thanks. You will have to go through life laden with our gratitude."

Celia got up and gave me her hand.

"You do not want me to say anything now, papa," she said. "We will go. Come, Laddy."

We closed the door of the office behind us, and escaped into the garden, where the apple blossoms were in their pink and white beauty; through the gate at the end, to our own resort and rest, by Celia's Arbour. We leaned against the rampart and looked out, over the broad sloping bank of bright green turf, set with buttercups as with golden buttons, across the sunny expanse of the harbour. The grass of the bastion was strewn with the brown casings of the newly-born leaves, the scabbards which had kept them from the frost. We could not speak. Her hand held mine.

Presently she whispered.

"Laddy, is it real? Does papa mean it?"

"Yes, Celia."

"And yesterday I was so happy."

Then we were silent again, for I had no word of comfort.

"Laddy," she cried, with a start of hope, "what is to-day? The first of June. Then in three weeks' time Leonard will be come again. I will give no answer for three weeks. Leonard will help us. All will be right for us when Leonard comes home."

CHAPTER XVIII.
FROM THE ORGAN-LOFT.

IN three weeks. Leonard would be home in three weeks. We had been so long looking forward that, now the time was close at hand, the realisation of its approach came on us like a shock.

We stared at each other.

"Three weeks, Cis! How will he come home?"

"I do not know. He will come home triumphant. Laddy, a moment ago I was so wretched—now I am so hopeful. He will come home and help us. We are like shipwrecked sailors in sight of land."

We did not doubt but that he would be another Perseus to the new Andromeda. What he was to do, more than we could do ourselves, we did not know. But he would do something. And that conviction, in the three weeks which followed, was our only stay and hope. We could not take counsel with the Captain, and even Mrs. Tyrrell was not informed of what had happened. She was to be told when Celia gave her answer. Meantime, Celia's lover made for the moment no sign of impatience. He came to the house in the evenings. He listened to Celia's playing and singing; he ventured with deference on a little criticism; he treated her with such respect as a lady might get from a *preux chevalier* of the old school; he loaded her with *petits-soins*; he never alluded in the slightest way to their interview in the office; his talk was soft, and in the presence of the girl he seldom displayed any of the cynical sayings which generally garnished his conversation; and he assumed the manner of a Christian gentleman of great philanthropic experience, and some disappointment with human nature. I was a good deal amused by the change, but a little disquieted because it showed that he was in earnest. There was to be no brutal force, no melodramatic marriage by reluctant consent to save a father from something or other indefinite. He was laying siege in due form, hoping to make the fortress surrender in due time, knowing that the defences were undermined by the influence of her father.

The Sunday after the first breaking of the matter he astonished me by appearing in the Tyrrells' square pew. I saw him from the organ-loft, and watched him with the utmost admiration. He was certainly a well set-up man, tall and straight. His full white moustache gave him a soldierlike look. He wore a tightly-buttoned frock, which was not the fashion of the day, with a rosebud in the button-hole, and new light lavender gloves. The general effect produced was exactly what he desired, that of a man no longer young, but still in vigorous life; a man remarkable in appearance, and probably remarkable, did the congregation know it, for his personal history. In church he laid aside the blue spectacles which he always wore in the street. His manner was almost theatrically reverential, although he showed a little uncertainty about getting up and sitting down. I have already explained that this was leisurely among occupants of the square pews at St. Faith's, so that his hesitation was less marked than it would be in an advanced church of the more recent type. I do not know whether he sang, because my back was necessarily turned to the congregation while I played for them, and among the curious mixture of discordances which rose to the organ-loft, and together made up the hymn, I could not distinguish the German's deep bass with the unmistakable rasp in it. There was the squawk of the old ladies who sat along the aisle—you made that out easily by reason of their being always half-a-dozen notes behind; there was the impetuous rush of those irregular cavalry, the charity children, who sat round the altar rails, and always sang a few notes in advance; there was the long-drawn hum of the congregation "joining in," which, taken in the lump, as one got it up in the organ-loft, was like the air played slowly on a barrel organ with a cold, or like a multitude attempting a tune through their noses. And there were sporadic sounds, issuing, I had reason to suppose, from individual singers, from him who tried tenor, and from her who attempted an alto. And sometimes I thought I could distinguish the sweet voice of Celia, but that was probably fancy.

The hymn over, I was free to turn round, and through an uplifted corner of the red curtain to watch Herr Räumer. The preacher on this Sunday was the Rev. John Pontifex, and it was a pretty sight to see the rapt attention with which the Teutonic proselyte followed the argument, as if it was something strange, original, and novel. As a matter of fact, it was Mr. Pontifex's one sermon. He only had one. Like Single-speech Hamilton, he concentrated all the logic at his command into one argumentative discourse. Unlike Single-speech, he went on preaching it whenever he was asked to preach at all. To be sure, he introduced variations in the text, in the exordium, and in the peroration. But the body of the discourse was invariably the same. And it was not a cheerful sermon. On the contrary, it was condemnatory, and sent people home to their dinners with a certainty about the future which ought to have taken away all their appetites.

Up in the organ-loft you had advantages over your fellows. The church lay at your feet, with the people in their pews sitting mute and quiet, and yet each man preserving in his attitude, in his eyes, in the pose of his head, his own individuality. Mr. Tyrrell, for instance, showed that he was ill at ease by his downcast eyes and drooping head. His daughter and I alone knew the reason of his disquietude, with that stranger who sat in the same pew with him. Behind Mr. Tyrrell was the Captain in a long pew. Years before he had sat there Sunday after Sunday with two boys. Was the old man thinking that in three more Sundays he might sit there with the wanderer back again? He entertained great respect for a sermon, as part of a chaplain's duties ashore, but it would have been difficult to discover from any subsequent remarks that he ever listened. Looking at him now, from my lofty *coign* of vantage, I see from his eyes that his thoughts are far away. Perhaps he is with Leonard, perhaps he is tossing on a stormbeat sea, or slave-chasing off the West Coast, or running again into Navarino Bay on a certain eventful afternoon. There is a calm about the old man's face which speaks of peace. What are the denunciations of the Rev. John Pontifex to him?

"Whither you will all of you—alas!—most infallibly go unless you change your ways—"

Within the communion rails, the Rev. Mr. Broughton, his legs stretched out, his feet upon a footstool, and his hands clasped across his portly form, is sitting comfortably. His part of the morning exercises is finished. His eyes are closed and his head nodding. Happy Perpetual Curate! On the red baize cushions round the rails are twenty or thirty school children, recipients of some charity. Why do they dress the poor girls in so perfectly awful a uniform? And why is the verger allowed to creep round during the sermon, cane in hand, to remind any erring infant that he must not sleep in church? It ought not to be allowed.

Look at the faces of the congregation as they are turned up vacantly to the roof. No one is listening—except Herr Räumer. What are they all thinking about? In this hive of a thousand people, there is not one but has his heart and brain full of his own hopes and fears. What are the terrible forebodings of the preacher—"No hope for any but the Elect. Alas! They are very few in number. For the rest of you, my brethren—" What are these words, which ought to generate a maddening despair, to the present anxieties and troubles of the people! The fat and prosperous grocer in the square pew is worried about a bill that falls due to-morrow; his daughter is thinking that a dear friend has treacherously copied the trimmings of her bonnet; the boys are wishing it was over; and so on. Did such words as the Rev. John Pontifex is now uttering ever have any real meaning? Or did they always lose their force by being applied, as we apply them now, to our neighbours? "Elect? Well, of course, I am one. Let us hope that all our friends are also in the number. But I have my fears." We are in a Dead Church, with a preacher of Dead Words; the old Calvinistic utterances drop upon hearts which have fallen away from the dogma and are no longer open to their terrors. Such a sermon as the one preached by the Rev. John Pontifex on that Sunday morning would be impossible now. Then it was only part of the regular Church business. Well, that is all changed; we have new dangers and new enemies; among them is no longer the old listlessness of service.

"Lastly, my brethren—" See, Mr. Broughton wakes up; the children nudge each other; the Captain's eyes come back to the present, and he instinctively gathers together the "tools," and puts them back into their box; a twitter of expectancy, with a faint preliminary trustle of feminine garments, ascends to my perch.

"Remember, that you, too, are included, one and all, in the sentence upon Ca—per—na—um."

So; he has finished. Herr Räumer sits back with a long breath, as if the argument had convinced him. Mrs. Tyrrell shakes her head solemnly. The clerk gives out the final hymn.

"Oh! may our earthly Sabbaths prove
A foretaste of the joys above."

Poor charity children! They go home to a cold collation insufficient in quantity; they have been caned for inattention; they have to attend three services like this every Sunday. And yet they pray for a continuance of these

"Oh! Ladislas," cries Mrs. Tyrrell, with a sigh of rapture, when I came up with the party after playing them out. "What a sermon! What Gospel truth! What force of expression! It is astonishing to me that Uncle Pontifex has never been made a bishop. He is coming to dinner on Tuesday," she resumes, with an entirely secular change of voice, "with Aunt Jane. Come, too, Ladislas, and talk to aunt. There will be the loveliest pair of ducks."

Herr Räumer is walking beside Celia. She is pale, and from the manner in which she carries her parasol, I should say that she is a little afraid lest her suitor should say something. But he does not. He is content to hover round her; to be seen with her; to accustom people to the association of himself with Celia Tyrrell. It is easy to divine his purpose. Suddenly to announce an engagement between an elderly man of sixty and a girl of less than twenty would be to make a nine days' wonder. Let them be seen together, so that when the right moment shall arrive to make the announcement, there shall seem nothing strange about it.

One thing let me say. I have, least of all men, reason to love this German. That will be presently apparent. But I wish to be just to him. And I think he loved Celia honestly.

I am, indeed, sure he did. I saw it in the way he followed her about with his eyes, in the softened tone of his voice; in the way in which he sought me out, and tried to learn from me what were her favourite books, her music, her tastes, so that he might anticipate them. The jealousy of my own affection for Celia sharpened my senses. What I saw in him I recognised as my own. I wonder how much that strange passion of love might have done to softening the man. For as regards the rest of the world he remained the same as before, cold, cynical, emotionless, without affections or pity. A man turned out by a machine could not have been more devoid of human sympathy. For instance, he was lodged on Augustus Brambler's first floor, and he was waited on by the best and prettiest of all Augustus's numerous olive branches, little Forty-four. She was like her father, inasmuch as she was unceasingly active, always cheerful and brave, always patient and hopeful, always happy in herself. Unlike her father, the work she did was good work. She kept her lodger in luxuriant comfort, cooked his dinner as he loved it, and left him nothing to desire.

Yet he never spoke a word to her that was not a command, never thanked her, never took the slightest notice of her presence. This bright-eyed, pleasant-faced, obliging girl, who did a hundred things for him which were not in the bond, was, in fact, no more to him than a mere machine. Sometimes, observing this strange disregard of all human creatures, it occurred to me that he might have learned it by a long continuance in military service. A soldier is a creature who carries out orders—among other things. Perhaps the soldiers in Herr Räumer's corps were nothing else. That would be a delightful world where all the men were drilled soldiers, and military manoeuvres the principal occupation, the art of war the only study, and victory the only glory. And yet to this we are tending. Whenever I tried to interest him in his landlord's family he would listen patiently and change the subject.

"The Brambler people?" he asked with no show of interest. "Yes—I have seen them—father who runs messages." Poor Augustus! This all the majesty of the Law? "Uncle who reports for paper—children who fall down the stairs. What have I to do with these *canaille*?"

I ventured to suggest that they were poor and deserving —that, &c.

"Bah!" he said. "That is the cant of English charity, my young friend. You will tell me next that men are all brothers. Do not, I beg, fall into that trap set for the benevolent."

"I will not, with you," I said. "I suppose you think that men are all enemies."

I said this with my most withering and sarcastic smile.

"I do," he replied solemnly. "All men are enemies. For our own advantage, and for no other reason, we do not kill each other, but unite in societies and kill our neighbours. Come, you want me to pretend benevolent sympathy with the people in this house, because the father is a fool and they are poor. There are an infinite number of poor people in the world. Some of them, even, are starving. Well, it is not my fault. Let them starve. It is my business to live, and get the most out of life."

"Do all your countrymen think like you?" I asked.

"All," he replied. "In Berlin we are a clear-sighted people. We put self-preservation first. That means everything. I do not say that we have no delusions. Machinery called charitable exists; not to so extensive and ruinous a degree as in England: still there is hope for the weakest when he goes to the wall that some one will take care of him."

"You would let him die."

"I do not actively wish him to die. If I saw that his life would be of the slightest use to me, I should help him to live. Let us talk of more agreeable things. Let us talk of Celia. Take a glass of hock. So."

He lit another cigar, and lay back in his chair, murmuring enjoyable words.

"You told me, a little while ago, that the man you admired most in the world, the noblest and the best, I think you said, after the Captain, was Mr. Tyrrell. Do you think so now?"

I was silent.

"You do not. You cannot. That is a lesson for you, Ladislas Pulaski. Remember that there is no man noblest and best. Think of yourself at your worst, and then persuade yourself that all other men are like that."

I said nothing to that, because there was nothing to say. It is one way of looking at the world; the best way, it seems to me, to drag yourself down and to keep down everybody round you.

"I said then, but you were too indignant to accept the doctrine, that every man had his price. You may guess Mr. Tyrrell's. Every woman has hers. Celia's price is—her father: I have bought her at that price, which I was fortunately able to command."

"You do not know yet."

"Yes, I do know. All in good time. I can wait. Now, Ladislas Pulaski, I will be frank with you. I intended this coup all along, and have prepared the way for it. I admire the young lady extremely. Let me, even, say that I love her. She is, I am sure, as good and virtuous as she is pretty.

Of all girls that I have ever seen, I think Celia Tyrrell is the best. It is, I know, partly due to your training. She is the pearl of your pupils. Her manner is perfect: her face is perfect; her conversation is admirable; her general cultivation is good."

"She is all that you say," I replied.

"You love her, I believe, like a brother. At least Celia says so. When I was your age, if I did not love a young lady like a brother I made it a rule always to tell her so at the earliest opportunity. That inability to love a girl after the brotherly fashion has more than once endangered my life. Like a brother, is it not?"

"Like a brother," I murmured, passing over the covert sneer.

"Very well, then. It is a weakness on my part, but I am willing to make sacrifices for this girl. I will study her wishes. She shall be treated with the greatest forbearance and patience. I do not expect that she will love me as I love her. That would be absurd. But I hope that, in a little while, a month or two,"—I breathed freely, because I feared he was going to say a day or two,—"she will receive my attention with pleasure, and learn to give me the esteem which young wives may feel for elderly husbands. I am not going to be ridiculous; I am not a Blue Beard; I know that women can be coaxed when they cannot be forced—*j'ai conté fleurettes*—it is not for the first time in life that one makes love at sixty."

"After all," he went on cheerfully, "Celia ought to be a happy girl. I shall die in ten years, I suppose. She will be a widow at eight-and-twenty. Just the age to enjoy life. Just the time when a woman wants her full liberty. What a thing—to be eight-and-twenty, to bury an old husband, and to have his money!"

CHAPTER XIX.
THE PONTIFEX COLLECTION.

IN the days that followed things went on externally as if nothing had happened. Celia's suitor walked with her in the town, was seen with her in public places, appeared in church morning and evening—the second function must have exercised his soul heavily—and said no word. Mr. Tyrrell, deceived by this appearance of peace, resumed his wonted aspect, and was self-reliant, and sometimes as blusterous as ever. Celia alone seemed to remember the subject. For some days she tried to read and talk as usual, but her cheek was paler, and her manner *distraite*. Yet I could say nothing. The wound was too fresh, the anxiety was still there; it was one of those blows which, though their worst effects may be averted, leave scars behind which cannot be eradicated. The scar in Celia's soul was that for the first time in her life a suspicion had been forced upon her that her father was not—had not been—. Let us not put it into words.

To speak of such a suspicion would have been an agony too bitter for her, and even too bitter for me. Yet I knew, by the manner of the man, by the words of the German, that he was, in some way, for some conduct unknown, of which he was now ashamed, under this man's power. I could not tell Celia what I knew. How was she to tell me the dreadful suspicion that rose like a spectre in the night, unbidden, awful? We were only more silent, we sat together without speaking; sometimes I caught her eye resting for a moment on her father with a pained wonder, sometimes she would break off the music, and say with a sigh that she could play no more.

One afternoon, three or four days after the first opening of the business, I found her in the library, a small room on the first floor dignified by that title, where Mr. Tyrrell kept the few books of general literature he owned, and Celia kept all hers. She had gathered on the table all the books which we were so fond of reading together—chiefly the poets—and was taking them up one after the other, turning over their pages with loving, regretful looks.

She greeted me with her sweet smile.

"I am thinking, Laddy, what to do with these books if— if—I have to say what papa wants me to say."

"Do with them, Cis?"

"Yes," she replied, "it would be foolish to keep things which are not very ornamental and would no longer be useful."

"Our poor poets are a good deal knocked about," I said, taking up the volumes in hope of diverting her thoughts; "I always told you that Keats wasn't made for lying in the grass," and indeed that poor bard showed signs of many dews upon his scarlet cloth bound back.

"He is best for reading on the grass, Laddy. Think of the many hours of joy we have had with Hyperion under the elms. And now, I suppose, we shall never have any more. Life is very short, for some of us."

"But—Cis—why no more hours of pleasure and poetry?"

"I do not know when that man may desire an answer. And I know that if he claims it at once—to-morrow—next day—what answer I am to give. I watch my father, Laddy, and I read the answer in his face. Whatever happens, I must do what is best for him."

"Put off the answer, Cis, till Leonard comes home."

"If we can," she sighed—"if we can. Promise me one thing, Laddy—promise me faithfully. If I have—if I must consent—never let Leonard know the reason: never let any one know; let all the world think that I have accepted—him—because I loved him. As if any woman could ever love him!"

Then he had not deceived her with his smooth and plausible manner.

"I promise you so much at least," I said. "No one shall know, poor Cis, the reason. It shall be a secret between us. But you have not said 'Yes,' to him yet?"

"I may very soon have to say it, Laddy. I shall give you all this poetry. We have read it together so much that I should always think of you if I ever try and read it alone. And it would make me too wretched. I shall have nothing more to do with the noble thoughts and divine longings of these great men: they will all be dead in my bosom; I shall try to forget that they ever existed. Herr Räumer—my husband," she shuddered—"would not understand them. I shall learn to disbelieve everything: I shall find a base motive in every action. I shall cease to hope: I shall lose my faith and my charity."

"Celia—my poor Celia—do not talk like that."

"Here is Keats." She opened him at random, turned over the leaves, and read aloud—

" 'Ah! would 'twere so with many
A gentle girl and boy!
But were there ever any
Writhed not at passèd joy?'

"Passed joy! We shall not be able to go out together, you and I, Laddy, any more, nor to read under the elms, nor to look out over the ramparts up the Harbour at high tide, and you will leave off giving me music lessons—and when Leonard comes home he will not be my Leonard any more. Only let him never know, dear Laddy."

"He shall never know, Cis. But the word is not spoken yet, and I think it never will be."

She shook her head.

"There is our Wordsworth. Of course he must be given up too. When the whole life is of the earth earthy, what room could be there for Wordsworth! Why," she looked among the sonnets, "this must have been written especially for me. Listen:

" 'O Friend! I know not which way I must look
For comfort, being, as I am, opprest
To think that now our life is only dressed
For show . . . .
. . . . .
The homely beauty of the good old cause
Is gone: our peace, our fearful innocence
And pure religion breathing household laws.'

"Fancy the household laws of Herr Räumer," she added bitterly.

She was in sad and despairing mood that morning.

I took the book from her hand—what great things there are in Wordsworth, and what rubbish!—and found another passage.

"Those first affections,
Those shadowy recollections,
Which be they what they may
Are yet the fountain light of all our days,
Are yet a masterlight of all our seeing,
Uphold us—cherish—and have power to make
Our noisy years seem moments in the being
Of the eternal silence: truths that wake
To perish never:
Which neither listlessness uor mad endeavour,
Nor man nor boy,
Nor all that is at enmity with joy
Can utterly abolish or destroy."

"Do you think, you silly Celia, if things come to the very worst—if you were—let me say it out for once—if you were tied for life to this man, with whom you have no sympathy, that you would forget the beautiful things which you have read and dreamed? They can never be forgotten. Why, they lie all about your heart, the great thoughts of God and heaven, what this beautiful earth might be and what you yourself would wish to be; they are your guardian angels, who stand like Ithuriel to ward off evil dreams and basenesses. They cannot be driven away because you have placed them there, sentinels of your life. If—if he—were ten times as cold, ten times as unworthy of you as he seems, he could but touch your inner life. He could only make your outer life unhappy. And then, Celia, I think —I think that Leonard would kill him."

"If Leonard will care any more about me," she murmured through her tears. "But he will not. I shall be degraded in his eyes. He will come home with happier recollections of brighter scenes and women far better and more beautiful than I can be, even in his memory."

"Celia," I cried hotly, " that is unkind of you. You cannot mean it. Leonard can never forget you. There will be no scenes so happy in his recollection as the scenes of the boyhood; no one whom he will more long to see than little Celia—little no longer now, and—oh! Cis—Cis, how beautiful you are!"

"Laddy, you are the best brother in all the world. But do not flatter me. You know I like to think myself pretty. I am so vain."

"I am not flattering you, my dear. Of course, I think you are the most beautiful girl in all the world. Ah! if I could only draw you and put all your soul into your eyes as a great painter would. If I were Raphael I would make you St. Catharine—no, St. Cecilia—sitting at the organ, looking up as you do sometimes when we read together, as when I play Beethoven, and your soul opens like a flower."

"Laddy—Laddy."

"I would make your lips trembling, and your head a little bent back, so as to show the sweet outlines, and make all the world fall in love with you. . . . Don't cry, my own dear sister. See, Leonard will be home again soon triumphant, bringing joy to all of us. Our brave Leonard—and all will be well. I know all will go well. And this monstrous thing shall not be done."

She put her arms round my neck, and laid her cheek against mine."Thank God," she said simply, "for my brother."

By this time I had mastered my vain and selfish passion. Celia was my sister, and could never be anything else. As if in the time when companionship is as necessary as light and air, it was not a great thing to have such a companion as Celia! In youth we cling to one another, and find encouragement in confession and confidence. David was young when he loved Jonathan. It is when we grow older that we shrink into ourselves and forget the sweet old friendships.

This little talk finished, Celia became more cheerful, and we presently stole out at the garden gate for fear of being intercepted by the suitor, who was as ubiquitous as a Prussian Uhlan, and went for a ramble along the beach, where a light breeze was crisping the water into tiny ruffles of wavelets, and driving about the white-sailed yachts like butterflies. The fresh sea air brightened her cheek, and gave elasticity to her limbs. She forgot her anxieties, laughed, sang little snatches, and was as merry as a child again.

"Let us go and call at Aunt Jane's," she cried, when we left the beach, and were striking across the furze-covered common.

To call upon Mrs. Pontifex was never an inspiriting thing to do. She had a way of picking out texts to suit your case and hurling them at your head, which sent you away far more despondent about the future than her husband's sermons. There is always this difference between a woman of Aunt Jane's persuasion and a man of the same school; that the woman really believes it all, and the man has by birth, by accident, by mental twist, for reasons of self-interest, talked himself into a creed which he does not hold at heart, so far as he has power of self-examination. Mr. Pontifex had lost that power, I believe.

They lived in a villa overlooking the common. Mrs. Pontifex liked the situation principally because it enabled her to watch the "Sabbath-breakers," viz., the people who walked on Sunday afternoon, and the unthinking sinners, who strolled arm in arm upon the breezy common on summer evenings. The villa had formerly possessed a certain beauty of its own, being covered over with creepers, but Mrs. Pontifex removed them all, and it now stood in naked ugliness, square and flat-roofed. There was a garden in front, of rigid and austere appearance, planted with the less showy shrubs, and never allowed to put on the holiday garb of summer flowers. Within, the house was like a place of tombs, so cold, so full of monumental mahogany, so bristling with chairs of little ease.

To our great joy, Mrs. Pontifex was out. Her husband, the servant, said, with a little hesitation, was at home.

"Then we will go in," said Celia. "Where is he, Anne?"

"Well, Miss," she said in apology, "at present master's in the front kitchen."

In fact, there we found the unhappy Mr. Pontifex. He was standing at the table, with a most gloomy expression on his severe features. Before him stood a half-cut, cold-boiled leg of mutton. He had a knife in one hand and a piece of bread in another.

"This is all," he said sorrowfully, "that I shall get to-day. Mrs. Pontifex said that there was to be no dinner. She has gone to a Dorcas meeting—No, thank you, Anne, I cannot eat any more—ahem—any more boiled mutton. The human palate—alas! that we poor mortals should think of such things—does not accept boiled mutton with pleasure. But what is man that he should turn away from his food? A single glass of beer, if you please, Anne."

"Do have another slice of mutton, sir," said the servant, in sympathising tones.

"No, Anne"—there was an infinite sadness in his voice. "No, I thank you."

"There's some cold roly-poley in the cupboard, sir. Try a bit of that."

She brought it out. It was a piece of the inner portion, that part which contains most jam.

Mr. Pontifex shook his head in deep despondency.

"That is not for ME, Anne," he said; "I always have to eat the ends."

"Then why do you stand it?" I said. "You are a man, and ought to be master in your own house."

"You think so, Johnny?" he replied."You are young. You are not again like St. Peter—ahem—a married man. Let us go upstairs."

He led us into his study, which was a large room decorated with an immense quantity of pictures. The house, indeed, was full of pictures, newly arrived, the collection of a brother, lately deceased, of the Rev. John Pontifex. I am not learned in paintings, but I am pretty sure that the collection on the walls were copies as flagrant as anything ever put up at Christy's. But Mr. Pontifex thought differently.

"You have not yet seen my picture gallery, Johnny," he said. "The collection was once the property of my brother, the Rev. Joseph Pontifex, now, alas!—in the bosom of Abraham. He was formerly my coadjutor when I was in sole charge at Dillmington. It was commonly said by the Puseyites, at the time, that there was a Thief in the Pulpit and a Liar in the Reading-desk. So great—ahem !—was our pulpit power that it drew forth these fearful denunciations. I rejoice to say that I was the—ahem!—the—Liar."

It was hard to see where the rejoicing ought properly to come in. But no doubt he knew.

"They are beautiful pictures, some of them," said Celia kindly.

Mr. Pontifex took a walking stick, and began to go round like a long-necked, very solemn showman at a circus.

"These are 'Nymphs about—ahem—to Bathe.' A masterpiece by Caracci. The laughter of those young persons has probably long since been turned into mourning.

"'The Death of St. Chrysostom,' supposed to be by Leonardo da Vinci. The Puseyites go to Chrysostom as to a father. Well; they may go to the muddy streams if they please. I go to the pure—the pure fountain, Johnny.

"'Pope Leo the Tenth,' by one Dosso Dossi, of whom, I confess, I have never heard. I suppose that there are more Popes than any other class of persons now in misery."

He shook his head, as he said this, with a smile of peculiar satisfaction, and went on to the next picture.

"A soldier, by Wouvermans, on a white horse. Probably the original of this portrait was in his day an extremely profligate person. But he has long since gone to his long—no doubt his very long account.

"That is 'The Daughter of Herodias Dancing.' I have always considered dancing a most immoral pastime, and in the days of my youth found it so, I regret to say.

"'The Mission of Xavier.' He was, alas! a Papist, and is now, I believe, what they are pleased to call a saint. In other respects he was, perhaps, a good man, as goodness shows to the world. That is, a poor gilded exterior, hiding corruption. How different from our good Bishop Heber, the author of that sweet miss—i—o—na—ry poem which we all know by heart, and can never forget.

" 'From Greenland's icy mountains—
From Greenland's icy mountains—
From Greenland's—ahem !—icy—'

—but my memory fails me. That is, perhaps, the result of an imperfect meal."

"Sit down, my dear uncle," said Celia. "You must be fatigued. What was Aunt Jane thinking of to have no dinner?"

"Your great-aunt, Celia," said Mr. Pontifex, with a very long sigh,"is a woman of very remarkable Christian graces and virtues. She excels in what I may call the—the—ahem —the very rare art of compelling others to go along with her. To-day we fast, and to-morrow we may be called upon to subdue the natural man in some other, perhaps—at least I hope —in a less trying method."

We both laughed, but Mr. Pontifex shook his head.

"Let me point out one or two more pictures of my collection," he said. "There are nearly one thousand altogether, collected by my brother Joseph, who resided in Rome, the very heart of the Papacy—you never knew Joseph, Celia—during the last ten years of his life. That landscape, the trees of which, I confess, appear to me unlike any trees with which I am personally acquainted—is by Salvator Rosa; that Madonna and Child—whom the Papists ignorantly worship—is by Sasso Ferrato; that group" (it was a sprawling mass of intertwisted limbs) "is by Michael Angelo, the celebrated master; the waterfall which you are admiring, Celia, is a Ruysdael, and supposed to be priceless; the pig—alas! that men should waste their talents in delineating such animals—is by Teniers; the cow by Berghem; that —ahem—that infamous female" (it was a wood nymph, and a bad copy) "is a Rubens. The Latin rubeo or rubesco is—unless my memory again fails me—to blush. Rightly is that painter so named. No doubt he has long since—but I refrain."

"Do you think, Celia," I asked on the way home, "that Mr. Pontifex dwells with pleasure in the imagination of the things which are always on his lips?"

CHAPTER XX.
THE RIGHT OF REVOLT.

THE Polish Barrack in 1858 had ceased to exist. There were, in fact, very few Poles left in the town to occupy it. A good many were dead. Some went away in 1854 to join the Turks. Some, grown tired of the quasi-garrison life, left it, and entered into civil occupations in the town. Some, but very few, drifted back to Poland and made their peace with the authorities. Some emigrated. Of all the bearded men I knew as a boy scarcely twenty were left, and these were scattered about the town, still in the "enjoyment" of the tenpence a day granted them by the British Government. I seldom met any of them except Wassielewski, who never wearied of his paternal care. The old man still pursued his calling—that of a fiddler to the sailors. The times, however, were changed. Navy agents were things of the past—a subject of wailing among the Tribes. Sailors' Homes were established; the oiled curls had given way to another and a manlier fashion of short hair. The British sailor was in course of transformation. He no longer made it a rule to spend all his money as fast as he received it; he was sometimes a teetotaler; he was sometimes religious, with views of his own about Election; he sometimes read; and though he generally drank when drink was in the way, he was not often picked up blind drunk in the gutter. The Captain said he supposed men could fight as well if they were always sober as if they were sometimes drunk; and that, always provided there were no sea-lawyers aboard, he saw no reason why a British crew should not be all good-character men, though in his day good character often went with malingering. The trade of fiddling, however, was still remunerative, and Wassielewski—Fiddler Ben, as the sailors called him—the steadiest and liveliest fiddler of all, had a large clientele.

At this juncture the staunch old rebel, as I have explained, was in spirits, because he had wind of a new movement. The Poles were to make another effort—he was really five years too early, because the rebellion did not begin till 1863, but that was not his fault; it would be once more the duty of every patriot to rally round the insurrection and strike another blow for Fatherland. Not that he looked for success. No one knew better than this hero of a hundred village fights that the game was hopeless. His policy was one of simple devotion. In every generation an insurrection—perhaps half a dozen—was to be got up. Every Pole who was killed fertilised the soil with new memories of cruelty and blood. It was the duty, therefore, of every Pole to get killed if necessary. No Red Irreconcilable ever preached a policy so sanguinary and thorough. Out of the accumulated histories of rebellion was to arise, not in his time, indignation so universal that the whole world would with irrepressible impulse rush to rescue Poland from the triple grasp of the Eagles. To bring about this end, but one thing was needed —absolute self-sacrifice.

I knew when he met me, the day after Celia's birthday, and told me that the time was coming, what he meant. I, like himself, was to be a victim to the Holy Cause. I was a hunchback, a man of peace, even a Protestant. That did not matter. I bore an historic name, and I was to give the cause the weight of my name as well as the slender support of my person. And, as I have no desire to pose as a hero, I may at once confess that I felt at first little enthusiasm for the work, and regarded my possible future with feelings of unworthy reluctance.

I suppose that Wassielewski saw this, because he tried to inflame my passion with stories of Russian wrong.

As yet I knew, as I have said, little or nothing about my parentage or the story of my birth. That I should be proud because I was a Pulaski; that I should be brave because I was a Pulaski; that I owed myself to Poland because I was a Pulaski—was all I had learned.

I suppose, unless the old patriot lied—and I do not think he did—that no more revolting story of cruel repression exists than that of the Russian treatment of Poland between the years 1830 and 1835. Wassielewski, with calm face and eyes of fire, used to pour out these horrors to me till my brain reeled. He knew them all; it was his business to know them, and never to forget them or let others forget them. If he met a Pole he would fall to reviving the old memories of Polish atrocities—if he met a "friend of Poland" he would dilate upon them as if he loved to talk of them.

History is full of the crimes of nations, but there is no crime so great, no wickedness in all the long annals of the world, worse than the story of Russia after that revolution of hapless Poland. We are taught to believe that the wickedness of a single man, in some way, recoils upon his own head, that sooner or later he is punished—*raro antecedentem scelestum*—but what about the wickedness of a country? Will there fall no retribution upon Russia, upon Prussia, upon Austria? Have the wheels of justice stopped? Or, in some way in which we cannot divine, will the sins of the fathers be visited upon the children for the third and fourth generation? We know not. We see the ungodly nourish like a green bay tree, his eyes swelling out with fatness, and there is no sign or any foreshadowing of the judgment that is to fall upon him. We do not want judgment and revenge. We want only such restitution as is possible; for nothing can give us back the men who have died, the women who have sorrowed, the children who have been carried away. But let us have back our country, our liberty, and our lands.

A dream—an idle dream. Poland is no more. The Poles are become Austrians, Prussians, and, above all, Muscovites.

Wassielewski, a very Accusing Spirit, set himself to fill my mind with stories of tyranny and oppression. The national schools suppressed, a foreign religion imposed, the constitution violated, rebels shot—all these things one expects in the history of conquest. What, however, makes the story of Russian barbarism in Poland unique in the History of Tyranny seems the personal part taken by the Czar and the members of his illustrious family. It was the Czar who ordered, in 1824, twenty-five thousand Poles to be carried to the territory of the Tchernemovski Cossacks. The order was issued, with the usual humanity of St. Petersburg, in the dead of winter, so that the most of them perished on the way. It was the Czar who, in 1830, on the occasion of a local outbreak in Sebastopol, ordered with his own hand that the only six prisoners—who had been arrested almost at random—should be shot: that thirty-six more were to be apprehended and knouted: that all the inhabitants without distinction should be expelled the town and sent to the villages of the Crimea: and that the place should be razed to the ground. Every clause except the last was exactly carried into effect. It was the Czar who ordered the library of Warsaw to be transported to St. Petersburg. It was the Czar who formed the humane project of brutalising the Polish peasantry by encouraging the sale of spirits by the Jews. It was the Czar who transported thousands of Polish nobles and soldiers to Siberia. And it was the Czar's brother, the Grand Duke Constantino, whose brutality precipitated the rebellion of 1832.

There were two things which Wassielewski as yet hid from me, because they concerned myself too nearly, and because I think he feared the effect they might have upon me. That, so far, was kind of him. It would have been kinder still had he never told them at all. Even now, nearly twenty years since I learned them, I cannot think of them without a passionate beating of the heart; I cannot meet a Russian without instinctive and unconquerable hatred: I cannot name Czar Nicholas without mental execration: and not I only, but every Pole by blood, scattered as we are up and down the face of the world, hopeless of recovering our national liberty, content to become peaceful citizens of France, England, or the States, cannot but look on any disaster that befalls Russia as a welcome instalment of that righteous retribution which will some day, we believe, overtake the country for the sins of the Romanoffs.

In those days, however, I had not yet learned the whole. I knew enough, in a general way, to fill my soul with hatred against the Russian name and sympathy with my own people. I had, as yet, received no direct intimation from the old conspirator that he expected me, too, to throw in my lot with him. But I knew it was coming.

I was certainly more English than Polish. I could not speak my father's language. I belonged to the English Church, I was educated in the manners of thought common to Englishmen, insular, perhaps, and narrow; when the greatness of England was spoken of, I took that greatness to myself, and was glad. England's victories were mine, England's cause my own, and it was like the loss of half my identity to be reminded that I was not a Briton at all, but a Pole, the son of a long line of Poles, with a duty owed to my country. Like most men, when the path of duty seems confused, I was content to wait, to think as much as possible of other things, to put it off, always with the possible future unpleasantly visible, a crowd of peasants armed with scythes and rusty firelocks—I among them—a column of grey coats sweeping us down, old Wassielewski lying dead upon the ground, a solitary prisoner, myself, kneeling with bandaged eyes before an open grave with a dozen guns, at twenty paces, pointing straight at my heart. Nor did I yet feel such devotion to Poland as was sufficient to make the prospect attractive. Also I felt, with some shame, that I could not attain to the exasperation at which Wassielewski habitually kept his nerves.

"I hear," said Herr Räumer one evening, "I hear that your friends in Poland are contemplating another insurrection."

"How do you learn that?" I asked.

"I happened to hear something about it from a foreign correspondent," he replied carelessly. "The Russians, who are not fools, generally know what is going on. Up to a certain point things are allowed to go on. That amuses people. It is only by bad management that conspiracies ever get beyond that point. The Grand Duke Constantine in '31 made enormous mistakes. Well, I had a letter from Berlin to-day, and heard something about it. Here we are at the respectable Bramblers'. Come upstairs and talk for half-an-hour."

"Besides," after he had lit a cigar, got out his bottle of Hock, and was seated in his wooden arm-chair—"Besides, one gets foreign papers, and reads between the lines if one is wise. There is a bundle of Cracow papers on the table. Would you like to read them?"

I was ashamed to confess that I could not read my native tongue.

"That is a pity. One multiplies oneself by learning languages."

"Music has only one language. But how many do you know?"

"A few. Only the European languages. German, Russian, French, English. I believe I speak them all equally well. Polish is almost Russian.

He who speaks German easily learns Danish, Swedish, and Dutch. Turkish, I confess, I am only imperfectly acquainted with. It is a difficult language."

"But how did you learn all these languages?"

He smiled superior.

"To begin with," he said," the Eastern Europeans—you are not yourself a stupid Englishman—have a genius for language. There we do not waste our time in playfields, as these English boys do. So we learn—that is nothing—to talk languages. It is so common that it does not by itself advance a man. It is like reading, a part of education. Among other things you see it is useful in enabling me to read papers in Polish, and to get an inkling how things look in that land of patriots. But you do not want papers, you have your friends here. Of course they keep you informed?"

"I have one or two friends among the few Poles that are left. Wassielewski, my father's devoted servant, is one of them."

"Your father's devoted servant! Really! Devoted? That is touching. I like the devotion of that servant who leaves his master to die, and escapes to enjoy an English pension. One rates that kind of fidelity at a very high value."

The man was nothing unless he could sneer. In that respect he was the incarnation of the age, whose chief characteristic is Heine's "universal sneer." No virtue, no patriotism, no disinterested ambition, no self-denial, no toil for others, nothing but self. A creed which threatens to grow, because it is so simple that every one can understand it. And as the largest trees often grow out of the smallest seeds, one cannot guess what may be the end of it.

"You are right, however," he went on, nursing his crossed leg. "At your age, and with your imperfect education, it is natural that you should be generous. It is pleasant in youth to think that a man can ever be influenced by other than personal considerations. I never did think so. But then my school and yours are different."

"Then what was the patriotism of the Poles?"

"Vanity and self-interest, Ladislas Pulaski. Desire to show off—desire to get something better. Look at the Irish, Look at the Chartists. Who led them? Demagogues fighting for a Cause, because the Cause gives them money and notoriety."

"And no self-denial at all?"

"Plenty. For the satisfaction of vanity. Vanity is the chief motive and power in life. All men are vain; all men are ambitious; but most men in time of danger—and this saves us—are cowards. I am sixty-two years of age. I have seen—" here he hesitated a moment—"I have seen many revolutions and insurrections, especially in 1848. What is my experience?

This. In every conspiracy, where there are three men, one of them is a traitor and a spy. Remember that, should your friends try to drag you into a hopeless business. You will have a spy in your midst. The Secret Service knows all that is done. The other two men are heroes, if you please. That is, they pose. Put them up to open trial, and they speechify; turn them off to be shot, and they fold their arms in an heroic attitude. I believe," he added, with a kind of bitterness, "that they actually enjoy being shot!"

"You have really seen patriots shot?"

"Hundreds," he replied, with a careless wave of his hand. " The sight lost its interest to me, so much alike were the details of each."

"Where was it?"

"In Paris," he replied. "Of course the papers said as little as could be said about the shootings. I am sure, in fact, now I come to remember, that they did enjoy being shot. The Emperor Nicholas, whose genius lay in suppressing insurrections, knew a much better plan. He had his rebels beaten to death; at least after a thousand strokes there was not much life left. Now, not even the most sturdy patriot likes to be beaten to death. You cannot pose or make fine speeches while you are walking down a double file of soldiers each with a stick in his hand.

The man's expression was perfectly callous: he talked lightly and without the slightest indication of a feeling that the punishment was diabolical.

"Except the theatrical heroes, therefore, the gentlemen who pose, and would almost as soon be shot as not, provided it is done publicly, every man has his price. You have only to find it out."

"I would as soon believe," I cried, "what you said last week—that every woman has her price, too."

"Of course she has," he replied. "Woman is only imperfect man. Bribe her with dress and jewels; give her what she most wants—Love—Jealousy—Revenge—most likely she is guided by one of those feelings, and to gratify that one she will be traitor, spy, informer, anything."

I suppose I looked what I felt, because he laughed, spoke in softer voice, and touched my arm gently.

"Why do I tell you these things, Ladislas Pulaski? It is to keep you out of conspiracies, and because you will never find them out for yourself. You have to do with the *jeunes élèves*, the *ingénues*, the *naïves*, the innocent. You sit among them like a cherubin in a seraglio of uncorrupted houris. Happy boy!

"Keep that kind of happiness," he went on. "Do not be persuaded by any Polish exile—your father's servant or anybody else—to give up Arcadia for Civil War and Treachery. I spoke to you from my own experience. Believe me, it is wide. If I had any illusions left, the year of Forty-eight was enough to dispel them all. One remembers the crowd of crack-brained theatrical heroes, eager to pose; the students mad to make a new world; the stupid rustics who thought the day of no work, double pay, and treble rations was actually come. One thinks of these creatures massacred like sheep, and one gets angry at being asked to admire the leaders who preached the crusade of rebellion."

"You speak only of spies, informers, and demagogues. How about those who fought from conviction?"

"I know nothing about them," he replied, looking me straight in the face."My knowledge of rebels is chiefly derived from the informers?"

It was a strange thing to say, but I came to understand it later on.

He threw his cigar-ash into the fireplace, and poured out a glass of pale yellow wine which he so much loved.

"Never mind my experience," he said, rising and standing over me, looking gigantic with his six feet two compared with my bent and shrunken form, crouched beneath him in a chair. "I am going to rest and be happy. I shall do no more work in the world. Henceforth I devote myself to Celia. Here is the health of my bride. Hoch!"

CHAPTER XXI.
THE WORLD AND THE WORD.

"COME to us, Cis, for a day or two," I said. "It will be a little change if it only keeps you out of the way of your persecutor."

It was a custom of old standing for Celia to spend a day or two with the Captain—it did us good in brightening up the dingy old house. When Celia was coming we put flowers on the mantel-shelf, the Captain went round rigging up the curtains with brighter ribbons, and he called it hoisting the bunting. The usual severity of our daily fare was departed from, and the Captain brought out, with his oldest flask, his oldest stories.

"He follows me about," she replied. "I can go nowhere without meeting him. If I go into a shop he is at the door when I come out—it is as if I was already his property."

"But he says nothing—he shows no impatience."

"On Sunday evening I spoke to him. I asked him to give up his pursuit—I appealed to his honour—to his pity."

"He has no pity, Cis."

"To his very love for me, if he really loves me. I told him that it was impossible for me to give my consent. I burst into tears—what a shame to cry before him!—and he only laughed and called me his little April girl. 'Laugh, my little April girl, it rejoices me to see the cloud followed by the sunshine.' Then he asked me to tell him what I wanted him to do and he would do it. 'To tell my father that you have given up your project—to go away and leave me.' He said that he would do anything but give up the project; that his hope was more firmly grounded than ever, and that time would overcome my last objections to making him happy. What kind of love can that be which looks only to a way of making oneself happy?'

That had been my kind of love not very long before.

"I cannot speak to my father, but I see that he is changed. Not in his kindness to me, not that—but he is irritable: he drinks more wine than he should, and he is all the evening in his office now—and sometimes I see his eyes following me—poor papa!"

"What is the meaning of it, Laddy? People do not usually promise their daughters to old men when they are eight years of age. Yet this is what he says papa did. Why did he do it? Do you think he lent papa money? You know we were not always so well off as we are now."

"I dare say money has something to do with it," I replied. "It seems to me that money has to do with everything that is disagreeable."

"It has," she said. "Why cannot people do without money altogether? But, if that is all, Aunt Jane and my Uncle Pontifex have plenty of money, and they would help me, I am sure."

"We cannot go to them for help yet. Patience, Cis—patience for a fortnight; we will tell Leonard when he comes home, and perhaps the Captain too."

"Patience," she echoed. "One tries to be patient, but it is hard. It is not only that I could never love Herr Räumer, Laddy, but the very thought of passing my life with him makes me shake and tremble. I am afraid of him, his manner is smooth but his voice is not, and his eyes are too bright and keen. I have seen him when he did not think it necessary to keep up that appearance of gentleness. I know that he despises women, because I once heard him make a cruel little sneer about us. And he pretends—he pretends to be religious, to please mamma. What sort of a life should I have with him? What an end, then, would there be to our talks and hopes!"

I murmured something weak about the higher life being possible under all conditions, but I did not believe it. Life with Herr Räumer—the man who believed religion to be the invention of the priests—that this life was the beginning and the end; that there was nothing to be looked for from man and womankind, but from love of self, no honour, no virtue. What could the future of a girl exposed to daily and hourly influences of such a man be like?

Love of self? Would it be, then, for love of self that Celia would accept him?

I suppose for strong natures life might be made to yield the fruits of the most sublime Christianity anywhere, even in a convict hulk; but most of us require more fitting conditions. It is happy to think that no man is tried beyond his strength to bear, although in these latter days we have gone back to the old plan of making new hindrances to the maintenance of the higher spiritual levels, and calling them helps. There are plenty of daily crosses in our way, which call for all our strength, without adding the new and barbaric inconveniencies of hunger and small privations. Fasting, as a Ritualist the other day confessed to me, only makes people cross. I should have pitied any girl, even the most commonplace of good English girls, whom Fate might single out to marry this cynical pessimist; how much more when the girl was one whose standard was so high and heart so pure! Should the clear current of a mountain stream be mingled with the turbid water of a river in which no fish can live, foul from contact with many a factory by which it has wound its way, and from which it brought nothing but the refuse and the scum? Are there not some men—I am sure Herr Räumer was one—who, as they journey through the world, gather up all its wickedness, out of which they construct their own philosophy of existence? And this philosophy it was which he proposed to teach Celia.

"I shall instruct that sweet and unformed mind," he said to me one evening in his lordly way, as if all was quite certain to come off that he proposed, "in the realities of the world. She is at present like a garden full of pretty delicate flowers—your planting, my young friend; they shall be all pulled up, and we shall have instead—well—those flowers which go to make a woman of the world."

"I do not want to see Celia made into a woman of the world."

"You will not be her husband, Ladislas Pulaski. You only love her like a brother, you know. Ha! ha! And that is very lucky for me. And you do not know what a woman of the world is."

"Tell me what she is."

"I shall not go on living here. I shall live in London, Paris, Vienna, somewhere. My wife shall be a woman who will know from my teaching how to deal with men, and how to find out women. As for the men, she shall play with them like a cat with a mouse. She shall coax their little secrets out of them, especially if they are diplomats; she shall make them tell her what she pleases."

"Why should they not tell her what she pleases? What secrets would Celia wish to hear?"

"*Jeune premier—Cherubin*—you know nothing. They will be political secrets, and my wife will learn them for me. It is only France and Russia which really understand the noble game of feminine intrigue. I shall take my bride away, train her carefully, and with her take my proper place."

Always in the Grand Style; always this talk about diplomacy, secret service and intrigue, and sometimes betraying, or perhaps ostentatiously showing, a curiously intimate acquaintance with Courts and Sovereigns. What, I wondered, was the previous history of this strange man?

"Celia has everything to learn, and a good deal to unlearn, "he went on thoughtfully. "I do not blame you in any particular, Ladislas. You have done your best. But she has to forget the old-fashioned provincial—or insular—axioms."

"God forbid."

He laughed.

"You forget that you are not an Englishman, but a Slav. They are very pretty—these insular notions—that people marry for love—that people must always answer truthfully, whatever comes of it—that if you want to get a thing you have only to march straight forward—that you must let your friends know all you intend to do—that men care for anything but themselves—that—"

He stopped for want of breath.

"Pray go on," I said; "let us have the whole string of virtues dismissed as insular."

"Marriage for love! Was there ever greater nonsense? The best union that the history of the world speaks of was that of the Sabine maidens carried off by the Romans—carried off by perfect strangers. Picture to yourself the feelings of a proper English young lady under such circumstances. Celia certainly will never love me, but in time, in a short time, you shall see. When a girl sees that a man is in earnest, that if she appeals to his pity, he laughs; if to his mercy, he laughs; if to such trifles as disparity of religion or of age, he laughs—why, you see that woman ends by giving in.

Besides it is a compliment to her. I know that I have not your influence or good wishes. I did not expect them, and can do without them. You are as *romanesque* as your pupil—*ça va sans dire*. But I have her father's. She looks very pretty—very sweet indeed—when she gives me one of those upward looks of hers which mean entreaty. What will she be when I have trained her to use those eyes for political purposes?"

It reminded me of a boy with a mouse in a trap. You know how pretty the creature is, her eyes bright with terror and despair, looking at you through the bars which she has been frantically gnawing all the night. Shame and pity to kill the pretty thing. One might tame her. So Herr Räumer, like the schoolboy, admired his prisoner. She was caught in his cage: at least he thought so: she amused him: she pleased his fancy: he would keep her for himself, caged and tamed.

So Celia came to us.

"I am in trouble," she said to the Captain, "and I came here. Laddy knows what sort of trouble it is, but we ought not to speak of it just yet. Say something, dear Captain, to help us."

The Captain in his simple way took her in his arms and kissed her.

"What trouble can you have that your friends cannot get you out of? I won't ask. There are troubles enough of all sorts. All of them come from somebody disobeying orders. Have you followed the instructions, my dear?"

"I have tried to, Captain."

"Then there will be no great harm done, be sure. 'Like a tree planted by the rivers of water, his leaf shall not wither.' Now I tell you what we will do. We will blow some of the trouble away by a sail up the harbour. First let us have tea."

"I remember," the Captain said, when he had finished his tea; "I remember in the action of Navarino, which you may have heard of, my pretty Laddy, what are you sniggering at? Of course Celia has heard of Navarino. Very well, then, you shall not hear that story, though it might be brought to bear upon the present trouble. The best of sea actions is the use they can be put to in all sorts of private affairs. That is not generally known, Celia, my dear: and it makes an action the more interesting to read. Nelson's example always applies. Lay your guns low—nail your colours to the mast—pipe all hands for action: and then— alongside the enemy, however big she is. As to the rest, that's not your concern—and it's in good hands."

"I wish I knew what my duty was," said Celia.

"I wish you did, my dear. And you will know, turning it over in your own mind. I thank God that my life has been a simple one. I never saw any doubt about the line of duty. My orders have always been plain. My children," he added, solemnly, "we all start in life with sealed orders. Some men, when they open them, find them difficult to understand. Now the way to understand them—they are all here"—he laid his hand upon a certain book on the small table beside him—"is to remember, first of all, that duty has got to be done, and that we are not always out on a holiday cruise in pleasant waters."

"I know," said Celia, "I know, Captain"—the tears standing in her eyes.

"They talk about church-going and sermons," the Captain went on,"well it's part of the discipline. Must have order; church belongs to it—and I'm a plain man, not asked for an opinion. But, Cis, my dear, and Laddy, there's one thing borne in upon me every day stronger. It is that we've got a model always before us. As Christ lived, we must live; those who live most like Him talk the least, because they think the more. I read once, in a book, of a statue of Christ. Now whoever went to see that statue, however tall he was, found it just a little taller than himself. It was a parable, Celia, I suppose. And it means that the nearer you get to Christ the more you find that you cannot reach Him. Be good, my children. And now, Celia, if you will put on your hat, we will start. It's a fine evening, with a fair breeze, and we need not be back before nine. No more talk about troubles till to-morrow."

CHAPTER XXII.
A NIGHT UP THE HARBOUR.

THE sun was still high, but fast sloping westwards; there was a strong breeze blowing up the harbour from the south-west, the tide was full, the water was bright, its wavelets touched by the sunshine, each one sparkling like a diamond with fifty facets, the old ships, bathed in the soft evening light, looked as if they were resting from a long day's work, the hammers in the Dockyard were quiet, and though the beach was crowded it was with an idle throng who congregated together to talk of ships, and they naturally tended in the direction of the beach because the ships were in sight as illustrations. We kept our oars and mast with the running-gear in safety in one of the houses on the Hard behind a shop. It was a strange and picturesque shop, where everything was sold that was useless and interesting —a museum of a shop; in the window were Malay creases taken in some deadly encounter with pirates in the narrow seas; clubs richly carved and ornamented for some South Sea Island chief; beads worked in every kind of fashion; feathers, bits of costume, everything that a sailor picks up abroad, brings home in his chest, and sells for nothing to such an omnivorous dealer as the owner of this shop. He, indeed, was as strange as his shop. He had been a purser's clerk, and in that capacity had once as strange an experience as I ever heard. He told it me one evening when, by the light of a single candle, I was looking at some things in his back parlour. Some day, perhaps, I will tell you that story. Not now. Some day, I will write down what I can recollect of the stories he told me connected with his collection. There is no reason now for suppressing them any longer; he is dead, and all those whose mouthpiece he was are dead too. I think that in every man over forty there lies, mostly only known to himself, a strange and wondrous tale. Could he tell it as it really happened, it would be the story of how events perfectly commonplace in the eyes of other people acted upon him like strokes of Fate, crushing the higher hope that was in him, and condemning him to penal servitude for life, to remain upon the lower levels. Because it is mostly true that many run, but to one only is given the prize. Am I—are you—the only one whom fortune has mocked? *Nos numerus sumus*, the name of the Unfortunate is Legion; no one has the exclusive right to complain. To fifty Fate holds out the golden apples of success, and one only gets them.

We took our sculls and sails from the shop, and rigged our craft. She was built something on the lines of a wherry, for sea-worthiness, a strong, serviceable boat, not too heavy for a pair of sculls, and not too light to sail under good press of canvas. Everybody knew us on the beach —the boatmen, the old sailors, and the sailors' wives who were out with the children because the weather was so fine, all had a word to say to the Captain, touching their forelocks by way of preface. One carried our oars, another launched the boat, another sent a boy for a couple of rough sea-rugs, because the wind was high and the young lady might get wet, and in the midst of the general excitement we jumped in, and pushed off.

Celia sat in the stern, one of the rugs serving as a cushion, and held the rudder-strings. The Captain sat opposite her. I took the sculls to row her clear of the beach, until we could hoist our sail.

"This is what I like," said the Captain, dragging a little more of the waterproof over Celia's feet in his careful way. "A bright day, a breeze aft, but not dead aft—Laddy, we shall have some trouble getting back—a tight little boat, and a pretty girl like little Cis in command. Aha! Catch an old salt insensible to lovely woman.

" 'Blow high, blow low, let tempests tear
The mainmast by the board;
My heart with thoughts of thee, my dear,
And love well stored.' "

Celia laughed. Her spirits rose as each dip of the sculls lengthened our distance from the shore, and made her certain of escaping, at least for one evening, from her persecutor.

She wore some pretty sort of brown Holland stuff made into a jacket, and braided with a zig-zag Vandyke pattern in red. I do not know how I remember that pattern of the braid, but it seems as if I remember every detail of that evening—her bright and animated face flushed with the pleasure and excitement of the little voyage, rosy in the evening sunshine, the merry eyes with which she turned to greet the Captain's little compliment, the halo of youth and grace which lay about her, the very contour of her figure as she leaned aside, holding both the rudder strings on one side. I remember the little picture just as if it was yesterday.

Outside the ruck of boats which came and went between the opposite shores of the port we were in free and open water, and could ship the sculls and hoist our sail for a run up the harbour.

The sail up, I came aft, and sat down in the bottom of the ship, while the Captain held the rope and Celia the strings. And for a space none of us talked.

Our course carried us past the Docks and the shore-line buildings of the Dockyard. There were the white wharves, the cranes, the derricks, and all sorts of capstans, chains, and other gear for lifting and hoisting; the steam-tugs were lying alongside; all as deserted and as quiet as if the Yard belonged to some old civilisation. Bright as the evening was, the effect was rather ghostly, as we glided, silent save for the rippling at the bows, along the silent bank. Presently we came to the building-sheds. Some of them were open and empty; some were closed; within each of the closed sheds lay, we knew, the skeleton, the half-finished frame, of a mighty man-o'-war—some of them but just begun; some ready to be launched; some, the deserted and neglected offspring of some bygone First Lord's experimental ignorance, lying as they had lain for thirty years, waiting for the order to be finished off and launched.

"Think of the twilight solitude in those great empty sheds, Cis," I whispered. "Think of the ghosts of wrecked ships haunting the places where they were built when the moonlight streams in at the windows. Fancy seeing the transparent outline of some old three-decker, say the great Victory, as she went down with a thousand men aboard, lying upon the timber-shores—"

"With the ghosts of the old ship-builders," said Celia, "walking about with their hands behind them, criticising the new-fashioned models."

"More likely to be swearing at steam," said the Captain. The new-fashioned models! Where are they now, the ships which were on the slips twenty years ago? The *Duke of Marlborough*, the *Prince of Wales*, the *Royal Frederick*, the *Royal Sovereign*.—Where is last year's snow? They are harbour ships, ships cut down and altered into ironclads, and of a date gone out of fashion.

There were many more ships in harbour then than now; we had not yet learned to put all our trust in iron, and where we have one serviceable fighting vessel now we had twenty then. No hulk in the good old days, that could float and could steer but could fight; there were no torpedoes, no rams, no iron vessels, no venomous little monitors. To lay yourself alongside an enemy and give broadside for broadside till one tired of it, was the good old fashion of a naval battle. What is it now?

Again, twenty years ago they did not break up and destroy every vessel that seemed to be past service. She was towed up harbour and left there moored in her place, to furnish at least house accommodation for a warrant officer, if she could be of no other use. There were hundreds of ships there lying idle, their work over; some of them were coal hulks, some convict hulks, some receiving hulks; most were old pensioners who did no work any more, floating at high tide, and at low lying in the soft cushion of the harbour mud. Presently we ran among them all, passing in and out, and through their lines. Then I took the rudder-strings so that Celia might look while the Captain talked.

He pushed his hat well back, sat upright, and began to look up and down the familiar craft with the eye of an old friend anxious to see them looking their best. It was not much they could show in the way of decoration, but the figure-heads were there still, and the balconies and carvings of the stern were mostly uninjured. As for the hull, it had generally been painted either black, white, or yellow. There were masts, but they had jurymasts to serve as derricks on occasion. "That is the *Queen Charlotte*, my dear. She was flagship at Algiers when Lord Exmouth showed the Moors we would stand no more nonsense. We've fought a good many naval actions, but I think that business was about the best day's work we ever did. I was chasing Arab dhows and slavers off Zanzibar, and hadn't the chance of doing my share of the work. In 1816, that was

"Look—look—Celia! Look, children. There's the old *Asia*. God bless her! Flagship, Celia, at Navarino. My old ship—my one battle. Ah! Navarino. They say now it was a mistake, and that we only played the Russians' game. No chance of doing that again. But anyhow it was a glorious victory." The recollection of that day was always too much for the Captain, and he might have gone on the whole evening with personal reminiscences of the battle, but for the breeze which freshened up and carried us past the *Asia*.

"No confounded steam," he growled, "no wheels and smoke spoiling the decks; quiet easy sailing, and no noise allowed aboard until the guns began to speak. Forty people were drowned when she was launched; and a good many more went below when she made herself heard at Acre. I was not there either, more's the pity. I was cruising about the narrow seas picking up pirates off Borneo.

"There is the *Egmont*. She fought the French fleet in 1795, and the Spaniards in 1797. Good old craft. Stout old man-o'-war.

"That is the *Illustrious*, moored in line with the *Egmont*. She was with her in '95, and I think she helped to take Java in 1811. We used, in those days, you see, Celia, if we wanted a place that belonged to the enemy, just to go and take it. Not that we were so unmannerly as not to give them a civil choice. We used to say, ' Gentlemen, Señors Caballeros, Mynheer Double Dutchmen,' as the case might be, 'we've come to haul down your bunting and run up the Union Jack over your snug quarters. So, as perhaps you would not like to give in without a bit of a fight, you had better ram in your charge, and we'll give you a lead.' Then the action began, and after a respectable quantity of powder was burned they struck their colours, we went ashore, the men had a spree, and the officers made themselves agreeable to the young ladies."

"Did not the young ladies object to making friends with the enemy?"

"Not at all, my dear. Why should they? We did them no wrong, and we generally represented the popular side; they wanted to be taken by the British Fleet, which meant safety as well as flirtation. And we enjoyed our bit of fighting first. Did you ever hear of Captain Willoughby in Mahébourg Bay, Island of Mauritius? Well, that's an unlucky story, because it ended badly, and instead of Willoughby taking the island the island took him. Ran his ship ashore. She turned on her side, so that her guns couldn't be brought to bear. They found the captain with one eye out and a leg shot off. The French captain had a leg shot off too, and so they put them both in the same bed, where they got better, and drank each other's health. The worst of it was that what we sailors got for England the politicians gave away again when they signed a peace. We let the Dutch have Java, we let the French have Bourbon and Guadaloupe. I wonder we didn't give New Zealand to the Americans, and I daresay we should if they had thought of asking for it.

"That is the *Colossus*, my dear. Good old ship, too; she was at Trafalgar. There is the *Alfred*, who helped to take Guadaloupe in 1810, and the *Æolus* frigate. She fired a shot or two at Martinique the year before. Look at them the row of beauties; forty-two-pounders, the handiest and most murderous craft that ever went to sea; and look at the sloops and the little three-gun brigantines. I had one under my command once. And there is the *Columbine*."

The Captain began to sing :

" 'The *Trinculo* may do her best,
And the *Alert* so fleet, sir,
Alert she is, but then she's not
Alert enough to beat, sir.

. . . .

The *Acorn* and the *Satellite*,
Their efforts, too, may try, sir,
But if they beat the *Columbine*,
Why, dash it!—they must fly, sir.'

"They will build no more such ships; seamanship means poking the fire. Look at those things now."

He pointed with great contempt to the war steamers. Those of 1858 would be thought harmless things enough now. Two or three had screws, but most had the old paddles. The *Duke of Wellington* of 130 guns carried a screw; so did the *Blenheim*, the *Archer*, and the *Encounter*, all of which were lying in the harbour. But the *Odin*, the *Basilisk*, and the *Sidon* were splendid paddle steamers. Among them lay the *Megœra*, a troopship, afterwards wrecked on St. Paul's Island; the Queen's steam yacht, the

Fairy, as pretty a craft as ever floated, in which her Majesty used to run to and fro between Osborne and the port; the *Victoria* and *Albert*, the larger Royal yacht; and the pretty little *Bee*, smallest steamer afloat, before they invented the noisy little steam launches to kill the fish, to tear down the banks of the rivers, and to take the bread out of the mouths of the old wherry-men in our harbour.

We were drawing near the last of the big ships.

"There, Celia, look at that craft," cried the Captain. "Do you see anything remarkable about her?"

"No; only she is yellow."

"That is because she is a receiving hulk," he informed her, with the calmness that comes of a whole reservoir of knowledge behind. "It is in her cut that I mean. Don't you remark the cut of her stern, the lines of her bows?"

She shook her head, and laughed.

"Oh! the ignorance of womankind," said the Captain. "My dear, she's French. Now you see?"

Again Celia shook her head.

"Well," he sighed," I suppose it's no use trying to make a young lady understand such a simple thing. If it had been a bit of lace now, or any other fal-lal and flapdoodle—never mind, my pretty, you're wise enough upon your own lines. That is the *Blonde*, my dear, and she is one of the very last of the old prizes left. When she is broken up I don't know where I could go to look for another of the old French prizes. My father, who was a Master in the Navy, navigated her into this very port. She struck her flag off Brest.

"It is a page of history, children," he went on, "this old harbour. They ought to keep all the ships just as they are, and never break up one till she drops to pieces. The brave old ships! It seems a shame, too, to turn them into coal hulks and convict hulks. I would paint them every year, and keep them for the boys and girls to see. 'These are the craft of the old fighting bulldogs,' I would tell them. 'You've got to fight your own battles in a different sort of way. But be bulldogs, however you go into action, and you'll pull through just as your fathers did.'

"I saw a sight when I was a boy," the Captain went on, "that you'll never see again, unless the Lords of the Admiralty take my advice and give over breaking-up ships. I saw the last of the oldest ship in the service. She was the *Royal William*, eighty guns. That ship was built for Charles the Second, sailed for James the Second, and fought off and on for a hundred and forty years. Then they broke her up —in 1812—because, I suppose, they were tired of looking at her. She ought to be afloat now, for sounder timber you never saw."

"Shall we down sail and out sculls?" I asked.

The Captain answered by a gesture, and we kept on our course. The tide was running out rapidly.

"Five minutes more, Laddy," he said. "We've time to go as far as Jack the Painter's Point, and then we'll come down easy and comfortable with the last of the ebb."

We had left the lines of ships and hulks behind us now, and were sailing over the broad surface of the upper harbour, where it is wise even at high tide to keep to the creeks, the lines of which are indicated by posts. In these there lay, so old that they had long since been forgotten, some half a dozen black hulls, each tenanted by a single ex-warrant officer with his family. Even the Captain, who knew most ships, could not tell the history of these mysterious vessels. What life, I used to think as a boy, could compare with that of being the only man on board one of these old ships? Fancy being left in charge of such a vessel, yourself all alone, or perhaps with Leonard moored alongside, also in charge of one. Robinson Crusoe in his most solitary moments could not have felt happier. Then to wander and explore the great empty ship; to open the cabin and look in the old lockers; to roam about in the dim silences of the lower deck, the twilight of the orlop; the mysterious shades of the cockpit, and to gaze down the impenetrable Erebus of the hold.

To this day I can never go on board a great ship without a feeling of mysterious treasures and strange secrets lurking in the depths below me. And what a place for ghosts! think, if you could constrain the ghosts on those old ships to speak, what tales they could tell of privateering, of pirating, of perils on the Spanish Main, of adventure, of pillage, and of glory. There may be a ghost or two in old inns, deserted houses, ruined castles, and country churchyards. But they are nothing, they can be nothing, compared with the ghosts on an old ship lying forgotten up the harbour. Cis shudders, and thinks she can get on very well without ghosts, and that when she wants their society she would rather meet them ashore.

"That ships may be haunted," said the Captain gravely, "is true beyond a doubt. Every sailor will tell you that. Did you never hear how we were haunted aboard the *Fearnought* by the ghost of the purser's clerk?"

I have always regretted, for Celia's sake, that we did not hear that story. The Captain stopped because we were close on Jack the Painter's Point, and we had to attend to the boat.

The Point was a low-lying narrow tongue of land with one solitary tree upon it, running out into the harbour. It had an edging or beach of dingy sand, behind which the turf began, in knots of long coarse grass, between which, at high tide, the ground was soft and marshy; when the water was out it was difficult to tell where the mud ended and the land began. Now, when the tide was at its highest, the little point, lapped by the waves, and backed by its single tree, made a pretty picture. It was a lonely and deserted spot, far away from any house or inhabited place; there was not even a road near it; behind was a barren field of poor grass where geese picked up a living with anxiety and continual effort; and it was haunted by the gloomiest associations, because here the ghost of Jack the Painter walked.

It was not a fact open to doubt, like some stories of haunted places; Jack had been seen by a crowd of witnesses, respectable mariners, whose testimony was free from any tinge of doubt. It walked after nightfall; It walked backwards and forwards, up and down the narrow tongue of land; It walked with Its hands clasped behind Its neck, and Its head bent forward as if in pain. Anybody might be in pain after hanging for years in chains. Imitate that action, and conjure up, if you can, the horror of such an attitude when assumed by a ghost.

The story of Painter Jack was an episode in the last century. He belonged to the fraternity of ropemakers, a special Guild in this port, the members of which enjoyed the privilege, whenever the Sovereign paid the place a visit, of marching in procession, clad in white jackets, nankeen trousers, and blue sashes in front of the Royal carriage. The possession of his share in this privilege ought to have made Jack, as it doubtless made the rest of his brethren, virtuous and happy. It did not: Jack became moody, and nursed thoughts of greatness. Unfortunately, his ambitions led him in the same direction as those of the illustrious Eratostratus. He achieved greatness by setting fire to the rope-walk. They found out who had done it, after the fire was over and a vast amount of damage had been done, and they tried the unlucky Jack for the offence. He confessed, made an edifying end, and was hanged in chains on that very point which now bears his name. It was in 1776, and twenty years ago there were still people who remembered the horrid gibbet and the black body, tarred, shapeless, hanging in chains, and swinging stridently to and fro in the breeze. Other gentlemen who were gibbetted in the course of the same century had friends to come secretly and take them down. Mr. Bryan, for instance, was one. He for a brief space kept company with Painter Jack, hanging beside him, clad handsomely in black velvet, new shoes, and a laced shirt. He was secretly removed by his relations. Williams the Marine was another; he was popular in the force, and his comrades took him down. So that poor Jack was left quite alone in that dreary place, and partly out of habit, partly because it had no more pleasant places of resort, the ghost continued to roam about the spot where the body had hung so long.

"Down sail, out sculls," said the Captain. "Hard a-port, Celia. We'll drop down easy and comfortable with the tide. How fast it runs out!"

It was too late to think of tacking home with the wind dead against us, and the tide was strong in our favour. I took the sculls and began mechanically to row, looking at Celia. She was more silent now. Perhaps she was thinking of her persistent lover, for the lines of her mouth were set hard. I do not know what the Captain was thinking of; perhaps of Leonard. However that may be, we were a boat's crew without a coxswain for a few minutes.

"Laddy!" cried the Captain, starting up, "where have we got to?"

I held up and looked round. The tide was running out faster than I had ever known it. We were in the middle of one of the great banks of mud, and there was, I felt at once, but a single inch between the keel and the mud. I grasped the sculls again, and pulled as hard as I knew; but it was of no use. The next moment we touched; then a desperate struggle to pull her through the mud; then we stuck fast, and, like the water flowing out of a cup, the tide ran away from the mud-bank, leaving us high and dry, fast prisoners for six hours.

We looked at each other in dismay.

Then the Captain laughed.

"Not the first boat's crew that has had to pass the night on the mud," he said cheerfully. "Lucky we've got the wraps. Celia, my dear, do you think you shall mind it very much? We will put you to sleep in the stern while Laddy and I keep watch and watch. No supper, though. Poor little maid! Poor Celia!"

She only laughed. She liked the adventure.

There was no help for it, not the slightest. Like it or not, we had to pass the night where we were, unless we could wade, waist deep, for a mile through black mud to Jack the Painter's Point.

The tide which had left us on the bank had retreated from the whole upper part of the harbour. But the surface of the mud was still wet, and the splendour of the setting sun made it look like a vast expanse of molten gold. One might have been on the broad ocean, with nothing to break the boundless view but a single solitary islet with a tree on it, for so seemed the Point of Painter Jack. The sky was cloudless, save in the west, where the light mists of evening were gathered together, like the courtiers at the *coucher du roi*, to take farewell of the sun, clad in their gorgeous dresses of pearl-grey, yellow, crimson, and emerald. Athwart the face of the setting sun, a purple cleft in light and cloud, stood up the solitary poplar on the Point. Bathed and surrounded by the western glory, it seemed to have lost all restraints of distance, and to form, in the far-off splendour, part and parcel of the sapphire-tinted west.

As we looked, the sun sank with a plunge, the evening gun from the Duke of York's bastion over the mouth of the harbour saluted the departure of day. The courtier clouds did not immediately disperse, but slowly began putting off their bright apparel.

In a quarter of an hour the outside clouds were grey; in half an hour all were grey; and presently we began to see the stars clear and bright in the cloudless sky.

"The day is gone," murmured Celia, "morn is breaking somewhere beyond the Atlantic. We ought not to let the thoughts of our own selfish cares spoil the evening, but when the sun sank, my heart sank too."

"Faith and Hope, my pretty," said the Captain. "Come, it is nearly nine o'clock. Let us have, evening prayers and turn in."

This was our godly custom before supper. The Captain read a chapter —he was not particular what—regarding all chapters as so many Articles or Rules of the ship, containing well-defined duties, on the proper performance of which rested the hope of future promotion. On this occasion we had no chapter, naturally. But we all stood up while the Captain took off his hat and recited one or two prayers. Then Celia and I sang the Evening Hymn. Our voices sounded strange in the immensity of the heavens above us—strange and small.

And then we sat down, and the Captain began to wrap Celia round in the waterproofs. She refused to have more than one, and we finally persuaded him to take one for himself—they were good-sized serviceable things, fortunately—and to leave us the other. We all three sat down in the stern of the boat, the Captain on the boards with his elbow on the seat, and Celia and I, side by side, the rug wrapped round us, close together.

Ashore the bells of the old church were playing their hymn tune, followed by the curfew.

"The bells sound sweetly across the water," murmured Celia."Listen, Laddy, what do they say?"

"I know what the big bell says," I reply. "It has written upon it what it says:

" 'We good people all
To prayers do call.
We honour to king,
And bride's joy do bring.
Good tidings we tell,
And ring the dead's knell.' "

"'Good tidings we tell,'" she whispers. "What good tidings for us, Laddy?"

"I will tell you presently," I say, "when I have made them out."

The bells cease, and silence falls upon us. It has grown darker, but there is no real darkness during this summer night, only a twilight which makes the shadows black. As we look down the harbour, where the ships lie, it is a scene of enchantment. For the men-o'-war's lights, not regular, but scattered here and there over the dark waters, light up the harbour, and produce an effect stranger than any theatrical scene.

Said the Captain, thinking still of the ships—

"A ship's life is like a man's life. She is put in commission after years of work to fit her up—that's our education. She sails away on the business of the country, she has storms and calms, so have the landlubbers ashore; she has good captains and bad captains; she has times of good behaviour and times of bad; sometimes she's wrecked;—well, there's many a good fellow thrown away so; sometimes she goes down in action—nothing finer than that—and sometimes she spends the rest of her life up in harbour. Well for her if she isn't made a convict hulk. Celia, my dear, you are comfortable, and not too cold?"

"Not a bit cold, Captain, thank you, only rather hungry."

There was no help for that, and the Captain, announcing his intention to turn in, enjoined me to wake him at twelve, so that we two could keep watch and watch about, covered his head with the rug, and in five minutes was fast asleep.

Then Celia and I had the night all to ourselves.

We were sitting close together, with the waterproof round our shoulders. Presently, getting a little cramped, Celia slipped down from the seat, and curled herself up close to the sleeping Captain, resting her head upon my knees, while I laid my arm round her neck.

Was it treachery, when I had striven to beat down and conquer a passion which was not by any means fraternal, for me to feel as if there had never been a perfect night since the world for me began till this one? I wished it would last for ever. When before had I had my queen all to myself in the long sweet silences of a summer night? And none to hear what we said.

There was no word of love, because that was all on one side, but there was talk. We did not sleep that night. The air was soft and warm, though sometimes came a cold touch of wind which made us pull the wraps tighter, and nestle close to each other. But we talked in low whispers, partly because the night is a sacred time, and partly because we were careful not to wake the Captain.

"Tell me now," she whispered, "tell me the good tidings of the bells."

I thought of Leonard's last secret which he told me when he left me on the platform of the station. "Tell Cis?" he said; "that would spoil all." Yet I did tell Cis. I told her that night.

"The bells said, Cis, that there only wanted a fortnight to Leonard's return. He will come back brave and strong."

"And he will make all right," she cried eagerly, clasping my hand in hers. "Go on, Laddy dear."

"He will make all right. The German shall be sent about his business, and—and—"

"And we all will go on just as we used to, Laddy."

"N—not quite, Cis. When Leonard went away, he told me a great secret. I was not to tell anybody. And I should not tell you now, only that I think it will do good to both of us, that you should know it. Tell me, my sister, you have not forgotten Leonard?"

"Forgotten Leonard! Laddy, how could I?"

"You think of him still. You remember how brave and true he was; how he loved—us both—"

"I remember all, Laddy."

"When he left me, Cis—he told me—Hush! let me whisper—low—low—in your ear—that his greatest hope was to come back in five years' time, a gentleman—to find you free—and to ask you—to ask you, Cis—to marry him."

She did not answer, but as she lay in the boat her hands holding mine, her face bent down, I felt a tear fall on my finger; I do not think it was a tear of sorrow.

"You are not offended, Cis dear?" I whispered. "I have done wrong not in telling you?"

"Let it be a secret between you and me, Laddy," she said presently. "Do not let us ever speak of it again."

"Cis, you told me once that you would hide nothing from me. Tell me—if Leonard asked you—"

She threw her arms round my neck, and hid her face upon my shoulder. "Laddy," she whispered, "there is no day, in all these five years, that I have not prayed, night and morning, for Leonard."

Then we were silent.

The hours sped too swiftly, marked by the bells of the ships in commission. About two in the morning the tide began to turn, and the day began to break. First, the dull black surface of flats became wet and glittered in the light. Then the water crept up and covered all; it took time to reach us, because we were on a bank. And all the time we watched, the grey in the east grew tinged with all colours; and the wild-fowl rose out of their sleeping-places by the shore, and flew screaming heavenwards in long lines or arrow-headed angles. And presently the sun arose, splendid.

"Laddy," whispered Celia, for the Captain still slept, "this is more glorious than the evening."

At six bells, which is three in the morning, we floated. I noiselessly stepped over the sleeping form of the Captain and took the sculls, dipping them in the water as softly as I could. He did not awake until half an hour later, when our bows struck the beach, and at the noise the Captain started up. It was nearly four o'clock; no boats were on the harbour; the stillness contrasted strangely with the light of the summer morning.

"Laddy," grumbled the Captain, "you've kept double watch. You call that sailor-like?—Celia, my dear, you have not caught cold?"

When we reached home, the Captain insisted on our going to bed.

"We have passed a night I shall never forget, Laddy," said Celia at the door.

"A sacred night, Cis."

She stooped down, my tall and gracious lady, and kissed my forehead.

"What should I do without you, Laddy? To have some one in the world to whom you can tell everything and not be ashamed, not be afraid. To-night has brought us very close together."

I think it had. After it we were more as we had been when children. My Celia, the maiden of sweet reserve, came back to me a child again, and told me all.

No need to speak again of Leonard. It remained only to look forward and hope and long for the weary days to pass away.

CHAPTER XXIII.
MRS. PONTIFEX ASKS WHAT IT MEANS.

THAT was a night consecrated to every kind of sweet memories. It was quite in the nature of things that it should be followed by one of a more worldly kind. In fact, the next day, to put the matter in plain English, we had a great row, a family row.

It began with Aunt Jane. She came to tea, accompanied by her husband; and she came with the evident intention of speaking her mind. This made us uneasy from the beginning, and although Mrs. Tyrrell attempted to pour oil on the troubled waters by producing her very best tea service, an honour which Mrs. Pontifex was certain to appreciate, she failed. Even tea services in pink and gold, with the rich silver teapot, accompanied by a lavish expenditure in seedcake, and Sally Lunns, and muffins, failed to bring a smile to that severe visage. Mrs. Pontifex was dressed for the occasion in a pyramidal cap trimmed with lace, beneath which her horizontal curls showed like the modest violet peeping between April leaves of grass. She wore her most rustling of black silk robes, and the most glittering of her stud-clasps in the black velvet ribbon which girt her brow. She sat bolt upright in her chair; and such was her remarkable strength of character, testimony to which has already been given by her husband, that she struck the key-note to the banquet, and made it joyless.

Who could be festive when Mrs. Pontifex icily refused sugar with her tea, and proceeded to deny that luxury to her husband?

"No, John Pontifex," she said. "It is high time to set less store upon creature comforts. No sugar, Celia, in my husband's tea."

Mr. Pontifex meekly acquiesced. He was already in the most profound depths of depression when he arrived, and a cup of tea without sugar was only another addition to his burden of melancholy. I conjectured that he had passed the afternoon in the receipt of spiritual nagging. In this art his wife was a proficient; and although nagging of all kinds must be intolerable, I think the religious kind must be the most intolerable. The unfortunate man made no effort to recover his cheerfulness, and sat silent, as upright as his wife, the cup of unsweetened tea in his hand, staring straight before him. Once, his wife looking the other way, he caught my eye and shook his head solemnly.

Under these circumstances we all ran before the gale close reefed.

It was a bad sign that Mrs. Pontifex did not talk. If she had been critically snappish, if she had told her niece that her cap was unbecoming, or Celia that her frock was unmaidenly, or me that an account would be required of me for my idle time—a very common way she had of making things pleasant—one would not have minded. But she did not speak at all, and that terrified us. Now and then she opened her lips, which moved silently, and then closed with a snap, as if she had just framed and fired off a thunderbolt of speech. Her husband remarked one of these movements, and immediately replacing his cup upon the table, softly rose and effaced himself behind the window curtains, where he sat with only a pair of trembling knees visible. Mr. Tyrrell pretended to be at his ease, but was not. His wife was not, and did not pretend to be.

As soon as we reasonably could we rang the bell for the tea-things to be removed, and began some music. This was part of the regular programme, though no one suspected Mrs. Pontifex or her husband of any love for harmony. And while we were playing came Herr Räumer, at sight of whom Mrs. Pontifex drew herself up more stiffly than before, and coughed ominously.

He looked very fresh and young, this elderly foreigner. He was dressed neatly in a buttoned frock (no one in our circle wore evening dress for a gathering under the rank of dinner-party or dance), and had a rose in a button-hole. A little bit of scarlet ribbon in his breast showed that he was the possessor of some foreign Order. In his greeting of Celia he showed a Romeo-like elasticity and youthfulness, and he planted himself on the hearth-rug with an assured air as if the place and all that was in it belonged to him.

In front of him, upon a small couch, sat Mrs. Pontifex, her lips moving rapidly, and her brow darker than ever. Either Herr Räumer was going to interrupt the battle, or he was himself the cause of it. Celia rose from the piano, and sat beside her great-aunt. Mr. Tyrrell was in an easy-chair on one side the fireplace, and his wife on the other, fanning herself, though it was by no means a warm night. As I said before, Mr. Pontifex was in hiding. I sat on the music-stool and looked on. Had there been any way of escape I should have taken advantage of that way. But there was none.

The awful silence was broken by Aunt Jane.

"'Be ye not yoked unequally with unbelievers,'" she said. Then her lips closed with a snap.

No one answered for a while. The curtain alone, behind which was her husband, showed signs of agitation.

"John Pontifex," said his wife, "assist me."

He obeyed immediately, and took up a position behind her, standing opposite to the German. He looked very, very meek.

"John Pontifex and I were talking this afternoon, Clara Tyrrell and

George Tyrrell, and we naturally discussed the strange—the very strange—rumours that are afloat with regard to Celia. Her name, George Tyrrell, has been coupled with that of this—this foreign gentleman here."

Mr. Pontifex shook his head as if more in sorrow than in anger.

"It is—alas!—the fact that such rumours are prevalent."

"You hear, George Tyrrell?" she went on.

"I hear," he replied. "The rumours are not without foundation."

Poor Celia!

"I announced to John Pontifex, this afternoon, my intention of speaking my mind on this matter, and speaking it in the actual presence of Herr Räumer himself, if necessary."

"I am infinitely obliged to you, madam," said that gentleman, with a bow. "I wish that I was already in a position to ask for your congratulations."

"Flap doodle and fudge," said Aunt Jane. I do not defend this expression, but it was her own, reserved for use on those occasions which required the greatest strength of the English language.

All trembled except the German. Celia, by the way, except that she looked pale, took no apparent interest in the conversation.

"Congratulations are useless ornaments of conversation," he said. "That, I presume, is what you mean, Mrs. Pontifex?"

She snorted.

"Pray, sir, will you tell us first, to what religious persuasion you belong?"

The unexpected question staggered him for a moment. I thought he was lost. But he recovered.

"My excellent parents," he said, "who are now no longer living, brought me up in the strictest school—Mrs. Pontifex is, I believe, a member of the Anglican Church—of German Calvinism."

"And what church do you attend in this town?"

"Unfortunately, there is no church of my views in this town. The English churches, however, approach my distinctive doctrines near enough for me." He said this meekly, as if conscious of a superiority which he would not press.

"No blessing shall come from me on any marriage where both members are not communicants of the English Establishment."

She said that with an air of determination, as if the matter was settled.

Herr Räumer laughed softly.

"If that is your only objection, my dear madam, it is easily removed. *Mademoiselle vaut bien une messe*."

"I do not understand French."

"I mean that love, coupled with a short conversation with your learned husband over a few doctrinal difficulties, would permit me to present myself to you in the novel character of a communicant."

He overacted the speech, and no one could fail to see the sneer behind it.

"John Pontifex."

"My dear, I am—in point of fact—behind you."

"You hear what this gentleman says. You can hold a discussion with him in my presence. If, in my opinion, he proves himself worthy of our communion, I shall withdraw that part of my objection."

"It is true," said John Pontifex, "that I am not at the present moment—alas !—deeply versed in the points which—ahem—separate us from German Calvinism. But no doubt Herr Räumer will enlighten me."

"Or," said the suitor, rolling his head,"let me refer myself to a fairer theologian. Celia herself shall convert me."

Celia made no sign.

"This is mockery," Mrs. Pontifex ejaculated. "But it is what I expected, and indeed said to John Pontifex as we drove here. That a foreigner should value Christian privileges is hardly to be looked for."

"That is, I believe," said Herr Räumer, with the faintest possible suspicion of contempt in his smooth tones, "the prevalent belief among English people. And yet no Englishman has yet publicly doubted that even a foreigner has a soul to be saved."

"Or lost," said Mrs. Pontifex sternly.

Her husband, who was still standing meekly beside her, his long arms dangling at either side, looking exactly like a tall schoolboy afraid of his schoolmaster, groaned audibly.

"Or lost," echoed Herr Räumer.

"And pray, sir, if I may ask, what are your means of existence? No doubt Mr. Tyrrell knows all about your family and the way in which you get your living, but we have not yet been informed, and we also have an interest in Celia Tyrrell."

"I have private property," he replied, looking at Mr. Tyrrell, "on the nature of which I have satisfied the young lady's father."

"Perfectly, perfectly," said Mr. Tyrrell.

"How do we know but what you have a wife somewhere else—in Germany, or wherever you come from?"

"Madam's intentions are no doubt praiseworthy, though her questions are not perhaps quite conventional. However, there is no question I would not answer to secure the friendship of Celia's great-aunt. I have no wife in Germany. Consider, Mrs. Pontifex, I have resided in this town for some twelve years. Would my wife, if I had one, be contented to languish in solitude and neglect? Would you, Mrs. Pontifex, allow your husband to live as a bachelor—perhaps a wild and gay bachelor—at a distance from yourself?"

The Rev. Mr. Pontifex smiled and sighed. Did he allow his imagination even for a moment to dwell on the possibility of a wild and rollicking life away from his wife?

"My wild oats," he said, very slowly, with emphasis on each word, and shaking his head. "My—wild—oats—are long since—ahem!—if I may be allowed the figure of speech —sown."

"John Pontifex," said his wife, "we are not interested in your early sins."

"I was about to remark, my dear, that they have produced—alas!—their usual crop of repentance—that is all. The wages of youthful levity—"

"We will allow, Herr Räumer," Mrs. Pontifex interrupted her husband, "that you are what you represent yourself to be. You have means, you are a bachelor, and you are a Christian. Well—my questions are not, as you say, conventional, but Celia is my grand-niece, and will have my money when my husband and I are called away. It is no small thing you are seeking."

"I am aware of it," he replied."I am glad for your sake that your money is not a small thing."

This he should not have said, because it was impolitic.

"I have one question more to ask you," said Mrs. Pontifex, drawing herself more upright than ever. "You are, I understand, some sixty years of age."

"I am sixty-two," he replied blandly. "It is my great misfortune to have been born forty-four years before Miss Celia Tyrrell."

"Then in the name of goodness," she cried, "what on earth do you want with a young wife? You are only three years younger than I. You might just as well ask me to marry you."

"My dear!" cried John Pontifex, in natural alarm.

"I cannot, madam," Herr Räumer replied—"however much one might desire such a consummation—I cannot ask you in the very presence of your husband."

Everybody laughed, including Celia, and Aunt Jane drew herself up proudly.

"You disgraceful man! " she said. "How dare you say such things to me? If John Pontifex were not in Holy Orders I should expect him to—to —"

"I fear I should do so, my dear," John Pontifex interposed. "I am sure, in fact, that, without the—ahem!—the deterrent influence of my cloth, I should do so."

"I am unfortunate this evening," the German went on, still bland and smiling. "I am advanced in years. All the more reason why a young lady—of Christian principles— should assist me in passing those years pleasantly."

"Pleasantly?" she echoed. "Is all you think of—to pass the last years of your life pleasantly? Would I allow my husband to pass his time in mere pleasantness?"

"You would not, my dear," said John Pontifex firmly.

"Mere pleasantness: a Fool's Paradise. George and Clara Tyrrell, I am your aunt, and entitled, I believe, to be heard."

"Surely," said Mr. Tyrrell. "Pray say what you think."

Celia laid her hand on her aunt's arm.

"Dear Aunt Jane," she said, "Herr Räumer has done me the very great honour of asking me to be his wife. He has also very kindly consented not to press for an answer. I feel—I am sure he feels himself—the many difficulties in the way. And if those difficulties prove insuperable, I trust to his generosity—his generosity as a gentleman—not to press me any longer."

"To be sure," said Aunt Jane, "people can always be put off. We can tell them that Herr Räumer felt for you the affection of a grandfather."

The German winced for a moment.

"Thank you, dear Mrs. Pontifex," he said. "You would smooth all the difficulties for us, I am sure."

He shrugged his shoulders.

"Let us have no more explanations. I have to thank Celia—Miss Tyrrell—for putting the position of things clearly. If she cannot see her way to accepting my addresses—there is an end—and things"—looking at Mr. Tyrrell—"must take their own course. If she can, she will have in me a devoted husband who will be proud to belong to the families of Tyrrell and Pontifex."

Aunt Jane was not, however, to be mollified. She kissed Celia on the forehead. "You are a sensible girl, my dear, and you will know how to refuse a man old enough to be your grandfather,"—then she gathered her skirts together. "George and Clara Tyrrell, when you have got over this folly, we shall be glad to see you at our house again. If it comes to anything further I shall alter my will. John Pontifex, I am ready."

She swept out of the room followed by her husband.

Then Mrs. Tyrrell sat up and began to express her indignation.

"When young people desire to marry," she said to her future son-in-law, who was not much more than twenty years older than herself, "they speak to each other, and then to their parents. That is regular, I believe?"

"Quite regular," said the Herr.

"When they have asked each other, and then spoken to the parents," she went on, exhausting the subject, "what else remains to be said?"

"Clearly nothing."

"There certainly is a difference in age," said the good lady. "But if Celia does not mind that—"

"Quite so," he interrupted.

"Religion, too, the same," she went on.

"Actually a coincidence in religion."

"Then what Aunt Jane meant by going off in that way, I cannot conceive. The very best tea-things, too!"

"My dear mamma," said Celia, "the conversation is useless. I am not engaged to Herr Räumer."

Nothing more was said, and the lover presently withdrew.

Mr. Tyrrell led me downstairs to his own office.

There he took the step common among Englishmen who are anxious and nervous, especially when they want to deaden repentance. He drank a tumbler and a half of brandy-and-water strong.

"I wish he was dead, Laddy," he murmured; " I wish he was dead."

"Can you do nothing?"

"I can put him off—I can gain time—and perhaps something will happen. If not she must marry him. She must. Else "

He finished his glass of brandy-and-water.

"She must not. Face anything rather than bring such a fate upon your daughter."

"Face anything," he repeated. " What do you know about it?"

"At least I know that there is nothing in common with him and your daughter."

"What have I in common with my wife? Stuff and nonsense. What has any man in common with his wife? The husband and the wife lead different lives. When they are together in what they call society, they pretend. Rubbish about things in common."

"Then look at the difference of age."

"So much the better, Ladislas," said Mr. Tyrrell fiercely. I hardly knew him to-night in this unusual mood. "So much the better. He will die soon perhaps; the sooner the better."

"Will he treat her kindly?"

"They will live in this town. I shall watch them. If he ill-treats my little girl—my pretty Celia—I will—I will—but that is nonsense. He will make her his plaything."

"Is that what Celia looks for in marriage."

"Will you have some brandy-and-water? No. I take it now, just for the present while this business worries me, to steady the nerves."

He mixed himself another tumbler.

"Why, Ladislas," he resumed his talk, "how foolishly you talk. One would think you were a girl. What Celia looks for in marriage! What is the use of looking for anything, either from marriage or anything else in this world? Disappointment we shall get—never doubt it—and punishment for mistakes—never doubt that. Probably also bad men, unscrupulous men, will get a hold of you, and make you do things you would rather afterwards not have done.

"If I had the key of that safe," he murmured, sinking into a chair; "if I only had the key of that safe"—it was the small fireproof safe, with Herr Räumer's name upon it—"Celia should be free."

I came away sick and sorry. I had heard enough, and more than enough. I knew it all along. My poor Celia!

"If I had the key of that safe!"

Then it occurred to me that the German must have it somewhere. I went to bed and dreamed that I was prowling round and round his room, looking for a key which I could not find.

CHAPTER XXIV.
THE CONSPIRATOR.

THE Polish question was not forgotten. In truth, it was not easy altogether to forget it. The burning fervour of Wassielewski, his glorious indifference to the probabilities of death, his scorn of failure provided the sacred fire was kept burning, all this could not but impress the imagination. When I thought of them my heart burned within me, and it seemed for the time a light thing to join my countrymen, and march with them to certain death, if only to show the world that Poland was living yet. Celia thought this kind of patriotism, this carrying on of a vendetta from father to son, was unworthy. But I never could get her to see the beauty of war, even in the balmy days of Crimean victory.

I laid my case before her, as much as I knew of it, then but little—the loss of my inheritance, the death of my father, my long line of brave progenitors, the obligations of a name.

She could not be persuaded.

"You are not a soldier, Laddy," she said. "You are a musician and an artist. It is not for you to go fighting. And think of all the misery that you and I have seen. Why does not every man resolve that he for one will not fight unless he has to defend himself? Be one of the peacemakers. After all, you foolish boy, it is not you that the Russians have injured, and you have grown up an Englishman. Why, you cannot even speak your own language."

"Wassielewski will be my interpreter."

"Poor old Wassielewski! He will run against the first Russian bayonet he meets, and be killed at the very beginning."

That was, indeed, just what the old man would do. He came to see me one day, with eyes full of fervour, and a voice trembling with excitement.

"Come out, Ladislas, I have much to say to you."

He took me into St. Faith's Square, a large irregular place, with the red brick church at one end. He dragged out of his pocket a pile of papers and letters tied round with ribbon. It struck me disagreeably that Herr Räumer was walking on the other side of the Square.

"They are all with us," he whispered. "See, here are the men from Exeter, here are the London men, here are the Paris men; we have emissaries in Vienna and in Rome; for the present, the country is kept quiet, no suspicions are awakened yet; no movement of Russian troops has been made towards Poland; we shall strike a desperate blow this time."

I mechanically took the papers which he gave me to read. There were lists of names, copies of compromising letters, mysterious notes dated Paris, Vienna, Rome. This old enthusiast was a sort of Head Centre, or, at least, a confidential and trusted agent of a wide-spread conspiracy. My heart sank when I saw my own name at the head of a long list.

"The plan of the campaign is being considered. I have sent in my ideas. They are, after making a feint in Warsaw, to—"

We will not follow the conspirator's plans through all its details. I thought five years later, when the rising of 1863 took place, of Wassielewski's projected campaign, and for my country's sake regretted that they had not been adopted.

"In a very short time—it may be to-morrow—it may be in six months—we shall receive our orders to move."

"And am I to see no one first—-to obey orders blindly?"

"Not blindly, Ladislas Pulaski. I shall be with you."

I suppose there was something of uncertainty in my face, for he quickly added:

"You shall see some of our people before you go. Ladislas, your heart is not yet wholly with us. I have seen that all along. It is my fault. I ought to have educated you from the beginning into hatred of the Muscovite. There ought to have been no single day in which you should not have recited the catechism of Poland's wrongs. My fault—mine."

"Forgive me, Wassielewski."

"But another day of retribution is coming. There will be another massacre of Polish patriots to rouse Poland out of her sleep, and fill the hearts of Polish women with renewed hatred, you and I shall be among the slain, and yet you do not rejoice."

He looked forward to his own death with exultation, much as a Christian martyr brought before Nero may have looked to the cross or the stake, with a fiery fervour of a confessor who glorifies the faith. And he lamented that I, fifty years younger than himself, with no personal memories of struggle and of wrong, could not rise to his level of self-sacrifice.

"I do not rejoice, Wassielewski. I have no wish, not the slightest, to be killed, even for Poland."

He groaned.

"You must wish. You must go with me as I go, ready to be killed—because we shall not succeed this time—for the cause. You must feel as I feel. The others think we shall not fail; they know nothing; those of us who have better information know that Russia is too strong. I want to take you with me knowing all. I pray, night and morning, that you may come to me of your own accord, saying, 'Son of Roman Pulaski and the Lady Claudia, I belong to Poland.'"

I was deeply moved by the old man's eagerness.

"What can I say, Wassielewski? When I am with you my spirit leaps up at your words. Helpless hunchback as I am, I am ready to go with you and do what you command. Away from you, my patriotism is feeble, and I care little for Poland. Forgive me, but I tell you the simple truth."

"There is one thing I have never told you. I meant to keep it till I landed you on the sacred soil of Poland. But I will tell you now. No; not now. I must go home and think before I can tell you that. Come to me to-morrow at this time, to my room, where you and I can talk alone. You will need to be alone with me when you hear all, Ladislas Pulaski—with that knowledge ringing in your brain, the scales will fall from your eyes and you shall see."

What was he to tell me? Were there not horrors enough that I had heard already; men beaten to death; men tortured by the knout; men sent by thousands in exile; women insulted; brides robbed of their bridegrooms, mothers of their sons; was there one single outrage in the long list of possible crimes that had not been committed in that dark story of Polish revolt and Russian repression? Needs must, but war brings misery. The annals of the world are red with tears of blood; "woe to the conquered" is the inevitable law; but such woe, such tears, such misery, as fell upon Poland by the will of the Czar are surely unequalled since the days when a conquered people all fell by the sword, or were led away to a hopeless servitude. What more had Wassielewski to tell me?

By some strange irony I always met Herr Räumer after Wassielewski had been with me. That same evening, as I came home from a walk with Celia, I was saluted by him. He looked down upon me with his white shaggy eyebrows and his green spectacles, as if half in pity, half in contempt. In his presence I felt a very small conspirator indeed.

"I saw you this morning," he said, "walking and talking with your old rebel, Wassielewski. Brave old man! Energetic old man! Useful to his friends. And oh! how useful to his country!"

Nothing could surpass the intense scorn in his voice.

"He is getting up another little rebellion, I gather from certain Cracow papers. At least, there are indications of another rising, and it is not likely that Wassielewski will be out of it. Such a chance does not come often."

"You mean such a chance for Poland?"

"No—I mean for a conspirator. You do not understand—how can you? —the charm of rebellion. Once a rebel— always a rebel. It is like acting. Those who have faced the footlights once are always wanting to go on again. Wassielewski is seventy years of age, and for sixty, or thereabouts, has been conspiring. It would have been a good thing for Poland had some one knocked him on the head when he first began. And a good thing for you."

Why for me?"

"Because Roman Pulaski would still be living and still be a great proprietor in Poland; because you would have been, as he was, a friend and *protégé* of the Imperial Court."

"How do you know so much about me?"

He laughed.

"I have read current history. I read and I remember. And I know the story of Roman Pulaski. It was Wassielewski who took your father from his quiet château, and launched him on the stormy waters of rebellion. Thank him, then, not Russia, for all your misfortunes. You ought to be very grateful to that old man."

This was a new view of the case, and, for the moment, a staggerer.

"That is for the past, Ladislas Pulaski. Now for the future."

"What of the future?"

"It is a Paradise of Fools. In the Future, Poland will be restored; there will be no more wars; nationalities will not be repressed in the Future—"

"At all events, it is better to believe in the Future than in the Present."

"You think so? That is because you are young. I believe in the Present because I am old. I love the Present, and work for it. When I am dead people may say of me what they like, and may do what they like. That is their own business. I eat well; I drink good wine; I read French novels; I smoke excellent tobacco: what more can the Future give me? Your friend Wassielewski fought once for the Future. He gets tenpence a day for his reward; he fiddles for sailors; he conspires for Poland; he will die in some obscure field leading peasants armed with scythes against Russian troops armed with rifles."

"I would rather be Wassielewski than—"

"Than I? *Ça va sans dire*. You are young," he laughed, and showed his white teeth. "Meantime, remember what I told you. Where there are three conspirators there is one traitor. Have nothing to do with them; refuse to be murdered for Poland; go on with your music-lessons—anything you like, but do not join conspiracies."

He seemed to know everything, this man. For the first time a strange thought crossed my brain. Could he have received intelligence of the intended rising?

"I mean well by you, Ladislas Pulaski, although you suspect me, and do not love me. That does not matter. I wish to see you kept out of the fatal business which killed your father.

"Crack-brained idiots!" he ejaculated. "There is in the Kremlin a box. In the box is a most valuable document, shown to strangers as a curiosity. It is the Constitution of Poland. Reflect upon that fact. Again, there is outside Cracow a mound, erected in immortal memory of Kosciusko. It is a mound so high that it dominates the town. Therefore the Austrians have turned it into a fort by which, if necessary, to crush the town. That is another inspiriting fact for a Pole to consider."

"It is like the Austrians."

"Doubtless. Otherwise they would not have built their fort. You would have preferred seeing them sympathise with the fallen hero. England and France have made of Poland a beautiful theme for the most exalted sentiments and speeches. But they do not fight for Poland. Voltaire, who did not share in the general enthusiasm, even wrote a burlesque poem on the Poles. Then England put clauses in the Treaty of 1815 to ensure the government of the country by her Constitution. When Nicholas laughed at the clauses and tore up the treaty, England and France did not fight. Who keeps treaties when he is strong enough to break them? Who goes to war for a broken treaty when he is not strong enough? What does the new Czar say to the Poles? 'No dreams, gentlemen.' It is a dream to believe that Poland is not abandoned. It is a dream that a few madmen can get up a successful rebellion. *Finis Poloniæ!*"

He inhaled a tremendous volume of smoke, and sent it up in the air in a thick cloud.

"Look There goes the liberty of Poland. Say I well, Ladislas Pulaski?"

"No," I replied bluntly.

"Did you ever hear what a great Pole said when they wanted him to conspire? *'Mourir pour la patrie? Oui, je comprend cela; mais y vivre? Jamais.'* And he did neither."

I was filled with strange forebodings; with that feeling of expectancy which sometimes comes over one at moments when there seems impending the stroke of Fate; I could not rest; wild dreams crossed my brain. Nor was Celia happier. We wandered backwards and forwards in the leafy and shady retreat, restless and unhappy. The great elms about us were bright with their early foliage of sweet young June; the birds were flying about among the branches where they were never disturbed; the thrush with his low and cheerful note, surely the most contented among birds; the blackbird with his carol, a bird of sanguine temperament; the blue tit, the robin, the chaffinch—we knew every one of them by sight because we saw them every day. And the meadows at the foot of the walls were bright with golden cups.

"How can I give it up, Cis?" I asked.

She answered with her sweet sad smile. We had both been brooding in silence.

"I am selfish," she said. "I think of nothing but my own troubles. You must not give it up, Laddy. You belong here, to the Captain, and to me. You must not go out among strangers."

I shook my head.

"Wassielewski says I must. It would be hard to tear myself away, Cis—not to talk to you ever again, to see you no more."

"Why no more, Laddy?"

"I am to give more than my presence to the revolt, Cis. I am to give what Wassielewski gives—my life."

Just then we saw him marching along the ramparts towards us. His eyes were upon us, but he saw nothing. He came nearer and nearer, but he took no notice; he swung his arms violently to and fro; his long white hair streamed behind him in the wind; he carried his black felt hat in one hand; he halted when he came to the wall of the bastion, leaned for a moment upon the rampart, gazing fixedly out upon the bright waters of the harbour. What did he see there? Then he turned and faced us, but spoke as if he saw us not.

"The time is at hand," he murmured, in the low tones of a prophet. "The wolves and the ravens may gather in the woods and wait for the dead. The mothers shall array their sons—the wives shall buckle the sword for their husbands, the daughters for their lovers; once in every generation the sacrifice of the bravest and noblest, till the times comes; till then the best must die."

"Not Ladislas," cried Celia, throwing herself in front of me. "Take any one else, take whom you please to be murdered. But you shall not take my brother Ladislas."

He made no answer; I suppose he did not hear. Presently he stepped lightly from the breastwork, and walked slowly away, still waving his arms in a sort of triumph.

"He is mad, Laddy," Celia whispered. "You must not trust your fate to a madman."

"He is only mad sometimes, Cis. It is when he thinks too much about the past."

"Laddy, if you go away and leave me; if Leonard—but that is impossible. God will be good to us—yet. I could not bear my life without you."

"Tell me, Cis dear, has he pressed for an answer?"

She shook her head.

"It is not that," she said. "He is patient. But it is my father. Do not put my thoughts into words, Laddy. They are too dreadful. And my mother sees nothing."

CHAPTER XXV.
WASSIELEWSKI'S SECRET.

THE Polish newspapers at one time, and until they were ordered to desist, used to print the words Past and Future in very big capitals, while they spoke of the present in the smallest possible type. That was Wassielewski's method. The Past was radiant with Polish glory and Polish struggles set in a black background of Russian atrocities. Like one of the new-fashioned "Arrangements in Brown," the details were smudged. The Future, after a good deal more of fighting and bloodshed, was also to be a chronicle of great glory. As for the present, it did not exist, it was a dream.

For himself, he was almost the last of the Poles whom I remembered as a child in the old black barrack. The barrack itself was gone, and the Poles dispersed. Those who were left lived about the town singly. Wassielewski alone among them still nourished thoughts of revenge and patriotism. He was certainly the only man of all the exiled Poles capable of giving life to the cause in a hopeless effort, where the only object was to keep alive the spark of rebellion. He also never flagged or lost heart, because he knew what he had to give, and he knew what he was going to get. I was accustomed to his fanaticism. If he met me when I was a child, he was wont to say, parenthetically, "Ladislas, Poland is not dead, but sleeping," and then pass on without waiting for an answer. He was like a bird which has but one tune; his one idea was the resuscitation of his country. Sometimes he would stop me in the street, and take off his hat, standing like a prophet of Israel with his deep-set eyes, his long white locks, and his passionate look, keeping me beside him while he whispered in earnest tones, "Listen, Ladislas Pulaski, there is a stir in her limbs. She will spring to her feet again, and call upon her children to arise and fight. Then let all the Poles scattered over the broad face of the earth, the Poles of Gallicia, the Poles of the Kingdom, join together. We are the children of those who fought with Kosciusko, and we are the grandchildren of those who followed Sobieski. If we die, the tradition of hate will be preserved. Let us die, if Heaven so will it."

I was therefore trained in the traditional hatred of Russia, almost as much as if I had been brought up in Warsaw among those Polish ladies who go in mourning all their days, and refuse to dance or have any joy. But my own feeling was of the passive kind, which is not fertile in action. By temperament as well as physique I was inclined to the contemplative life; if I regarded the Muscovite with patriotic hatred, I was by no means prepared to leave my own ease, and put on the armour of a soldier. Besides, to all intents I was an Englishman, with English ideas, English prejudices; and the Poles were foreigners to me, although I was of Polish blood, and—I was a cripple.

Wassielewski saw with pity that his most fiery denunciations, his most highly-coloured narratives of blood, failed to rouse me to the level of his own enthusiasm, and therefore the old conspirator had recourse to his last and most desperate measure. If that failed I was hopeless. He told me the secret that had been religiously kept from me by the Captain, Mr. Broughton, and the few who knew it—the tragedy of my birth.

I wish he had not told me; I ought to have been spared the bitter knowledge; it was with kindness that it had been kept from me. For the story fired my blood, and maddened me for a while with the thirst of vengeance.

It was about four o'clock one afternoon—a week before Leonard's return, that I went to Wassielewski's lodgings—at his own request. I went unwillingly, because it pained me to see him so eager, and to feel myself so lukewarm over the wrongs of my country; but I went.

His one room was furnished with a narrow bed, a chair, a table, and a music-stand. A crucifix was hanging on the wall—Wassielewski was a Catholic—a sword hung below it; at the head of the bed was a portrait in water-colours, which I had never seen before, of a young lady, dressed in the fashion of the Thirties. She had a sweet, calm face, and her eyes, which fell upon me when I entered the room, seemed to follow me about. They were large eyes, full of thought and love.

"That is your mother, Ladislas Pulaski," said the old man slowly. "Your sainted mother, one of the martyrs of Poland. Claudia, wife of Roman Pulaski."

My mother! I, who never knew a mother, and hardly ever gave her memory one filial thought. A strange yearning came over me as I gazed at the face, and saw it blurred through the tears that crowded in my eye.

"My mother! Wassielewski, why have you never shown this to me before?"

"Because I waited for the moment to come when I could give you her portrait, tell you her story, and send you forth to kill Russians in revenge. Sit down, poor boy. I have much to say, and nothing that is not sad."

I sat down with strange forebodings. But I took the portrait of my mother from the wall.

"You will give this to me, Wassielewski?"

"When I die, or when we go together to Poland."

Ah! The tender sweetness of the face; the kind face; the noble face. Ah!

the good and true eyes that saw her son after so many years; so bright, and yet so sad. For they had the sadness which seems to lie in the eyes of all whom death takes young. Death! How did my mother die? And while I looked I felt that the poor old man who loved her so much—else he could not have been so careful for me—was looking with me in her face, and dropping tears upon my head.

"Do not tell me, Wassielewski—not now—if it pains you so much."

"That will pain you more," he groaned. "Day and night for twenty years it has been ever before my eyes. I was only her humble friend and servant. You are her son. How shall I tell you the shameful story.

"Sit so, Ladislas Pulaski, with your eyes upon the face of your dead mother—perhaps she will smile upon you as she does upon me sometimes in moonlight nights when I lie awake and listen for the call from Poland. So—so—while I try to tell you how she died and how your father died."

His voice was calm and steady, but his eyes were wild. I looked at him no more, but kept my eyes upon the picture, awed and expectant.

He took his violin from the case, and played a few bars walking up and down the room.

"That is a Polish waltz. We used to dance a great deal in Poland before 1830. We were Russian subjects, it is true, but we were happier than our brothers who were under Prussia. Some of us were young, too—not I. I am seventy-five now, and I am talking of events which took place only five-and-twenty years ago. But I was not too old to join in the dances of the people. And I was happy in my stewardship of the Lady Claudia. She was an only child, like your father, Roman Pulaski, and I was the steward of her father, and had special charge of the young lady. There is a girl in this place; I often see you with her."

"Celia Tyrrell?"

"Yes—perhaps. She has the eyes of your mother and her sweet face. I think she must be good, like her.

"Lady Claudia was not proud. We went about together, her father and she and I, to all the peasants' festivals. I was but a peasant born, but she, it is true—oh! she was a great lady. When we had a wedding it lasted a week, and we danced all night; we wore our national dress; we sang our national songs—this was one of them."

He played a quaint delightful air, full of sweetness and character.

"We ate our *bigos* and *cholodiec*; we laughed and joked. And with the Muscovites we were friends. You would have been a happy child, Ladislas Pulaski, could you have been brought up among your own people, and learned their customs—such as they were. Now, it is all changed. The national costume is forbidden; we may not sing the Polish hymns—Listen to one. Ah! you cannot understand the words."

He played a hymn with soft and melancholy cadences, crooning rather than singing the words which I could not, as he said, understand.

"We dance no longer; even the young Polish girls, who loved dancing more than any girls in the world, dance no more; we go in mourning all our days; even the young Polish girls, whose dress was so gay and bright, wear black all their lives; we laugh no more, but sit with weeping eyes; we go to church, not to pray for good harvests and joy, but for the hour of revenge."

He paused a moment.

"That is what you know already. Up to the age of nineteen, my young lady was as happy as the day is long. She was as happy as God ever allowed any human being to be. For when she was eighteen she was married—to your father.

"Roman Pulaski was worthy of her—he, alone among men. He was of a good descent; he was as rich, he was as handsome, he was as strong and brave as she was true and good. They were married, and you were born—a strong and straight-backed boy—a true Pulaski, with curly brown hair, and plenty of it, when you were but a little baby. And who so happy as your mother? All day long she held you in her arms; all day and all night; it made the tears come into my eyes only to see how pleased and happy she was with her child.

"That lasted two years. Then came the insurrection. Of course your father joined it. How could he keep out of it? And the Lady Claudia wove silk banners, and brought her jewels to buy arms, and gave all she had to the brave rebels.

"One day, after three months of fighting, I came back— alone. Your father had disappeared; our men were all killed; and the Russians were marching upon the castle to destroy it. I remembered how, once, they set fire to a house full of Poles, and killed all who tried to escape. So I hurried your mother away; we carried the child between us, and escaped into the woods, where we wandered backwards and forwards through the bitter cold night, and watched at nightfall the red glow in the sky, which marked our burning castle. So you no longer had a house, you and the Lady Claudia.

"In the morning, finding that the Cossacks were gone, I took her home to our village. It was a place full of women and children; not a man left in it; only a few boys of ten and old men of seventy; but because there were no men, I thought she would be safe. She was brave—always brave—and in her pale face there was no thought of repentance. They weighed the cost, and joined the losing side. Her husband gone—perhaps dead; her house destroyed; nothing left in the world but her year old child. Yet she never lamented. Only the second day, she sent me away. 'Old friend,' she said, 'go—and, if you can, bring me news of Roman Pulaski. If he is dead we will mourn for him as those who mourn for the dead in Christ.'

"I left her—in safety, as I thought—I crept cautiously through the woods, from village to village, and asked of the women and old men in each place for news. For a time I could learn nothing, but one day I found a newspaper, and read that Roman Pulaski was not dead but a prisoner.

"It would have been better for him had he died in battle. You have heard—I have told you over and over again—how the Czar Nicholas hated the very name of Pole; how there was no cruelty practised by his officers, no severity so great towards the Poles that it should displease him. But the case of one who stood so high as your father was too important to be decided upon even by the Archduke Constantino's favourite, General Kuruta.

"Roman Pulaski had been a favourite in the St. Petersburg Court; he had attracted the notice of the Empress, who hoped to attach him to the Russian cause; his rebellion incensed the Czar more than the defection of all the other Poles put together. Imagine, therefore, his satisfaction at having his enemy in his own power. At first he ordered that the prisoner should be shot. This order was immediately afterwards commuted, as he called it, to hard labour in the mines of Siberia for life, which was called the Czar's clemency.

Even the Russians were appalled at such a sentence, which condemned a gentleman to the lowest degradation of companionship with criminals. They drew up a petition; it was represented that the Count Roman Pulaski was young and hotheaded; they said he had been drawn into the rebellion by disaffected advisers and by misrepresentations. The Czar refused to receive the petition. Then the Empress herself, his own wife, threw herself on her knees at his feet and implored mercy.

"'You ask mercy for a Pole,' he cried. 'Then this is what you shall get for him.' He took the paper containing the sentence, and added to it in his own handwriting, 'And the prisoner shall walk the whole way.'"

"Walk?—walk the whole way from Warsaw to Siberia?"

"Walk. Think of it quietly if you can, for a while. Try to understand something of what it means. To be one of a gang of murderers and common thieves, because they did not allow him to perform his journey with brother Poles; to step side by side, manacled together at the wrist, with one of the worst of these criminals; to sleep with him at night on a sloping bench; to eat and drink with him; never to be separated from him; to be driven along the never-ending road by Cossacks armed with whips; to endure every indignity of blows and curses; to have no rest by day, no repose by night; to eat the vilest and commonest food; to spend the winter—it was in the winter that he started— pacing for ever along the white and frozen snow; to be on the road when spring returned; to be still walking always with the thieves and murderers, in the glaring summer.

"Take a map, measure the distance from Warsaw to Moscow, from Moscow to Astrakhan, from Astrakhan to Tobolski, and thence to the mines. You will say to yourself, fifteen miles a day; that makes—how many months of walking? Left behind him a wife, young and beautiful as the day; a boy not old enough yet to do more than look in his father's face, and cry, 'Papa—Wassielewski!'

"Wife and boy gone—happiness gone for ever—no hope—before him the long road—with the horrible daily and nightly companions, and after the road? Perhaps after the road the worst part of the sentence; for in the road there is change, in the mines none; day after day the same work; day after day the same hopeless toil; day after day the same gloom; day after day the same wretched fellow-prisoners; the same faces; the death in life.

"They used to go mad, some of them; they used to commit suicide; some would murder a soldier or a gaoler for the mere excitement of being flogged to death. Some tried to run away. It was fortunate for those who made their escape in winter, because when night fell they lay down in the snow—out on the free white snow, which covered them up and hid them after the cold winter wind had fanned them to sleep, and when they were found in the spring they were dead corpses covered over with tall grasses and pitiful flowers. Those who neither went mad, nor were knouted, nor were frozen to death, nor committed suicide, dropped away and died day by day, like your father, and for the last few months of their lives, God, more merciful than the Czar, made them stupid."

Wassielewski stopped. I looked up at him with beating heart and flashing eyes. His own eyes, deep-set and stern, were glowing with the intensity of his wrath, and the red gash on his cheek was a long white line.

"Go on, Wassielewski," I cried,"tell me more."

"I have thought upon that journey," he continued in a calm voice, "till I seem to know it every step. And he was so tall, so brave, so handsome.

"News came, later on—not for a long time—about him. More than half the convicts died upon the road; the man to whom he was manacled threw himself down upon the road one day, and refused to move another step; they flogged him till he could not have walked if he had tried; but he still refused, and then they flogged him again until he died. That was part of the Czar's clemency. Your father was one of the few who survived the journey, and reached Siberia in safety. He sent home by a sure hand a little wooden cross, on which he had carved—the names of Claudia his wife, and Ladislas his boy."

"Stop—stop! Wassielewski, I cannot bear it."

"I shall not stop," he replied, "you must bear this, and more. There is worse to hear. Do you think it is for nothing that I tell you all these things? The cross was to show his wife that he was alive, and that he still thought of them. But when it arrived his wife was dead, and the child was in exile. The cross,"—he opened a little cabinet which stood upon a chest of drawers—"the cross is here. I have kept it for you."

It was a roughly-carved cross, eighteen inches long, of a dark-grained wood, a Latin cross. On the longer limb was carved in letters rude, but deeply cut in the wood, "Roman to Claudia," and on the transverse limb the single word, "Ladislas."

"See, from his grave your father calls you."

"From his grave?"

"He died, like all the prisoners in the mines, of hard work, of despair, of misery, and neglect. He could write no letters, he could receive none; he had no longer anything to hope for in this world. Roman Pulaski died. Grey, deaf, and blind, my poor old master died. He was not thirty years of age.

"When he was dead, lying news was published in the papers by the command of Nicholas. They said that he had been released from the mines, that he had voluntarily entered as a private soldier in a Caucasian regiment, that he had fallen in action. Lies! Lies! No one believed them. As if Roman Pulaski would not have written to Poland for news of his wife and son; as if he would not have flown along the road as soon as he obtained his liberty, to learn if they were dead or living. No! In the darkest and deepest mine, with the foulest thieves of a Muscovite crowd, Roman Pulaski lived out his wretched years, and died his wretched death. And you are his son.

"Before you go home, remember this: he died for Poland; his death is not forgotten; for fifty generations, if need be, the story shall be told of the Czar's revenge."

He paused for a moment.

CHAPTER XXVI. THE MASSACRE OF THE INNOCENTS.

I HAVE more to tell you," he went on, wiping the beads from his brow wearily. "More to tell you, more that I cannot tell without the bitterest pain, and that will sadden all your after years. But you must learn it, you must learn it, before you become a true child of Poland."

He leant over me and kissed my head.

"Poor boy! I thought at one time that you might be spared. The good Captain said to me when you went away to live with him, 'Let him not know, Wassielewski; let him never know.' I said, 'He shall never know, Captain; no one shall tell him:—unless his country ask for him. Then he shall know, because the knowledge will fire the blood, and make him fight like ten men. We are all like ten men when we rise to fight the Muscovite.' So I promised and I prayed of a night to the Lady Claudia, who is now a saint in Heaven, and hears what sinners ask, that she would guard her son from harm. 'Because,' I said on my knees, 'he is not a strong man like your husband or your servant; he is afflicted, he is feeble, he is a boy of peace and fond of music, and he has made good friends.' I knelt by the bed, and I looked on that face.

"The face changed as I prayed, and sometimes, by candlelight, or by moonlight, I could see the eyes of my mistress shining upon me, or see her lips move as if to speak or to smile. And always happy. Ladislas, happy are those who forgive."

"But we cannot forgive," I said.

"Never, boy, never. We are God's instruments of wrath. And now the time has come, and Poland asks for you. So I must tell you, Ladislas," he added pitifully, "I must tell you, in addition, how your mother died. You will think over the story every day for the rest of your life. And you will understand, henceforth, how Russia may become the Protector of Christians—out of her own country.

"It happened while I was away, looking for certain news of your father. I left her in safety, as I thought, among the women and children. Even I did not know how far the Czar could carry his revenge. Not even the little children were safe. An order came from St. Petersburg that all orphan Polish children—all those whose fathers had fallen in the insurrection—all who were a burden to the State— should be carried away and brought up in military schools. That was a master-stroke. The little Poles were to become Russians, to fight their brothers.

"You were not an orphan, nor a burden on the State; you did not fall within that law. It was by the great, by the divine clemency of the Czar that that ukase was issued, to save the children whom every Polish household would have welcomed, to relieve the State of a burden which did not exist. But the order did not affect you, and if I had known of it I should not have been disturbed. You were safe, safe with your mother, and she was safe among her own people, the women who knew her and loved her.

"As the order was issued it had to be carried out, and the soldiers were sent to find orphan children, begging their bread, and a burden on the State. But there were none: yet the order must be obeyed. So they began to carry off all the children they could find, whether they were orphans or not, whether their mothers wept and shrieked, or whether they sat silent, struck with the mad stupor of a misfortune greater than they could bear.

"When Herod slew the infants in Bethlehem, there were some thirty killed. When Nicholas murdered the innocents in Poland, there were thousands. Perhaps, when one crime becomes as well known as the other, that of the Czar will take its proper rank.

"In the afternoon, when the day was sinking, there came clattering up to the village where your mother had taken refuge a long cavalcade of carts, horses, and cavalry. In the carts were infants; it was a day of winter, and the snow was lying over the fields and in the branches of the pines. The carts were covered, it is true, and within them the children cried and moaned, huddled together against each other for warmth; some mere infants in arms; some five or six years of age, who carried the smaller ones; some little toddling things of two. They had spread rough blankets on the floors of the carts, but still the helpless babes were cold. And their only nurses were the soldiers, who had small pity.

"The women of the village came out crying over the poor children, bringing them bread and milk. With them they carried their own. They had better have stayed indoors; better still have fled into the woods, and hidden there till the Cossacks went away. For presently, the soldiers began picking up the children of the village and tossing them, too, into their carts. Among them, led by an older child, wrapped in furs, was a little boy of two years old—you, Ladislas Pulaski.

"You were straight-backed then, poor boy; straight and comely, like your father—

"When they rode away, the carts lumbering along the roads, the children crying, the soldiers swearing, they were followed by a stream of women, who shrieked and cried, and first among them all ran and cried your mother—the Lady Claudia. Yes—she was brave when her beautiful home was burned with all the sweet things she had grown up amongst; but when she saw the boy torn from her, she became, they told me, like a mad woman. They were all mad women.

"It was twenty-four hours later when I returned and heard what had happened. The carts had all that much start of me; also I had to be careful, because near the villages I might be recognised and arrested. I followed on the high-road when I could—through forests when I could find a faithful guide—anyhow so that I followed. After two days of pursuit, I found—courage, Ladislas—courage, boy—so—drink this water—lie down for a moment—sob and cry—it will do you good as it did me, when I found her—the tale is almost told.

"I found her lying cold and dead in the road. She was bare-headed, and her long hair lay blown about her beautiful head; her face was looking with its pale cold cheeks and closed eyes—looking still along the road in the direction of the carts—one arm was bent under her, one hand upon her heart; one lay extended, the fingers clutched in the snow, as if she would drag herself along the way by which she could no longer creep; her shoes had fallen from her feet, she was frozen;—in the night she had fallen, and, too weak to rise, must have died in the painless sleep that swiftly closes the eyes of those who lie down in our winter snow. I lifted her and bore her to the edge of the forest, where, because I could not dig her a grave, I made a hole in the snow, and covered her over with branches to keep off the wolves. I knelt by her dead form and called Heaven to witness that such revenge as I could work upon the people who had killed her I would work—it is a vow which I have renewed from day to day; and after many years, the time has come at last. It always comes to those who have faith and patience.

"When I had buried your mother, I hurried along the road still in pursuit of the train of children. These trains do not move quickly, and I knew that I should come up with it—sooner or later. The roads were very still and quiet; it was not only the snow that lay on the earth, but the dread and terror of the Cossacks. Death was in the air; in the woods lay the bodies of the men: in the villages lay the women weeping; on the cold roads lumbered the long lines of kibitkas that carried away the children. Somewhere on that road marched the train of convicts manacled wrist to wrist, your father among them.

"Presently—it may have been a day, it may have been an hour, after I left your dead mother—I heard far off the dull dead sound of the carts, the cracking of whips, and the curses of the drivers. Then I stopped to think. If they saw me I should be shot, and that would be of no use to any one. Now, if I lost sight altogether of the train, how could I help you, who were in it?

"Walking and running, I kept up close behind the train; as the night fell again, I could get so close as to hear the wailing of the children, who cried for hunger and for cold. And Providence befriended us; for while I went along the road, I saw something move in the moonlight, and heard a faint cry. Ladislas, it was you. You had fallen from the cart, and they left you there to die. Perhaps they did not see you. Five minutes more, and you would have died, like your mother, of that fatal sleep of frost.

"There is nothing more to tell—I had a long and weary journey from village to village before I reached the Austrian frontier, and found a friend who would help us over mountains and by forests to Switzerland. All Europe was full of our sufferings, and we made friends wherever we went; there were societies called 'Friends of Poland,' who helped us with money and work; had they given us soldiers and arms we should have asked no other help—we passed from Switzerland to France, and from France we came to England. Always the same kindness from the people; the same indignation; and the same help. I wonder, now, if they have forgotten the cause of Poland; perhaps, because it is twenty years ago.

"Well, as the days passed on, I noticed something. At first it was not much, but as the time went on, I found that your back was round, and that you were—poor boy—deformed. It was done by the fall from the cart. Remember, Ladislas, that you owe that, as well as everything else—to the Czar. When you look in the glass, say to yourself, 'But for them I should be well and straight like my father:' when you pass a rich man's house you may say, 'My house stood among woods fairer than these, with more splendid gardens; the Czar burnt it, and took my broad lands.' When you stand upon the ramparts and see the lines of convicts, working, silent, in single file, think of your father dying slowly in the Siberian mines—and every evening and every morning, look at the face of your mother and think of her rushing along the frozen roads, catching at the hands of the soldiers, crying and imploring—to fall at last for very weakness on the ground and die in misery.

"Hush, boy—hush—strengthen your heart—rouse yourself—think that your arms are strong though your back is round; you can fire a gun; you can kill a Russian; you can fight, as men fight now; and you are a Pulaski.

"I thought, when I saw what you were, that Heaven had resolved to spare you the common lot of Poles. But that is not so—we must all go now."

"Yes, Wassielewski—all must go. I among the rest."

"I knew you would say that, when you had been told all. Look me in the face, boy, and swear it."

"I swear it," I murmured, in a broken voice. "By the portrait of my mother, Wassielewski, I will go with you to Poland, when you claim my promise. You shall take me back to my own people: you shall say to them that I am poor and deformed; that I can neither march with them, nor ride, nor stand upright among their ranks; that I cannot even speak my own language; but that I have greater wrongs to avenge than any of them; and that I ask leave just to crawl among them and load my rifle with the rest."

"Good—boy—good." The old man's eyes had an infinite tenderness in their depths while he took my hand. "I am taking you to Death. That is almost certain. I pray God that we may die together, and that we may die upon a heap of Russians while the enemy is flying before our faces scattered like the chaff before the wind. Then I can take you by the hand and lead you to Heaven, where we shall find them both, waiting for us—Count Roman and Lady Claudia—and I shall say, 'My master and my mistress, I have brought your boy home to you. And he died for Poland.'

"It is not that I have done this of myself," he went on. "For years a voice has been ringing in my ears which at first I could not understand,—it was only a voice, and indistinct. Gradually I began to hear and make out what it said. 'The time is coming,' it said, 'the time is coming. Prepare to end thy work. The time is coming.' That lasted for a long while, but I was patient, because I knew that it was the Lady Claudia who spoke to me at night, and she would have good reason for what she said. And now the voice says more. It says, 'Ladislas must be told; Ladislas must go with you; let Ladislas, too, fight for Poland.' We must obey a voice from Heaven, and so I have told you.

"Remember, I can promise you nothing—not even glory, not even a name. You may be killed in a nameless fight upon a village green; you may follow your father to Siberia; I know not. I partly read the future, but not all. I see fighting. I hear the Polish hymn; there are the accursed grey coats, there is the firing of guns, and all is finished. Among the patriots I do not see you, Ladislas, and I do not see myself'.

"You have sworn, and I will give you besides your father's cross, your mother's portrait. Take them with you to-night, put them in some safe place, pray with them in your hand, night and day. Remember, you are no longer a music-master in an English town; you are a child of Poland, and you teach music till you hear your country's call. And now, farewell; wait and expect."

. . . .

"Play something, Celia, my dear," said the Captain. " Soothe his spirit with music. Poor boy, poor boy! He should not have told you."

. . . .

I went home in a dream, bearing with me the precious relics which Wassielewski gave me. I think I was mad that evening. It was nine o'clock when I reached home, and Celia had waited for me all the evening. But I had no eyes for Celia, and no thought for anything but what I had heard. And then, in such language as came to me, with such passion and tears as the tale called up within me, I told my story and once more renewed my vow.

. . . .

There was no sleep for me that night, but in the morning I fell into a slumber broken by unquiet dreams. There was the lumbering, grinding roll upon the frozen snow of the children's train escorted by the mounted soldiers; there was the figure of my mother, lying stone dead on a road of ice; there was the gang of convicts limping along a road which seemed to have no beginning and no end.

. . . .

They would not let me go to my pupils; my hands were hot, my brow was burning. Celia came to sit with me, and we talked and wept together. I was fain to tell my story all over again. She held my hand while I told it, and when it was finished I saw in her face no wrath, none of the madness with which Wassielewski filled my soul the day before, but only a great sadness. I was still mad for revenge, but somehow I felt instinctively as if Celia's sorrow was not a higher thing than the old Pole's thirst for revenge. And I was ashamed in presence of her sad and sympathising eyes to renew my oath of vengeance.

"Poor Laddy!" she said, "what a tale of misery and wrong! Let us pity the soldiers who had to carry out such an order. Let us believe that the Czar did not know—could not know—how his order was obeyed. Do not dwell upon it, dear. Do not let cruel and revengeful thoughts grow out of the recollection. 'Vengeance is mine,' you know. Your mother's face—how beautiful it is!—does not make you think of revenge? See how calmly the sweet eyes look at you! And oh! dear, dear, Laddy, make no more rash vows, at least till Leonard comes home. And it wants but three days—three short, short days, and we shall see him again, and all will go well with us once more."

The Captain said nothing, but in his sad face I saw that he sorrowed for me, and in his grave eyes I read the warning which did not leave his lips.

CHAPTER XXVII.
THE DAY BEFORE.

THEY were very patient with me, the Captain and Celia, while the madness was in my blood. They let me talk as wildly as I pleased, and did not argue. But on the third day Celia put her foot down.

"I will hear nothing more, Laddy," she said. " You have spent three days in dreams of bloodshed and battle. Talk to me about your mother, if you please. I shall never tire of looking at her eyes. They are like yours—when you do not madden yourself with the recollection of that story. Let us picture the sweet life in the Polish village with the château beside it, and the girls dancing. Let us play their waltz, or let us go up to the wall and talk of Leonard. But no more battles."

It was a wise prohibition, and I had to obey. My thoughts were directed into a new channel, and the furies which had taken possession of me were, for the moment at least, expelled.

Four days, then, to the twenty-first. Four long, tedious days.

Then three.

Then the days became hours, and at last we were only a single day—only four-and-twenty hours from the fixed time when Leonard should come back to us. "In riches or in poverty"—somehow, in spite of all obstacles—he was to return to Celia's Arbour on the evening of the twenty-first of June, 1858. How would he come back, and what would be his history?

"If he is changed, Laddy," said Celia, "he will find us changed too. You, poor boy, under a promise to go out and get killed for Poland. Not that you shall go, in spite of the old patriot. And I—what am I, Laddy?"

"You are like Andromeda chained to the rock, waiting for the monster to come and devour her. Or you are like an Athenian maiden going out to the youth-devouring Minotaur. But patience; Perseus came to Andromeda, and Theseus killed the Minotaur. I fancy the Minotaur must have been a tall and rather imposing animal to look at, six feet high at least, with a heavy white moustache, and a military carriage. And very likely he wore blue spectacles out of doors."

"And what was Theseus like?"

"I think we will call him Perseus, and our monster shall be Andromeda's terror. There is an ugly story, you know, about Theseus and Ariadne."

Cis flushed a sweet rosy red.

"Then tell me what Perseus was like."

"He was about as tall as the monster, perhaps not quite. He was very handsome, had curly brown hair, perhaps he had a moustache, he was about four-and-twenty years of age; he was greatly esteemed by everybody because he was so brave and strong; there was a mystery about his birth which only made him more romantic; there was, you know, about a good many of the ancients. Theseus, for instance, Achilles, Œdipus—the damsels all fell in love with him because there was no one in all Greece or the Isles half so handsome; but he kept himself away from all of them. I believe there is a story about some Queen offering him half her throne if he would marry her, but he would not—declined in the most respectful, but unmistakable terms. When she received his answer, and sent half-a-dozen men to murder him—because terrible is the wrath of a woman whose beauty has been despised—he stood with his back against a wall, with his short sword held so, and with his shield held in the other hand, he made mincemeat of all those six murderers together, and went on his way without further molestation. There was a Dryad once, too, who met him in an Arcadian forest, and proffered him, in return for his love, half the balance of her life. She said she didn't know how much there was left to run, but she thought about fifteen hundred years, or so, when she and her sister, and the great God Pan, would all be snuffed out together. Perseus told her that Love was immortal and not a slave to be bought or sold. So he passed away, and the Dryad, sitting under a tree, slowly pined and pined till Orpheus found her at last changed into the strings of an Æolian harp, and sighing most melodiously when the western breeze blew upon it. Perseus—"

"Laddy, talk sense."

"I can't, Cis. I feel as if Leonard was coming home to lift a great weight from both our hearts. I do not know how. I feel it. Perseus, however, was not callous to female loveliness, only he had given his heart away five years before, Cis, five years before."

"Laddy, I forbid you to go on."

"It is not a made-up story, Cis. I am certain it is all true. Arthur and Barbarossa are coming some day, to remove the miseries of the people. Why not Leonard to take away our troubles? We had no troubles when he went away. Now we are hampered and fettered, by no fault of our own, and I see no way out of it."

"Does the Captain know that it is so near?"

"Yes, he has not spoken of it to me, and he will not, I am sure. But he knows, and is looking forward. Last night I heard his step for an hour in his room, after he had gone to bed. He was thinking of Leonard, and could not sleep. And this morning he told Mrs. Jeram that you were going to stay all night to-morrow."

"Did he? The kind old Captain!"

"And that there would be another guest, and she was to get supper, a magnificent supper. The other guest, he explained, was to have his own room, and you were to have the spare room. Then I interposed, and said that a better arrangement would be to put the stranger into the spare bed in my room, so that he would not have to turn out. He grumbled and laughed, but he gave way."

"So he knows—but no one else."

"No one else; not even poor old Mrs. Jeram."

"We have gained a little time," said Celia; "Herr Räumer has not asked yet for my decision; but he has not given me up; and I am sure he will not. My father says nothing; but he starts if I come upon him suddenly. How will Leonard be able to help us with him?"

How indeed? And yet, somehow he was going to help. I was quite sure of it.

"And how will Leonard help us?" I asked.

"It is no use hoping," said Celia. "Leonard can help neither of us."

"He will help you, somehow, Cis. Of that be very sure. But he cannot help me."

"He shall help you, Laddy. Do you think we are going to let you go off to be killed?"

"I must," I said. "I have partly got over the revengeful madness which filled my soul when Wassielewski told me my story. I can think of a Russian, now, without wanting to tear his heart out. But the old man is right; I owe my life to the same cause in which my father and my mother lost theirs. If I can do anything for Poland, I must. And if Wassielewski tells me that it will be good for my country if I go out to get shot in his name, why I must do that. And I have sworn to do it on the cross that my father carved."

"Sworn! Laddy, of what power is an oath made under those conditions? You were maddened when you swore that oath. That old enthusiast ought never to have told you the story."

"Cis, dear. If I were to break that oath, it would break his heart. There is no way out of it at all. I must go."

That was the real reason. Heaven knows that during the first transport of rage, while before my eyes moved, visible in all the details, the long line of carts full of children, escorted by cavalry, and followed by shrieking women, running blindly along in the snow, and among them my poor mother, there was no scheme of vengeance, however mad, into which I wouldn't have plunged with joy. With calmer thoughts came better judgment, and I hope I shall not be accused of insensibility because I listened to Celia when she said that the perils of hopeless insurrection were not what my mother's death called for. There is no blacker story in all the black record of Russia than that robbery and murder of those helpless children; no wail yet resounding within the vaults of space than my poor mother's last cry for her stolen child. And yet, oh sweet pure eyes; oh tender face; oh lips of soft and compassionate mould—would you wish in return for your death another tale of misery and retribution?

And if I did not go when the old man should think it the time to summon me, I should break his heart. It was the dream of his old age to carry back with him the son of his murdered mistress. He thought that because his own life had been spent in brooding over that cruel crime, all good Poles at home had done the same thing, and he dreamed that he had but to show himself with me beside him to say, "This is the child of Roman Pulaski, tortured to death in the mines, and Claudia, who died of cold and fatigue trying to save the child," and that thousands would rise from all quarters to die for Poland. For at least he entertained no illusions of possible success. Poland could not free herself in his lifetime; of that he was quite certain. All the more honour to those who, knowing the worst, were ready to brave the inevitable. When a man fixes his thoughts incessantly upon one thing, when day and night he is always dwelling upon a great aim, there comes or seems to come unto him, when his mind is charged with figures of the present and the future, the gift of prophecy. The mist which falls upon the spirit of the Highland seer is gloomy always, and full of woe. The prophet is always like him who would prophecy no good concerning Ahab, but only evil. As for me, I think:

> "Too dearly would be won
> The prescience of another's pain,
> If purchased by mine own."

Six years ago, when the maddest of all modern revolts, that of the Commune of Paris, was staggering to its doom in blood and flame, there was one man among the leaders, Delescluze by name, who out of a life of over sixty years had spent between thirty and forty in prison, for the sacred cause of the people. Twice had he travelled backwards and forwards on that cruel and stifling voyage between Brest and Cayenne. Many times had he been arrested on suspicion; he had been hauled before judges, brow-beaten, scoffed and punished; had he been in Prussia he would have had the administration of stick, with those cuffs, boxes of the ear, kicks, and addresses in the third person, which illustrate the superior sweetness and light of the land of *Geist*. Had he been in Russia he would have had the knout. As he was in France he only got prison, with insufficient food, and wretched lodging. There came the time of the Commune, prophesied by Heine, after the siege, when Delescluze for the first time in his life got his chance. It was really only the ghost of a chance, but he did his best with it. Of course he failed, as we know, and became, together with his party, a byword of execration, by him quite undeserved. When it was apparent, even to him, the most fervent believer in the Commune, that there really was no longer any hope left, the poor old man was sent forth to meet Death. He would not wait to be brought before a Court-martial, to have more questions to answer, more witnesses to hear examined, to listen to more speeches, to wait in suspense for the sentence which would do him to death, to go back to a miserable prison, and sit there till the hour struck, when in the cold grey of the spring dawn he was to be placed with his back against the wall of La Roquette and receive the bullets of the soldiers. All this was too wearisome. But he had to die. His work in the world was over. He had striven for the best; he had maintained his own ideal of purity and singleness of purpose; as he had lived for the Cause, so he would die amid its dying struggles. He descended into the street, took off his hat, as one should in the presence of Death, of God, and of the Judgment, and walked without a word along the way till he came to the first barricade. Up to this he climbed, and then standing, his long white hair streaming in the wind, his sorrowful eyes looking upwards, his face full of that great love for humanity which made him half divine, he awaited the bullet, which was not long in coming.

When I read the story of the death of Delescluze, when I conversed with a man who actually saw it, I thought of poor old Wassielewski, for such was he, as unselfish, as simple, as strong in his conviction, and careless of himself, if, by spending and being spent, he could advance the Cause.

With brave words and a great pretence at cheerfulness I comforted poor Celia, and prophesied her release; but I could not feel the assurance I pretended. How could Leonard, if he were ever so successful, free her so as to leave her father safe from the German's revenge? How could he release me from the oath which bound me to the old Pole, and yet not darken the last years of his life with the thought that the child of the Lady Claudia was a traitor to his mother's cause?

We had been living in a fool's paradise, expecting such great things; and now at the very time when they ought to be coming off, we were face to face with the cold truth.

"We must not think of ourselves any more, Laddy," said Cis, as if reading my heart. "If Leonard can help us, he will. At all events, he will be on our side. I shall wait patiently until I am called upon to give my answer, and then, Laddy—and then if for my father's sake "—she broke off and left the sentence unfinished. "You must both of you try not to think badly of me."

"We shall never think badly of you, whatever you do, Cis," I said, a little huskily.

"Come home with me, Laddy," she said, rising from the grass. "It is nearly eight o'clock. See, the tide is high; we shall have everything to-morrow evening just as it was five years ago; a splendid evening; a flowing tide; the light of a midsummer sunset on the water; the buttercups and daisies out upon the meadow; the long green grass waving on the ramparts and growing up before the mouth of the cavern; you and I, dear Laddy, standing by the old gun, waiting for him. What was it he promised? 'In velvet or in rags—in riches or poverty, I will come to see you on the 2 ist of June, 1858.' And now it is the 20th. Laddy—tell me how he will come."

"We shall see him first," I said, "crossing the meadow, just down there. We shall know him by the backward toss of his head. Presently we shall see his brown curls, and then his eyes and his mouth. He will see us then, and his lips and eyes will laugh a welcome before he runs up the slope. Then he will spring upon us in his old way, and— and—where he said good-bye, Cis, he kissed you."

"We are older now," said Cis. "And do not be silly, sir. As if men want to kiss like children!"

"It depends, my dear," I replied wisely, "on the object. However, that will be the manner of his return. And then we shall all three march off to the Captain's, Leonard between us; and should be singing as we went, but for the look of the thing: Leonard will be asking us questions about the dear old Captain and everybody—wait—Cis—wait for four-and-twenty hours."

I went home with her. Herr Räumer was talking to Mrs. Tyrrell in the drawing-room. We had a little music. The German played and sang one or two of his Volkslieder in his most sentimental manner, but we listened very little. Mr. Tyrrell was in his office, and I crept down to see him.

He was sitting in an attitude of profound melancholy before a pile of papers.

"Shut the door, Laddy, boy," he said wearily. "Who is upstairs?"

"Herr Räumer, Mrs. Tyrrell, and Cis."

He sighed.

"He is beginning to worry about an answer. What would Celia say?"

"Celia would be made wretched for life. It cannot be. Is it quite, quite necessary?"

"There is one way out of it," he murmured.

I stood still and looked at him.

"What is the one way out of it?"

"There are two ways—Death and Dishonour. Let no one know, Laddy. Think of me as you must, only think that for no other cause would I ask this thing of my child. Poor Celia! Poor Celia!"

He drew his hand across his forehead.

"I cannot sleep—I cannot work—I can think of nothing else. Do you believe I like to have that man here—that cold and selfish cynic—that I willingly tolerate him in my house, to say nothing of seeing him hang about my daughter? But I am a lost man, Ladislas. I am a lost and guilty man, and I must abide my lot."

A lost and guilty man! And this the most successful man in the town!

He pointed to the safe painted outside "Herr Räumer."

"The papers are there—locked up. If I only had the key for one minute Celia would be free."

CHAPTER XXVIII.
THE TWENTY-FIRST OF JUNE.

THE day fulfilled its promise of the evening: it was one of those most perfect and glorious days which sometimes fall in June, and make that month, in full summer and yet with all the hope and promise of the year before it, the most delightful of any. I rose early, because I could not sleep; but I found the Captain up before me, at work in the garden. But he prodded the ground nervously, and made little progress. At prayers he opened the Bible at random, and read what fell first before his eyes. It was a chapter of the Song of Solomon, and as he read his voice faltered.

"'The watchmen that go about the city found me: to whom I said, Saw ye him whom my soul loveth?

"'It was but a little that I passed from them, but I found him whom my soul loveth.'"

Then he stopped, having read only the first four verses of the chapter; and to him, as to me, they seemed to be of good omen.

He did not mention Leonard's name, but he presently went upstairs, and I knew he was gone to see that the room was in order for him. He brought out certain articles of family plate which only saw the light on grand occasions: and I caught him making extensive and costly preparations with a couple of bottles of champagne. All day he was very serious. Nor did he, as usual, go out upon those mysterious rounds of his, of which I have spoken.

"Celia will come here to dinner, sir."

"Ay—ay . The earlier the better. Celia cannot come too early or too often." He sat down in his wooden arm-chair and began to nurse his leg in a meditative fashion.

"Laddy Celia Tyrrell is a very beautiful girl."

"Have you only found that out to-day, sir?" I asked. "Why, she is the most beautiful girl in all the world, I believe."

"I was thinking—Laddy—if things are all right—and they must be all right, or else he would have written—when he comes home—he might—I know I should have done so at his age—he might—fall in love with her. She must have a good husband, the best husband that we can find for her. Look high or low, Laddy, I can see no one but Leonard that will do for her."

"But you have not seen him yet. And he may have fallen in love with some one else."

"Nonsense, boy. As if I did not know what he is like. Curs don't grow out of lion's cubs; you can't turn a white boy into a nigger; and a Portugee, as every sailor knows, is a Portugee by birth."

Then we began, as we had done the night before, speculating how the wanderer would return. He was above all things, according to the Captain, to be strong, handsome, and successful.

Celia came to our midday dinner, and when it was over we moved into the garden, and sat under the old mulberry-tree. The sun was streaming full upon the sheet of water before us, and a light breeze crisped the surface.

We spread the rugs on the grass, and all three sat down upon them, Celia lying with her head on the Captain's knees, while he sat with his back against the tree. It was peaceful and quiet, save for the boom of the mill hard by, and to that we were accustomed.

The excitement of the day touched Celia's cheek with a light flush, and heightened the brightness of her eyes. I had never before seen her more perfectly beautiful than on that afternoon. The Captain's eyes rested on her face, and his hand was in her hair with a gentle caress.

"This was where you were sleeping," she said in a low voice, "when he first came."

We did not say "Leonard" on this day, because our minds were full of him, and a pronoun was quite as useful as the noun.

The Captain nodded his head.

"Just here, my dear," he replied,"and just such an afternoon as this, without the breeze, and maybe a thought warmer. It was in August, when the mulberries are ripe. I came out after dinner. My dinners were solitary enough then, before I had the boys to mess with me, and I sat under the tree and smoked my pipe. Then I fell fast asleep. What woke me was the mulberries dropping on my face, and then I looked up and saw the pretty rogue laughing at me, with his mouth full of mulberries, and his face and hands stained black with mulberry juice. Ho! ho! and he began to laugh at once. What a boy he was! What a boy! Never any boy like him for spirit. A thousand pities he wasn't a sailor."

"And you never lost sight of him after that?" said Celia.

"No, my pretty—never after that. It was a matter of a year or two though before I found out that I was a lonely old bachelor, and wanted the boys with me. Wanted them badly, you may be sure. We had a good spell of fine weather, those years you were both of you at school, Laddy, hadn't we?"

"Indeed we had, sir."

"I was at sea when I was thirteen, and I hadn't much experience of shore-going boys till then. To be sure, I was always fond of watching boys at play, and talking to them— perhaps throwing in a word on the great subject of duty. But Lord! the things I learned from those two! The pretty ways of them when they were next door to babies! and their growing up to be boys together bit by bit. Then how they grew to be self-reliant, and how we all grew to understand each other! My dear," the good old man continued simply, "if I were to give you what is best for all of us, man or woman, I would give you children. You can't distrust the Lord when you have felt what it is for the little children to trust and love you. I never had a wife, but I have had two boys all the same. Both good sons to me—Laddy, there, will not be jealous—and to each his gifts; but Leonard was born, like Nelson, without fear."

"Always a brave boy, was he not, Captain?" Celia murmured.

"It's a rare gift. Most of us learn by experience how to go into action without fear, and a fight is a red-letter day for soldiers as well as sailors. But Leonard would have gone in laughing as a middy. It's a beautiful thing to see a plucky boy! You remember how he used to come home after a fight, Laddy? The other boy always struck his colours, eh?—and generous and thoughtful with it, too. Why did I ever consent to his going away for five years?"

"Patience!" said Cis. "Tell me more about him."

We kept the Captain amused all the afternoon with yarns of Leonard's school life, while in the quiet garden the big bumble bees droned, and the hollyhocks turned their great foolish faces to the sun, while the mill went grinding as the water ran out with the tide to the deep-toned music of its heavily-turning wheels, and the golden sunshine of June lay upon the rippled waters of the mill-dam, and lit with flashes of dazzling light the leaves of the trees upon the little island redoubt.

At six I brought out a table and chair, and we had tea in the garden, also under the mulberry tree. Cis made it for us; she always made it so much better than we did.

And then the time began to drag, and the Captain to look at his watch furtively. Presently the mill stopped, and everything became quite still. That meant that it was seven o'clock.

Then Celia and I rose from the table.

"We are going for a walk, Captain," said Cis.

"Mayn't I go too?" he asked wistfully.

She shook her head with decision.

"Certainly not. You have got to stay at home. We have got to go to the walls and—and walk about there—and talk. And we shall not be back till a quarter to nine, or perhaps later. Perhaps, Captain, we shall bring you some news—Oh! What news will it be?" she cried eagerly.

No one on the Queen's Bastion, when we got there; Celia's Arbour as deserted as any outwork of Palmyra; no one on the long straight stretch of wall between the gate and the Bastion—not even a nurse with children; and our own corner as green and grassy, as shaded by the great elm, as when, five years ago, Leonard bade us farewell there. Nothing changed here, at any rate.

"Laddy," whispered Celia, in awe-struck tones, "suppose, after all, he should not come."

"He will come, Celia; but we are an hour before our time."

"Oh! what a long day it has been! I am selfish. I have been able to think of nothing but my own troubles until to-day. And now they seem to be all forgotten in this great anxiety."

We walk up and down the quiet wall, talking idly of things unimportant, talking to pass the time.

Eight struck from half-a-dozen clocks, from the clock in the Dockyard, the clock on the Ordnance Wharf, the clock of St. Faith's, the clock of St. John's, from all of them. The splendid sun was sloping fast towards Jack the Painter's Point; the great harbour, for it was high tide, just as on that night when Leonard went away, was a vast lake of molten fire, with sapphire edging below our feet. We leaned against the rampart and looked out, but we were no longer thinking of the Harbour or the light upon it.

Five years since he left us, a tall stripling of seventeen, to seek his fortune in the wide and friendless world. Five years. Celia was a little girl who was now so tall and fair. In her, at least, Leonard would not be disappointed. And I? Well, I suppose I was much the same to look at. And for my fortunes, there was little to tell, and nothing to be proud of. Only a music-master in a provincial town; only an organist to a church; a composer of simple songs to please myself and Celia. But what would he be like? What tale would he have to tell us? What adventures to relate? In what part of the world had his fortunes drifted him?

Five years. They make a girl into a woman; a boy into a man; five links in the chain of time; time to make new friends, to form and lose new loves; to strengthen a purpose; to make or mar a life. Had they made or had they marred the life of Leonard?

"What will he say when he sees us?" murmured Celia."He will remember, Cis, the words of Spencer—

" 'Tell me, ye merchant's daughters, did ye see
So fair a creature in your town before?
So sweet, so lovely, and so mild as she,
Adorned with beauty's grace and virtue's store.' "

"Don't, Laddy, please. Let us talk only of him until he comes."

"Where is he now?" she whispered, looking round. "On the road walking quickly, so as to keep his promise to the minute? Is he in the train? Do you think he came last night, and has been hiding away in an hotel all day for fear of meeting us before the time? O Laddy! let us move about at least. I cannot stand here doing nothing."

The minutes passed slowly on. I looked at my watch.

"Twenty minutes more. Courage, Cis! Only twenty minutes. Where are your thoughts now?"

"I was thinking of the dear old time. Listening to his talk about the great world—it lay over there, you remember, behind the harbour and the hill. Wishing I had been a man, to go with him and fight the world beside him."

"Five years ago, Cis! Why, Leonard may have lost his faith in his own power, and—"

"Don't, Laddy. Not now. It is all we have to believe in. And—and—Laddy—please—do not tell him what you told me."

"I understand, dear Cis. I have forgotten that I ever told you."

"Not but that you made me happy and proud; any girl would be proud to think of having had, if only for a day, such a hope and such a love. But he must never know. And yet I should be ashamed to hide things from him."

"Until you tell him yourself then, Cis."

I looked at my watch again. Heavens! had Time tumbled down and hurt himself, so that he could only crawl? Only a quarter-past eight. Fifteen minutes more.

"Where are you now, Cis?"

"I am thinking what a difference he will see in us, and we in him. Why, I was only a child, a girl of fourteen, then, and you were only fifteen."

"At least," I said, "he will see no difference in me. I am no taller and no straighter. But you—oh! Celia, if you only knew how beautiful he will think you! "

"That is only what you think, dear Laddy. Beautiful? Oh! if I ever had any thoughts that are not common or mean, it is because you have put them into my heart. What should I be now, if I had not had you, all these five long years?"

She stooped, and kissed my cheek.

I could endure that now—I could kiss her in return—without that old passionate yearning which, a very little while before, had been wont to set the blood tingling in every pulse at very sight of her. The monks of old were quite right in one thing, though, as a Protestant, I am bound to think that they had a very confused and imperfect sort of perception. I mean that you may, by dint of resolution and patience—they would call it prayer and penance—quite beat down and entirely subdue any inclination of the heart or intellect. They started with the supposition that every man was bound to fall in love with every woman. That is absurd, but an intelligible position on the score of monkish ignorance. I, for my part, was only in danger once of falling in love. Having seen, known, and learned the sweet nature of one woman, it was not possible that I should ever fall in love with another.

We kissed each other on the lips, and then we sat with clasped hands upon the sloping bank, waiting. At last the clock struck the half-hour, and we turned together and looked across the green.

Suddenly came a figure, a ragged figure, walking swiftly across the grass.

Yes, as I had prophesied, by the backward fling of his head, by the proud carriage, by the firm and elastic walk, we knew him.

Celia clasped my hands convulsively, and I hers; and before she sprang to her feet she whispered—

"See, he is ragged—he is poor—he has failed. Not a word, not a look, Laddy, to let him see what we feel. Oh, my poor Leonard! my poor Leonard!"

She made a little moan, and then ran forward to meet him. For it was Leonard himself and no other, who, at sight of us, came bounding up the grass slope with quick and eager step, and in a moment was with us, holding Celia by both his hands, and gazing in her face with eyes that spoke of love— of love—of love. Who could mistake that look! Not Celia, who met the look once, and then dropped her eyes shamefaced. Not I, who knew by sad experience what love might be, how strong a king, how great a conqueror.

In one glance we caught the melancholy truth. He was in rags; there was no petty pretence of genteel shabbiness; there was no half-failure, he was in rags absolute. He wore a battered old felt hat, the brim of which, partly torn, hung over his right eye; he had on a coat which was a miracle for shabbiness; it was green where it ought to have been black; shiny where it had once exhibited a youthful gloss; and it had a great hole on the left shoulder, such a hole as would be caused by carrying a bundle on a stick. The coat, an old frock, was fastened by the two surviving buttons across his chest. One could see that he had no waistcoat, and his trousers were in the last stage of dilapidation and decay. He wore neither collar nor neck-tie. But it was Leonard. There was no mistake about him. Leonard come back to us on the day that he promised. Leonard, dressed as a beggar and stepping like a prince.

"Celia!—Laddy! "

"Leonard!"

Both hands; not one. And as he clasped her tight she drew nearer to him, and like a child who holds up his face to be kissed, she looked up at him. But there was no kiss. Men, as Celia said, are not like children, always wanting to kiss. Oho! Cis, as if you knew! Man's love is like the morning sun, which, falling on his bride, the earth, draws up sweet mists which rise to hide her blushes. Leonard was come back, and now I understood how in her mind Leonard was to make all straight, because Leonard loved her, and she loved Leonard. And he a beggar.

He got one hand free, and gave it to me.

"Laddy! Well? You at least are not changed. But look at Celia!"

"Take off your hat, Leonard," she said. "Let us look at your face. Laddy! He is just the same, except for that." She laughed, and patted her own upper lip with her fingers. Leonard had grown a great moustache. "And his face is bronzed. Where have you been, sir, to get your face so brown? Fie! What a bad hat! A great hole in the side of it, and look what a coat to come home in! Dear, dear, before we take him home to the Captain we must dress him up. What a pity he is too tall to wear your things, Laddy. Now we have found him again we will never let him go. Will we? He is our prodigal son, Laddy, who has come back to us—back to us," and here she broke down, and burst into tears. "We have so longed for you, have we not, Laddy? And the time has been so weary, waiting for you."

"But I am come at last, Celia," he said, with eyes that filled—I had never before seen a tear in Leonard's eyes—"I have kept my promise. See —in rags and tatters, with empty pockets." He turned them out.

"What does it matter," she cried, "so long as we have you, how you come?"

"And the Captain?"

"He is well," I told him, "and waiting at home for us all. Come, Leonard."

He hesitated, and looked with a humorous smile at his ragged habiliments.

"What will the Captain say to these rags? Dear old boy, it is not as he expects, is it? Nor as you expected, Celia."

"No, Leonard, I am sorry for your ill-success. But it wasn't your own fault?"

"No, certainly not my own fault," he replied, with a queer look. "Not my own fault. I have done my best. Celia and Laddy! How jolly it is to say the two names over again with their owners in the old place! And how often have I said them to myself, thousands of miles away,"—he had been a traveller, then. "Suppose you two go first to the Captain, and prepare him. Will not that be best? Say that he must not be surprised to find me coming home in a sad plight—all in rags, you know—tell him about the hat, Laddy, and then—I will only be a quarter of an hour after you—he won't be so very much shocked. Will you do this? Good. Then, in a quarter of an hour, I will be there."

He caught Celia's hand and kissed it, looking her in the eyes half lovingly, half amused, and ran down the slope as lightly as if he was come back a conquering prince.

We looked at each other in stupefaction. Was it really Leonard? Was it a strange dream?

"Can you understand it, Celia?"

"Not yet, Laddy, dear. Do not speak to me just now."

"His hands were white," I went on, unheeding, "like the hands of a gentleman; his boots were good and new, the boots of a gentleman; and his face—did that look like the face of a beggar, Celia?"

"Always the same face, Laddy. The dearest face in all the world to you and to me, isn't it? Poor and in rags. Poor—poor Leonard!"

"I don't know," I replied,"whether your face isn't dearer to me than Leonard's. That is because I have seen more of it, perhaps. But why is he in such a dreadful plight? He said he had been thousands of miles away. He must have been an emigrant in America, and failed."

Of course that was it. He must have gone to America as an emigrant and failed.

We crept slowly and sadly back, like a pair of guilty children. What were we to say to the Captain? Who should break the news?

CHAPTER XXIX.
"A SURPRISE."

THE Captain, dressed in his Sunday blue uniform coat and white ducks, was sitting at his table, pretending to read. At least he had a book open before him, but I observed that it was upside down, and it was not usual with the Captain to read with the book in that position. But it was getting dark; the sunset gun had gone half an hour before; and the twilight of the longest day was lying over the garden and the smooth waters of the Mill Dam. Perhaps, therefore, the Captain could see to read no more, and, indeed, his eyes were not so good as they had been. The candles were on the table, but they were not lit; and the cloth was laid for supper. He had been listening to our footsteps, and when we came in looked up with a quick air of expectation which changed to disappointment.

"You two?" he cried. "Back again?—And alone—alone?"

We had pretended, all day long, not to know who was coming in the evening, but the pretence broke down now.

Celia threw her arms round his neck and kissed him.

"Dear old Captain," she whispered; "yes, he has come back—our Leonard has come home again to us."

He started to his feet trembling.

"Where is he, then? Why do you look at me like that? Why does he not come to me? What is it, Laddy?"

"Perhaps, sir, he is ashamed to come."

"Ashamed? Leonard ashamed? Why?"

"Suppose," said Celia, laying her hand on the Captain's shoulder, "suppose, Captain dear, that our boy, after he had promised his friends to come back triumphant, found the world too strong for him, and had to come back—in poverty, and not triumphant at all?"

"Is that all?" cried the stout old Captain. "Leonard has failed, has he? That is nothing. Many a lad fails at first. Give him rope enough and no favour, and he'll do in the long-run. It's the confounded favour plays the mischief, ashore as well as afloat. Leonard has not had fair play. Where is the boy?"

And at this moment a step in the hall, and a scream, and a shuffle, showed that the "boy" was arrived, and in the arms of the faithful Jeram.

"Oh, my beautiful boy—oh! my bonnie boy. Let your old nurse kiss you once again—and you so tall and brave."

The Captain could restrain himself no longer.

"Leonard," he shouted, breaking through Celia's arms, "Leonard, ahoy! Welcome home, my lad."

We caught each other's hands and trembled, waiting for the moment when the Captain should discover the rags and tatters.

"Shall I light the candles, Laddy?"

"Not yet, Celia. Yes—do—it will be best so. The Captain must know all in a few minutes."

They were in the hall, laughing, shaking hands, and asking each other all round, and all at once, how they were, and how they had been.

"Supper at once, Mrs. Jeram," cried the jolly old Captain. "Supper at once. Such a feast we will make. And none of your fanteegs about not sitting down with Miss Celia, Mrs. Jeram, if you please. Now then, Leonard, my boy, come and talk to Laddy and Celia. Lord! how glad I am, how glad I am!"

We look at each other. One moment, and the rags would be visible to the naked eye.

"Poor Leonard—Oh, poor Leonard!" Celia whispered.

Then we started and cried out together, for the Captain and he came in together, the Captain with his hand upon Leonard's stalwart shoulder, and a face which was like the ocean for its multitudinous smile.

But where were the rags?

They were gone. Before us stood the handsomest man, I believe, in all the world. He was nearly six feet high, his light brown hair lay m short crisp curls upon his head, his eyes had the frankest, loyalest look in them that I have ever seen in any man, and at that moment the happiest look as well. I declare that I have never seen in all my forty years of life so splendid a man as Leonard was at five-and-twenty. As he did not look one-half so splendid in rags one is bound to admit that clothes do improve even the finest figure. And as he stood in the doorway with the Captain I was dazzled by the beauty and vigour of the man. As for his dress, it was nothing but a plain black coat, with light summer trousers, just as any gentleman might wear. That was it: any gentleman.

He had succeeded, then.

"I beg your pardon, Celia, and yours, Laddy," said Leonard. "The foolish thought came into my head to see how you would receive me if I were to return in poverty and rags. So I masqueraded. I meant to come on here and see the Captain too, just as I was. But I had not the heart when I saw the pain it gave you. So I made an excuse and gave up the silly trick. Forgive me, Celia."

Her eyes, which had been frank with pity, looked more shyly into Leonard's as she listened.

"What is there to forgive, Leonard? If we were glad to have you back again any way, how much more glad ought we to be that you have come back—as you are?"

"But you do not know me—as I am."

"Come, come, no explanations now," cried the Captain. "Supper first, talk afterwards. I am so glad. Here's something I found to-day in your room, Master Leonard. See if you have forgotten the old tune."

Of course he had not forgotten it. It was the old fife on which he used to play the "Roast Beef of Old England" every Sunday before dinner. Leonard laughed, took up his position at the door, and piped lustily while the maid brought in the supper.

We all sat down, I at the end, and Celia on the Captain's right, Leonard at his left, and Mrs. Jeram next him. I don't think we ate much at that supper, though it consisted of cold fowls and ham, the Captain's fixed idea of what a supper ought to be, but we had a bottle of champagne, a drink looked upon in those days as a costly luxury, to be reserved for weddings, Christmas dinners, and such great occasions. What greater occasion than the welcome home of the exile!

"No explanations till after supper," repeated the Captain. "Celia, my pretty, not a question. Take another wing, my dear. No? Then Leonard shall have it. Leonard, my boy, here's to you again. Your health, my lad. After supper, you shall tell us all. I am so glad."

Supper finished, I began.

"Now, Leonard."

"Not yet," said the Captain. "The Bible and Prayer-book, Laddy, my boy."

Putting on his glasses, the old man turned over the pages till he found what he wanted.

Then he laid his hand upon the place and looked up.

"Before I read the chapter," he said, "I wish to say that I thank God for my two boys, and for the trust that has always been with me, firm and strong, that the one who was away in the world would turn out as good in the matter of duty as the one who stayed with me."

And then, to our extreme discomfiture, he proceeded to read the story of the Prodigal Son. What on earth had the Prodigal Son to do with us at this juncture? Prayers despatched—he was always brief, after the manner of sailors, over prayers—he made another little speech.

"Since Leonard went away," he said, "which is five years to-day, as long a cruise as ever I made in the old days, I've been drawn towards this parable till I know it by heart. I've thought at times—What if Leonard were to come back like that young man with five years' neglect of duty upon his mind? How should we have to receive him? And here I find the directions laid down plain. Lord! Lord! how plain a man's course is marked out for him, with lighthouses along the coast, and the mariner's compass, and the stars to steer by at night—if only he would use his eyes. Well, Mrs. Jeram, ma'am, and Celia, and Laddy, it was clear what we all had to do. And though a dreadful thought crossed my mind when you came home without him, and beat about the bush, talking of failure and such things, which I now perceive to have been only the remains of the devilment that always hung about the lad, I went out into the passage bold, and prepared, I hope, to act according to open orders. Somehow, we generally think, when we read this Divine parable, of the young man. To-night, all through supper, I've been thinking about his father, and I have been pitying that father. What if his boy, who had been away from home for five years or thereabouts, came home to him, not as he did, in rags and disgrace, but proud and tall, bringing his sheaves with him, my dear—bringing his sheaves with him! Think of that; for I am so glad, Leonard, I am so glad and happy."

We were all silent while the good old man cleared his throat and wiped his eyes. Celia leaned her head upon his shoulder and wept unrestrainedly.

"Therefore I say," continued the Captain, "the Lord be thanked for all His mercies, and if Laddy will play the Hundredth Psalm, and Celia will sing it with him, I think it would do good both to Mrs. Jeram and to me."

"Thank you, my children," he said, when we had finished. "That hymn expresses my feelings exactly. And now, Leonard, that we've got the decks clear of all superfluous gear, and are shipshape, and have had supper, and drunk the champagne, and thanked God. I will light my pipe, and Celia shall mix me the customary—double ration to-night, my pretty—and you shall give us the log."

"Shall I begin at the end, sir, or at the beginning?" asked Leonard.

"The end," said Celia.

"The beginning," said the Captain, both in a breath.

"What do you say, Mrs. Jeram?" Leonard asked the old lady.

She said, crossing her hands before her, that, beginning or end, it would be all the same to her; that she was quite satisfied to see him back again, and the beautifullest boy he was that God ever made—flash o' lighting about the place just as he always had a done; and she was contented, so long as he was well and happy, to wait for that story for ever, so as she could only look at him.

"What do you say, Laddy?"

"Ask the Captain," I said. "He commands this ship, but Celia is our passenger."

"Good," said the Captain. "My dear, the ship's in luck to get such a lovely passenger as you. And you shall command the ship instead of me, so long as you don't run her ashore. Now then, Leonard, the end of the log first."

"First," said Leonard, "by way of preface to my log—you remember this?"

He drew a black ribbon from his neck with a gold ring upon it.

"A good beginning, my lad—your mother's ring."

"You remember what you said to me when you gave it to me? That it was an emblem of honour and purity among women, and that I was to wear it only so long as I could deserve it?"

"Ay—ay. This is a very good beginning of the end, Celia, my love. Go on, Leonard."

"I believe I have not forfeited the right to wear it still, sir."

"I never thought you would," said the Captain, with decision. "Go on, my lad—keep on paying out the line."

"Then the end is," he said modestly, "that I bear Her Majesty's Commission, and am a Captain in the Hundred and Twentieth. We disembarked from India a week ago, and are now lying in the Old Kent Barracks in this town. Here, sir, are my medals—Alma, Inkermann, Sebastopol, and India. I have seen service since I left you, and I have gone through all the fighting without a wound or a day's illness."

"You are a combatant officer in Her Majesty's service like myself?"cried the Captain, springing to his feet.

"I am Captain Copleston, raised from the ranks by singular good fortune; and five years ago a raw recruit sitting on a wooden bench at Westminster, with all my work ahead."

"Like me, he has seen service; like me, he holds Her Majesty's Commission; like me, he can show his medals."

He spread out his hands solemnly. "Children, children"— he spoke to Celia and to me—"did we ever dare to think of this?"

CHAPTER XXX.
LEONARD TELLS HIS STORY.

THEN Leonard began his story. The room was lit by the single pair of candles standing one each side of the model of the *Asia*, on the mantleshelf. The Captain sat with his pipe in his wooden chair, his honest red face glowing with satisfaction, and beside him Celia leaning on his shoulder and listening with rapt eyes. It was Dido listening to Æneas. "With varied talk did Dido prolong the night, deep were the draughts of love she drank. 'Come,' said she, 'my guest, and tell us from the first beginning the stratagems of the enemy and the hap of our country then, and your own wanderings, for this is now the *fifth* summer that carries you a wanderer o'er every land and sea.'" As Dido wept to hear, so did Celia sigh and sob and catch her breath as Leonard told his story. No Gascon, he; but there are stories in which the hero, be he as modest as a wood-nymph, needs must proclaim his heroism. And a hero at four-and-twenty is ten times as interesting as a hero of sixty.

"Oh, talk not to me of a name great in story,
The days of our youth are the days of our glory;
And the myrtle and ivy of sweet two-and-twenty
Are worth all your laurels, though ever so plenty."

And what is it when the myrtle and ivy of two-and-twenty have real laurels mixed up with them?

A philosopher so great that people grovel before his name, in a work on the Subjection of Women, makes the astounding statement that the influence of woman has always been in the direction of peace and the avoidance of war. Pity he had not read history by the light of poetry. Was there ever, one asks in astonishment, a time when women did not love courage and strength? It was not only in the days of chivalry that young knights fought before the eyes of their mistresses—

"Since doughty deeds my lady please,
Right soon I'll mount my steed;
And strong his arm and fast his seat
That bears frae me the meed."

How could it be otherwise? We love the qualities which most we lack.

If women ceased to be gentle, tender, soft—what we call womanly—we should leave off falling in love. That is most certain. Who ever fell in love with one of the unsexed women? And I suppose if men ceased to be strong and courageous, women would leave off accepting and rejoicing in their love. Dido drank deep draughts of love listening to the tale of Æneas which was, as Scarron many years afterwards remarked, extremely long and rather dull. So sat Celia listening to a much more wonderful story of battle and endurance. Or, I thought, she was more like the gentle maid of Venice than the proud Phoenician queen. With such sweetness did Desdemona listen when the valiant Moor told of the dangers he had passed. Did she, as John Stuart Mill would have us believe, incline to ways of peace? Quite the contrary; this sweet and gentle Desdemona wished "that Heaven had made her such a man," and when her lord, must go to slay the Turk she would fain go with him. My gentle Celia wept over the brave soldiers who went forth to fight, and again over those who were brought home to die; but her heart, womanlike, was ready to open out to the most valiant.

"I went up to town," he began, "with my ten pounds, as you all know. When I arrived at Waterloo Station I discovered for the first time that I had formed no plans how to begin. The problem before me was the old difficulty, how a man with a reasonable good education and no friends had best start so as to become a gentleman. I faced that problem for a fortnight trying to find a practical solution. I might become a clerk—and end there; a mechanical copying clerk in a City office!"

"Faugh! " said the Captain.

"Or an usher in a school—and end there."

"Fudge !" said the Captain.

"Or a strolling actor, and trust to chance to make a name for myself."

"Pshaw! " said the Captain.

"There were men, I knew, who made money by writing for the papers. I thought I might write too, and I found out where they mostly resorted, and tried to talk to them. But that profession, I very soon discovered, wanted other qualities than I possessed. Laddy might have taken to writing; but it was not my gift."

"Right," said the Captain. "Laddy, you remember the story of my old messmate who once wrote a novel. 'Twas his ruin, poor fellow. Never lifted his head afterwards. Go on, Leonard."

"All the time I was looking about me the money, of course, was melting fast. I might have made it last longer, I dare say; but I was ignorant, and got cheated. One morning I awoke to the consciousness that there was nothing left at all except the purse. Well, sir, I declare that I was relieved. The problem was solved, because I knew then that the only line possible for me was to enlist. I went down to Westminster and took the shilling. Of course I was too proud to enlist under any but my own name. Going a soldiering is no disgrace."

"Right," said the Captain.

"Well," he went on, "it is no use pretending I was happy at first, because the life was hard, and the companionship was rough. But the drill came easy to me who had seen so many drills upon the Common, and, after a bit, I found myself as good a soldier as any of them. One fretted a little under the rules and the discipline; that was natural at first. There seemed too much pipeclay and too little personal ease. One or two of the sergeants were unfair on the men too, and bore little spites. Some of the officers were martinets; I offended one because I refused to become a servant."

"You a servant, Leonard!" cried Celia.

He laughed.

"The officers like a smart lad; but it was not to be a valet that I enlisted, and I refused, as a good many others refused. Our lads were mostly sturdy Lancashire boys, proud of being soldiers, but had not enlisted to black other men's boots. It makes me angry now—which is absurd—to think that I should have been asked to become a lackey. Well, it was a hard life, that in the ranks. Not the discipline, nor the work, nor the drill—though these were hard enough. It was the roughness of the men. There were one or two gentlemen among us—one fellow who had been an officer in the Rifles—but they were a bad and hopeless lot, who kept up as best they could the vices which had ruined them. They were worse than any of the rough rollicking countryside lads. I can't say I had much room for hope in those days, Celia."

She reddened, but said nothing. I remembered, suddenly, what he might mean.

"Things looked about as black for a few months as they well could. Rough work, rough food, rough campaigning. I thought of Coleridge and his adventures as a private, but he turned back, while I, for there was nothing else to do—resolved to keep on. And then, bit by bit, one got to like it. For one thing, I could do all sorts of things better than most men—my training with the Poles came in there—it was found that I could fence: it got about that I played cricket, and I was put in the eleven—to play in the matches of the regiment, officers and men together; once, when we had a little row with each other, it was found that I could handle my fists, which always gains a man respect. And then they came to call me Gentleman Jack; and, as I heard afterwards, the officers got to know it, and the Colonel kept his eye upon me. Of course one may wear the soldier's jacket very well without falling into any of the pits which are temptations to these poor fellows, so that it was easy enough getting the good conduct stripe, and to be even made corporal. The first proud day, however, was that when I was made a sergeant, with as good a knowledge of my work, I believe, as any sergeant in the Line."

Mrs. Jeram shook her head.

"More," she said, "much more."

"A sergeant," said Leonard. "It sounds so little now, but to me, then, it seemed so much. The first real step upwards out of the ruck. The old dream that I should return triumphant somehow was gone long since, or it was a dream that had no longer any faith belonging to it. And I began to say to myself that to win my way after two years to a sergeant's stripes was perhaps as much honour as Providence intended for me."

The Captain murmured something about mysterious ways. Then he patted Celia's head tenderly, and begged Leonard to keep on his course.

"Well," said Leonard, "you have heard how the great luck began. It was just before the Crimean War that I got the stripes. We were among the first regiments ordered. How well I remember embarking at this very place, half afraid, half hoping, to see you all, but I did not."

"We were there, Leonard," said Celia, "when the first troops embarked. I think I remember them all going."

"It is a solemn thing," Leonard went on, "going off to war. It is not only that your life is to be hazarded—every man hazards his life in all sorts of ways as much as on a battlefield—but you feel that you are going to help in adding another chapter to the history of the world."

"Ay," said the Captain. "History means war."

"Let us pass over the first two or three months. We went to Varna, where we lost many men needlessly by cholera, waiting till the Generals could make up their minds. I suppose they could not avoid the delay, but it was a bad thing for the rank and file, and we were all right glad when the orders came to embark for the Crimea. We were amongst the earliest to land, and my first experience of fighting was at Alma. One gets used to the bullets after a bit; but the first time—you know, Captain—"

The Captain nodded.

"After Alma we might, as we know very well, have pushed straight on to Sebastopol. I doubt whether that would have finished the war, which had to be fought out somewhere. Russia had to learn that an immense army is not by itself proof of immense power. And so it was just as well, I believe, that we moved as we did.

"You know all about the battles—the Alma, Inkermann, Balaclava, and the rest. Our fellows went through most of the fighting, and, of course, I with the rest. The hardest day was Inkermann. We had just come in at daybreak from the trenches, where we had been on duty for four-and-twenty hours, when we were turned out to fight in the fog and rain. We fought in our greatcoats—well—all that is history. But the days of battle were red letter days for all of us, and what tried us most was the inaction, and the dreary waiting work in the trenches. And yet it was that work which got me my commission.

"You know what it was we had to do. Before the Redan and the Malakoff were our batteries, the French attack on the Mamelon and the Malakoff was on our right. Separating our right from our left attack was the valley which they called the Valley of the Shadow of Death, along which they carried the wounded, and where the Russian shells, which went over the Twenty-one Gun Battery, fell and rolled till the place was literally paved with shells. It was a dangerous way by which to carry wounded men, and at night the troops went down by the Woronzow Road. It was easy work comparatively in the battery; you could see the shells flying over, and long before they fell you had plenty of time to dodge behind the next traverse; after a while, too, a man got to know exactly if a cannon-shot was making in his direction; sometimes the bombardment went on for days on both sides without any apparent result. There was the Naval Brigade—you would have liked to see them, Captain, in the Twenty-one Gun Battery under Captain Peel, the coolest officer in the whole navy—they were handier with the guns and a great deal readier than our men.

"In front of the battery were the trenches, and in advance of the trenches were the rifle-pits. You could see before you the venomous little Russian pits out of which so many brave fellows were killed, dotted about with sandbags, and where the Russians lay watching our men working from parallel to parallel, and in the zig-zags. There was one rifle-pit in particular—I shall come to it directly—which gave us more annoyance than any other, on account of its position. It was close to the Quarries. The fire from it interfered with the approach of our trenches, and we had lost our men in numbers in the advanced sap at this point. It was for the moment the *bête noir* of our engineer officers. Of course, you have read in the papers what sort of work we have had in the trenches. On a quiet night, when the batteries were silent and the weather fair, it was pleasant enough. We sat round a fire smoking, telling yarns, or even sleeping, but always with the gun in readiness. In wet and bad weather it was a different thing, however. Remember that we only had ammunition boots, made by contract, which gave out after a week. The mud got trodden about deeper and deeper, till it was pretty well up to the knees: and when snow fell on top of it, and rain on top of that, and all became a wet pool of thick brown mud, it was about as lively work as wading up and down the harbour at low tide, even if you did happen to have a "rabbit," that is, one of the coats lined with white fur. And if it was a hot night you had the pleasure of listening to the cannonade, and could see nothing on the Russian side but the continuous flash of the guns. And there was always the excitement of a possible sortie.

"We went out for night work in the trenches with heavy hearts, I can tell you, and many a man wished it were day again, and he was back in safety. We grew every day more badly off, too. Not only did the boots give out, but the greatcoats dropped to pieces, and the commissariat fell short. You have heard all that story. Jack of the Naval Brigade did not mind so much as regards the greatcoats, because he could patch and mend. He used to sell his slops for brandy, and cobble his old garments with the brown canvas of the sandbags. But the redcoats were not so handy —I have often thought it a great pity that our fellows don't imitate the sailors, and learn how to do things for themselves—we suffered terribly. That you know, too; and any national conceitedness about the pluck of our fellows in fighting so well under such conditions has to be pulled up by the thought that what we did the French and Russians did, too. After all, there is no such thing as one nation being braver than another."

"Our sailors were stronger than the French," said the Captain. "When it came to pounding with the big guns, they held out longer."

"Let me come to my piece of great good fortune," Leonard went on, "or I shall be talking all night. I have told you of the rifle-pit by the Quarries which caused us such a lot of trouble. Now I am going to tell you how I took it. It was an afternoon in April 1855. We were in the trenches; there had been joking with a lot of 'griffs,' young recruits just out from England; the men used to show them the immense wooden spoons with which the Russian soldiers eat their coarse black bread soaked in water, and declare, to Johnny Raw's terror, that the Russians had mouths to correspond. At that time the fighting between rifle-pits was the great feature of the siege, and to take a rifle-pit was one of the most deadly things possible, as it was also the most important. The 'griffs' went down to the most advanced trench; some of them had never been under fire before, and they were naturally nervous. Just after grog time—their grog had been taken down to them—a heavy firing began, and one of those curious panics which sometimes seize some veteran soldiers attacked these boys, and they bolted; left the trench and skulked back along the zig-zag, declaring that the enemy was out in force. That was nonsense, and I was ordered down with a dozen men to take their place. My fellows, I remember, chuckled at finding the grog still there, and made short work of it.

"We had not been in the trench very long before a sortie in force actually took place. We were in front of the Redan; before us, under the

Redan, stood the pit of which I have told you; on the right was the Malakoff. Suddenly a cannonade *d'enfer* began from the Mamelon and the Malakoff, and we began to suspect that something was going to happen; and then, between the two forts, we saw the advance of the great Russian sortie. To our great joy, they turned to the left, in the direction of the French. While we looked, a thought came into my head—an inspiration. I reflected that the holders of the enemy's rifle-pit would very likely be watching their own sortie, and that now was the moment to make an attempt. I took half-a-dozen of our men; we crept out of cover, and then, without a word, rushed across the ground between. It was as I thought: the Russians never saw us coming: they were watching their own friends, and we were on them—a dozen of them—before they knew what had happened. It was hand to hand fighting, but we were the assailants. You know, Captain, it is always better to be in the attacking force. I cannot give you the details; but in less time than it takes me to tell the story, the Russians were *hors de combat* and the rifle-pit was ours. Then came the turning of the position. You understand, Celia, that the rifle-pit was a little advanced kind of redoubt, consisting of perhaps a dozen gabions filled with earth and topped with sand-bags, enough to shelter two or three dozen men. These were of course all placed in front, towards the enemy. We had to reverse the position, and place them towards the Redan. By this time we were observed, and shots began to fly about. That was the most dangerous moment of my life. We worked steadily and swiftly; tearing up the gabions, lugging the sand-bags round, getting such protection as we could while we worked. I do not know how long it lasted, but by the time we had finished there was only myself and one other left, and he was wounded in the right wrist. But the rifle pit was ours, and our men in the trench behind were cheering like madmen."

CHAPTER XXXI.
LEONARD CONTINUES HIS STORY.

LEONARD stopped for a moment. The Captain's eyes were kindling with the light of battle, Celia's with the light of admiration.

"It did not take long to do. It takes no time to tell. The whole thing was a happy accident; but it was the one fortunate moment of my life. Our men, watching from the trenches, cheered again; a rush was made, and that rifle-pit never went back to the Russians."

"They ought to have given you the Victoria Cross, Leonard," I cried.

"No, no," he replied, "that was given for braver actions than mine. Captain Bouchier got it for taking the 'Ovens, a rifle-pit which could hold a couple of hundred; such gallant fellows as Private Beckle, of the 41st, who stood over the body of his wounded Colonel against a dozen of the enemy—those are the things that make a man V. C. As for me, I was more than rewarded, as you shall hear.

"When we came off trench duty, and were marched to our own quarters, I was sent for by the Colonel. You may judge what I felt when he told me, after speaking of the affair in the kindest manner, that he should take care it was properly reported. He was better than his word, because the next day he ordered me to attend in the morning at Lord Raglan's head-quarters. I went up in trembling, but I had no occasion to fear. All the Generals were there, for a Council was to be held that day. General Burgoyne, when I was called in, very kindly explained to the Chief the importance of this rifle-pit, and how its occupation by our men would facilitate matters in our advanced approaches towards the Redan, and then he told Marshal Pelissier and Omar Pasha, in French and in the handsomest terms, what I had done. Lord Raglan spoke a few words to my Colonel, and then he said, in his quiet, steady way, what I shall never forget.—

"'Sergeant Coplestone, you have done a gallant action, and I hear a good report of you. I shall recommend you to the Field-Marshal Commanding-in-Chief for promotion. I am sure you will not disgrace Her Majesty's Commission.'

"I could not speak—indeed, it was not for me to speak. I saluted, and retired. Those words of the gallant old Chief —and that scene—I can never forget."

"Tell us," said Celia, "what he was like, Lord Raglan?"

"He was a grand old man," said Leonard, "with a grave face, squarely cut about the chin, overhanging brows, deep-set eyes, and wavy white hair, gone off at the temples; his nose was aquiline, and the expression of his face was one of great beauty. Every one trusted him, the French and Turks as much as the English. He had left one arm in the Peninsular War thirty years before, and he was about sixty-nine years of age. He was never so happy, his staff used to say, as when he was under fire, and yet he was careful of his soldiers' lives. What killed him was disappointment at his failure of the 18th June. He wanted to wipe out the memory of Waterloo from the minds of French and English by a victory as brilliantly attained by both armies side by side on the anniversary of that battle. It was a muddle and a mess. What was to be the grand success of the campaign proved the most serious reverse that the allied armies experienced in the Crimea. Out of five general officers commanding columns four were killed or mortally wounded, and out of one small force fifteen hundred gallant fellows were killed on that terrible day. Death was very busy with us just then. General Estcourt, Adjutant-General, a splendid man, and worthy companion in arms with Lord Raglan, died a week later. Captain Lyons, the son of Sir Edmund, died about the same day; on Thursday, the 28th, the Chief himself expired; and Colonel Vico, the French Aide-de-Camp attached to the English head-quarters, died also after this event, showing the depressing influence of even a temporary defeat on the best of men. Even one of the interpreters sickened and sank. It was a sort of murrain among those at headquarters.

"Well," Leonard went on after a pause, "that is all newspaper news. What the papers could not tell you was the grief of both armies and the profound sensation caused by Lord Raglan's death. There may have been better generals in the history of England's wars, but there never was one more loved and trusted. His life was perfectly simple; his headquarters contained nothing but camp furniture, a table on trestles, a red table-cloth, camp chairs, and no carpets; he was up at all hours, and he was without fear.

"Of the other generals I think Pelissier was the best. He was a little dumpy man, with a thick neck, and he was a little too fond of hurling his men at the enemy, but he did fight and fought well. They made him Duke of Malakoff afterwards, which is as if we were to make a man Duke of Jones."

"Why?"

"Because the Malakoff was named after a man who had once kept a tavern on the spot. Malakoff was a purser in the Russian Navy, and being kicked out of the service for drinking, swindling, and smuggling,—this last he did in smuggling ship's stores,—came ashore and started a drink-shop outside Sebastopol, where he could combine profit with the pursuit of his favourite occupation. And as his drink was cheaper than could be got anywhere else, for he had the advantage of his old smuggling experiences in the laying in of his stores, the place became a favourite resort of the Russian sailors when they came ashore to get drunk. After a while, the stony hill with Malakoff's sheebeen upon it became Malakoff's Redoubt. Sturdy Pelissier, however, did not look much like a duke, as we picture dukes. When Soyer the cook came out, he was so like the General that we used to ask which was the cook and which was the General. Only Soyer wore more gold lace, and distinguished himself in that way.

"My commission came out before the death of Lord Raglan. You may fancy what a trial it was to me, on that day, not to be able to write home, and tell you all about it. I did write, however; I wrote a full history of all I had done, with a note inside that it was to be sent to you, Captain, in case I fell. My brother officers gave me a hearty welcome, and we had a big dinner—as big as the materials at our disposal allowed, the day I joined—so to speak. I have been to many a better feast since, but none at which I was so entirely happy. I remember that the things to eat were scanty, as often happened in the year 1855—but I was eating what there was among gentlemen, with Her Majesty's commission in my pocket. We had no candlesticks fit to show on a mess table, but a dozen bayonets, with candles in them, stuck in the table, made a brilliant illumination."

Leonard paused again.

"The dinner was the last that some of us were to take together. On the 18th of June came our repulse at the Redan, when we lost half-a-dozen from our mess.

"As soon as quiet days came I took an opportunity of telling the Colonel my little history—how I was ignorant of my parentage, how I was a gutter child, wandering about the streets, living on the charity of a kind and good woman, herself poor, and how the Captain picked me up, educated me—and allowed me to go out into the world to seek my fortune; how I was to get home after five years, if I could, to report myself, and how my dream had been to go home, somehow, as a gentleman."

"Always the best of old Captains," said Celia, patting the old man's cheek.

"Nonsense, my dear," said the Captain. "Best of boys, you mean. Go on, Leonard."

"The Colonel will call on you to-morrow, sir. You will remember that he has been my constant and most steady friend and adviser throughout."

"Ay—ay," said the Captain. "I shall find something to say to him. Go on."

"Of all the fifty fellows that made up our mess when I got the colours, there are not a dozen left now. The winters, the trench work, the night-work, and its after effects, killed those whom the Russian bullets spared. They fell around me, and I passed through it unharmed; we were in almost everything, and I think every man in the regiment did his duty, sir, as well as any of your old sea captains."

"I doubt it not," said the Captain; "we belong to a fighting people."

"And so we finished that war and came home again. I was a Lieutenant when we landed at this very port and marched up the street, colours flying, amid the cheers of the people. I looked out for you again, sir, and for you, Celia and Laddy, but could not see any of you in the crowd. It was very hard not to call and tell you of my fortune, harder still not to ask for news of you, but only three years of the five were passed, and I had my promise to keep. We went to Chobham, and from there, after six months' rest, were ordered out to India.

"We will talk about the Mutiny another time. I got my company, as I had got my step, six months later, by death vacancies. The same good fortune followed me in India as in the Crimea. The sun did not strike me as it struck some of ours. I caught no fever or cholera which killed some, and I got through the fighting without a scratch; and the only thing that troubled me towards the end was the fear that I might not get home in time. We had a long and tedious passage, but we arrived at last, and I have kept my promise and my appointment, Celia."

After the first surprise the Captain took the stories of the fighting with unconcern. In the matter of battles he was a fatalist, like all men who have been in action. Every bullet has its billet; there is a time for every man; skulkers always get the worst of it—these were the simple axioms of his nautical creed. That Leonard should have gained a commission was to him so surprising an event as to swallow up all minor things. That he should have borne himself bravely was only what he expected, and that he should have been spared to return was the special act of Providence in return for many prayers for which he had given thanks already.

But to Celia—

> "'Twas passing strange;
> 'Twas pitiful, 'twas wondrous pitiful."

Leonard was no longer her old friend, her playmate, the boy to whom she had looked as a girl for protection, help, and guidance; he was now a man who had looked in the face of Death and quailed not. For the first time she talked with one who had fought in the way which had, so to speak, surrounded her later years.

She took the medals again, Leonard completed his tale, and kissed them reverently with glittering eyes before she gave them back to him.

"Leonard," she said, "when Laddy and I used to wonder where you were, and what you were doing, we never thought of this."

"And when we worked ourselves up into rages about the poor army starving in the cold of the Crimea, Cis," I said, "we never thought that Leonard was among them."

"We were all blind bats," said the Captain, "not to guess where he would go and what he would become. The only true profession for a gentleman is the profession of arms. There's no opening for volunteers in the navy, as there used to be, more's the pity. Cloudesley Shovel got on in that way, and in the good old times, Leonard, you might have risen to be a First Lieutenant by this."

"Are you not satisfied, sir?" asked Leonard, with a smile.

"Satisfied, my boy! Celia, my dear, tell him for me what we think."

Celia blushed very prettily.

"We are so proud and happy, Leonard," she said, "that we hardly know what we are saying. In all our talks about you we never hoped that you would be able to tell such a tale as this."

"Never," I repeated.

"We knew, did we not, Captain, that Leonard would bear himself bravely?"

"Ay, ay," said the Captain, laying his hand on Leonard's shoulder, "that we knew all along. We know sneaks and skulkers when we see them. Malingerers carry the truth in their faces, and by the same rule we know whom we can trust. Leonard and Laddy belong to them."

It was very good of the old fellow to say a word for me. Not that I wanted it, but it showed that he was anxious that I should not feel left out in the cold.

"Go on, Celia, my pretty," said the Captain; "is there any more to say?"

"No, sir," Celia replied. "Only—only—" And here her voice broke down, and her eyes were filled with tears. "Only to thank God, Leonard, again and again and all our lives, for keeping you safe through all these dangers, and for bringing you back to the Captain and Laddy—and to Mrs. Jeram—and to me."

"Amen," said the Captain; "that's very well put, Celia, my dear; and if you were to stay here altogether—and I wish you would—I should promote you to be chaplain. And now, Mrs. Jeram, you and I had better go off to bed, and leave these young people to talk as long as they will. It's past twelve o'clock, ma'am. Kiss me, pretty. Laddy, we've got something to talk about now, you and I, in winter evenings. Leonard, my son, good-night." He rested his hand on Leonard's head. "I am so glad, my lad; I am so glad."

They went away, and we three were left alone.

It was a night of full moon, without a cloud in the sky. We took our chairs into the garden and sat under the old mulberry tree, facing the mill-dam lake, and talked.

We talked all the brief night, while the bright moon hid the stars, and we could only faintly distinguish Charles' Wain slowly moving round the Polar light, until the moon herself was paled by the grey of the early morning, and even long after the sun had lifted his head above the sky and was pouring upon the sheet of water, making the little island redoubt upon it stand out clear cut against the sky, with a foreground of deep black shade.

What had we to talk about? Our hearts burned within us, even like those of the disciples at Emmaus. We three who had grown up together and loved each other,—we were met again, and all in early man and womanhood, and we loved each other still. I, with my jealous eye, watched Celia, and could see the sweet shy look that told me, what indeed I knew before, how only a word was wanted to flash a spark into a flame, how but a touch was needed before a maiden would yield. I saw, too, Leonard's eyes stealing every moment to rest upon her sweet face. It was with a natural pang that I saw this. Nobody knew, better than I, that Celia could be nothing to me but my dear sister, my true and most trusted friend. I had battled with my passion and it was dead. Now, I was ashamed of it. Who but Leonard was worthy of that sweet girl? She had no fault, nor has she any still, in my eyes. She is altogether incomparable. And who but Leonard, our hero, our Perseus, was fit to claim her for his own, love her, marry her, and keep her safe in his arms? Did I, sometimes, have thoughts, angry thoughts, of what might have been? Perhaps, we are but human; but on the whole I had learned by that time to look on Celia as my sister.

From time to time Leonard asked us about ourselves. We fenced with his question. It was not the season to parade Celia's troubles, nor mine. We were there to listen to his story, to be gladdened by his successes. What good to be talking of ourselves when every moment seemed sacred to his welcome home? The broad daylight found us still talking. Celia's eyes were brighter, her cheek a little paler. Leonard was handsomer, I think, by day than he had seemed by the light of our modest pair of candles. I went to the larder, and found there a whole chicken, with the Captain's second bottle of champagne, and we had a late supper, or an early breakfast, at four, with no one to look at us but the sparrows, who peeped over the housetops and chirped to each other that there would be a most unusual and festive chance in the way of crumbs as soon as the foolish humans should go to bed.

We should have sat till breakfast-time, but that Leonard looked at his watch and sprang to his feet.

"Cis," he cried, quite in his old tones, "do you know what time it is? Half-past five. You must go to bed, if only for a couple of hours. Good-night—till nine o'clock." He held her hand in his. "And—and—look in your glass when you go to your room—and think if you could have expected our little Cis to grow into—what you see there."

She shook her head, but did not answer, only holding out her hand timidly. But she was not displeased.

Then she ran away and left us.

"Laddy, old boy," said Leonard, "one doesn't come home to be made much of every day. I can't sleep if I go to bed. "What are we to do?"

"Let us go out to the Castle and bathe, and be back by eight when the Captain gets up."

"We will, Laddy. How splendid the dear old Captain is looking! Is there anybody like him in the world? And Celia—" Here he stopped. "You remember what I told you, Laddy, when I went away? Well, I have never forgotten it, and I mean it more than ever."

CHAPTER XXXII.
A FRIENDLY CHAT.

HOW fresh it is! And how jolly to be back in the old place!" Leonard cried, as we walked out into the silent streets.

Half-past five. The best part of the summer day. There was no one stirring yet, save here and there an early housemaid brushing away the morning dew upon the doorstep. Our feet echoed on the pavement with a clatter from wall to wall as if of many hundred feet, and when we spoke it was as if our voices were too loud as they reverberated along the houses. All just as it had been of old so many times when we two boys had run along the streets at six for a swim in the sea before school. Nothing changed save that the boy who used to run and jump, shouting in the overflow of strength and spirits, rejoicing in the breath of life, was become the splendid fellow who strode at my side. Of course I was just the same. A sleeping city and two boys going out to bathe. Nothing changed. The town asleep, and my brain filled with all sorts of weird fancies. I have read of deserted and ruined cities in the far-east Syrian plains, on the edge of the great and terrible wilderness where the lion of prophecy roams round the heaps of Kouyounjik. Some of these cities still stand, with their rooms and their staircases perfect as when the terrified inhabitants fled before some conquering Shalmaneser who came from the mysterious east destroying as he went. Now there is not a single soul left to mourn over the greatness of the past. You may hear the cry of the lizard, the shrill voice of the cigale; your feet echo as you stride along the silent footway, and you speak in a whisper, for this is an image of Death the conqueror. As I go along with Leonard I somehow think of these old ruins. There is no connection between a ruined Syrian city and a sleeping modern town, except the stillness which smites the soul as you pass along deserted pavements between houses closed and barred, which might be houses bereft of their inhabitants, soulless, empty, haunted. Within, the children lying asleep; the little faces flushed with sleep, and the little limbs tossed carelessly upon the sheets, the wondering eyes just about to waken for the glories and fresh joys of another day. Within, the young men and the maidens, the old men and the ancient dames, each wrapped in the solemn loneliness of sleep, when spirits even of lovers dwell apart, while the busy fingers of the restless Fates are weaving the many-coloured web and weft of life's short story. What stories behind those shutters! What dreams in those white-blinded rooms! What babble of infant voices to welcome the new-born day!

"What are you thinking of, Laddy? Dreamer, your eyes are always far away. This is just what we used to do years ago. Up at six and out across the common for a bathe! And you always dreaming! Look! there is the early bird. Good-morning, Molly. Fine morning for doorsteps—good for the complexion."

"Get along o' your nonsense," said Molly, not displeased.

"She's quite right; you're an officer now, Leonard, and it can't be allowed any more."

"Where is your mop, Molly?" he went on, with his light, boyish laugh.

"Mops have gone out," I replied, "so have pattens."

"Have they really? Not the clear old mop that they used to trundle up and down in their arms? I'm sorry for it, Laddy. The domestic mop used to be as good a weapon for the defence of housemaidenhood as any. And in a seaport town, too. Many is the time I've seen a too demonstrative Jack discomfited by a timely dab in the face from a dripping mop. Slaps and scratches are poor things compared with a dollop of wet mop. Even a Billingsgate broadside cannot be so effective. Something might be done, I dare say, with a garden hose, but, after all, nothing like a mop and a bucket. And even pattens gone, too,—the tinkling patten. I wonder no love-sick poet ever celebrated the musical clatter on the stones of the housemaid's patten. These are the losses of civilisation, Laddy."

We passed through the gate, our heels clanking across the iron drawbridge. Beyond the bridge, and between the walls and the advanced works, was the guard house, where stood a sentry, who saluted us with as much astonishment as discipline would allow, expressed upon a not remarkably mobile set of features. Why should an officer, who was not obliged to stand at a sentry-box during the small hours, be up and out so early? What good, in such a case, of being an officer at all?

And then we passed the awkward squad on their way to goose-step drill. They saluted, too, as we passed. The salute of those days was a thing of ceremony—extension of right arm, doubling of right elbow, hand square to the forehead, return double, drop of right arm. The Marines did it best, regulating the motions from a slovenly and irregular movement of the arm for a middy or a mate to a precise and clearly directed six-fold ceremonial, ending with a resonant slap of the right leg, for superior rank. They knew, the Marines, how to signify respect to rank. Any popular officer, particularly if he was also an Admiral, was saluted as he went down the street with a regular Kentish fire of open-handed slaps of right legs. That also is a thing of the past.

"I was like those honest fellows once," said our young Captain gravely.

"One of the awkward squad; sentry in the barracks; one of the rank and file; standing up to be drilled and ordered. Well; it's not a bad thing for a man."

"And the officers of the regiment, Leonard;—did that make any difference?"

"I became at once one of themselves— a brother officer. What else could their treatment be? I asked the Colonel as a personal favour, to tell them who I was. Every regiment has its 'rankers;' every ranker his story. I should be a snob if I were ashamed of having risen."

We crossed the broad common, where all the old furze had by this time been cut down and cleared away to make room for military evolutions; and we came to the Castle standing upon the edge of the sea. There was not a soul upon the beach, not even our old friend the cursing coastguard; we sat down under the slope of stone, for it was now low tide, and made ready for a dip.

"There go the last fumes of last night's long talk. Sitting up all night, even with Celia, does fog the brain a bit." Thus Leonard, coming out of the water all glorious like Apollo. I suppose it is because I am so unshapely that I think so much of beauty of form. Then we dressed, and Leonard took out a cigar-case, to my astonishment, for somehow I had never thought of him in connection with tobacco—heroes of imaginations neither smoke nor drink wine, as we all know—and then lying back on the shingle, he began to talk lazily.

"I am rather tired of telling about myself, Laddy; it is your turn now."

Of course I knew it was coming sooner or later.

"You do not expect to hear much about me," I said. "I am organist at St. Faith's; that is my official position, and it brings me in six-and-twenty pounds a year. For ten shillings a week I hear three services on Sunday and two in the week." .

"Poor old boy!" said Leonard. "Can't something better be got?"

"I rather like the church work. Then I give lessons in music and singing, and out of them I make about two hundred a year more."

"I see. But the house does not seem much improved by this enormous accession of wealth."

"No. The fact is, Leonard, that the Captain takes all the money, and I never ask what he does with it. If I made a thousand a year I am certain that extravagant old man would absorb it all."

"Ah! The crafty old Captain! Do you think he invests it in Russian stock or Turkish bonds?"

"No. I think he gives it away. Where does he go when every morning he disappears for three hours? Answer me that, Captain Leonard."

"He always did it, and he always will. He is an incorrigible old mystery."

"In the afternoon he stays at home, unless it is half-holiday, when he goes out on the common to see the boys play, and talk to them with his hands behind his back. To be sure he knows every boy in the town."

Leonard laughed.

"I remember an incident or two—years ago—when we were children in the house. There was a woman—she had black hair, I know—and she used to come in the evening and ask for money. I suppose, from my personal experience, that she was drunk one night when she came, and went on—I forget what about—like another Jezebel. She wanted money, and the Captain was so upset by her inconsiderate conduct that he—behaved as the Captain always does."

"What was that?"

"Went to the Sailing Directions. Remembered that every sinner had to be forgiven at least seventy times seven, and so added one or more to her score, which I should say must have already reached a pretty high total. He gives his money all away, Laddy, and if I were you I would not work too hard, because he will only give yours away too. The kind old man! What else have you to tell us about yourself?"

"I've been taking care of Cis," I said, evading the difficulty.

"So I saw last night. Good care, Laddy. There never was a better brother than you."

But he did not know all; and I could not tell him how near I had been, once, to betraying his trust.

"Cis—Celia—Oh! Laddy!" He threw away the cigar and started to his feet, gazing out to sea. "Did Heaven ever make a sweeter girl? Did you watch her face last night? And her eyes, how they softened and brightened!"

"Am I blind, Leonard?"

"Did you see how she lit up with pity and sympathy? Laddy, I must win the girl, or I shall not care what happens.

"I have never ceased thinking of her," he went on; "never since I left you five years ago. To be sure, when I was a private soldier, or even a non-commissioned officer, it seemed too absurd to think of her, but when my promotion came, then the old thoughts revived. All through the war I thought of her. In those dreadful nights when we sat and slept in the trenches, knee-deep in trampled mud and melting snow, I used to let my thoughts wander back to this old place. Always in Celia's Arbour, lying beneath the elms: play-acting beside the gun: running up and down the slopes with little Cis, wondering what she was like. You with her too, of course, with your great dreamy eyes and trusty face —Laddy and Cis. I suppose it was sentimental, all of it; but I am different from most men. There is no family life for you and me to look back on except that. In those days —I am not boasting—I had no fear, because it seemed as if every day brought me nearer to her, and higher up the ladder. In case of death I had a letter written to the Captain, enclosing one for you and one for Celia, telling you all about it. But I did not die. Then I had to come home and be near you, within a hundred miles, and yet not go to see you; that was very hard. When India came I lost my old fearlessness, and began to be anxious. It was want of faith, I suppose. At all events I escaped, and came out of the whole racket unwounded. Laddy, I should be worse than an infidel," he added solemnly,"if I did not see in my five years of fortune the protection of the Lord."

"We pray—we who stay at home—for the safety of those who go abroad; and perhaps our prayers are sometimes granted. Is that sentiment, too?" I asked.

He was silent for a little space; then he shook himself as one who would change the current of his thoughts.

"Let us go back, old boy; the Captain will be up by this time. And now tell me more about yourself; there must be more to tell than that you have become a musician. Haven't you fallen in love, Laddy?"

"Fallen in love! Who is there to fall in love with a man like me? Look at my shadow, Leonard."

It was a gruesome-looking shadow, with high back, and head, thrust forward. I think that if Peter Schlemihl had been hump-backed he would have made an easier bargain for the rolling up and putting away of his shadow. A small annuity, paid quarterly, would have been considered ample on the part of the purchaser. And as for awkward questions—well—there are secrets in every family, and it would soon be understood that the absence of shadow must not be remarked upon. I only know that my own was a constant shame and humiliation to me. Unless I walked with my face to the sun there was no getting out of the deformity.

"Bah! You and your shadow. Laddy, look in the glass. You have eyes that would steal away the heart of Penelope, and a musical voice, and you are a genius."

"Nonsense. I am only a plain musician, and as for falling in love, have I not been every day with Celia? How could I fall in love with any other girl when I had known her?"

"That is true," he said reflectively. "That is quite true. Who could? She is altogether sweet and lovely. After dreaming of her every day for five years I am afraid of her. And you have been with her, actually with her, for five years."

I think he guessed my secret, for he laid his hand affectionately on my shoulder.

"Cis and I are brother and sister," I said; "that you know very well. But you are right to be afraid of her. Men ought to be afraid of such a girl. Only the priest, you know," I added, following up a little train of allegory that arose in my mind," can touch the Ark of the Lord."

"You mean— "

"I mean that a man ought to be holy before he ventures upon holy ground."

"Yes; you are a Puritan, Laddy, but you are quite right. I have been saying to myself ever since she left us, 'She is only a woman after all.' And yet that does not seem to bring her any closer to me. It would bring all other women closer, but not Celia."

"She is only a woman to two men, Leonard, and to those two a woman of flesh and blood, with all sorts of hopes and fancies. One of these is myself, her brother, and the other—will be the man she loves. But there is a great trouble, and you ought to learn what it is."

I told him, in as few words as I could manage, part of the story. It seemed a breach of trust to tell him what I knew—though Celia only feared it—that this German had a hold upon Mr. Tyrrell which he threatened to use; but I was obliged to let him understand that Mr. Tyrrell wished her to accept the man, and I told how Celia suffered from the assiduity with which he followed her about, went to church with her, was everywhere seen with her, and how he hoped gradually to overcome, by quiet perseverance, the dislike which she, as well as her friends, would at first show to the marriage.

"He has not yet pressed for a reply," I concluded." But he will very soon now."

"Why now?"

I omit the remarks (which were un-Christian) made by Leonard during my narrative.

"Because you have come home. Because he will find out that Celia sat up all night with us talking. Because he will see her looking happier and brighter, and will suspect the cause."

"The cause, Laddy? Do you mean—"

"I mean nothing but that Celia is glad to see you back again, and if you expected anything less you must be very forgetful of little Cis Tyrrell. If you expected anything more, Leonard—why—perhaps you had better speak to her yourself."

"I remember Herr Räumer," Leonard went on. "He was always hanging about the streets with his blue spectacles and his big white moustache. I remember him almost as early as I remember anything. They used to say he was an exile from Germany for Republican opinions. During that year I spent learning French and Russian in the Polish Barrack he took an opportunity of speaking to me, was very friendly once or twice, and took a great interest in the Poles. I remember he wanted to know what they talked about. I wonder if he is a Russian spy?"

"Nonsense, Leonard. He dislikes the Russians."

"Does he? My dear Laddy, you know nothing about the country whose people are so pleasant, and whose government is so detestable. Russian spies are everywhere. The Russian Secret Service is like a great net spread over the whole world; they are the Jesuits of politics. Herr Räumer may not be one of the black gang, but he may be; and if he isn't, I should like to find out what keeps a German in this place, where we have got a great dockyard, and where improvements and new inventions are always being tried and talked of, where there are several regiments, half our fleet, and a lot of Poles. Do you think it is love of the town?"

"I suppose he is used to it," I said.

"What kind of man is he?"

"He is a cynic. He professes to live for his own enjoyment, and nothing else. Says the rest is humbug. I have never heard him say a generous thing, or acknowledge a generous motive. Yet he talks well, and one likes to be with him."

"I shall call upon him," said Leonard. "As for his own enjoyment and the selfish theory of philosophy, a good many Germans affect that kind of thing. They think it philosophical and intellectual, and above their fellow-creatures, to be wrapped in a cloak of pure selfishness. Well, Laddy, unless Celia wishes it—"

"She does not wish it."

"She shall not throw herself away upon this man. Great Heavens! my beautiful Celia," he said, "my beautiful Celia to be thrown to an old—" He checked himself. "No use getting angry. But if there is no other way of stopping it, we'll carry her off, Laddy, you and I together, and stand the racket afterwards. I can't very well call him out and shoot him. I don't mean that I see at present how it is to be prevented, but we will find out."

"Perseus," I said, "had to borrow of other people two or three little things to help him when he went on that expedition of his. You had better take the Captain, as well as myself, into your confidence. Here we are at home, and there is the jolly old Captain at the door, beaming on us like the morning sun."

"Come in, boys," he shouted, "come in to breakfast. Celia is ready, and so am I. Ho! ho! I am so glad, Leonard. I am so glad."

CHAPTER XXXIII.
A TRIUMPHAL PROCESSION.

THESE were the days of a grand triumphal procession, in which we led our hero about to be congratulated by his friends. There were not many of these, it is true. That made it all the better, because the chances of the hateful passion of envy being aroused were lessened. To be sure, there were none who could be envious. Leonard's road to honour is a Royal road, open to all. But it is beset with difficulties. Stout is the heart and strong the will of him who dares to tread that pipe-clayed and uncertain way. None of the boys with whom we had been at school knew Leonard as a friend, or even as an old acquaintance. The reserved school boy who fought his way to freedom from molestation was not likely now to search out the lads who had once stung his proud soul by references to the price of soap. They were now chiefly engaged in promoting the commercial interests of the town, and would have saluted the young officer, had they known who he was, hat in hand.

We went round, therefore, among our little circle of friends.

Mr. Broughton promptly invited us to dinner.

There were present at the banquet—to furnish it forth all the resources of the reverend gentleman's cellar were put under contribution—the Captain, Mr. Pontifex, Leonard, and myself. The dinner was simple, consisting of salmon, lamb and chicken, cutlets, with early peas and asparagus. A little light Sauterne, which his reverence recommended in preference to sherry, as leaving the palate clean for the port, accompanied the meal. There was also champagne, which, he said, was a wine as Catholic as the Athanasian Creed, inasmuch as it goes equally well with a simple luncheon of cold chicken, and with the most elaborate Gaudy. After dinner, solely in deference to the uncorrupted digestion of youth, he ordered a dish of strawberries.

"It is not the right time to eat them," he said, in a voice almost as solemn for the occasion as that of Mr. Pontifex. "Their proper place is after breakfast. A good dinner biscuit would be better. But young men expect these things. When you and I were undergraduates, Pontifex, we liked them." And then, while we absorbed the strawberries, he arose and brought from a sideboard, with great care and with his own hands, four decanters of port.

They stood all in a row before him, a label hanging from each. He put out his hands over them like a priest pronouncing a blessing.

"We ought, Brother Pontifex," he said, "to have a form of thanksgiving for port."

"When I was a young man," said Mr. Pontifex, with a sigh, "I was called by some of my reckless companions—ahem !—Two-Bottle Pontifex....Two-Bottle Pontifex—such was my appetite for port-wine at that period! I am now never allowed by Mrs. Pontifex—alas—even to taste the—ahem!—the beverage."

"This," said Mr. Broughton, affectionately caressing one of the decanters, "is a bottle of 1820. I sincerely wish, Leonard, that I could entertain the hope of bequeathing you a few dozens in token of regard to my old pupil. But I have not more than enough for my own use, always supposing that I reach the allotted time of three score years and ten. It is generous still, this wine." He poured out a glass, and held it to the light. "Mark the colour; refresh yourself with this bouquet; taste the noble wine." He suited the action to the recommendation. "What a combination of delight for all the senses at once! Nature never raised a sweeter colour —a more divine fragrance—a more Olympian taste than she has united—"

"Under Providence, Brother Broughton," said Mr. Pontifex, shaking his head.

"—united in this one glass of the finest wine ever grown. How my good grandfather, the Bishop—whose piety was only equalled by his taste for port—would have enjoyed this moment! The day before he died, his chaplain, on pouring him out his single glass—the Bishop was then too feeble for more—said, 'We shall drink, my lord, in a better world, a more delicious wine.' He was a learned and sound divine, but young, and with a palate comparatively untrained. 'We cannot,' said the good old Bishop. 'Better wine than this is not to be had.'"

"The next decanter," he went on with a sigh for the good Bishop's memory, "is a bottle of 1834. I do not know aright how to sing its praises. After what I have said of 1820 I would only say—

'O matre pulchra, filia pulchrior!'

"You shall taste it presently. Thirteen years later, we come to 1847. What a year for port; and to think that it should be followed—that year of generous and glorious vintages— by the year of rebellion and social upheaving! As if Heaven's choicest blessings were altogether thrown away upon ungrateful man! This last is a bottle of 1851, now four years in bottle and still a little too full. The four bottles do not make altogether a bottle a head—nothing to your old days, Pontifex—but we three are advanced in years, I am sorry to think, and the boys have been trained in a different school. Perhaps a better one.

"And now," he resumed, looking round with smiles twinkling in his eyes and playing over his jolly red face, "a Toast. The health of Leonard—our brave lad who has come home from the wars with medals and honours which make us all proud of him. It was in this room, my dear boy, that you first read the wars of antiquity told in heroic verse. It was here that your ear and your heart became attuned to the glorious aspects of heroism, and the din of battle. Remember, when you have some of your own, that nothing succeeds like putting a boy through the good old mill of Homer and Virgil. You were educated by me for your work, not by cramming yourself with a bundle of scientific facts, which they would persuade us is what soldiers want, but by the deeds of the great men of Greece and Rome. You have not forgotten Diomede, I hope."

"No, sir," said Leonard. "Nor Sarpedon, nor the cowardly Paris, nor Turnus, nor Nisus and Euryalus—nor any of them. Who can forget the jolly old battles?"

"When I was a schoolboy," Mr. Pontifex said solemnly. "I once fought a battle with another boy in which, I remember, I was worsted, owing to the superior strength of my antagonist. This breach of rules was subsequently discovered by the master of the school, and I was summoned before his presence. As I had nothing to say in—ahem!—vindication of the offence, I was instantly condemned to be— ahem !—in fact—birched! The—the necessary preliminaries having been performed, they proceeded to search for the rod, an instrument which was kept for that purpose under wet straw in the garden. When this had been found, I sustained a most fearful infliction."

We all laughed at this graphic reminiscence of a school battle and its consequences, and Mr. Broughton bade us charge our glasses and begin the '34. Mr. Pontifex grew more solemn as well as paler under the influence of the port as the evening went on, and Mr. Broughton more purple in the face, more jolly, and more animated. I had frequently seen this opposite effect of wine upon both clergymen. After the second bottle, the wine passed chiefly from one to the other, because the Captain had already exceeded a double ration, and Leonard was moderate in his libations.

In the course of the evening, the Perpetual Curate of St. Faith's pronounced a eulogium on the world generally, on those who know how to enjoy life, and on the good things life has to give. It was in the middle of the last bottle, and his face was a deep purple, while Mr. Pontifex, perfectly white, sat with his long upper lip grown half an inch longer, and the solemnity of Rhadamanthus upon his brow.

"What good things they are," he said enthusiastically, "to those few who know how to cultivate their senses. Wine such as this; the meats and fruits which come in their season; music such as Laddy here can play; the poetry of those divine men who made the language of a little peninsula survive for ever to fill our hearts with wonder and delight; the beauty of women to take us out of ourselves when we are young—you have been in love, Captain?"

The Captain laughed.

"Was there ever a sailor," he asked, "who has not been in love? And was there ever a lover like a sailor? What does the song say?" The Captain lifted up his pipe.

" 'And the toast—for 'twas Saturday night—
Some sweetheart or wife whom he loved as his life,
Each drank and he wished he could hail her.
But the standing toast
That pleased the most
Was the wind that blows,
And the ship that goes,
And the lass that loves a sailor.' "

"And the lass that loves a sailor," echoed Mr. Broughton, to his colleague's astonishment. "I knew you had, Captain. Catch a salt neglecting such a chance of completing his education. It did you good—own that; and it did me good, too, after the fit was over. Come, Pontifex, your wife is not here. Confess."

Mr. Pontifex shook his head very solemnly, and made answer with many parentheses.

"It is a sad—sad reminiscence of an ardent and perhaps (in this and in one or two other particulars which I have already at various times, as you may remember, Johnnie, in the course of conversation touched upon) ill-regulated youth, that I once imagined myself—actually in Love"—he spoke in a tone of the greatest surprise—"with a—a—in fact—a young person of the opposite sex, who vended perfumes, unless my memory greatly deceives me, at an establishment in the High—"

"And I dare say it was a very good thing for you," returned his jovial brother, interrupting the further particulars of this amour. "It was for me, and no worse for the girl I loved, because she preferred somebody else, and married him. It was an education for us all. As it is now, Captain, at our time of life we may say—

'Old as we are, for ladies' love unfit,
The power of beauty we remember yet.'

"And the sight of a pretty face, like that of Celia Tyrrell— bless her !—I drink this glass of the Forty-seven to her—is like the shadow of a rock in the wilderness. Age has its pleasures; they are, besides the drinking of good port, the contemplation of beautiful women and active youth. We have lived—let us sit down and watch those who are living. You, Leonard boy," he resumed the familiar tone of our old tutor, "you had the impudence to tell me, five years ago, that you would rather help to make history than to write it. And that is what you have been doing ever since. And it does us good—us old stagers, to see you doing it."

Presently he became more serious, and spoke from the Christian's point of view.

A Christian scholar and a gentleman. His race is nearly extinct now. But he had his uses, and many were his virtues. When I read Robert Browning's poem of "Bishop Blongram's Apology," I read for Blongram, Broughton. And yet he only touched that Right Reverend Father in a few points. Above all, a scholar; and with it, a kindly heart, a simple faith, and a robust, full nature, which enabled him to enjoy all that could be got from life. He is gone now, with his purple face, his short fat figure, and his dogmatic sermons. I do not like the present man—who is earnest—so well. Nor do I love the fussiness of the new school.

The next day we called upon Mrs. Pontifex, who received Leonard as cordially as that lady could make a greeting. Nothing was said about her husband's excesses in port the previous evening. She said that news had reached them of Leonard's happy return; that she rejoiced at his success, which was doubtless, she was good enough to say, deserved, though she wished it had been in more Christian fields; that the army was a bad school for those who wished to be serious; and that he must specially beware of that inflation which prosperity brings upon the heart. Then she said hospitably that she proposed, after consideration, to name an early day, for tea. Leonard laughed and accepted, leaving the day open. He always laughed, this favourite of Fortune. I do not think that festive gathering ever came off, owing to other circumstances which interfered. The Rev. John Pontifex, who was present, looking pale, and still preserving last night's solemnity, followed up the theme opened by his wife, giving us by way of illustration a few personal experiences, with copious parentheses.

"I observed the same dangerous tendency," he said, "when I was standing for my degree at Oxford; on which occasion, I may be permitted to add, though I now hope, having been chastened"—he looked at his wife —"without pride, I greatly distinguished myself"—he got a fourth. "I was treated, it is true, by the examiners with gross injustice, being required to translate passages ACTUALLY, though you may not perhaps credit the disgraceful circumstance, from the very end of the works both of Lucretius and Virgil!!! I was confronted, in fact, with the hardest portions of those authors." Mr. Pontifex spoke with great bitterness, and in the firm belief that Virgil, writing expressly for Academical candidates, contrived his books so as to form a series of graduated exercises. "And in spite of this I obtained a place of honourable distinction. On that occasion, I confess with repentance, my heart was greatly puffed up. It is an event to look back upon with profound Repentance. I observed a similar temptation to pride, when I dealt my Blow at the Papacy in fifty-three theses. A copy of this work shall be sent to you, Leonard, before you go again into Popish regions. I heard, indeed, that one so-called Father (I suppose because he has no sons)—a Papistical Priest—had presumed to answer. He said he was an enquirer. So, indeed, am I— but—but—he is a scoundrel, and will most certainly, some day—at least, I fear so—meet with his deserts."

This seemed carrying the *odium theologicum*, as well as literary controversy, a little too far. Mr. Pontifex had but one weapon, the threat of his one punishment.

In the afternoon of what Celia called "the day after," leaving the rest of the phrase to be filled up, Leonard's Colonel called upon us. There was one thing remarkable about the Captain. He was the simplest of sailors—no retired Bo's'n could be simpler—in his habits of thought, his speech, and his way of life. But with an officer of his own or the sister service, his manner changed instinctively. To the quiet simplicity of his habitual air he added the bearing and dignity of his rank. He was, he remembered on these occasions, a Captain in the Royal Navy, and the carpet of his dining-room became a quarter-deck.

The Colonel came to say great things of Leonard, and said them, Leonard not being present.

"He was observed by his officers, sir, from the first. Reported on his joining at his depot as a smart, well-set-up lad. Found to be of superior rank and education to the men. Proved himself excellent at drill. Made a corporal first and a sergeant shortly after. And, sir, if it were not for his own interests, I should say I wish he was a sergeant still.

"You have heard of his gallant action, I suppose," he went on. "Nothing finer ever done. Lord Raglan sent for him, sir. He has told you that, I dare say. But he did not tell you what the chief said afterwards. It was that if he had it in his power he would have knighted him on the field of battle. He has been a credit to the regiment since the first day he joined it. We are proud of him, sir: we are proud of him, and I am happy in being able, this day, to beat up your quarters and tell you so."

The Captain answered simply. He said that Leonard was always a brave and trustworthy lad: that for his own part he had endeavoured to make the boy think of duty before all things: that it gave him unspeakable pleasure to hear what the Colonel had said, and to know that it was the truth without exaggeration: that the boy was still young, and, as yet, only at the beginning of his career. I felt proud of the Captain as he made his little speech, full of dignity and good feeling.

"At all events, he owes everything to you," said the Colonel. "And now, will you dine with us to-morrow, you and Mr. Pulaski? It is guest-night."

The Captain accepted for both of us.

"I should like to ask," said the Colonel, "if it is not an impertinent question—do you think there is any chance of Copleston finding out something of his family?"

"I have thought of it more than once," the Captain replied. "His mother died in giving him birth; with the last breath she said his name was to be Leonard Coplestone, 'her husband's name.' It is not a very common name. To find him one would have to consult army and navy lists of five-and-twenty years ago. If we found him, what might we not find too? That his father was a scoundrel is certain to me, from the circumstance of the boy's birth. He may be dead; he may have dishonoured the name; he may be unwilling to recognise his son—why not let things go on as they have done, without further trouble. The boy bears the Queen's Commission; he is no disgrace, but a credit to his regiment. Let us remain satisfied."

The Colonel shook his head.

"I shall look up the lists," he said. "And if I find out anything I will tell you first. If it is anything calculated to do Coplestone harm, we will keep it to ourselves."

Guest-night at the Hundred-and-Twentieth. The tables covered with the regimental plate, and crowded with officers. The Colonel has our old Captain on the right, his own guest. I sit beside Leonard. The band is playing. There is a full assemblage. The younger officers are full of life and spirits. What is it like—this world I have never seen till to-night—this world of animal spirits, laughter, and careless fun? I look about me dreamily. This, then, I think was the kind of life led by my father, Roman Pulaski, of the Imperial Guard, before Nicholas exchanged it for the Siberian mines. It must be pleasant for awhile. These young fellows are neither creating, like artists; nor criticising, like scholars; nor working for money, like professional men; nor selling their wit and spirits, like authors; nor contriving schemes for making money, like merchants; they are simply living to enjoy things. They have had a hard time of it in India: a few of them—very few, alas!—had a hard time in the Crimea: now they are back to garrison and English life, and they are rejoicing as heartily as they fought.

They tell me that the officer of to-day is scientific, and plays Kriegspiel. I am sure he is not braver, more genial, kindlier, or more generous than Leonard's brothers in arms of twenty years ago. I dare say, even in those brainless times, even among the jovial faces around that mess table, there were some who cared about their profession, had strategic genius, and studied the art of war. At least one did. Everybody challenges the Captain. He was Copleston's guardian. Everybody knows all about him. Then they challenged me, and had I drained all the bumpers they came offering me, my course at that table would have been brief indeed.

"Gentlemen, 'The Queen!'"

It is the President, and then we fall into general talk.

What sort of mess would that be into which Wassielewski was going to introduce me? A mess of peasants sitting round a fire of sticks in a forest. Instead of the Queen's health we should drink to Poland, instead of claret we should have water, instead of a circle of faces in which the enjoyment of life—the mere fact of living—was the prevailing feature, I should see round me everywhere the grim and earnest faces of those who were looking forward sadly to defeat and death. I suppose when a man is going to be martyred he goes to meet his doom with a certain exaltation which enables him to pass through the agony of death with heroic mien. The most disagreeable part about it must be the steady looking forward to the supreme moment.

"Dreamer," whispered Leonard, "where are your thoughts?"

"I was thinking what sort of a regimental mess I should find in Poland," I replied, forgetting that Leonard knew nothing.

"What mess? Poland?" he asked. "What have you to do with Poland now?"

I told him in a few words. It was not the place or the time after dinner at a regimental mess to go into any heroics. Besides, I felt none—only a sad despondency at the necessity which was going to drag into the trouble one who had such small stomach for the fight.

Leonard was aghast.

"The thing is absurd, Laddy, ridiculous. You must not go."

"I have pledged my word," I said, "and I must. You would not have me break old Wassielewski's heart?"

"I don't know. It must be a tough old heart by this time. But I would rather break that than let him break your head. We will talk about it to-morrow, old boy. What with Celia's troubles and yours, it seems as if we shall have our hands full for awhile. Pray, has the Captain, by accident, got any secret sorrow?"

"No," I replied, laughing. It was beautiful to see the calm way in which Leonard faced difficulties.

"He is not engaged to Mrs. Jeram, I hope, or has not contracted a secret marriage with his cook? He's not going to be tried by court-martial for intoxication, is he? Really, Laddy, you have given me a shock. Are you sure there is no more behind?"

"Quite sure."

"Good. There is going to be a move. We will get away early. I will go and see this fire-eater, and appeal to his common sense."

It was twelve, however, before we escaped the kindly hospitalities of the mess, and the Captain came away amid a storm of invitations to dine with them again. He accepted them all, in great good spirits, and became a sort of privileged person in the barracks so long as that regiment stayed in the place, dividing his time in the afternoon between the officers and the boys at play. When the regiment was ordered away he returned entirely to the boys.

CHAPTER XXXIV.
AN APPEAL TO COMMON SENSE.

"WE will appeal," said Leonard, "to the man's common sense first. The thing is absurd and preposterous."

He did make that appeal to Wassielewski, and as it was a complete failure, I suppose the old conspirator had no common sense.

He called in the morning at his lodgings, that one room which I have described, where the old man told me my own story in all its hideous details, sparing nothing. The Pole was sitting at the table, the map of Poland in his hand, preparing for the campaign. Long lists and estimates lay beside him, with which he was estimating the progress and duration of the struggle. The longer the revolt, the more lives sacrificed, the greater the exasperation and cruelties of the Muscovs, the better for Poland. Tears of women, he used to say in his grim way, and blood of men together fructify the soil, so that it produces heroes.

At sight of a stranger he sprang to his feet, and clutched his papers.

"You do not remember me," said Leonard. "I do not," replied the old man, gazing keenly and suspiciously into his face. Spies and police assume so many forms that they might even be looked for beneath the guise of a young Englishman. "Who are you, and what do you want with me?"

"My name is Leonard Copleston. I am the old friend of Ladislas Pulaski. One of his only friends."

"He has many," said Wassielewski. "Friends in his own country."

"Friends who will make him the tool of their own purposes, and lead him, if they got their own will, to death. I am one of the friends who want him to live."

Wassielewski made no reply for a moment.

Then he seemed to recollect.

"I know you now," he said. "You went away to seek your fortune. You used to come to our barrack and learn things. The Poles were good to you then."

"Some of your people taught me French and Russian, riding, fencing, all sorts of useful things. I am grateful to them."

"And your fortune—it is found?"

"Yes; I am an officer in the army; I have been in the Crimea."

The old man's face brightened.

"Aha! you fought the Muscovite. We were watching, hoping to fight him too, but our chance never came. Why— why did you not make a demonstration in Poland?"

"We did what we could, and we got the best of it."

The Pole sighed. Then he resumed his suspicious look.

"Why do you come to see me? Can I fiddle for you? I can march before troops of your men playing a hornpipe. What else can I do for you? Ah! I see—I see," his face assumed a look of cunning. "You are a friend of Ladislas Pulaski, and you come here to persuade me not to take him. That is too late. He hast pledged himself, and he must keep his word. Say what you have to say, and leave me. I have much to think of."

"What I have to say is short. It is absurd to drag into the meshes of your conspiracy a man like Ladislas, the most peaceful, the most unpractical, the most dreamy of men. Even now, when you half-maddened him with some horrible story of death and torture, his sympathies are only half with you. He cannot speak Polish: he is a quiet English musician, as unfit for a campaign as any girl. Why do you seek to take away his life? What earthly good can his death do to Poland?"

"He is a Pulaski. That is why he must come with us. His father, Roman Pulaski, dragged out ten years of misery in a Siberian mine. Ladislas must strike a blow to revenge him."

"Revenge! revenge!" Leonard cried impatiently.

"Yes, young gentleman," Wassielewski rose to his full height, looking something like an eagle. "Revenge! That is the word. For every cruel and treacherous murder there shall be revenge full and substantial. Did Ladislas tell you the story of his father?"

"No, not yet."

"That is not well. His mother, too, was murdered when the Russians stole her boy, and she ran after the carts through the winter snow, bareheaded, crying and imploring for her child till she could run no longer, and so fell down and died. Did Ladislas tell you of his mother?"

"No."

"It is not well. Ladislas should tell everybody these things. He should repeat them to himself twice a day; he should never let them go out of his brain."

"Why did you disturb the current of his peaceful life with the story?"

"To fire his blood; to quicken his sluggish pulse. The boy is a dreamer. I would spur him into action."

"You cannot do that. But you might spur him into madness. What is the use of filling his thoughts with revenge which can only be dreamed of?"

"Only be dreamed of!" Wassielewski cried, almost with a shriek."Why, man, I have dreamed of revenge for twenty years and more. Only be dreamed of? Why we shall put the revenge into action at once. Do you hear?—at once— next week. We start next week—we—but you are an Englishman," he stopped short, "and you would not betray me."

"I betray no one. But Ladislas shall not go with you."

"I say he shall," Wassielewski replied calmly. " I have persuaded him. He is expected. Revenge! Yes; a long scourge from generation to generation."

"An unworthy thing to seek. I thought you Poles were patriots."

"It is because we are patriots that we seek revenge. How easy it is for you English, who have no wrongs to remember, to talk with contempt of revenge. What do you know of backs scarred and seamed with Russian sticks? What murdered sons have you for the women to lament? What broken promises, ruined homes, outraged hearths, secret wrongs, and brutal imprisonments? Go, sir; leave me along with my plans; and talk to no Pole about living in peace."

"He is deformed."

"So much the better. All the Pulaskis for centuries have been tall and straight. Who crippled the boy? The Russians. Let the people see his round back and hear his story."

"He is weak; he cannot march; he cannot even carry a gun."

"Yes; he is strong enough to carry a rifle, and use it, too."

"He is a dreamer. Let him dream away his life in peace."

"He may dream, if he likes—in the next world," said the conspirator grimly. "Poland claims all her sons—dreamers, and poets, and all. This is a *levée en masse*, a universal conscription, which knows of no exceptions. He must join the rest, and march to meet his fate. Shall a son of Roman Pulaski stay in inglorious exile while the Poles are rising again?"

Leonard made a gesture of impatience.

"It is madness. Man, it is murder."

Wassielewski sighed and sat down—he had been walking up and down the room. Resting one hand upon his papers, he looked up sorrowfully at Leonard, speaking in low tones of conviction and with softened eyes.

"It is what I have said to myself a thousand times. Ladislas is not a soldier: let him live. I say it still in the day-time. But at night, when I am quite alone in the moonlight, I sometimes see the form of his mother, the Lady Claudia. She is in white, and she points to Poland. Her face is not sad but joyous. Perhaps that is because she is going to have her son again, in Heaven—after the Russians have killed him. I asked her once, because I wished to save the boy, if he should go. She smiled and pointed her finger still. After that, I knew. She wants to have him with her."

"That was a dream of the night, Wassielewski."

"No—no," he shook his head and laughed: " I am not to be persuaded that it was a dream. Why, I should be mad indeed if I were to take the injunctions of my dear and long-lost mistress to be a dream."

"People are sometimes deceived," said Leonard, "by the very force of their thoughts—by illusions of the brain—by fancies—"

"It seems a cruel thing," Wassielewski went on unheeding, "but it cannot be cruel if his mother orders it. The boy must come with me: he must join the villagers: he must learn their language—if he has time: march with them: eat with them: and carry his life in his hand until Death comes for him. It will be bad for him at first, but he will grow stronger, and then he will feel the battle fever, so that when I am killed he will be better able to protect himself. And perhaps he will escape—a good many Poles have escaped. Then you will have him back again. But I do not think he will, because in the night I see visions of battles between the Russians and the Poles, and I never see him among them, even myself."

"Poor Wassielewski," said Leonard, touched with his fanatic simplicity.

"He is a good lad," the old man went on." I loved him first for his mother's sake, but learned to love him for his own. He has a tender soul, like a woman's, and a face like a girl's. We shall have to accustom him to scenes that he knows nothing of. We do not make war in Poland with kid gloves. We kill and are killed; we shoot and are shot: we use every weapon that we can find and call it lawful. We slaughter every Muscov who falls into our hands, and we expect to be slaughtered ourselves. It is war to the knife between us, and the Poles are always on the losing side."

"Then why make these mad attempts at insurrection?"

"Because the time has come round again. Once in every generation, sometimes twice, that time comes round. Now it is upon us, and we are ready to move. You wish to save your friend. It is too late; his name is here, upon the roll of those who dare to die."

"Why," said Leonard, "you are a worse dreamer than poor Ladislas. On whose head will the guilt of all this bloodshed lie, except on yours and the madmen among whom you work?"

Wassielewski shook his head.

"The crime be on the head of the Czar. Rebellion is my life. I think of it all day, and dream of it all night. By long thinking you come to learn the wishes of the dead. They whisper to me, these voices of the silent night, 'What we died for, you must die for; what we suffered for, you must suffer for; the soil of Poland is rank with the blood of her martyrs. Do you, too, with the rest, take the musket, and go to lie in that sacred earth.' They have chosen me, the noble dead; they have elected me to join in their fellowship. Ladislas shall sit beside me with them. I have spoken."

He finished, and pointed to the door. There was nothing more to be said, and Leonard came away disheartened.

"It is no use, Ladislas," he said. "The man is mad with long brooding over his wrongs. I have never been much in the conspiracy and rebellion line, but now I understand what a conspirator is like in private life, and I don't like him. When I read henceforth of Guy Fawkes, Damiens, Cassius, Brutus, and other gentlemen of their way of thinking, I shall always remember old Wassielewski, with his deep-set eyes, his overhanging eyebrows, that far-off look of his, and the calm way in which he contemplates being killed. Even Havelock and his saints never marched to death with greater composure. And killed he certainly will be, with all the madmen who go with him."

"I must go with him, Leonard. I have promised. I am pledged."

"We shall see," he replied.

The vague words brought a little hope to my soul. The thirst for revenge, alien to my nature, was gone now, despite the burning wrongs, the shameful and horrible history which the old man had told me. I looked forward with unutterable disgust to a campaign among Polish rebels. I was indeed an unworthy son of Poland.

CHAPTER XXXV.
A DIPLOMATIST.

IT was not with any view of appealing to Herr Räumer's generosity that Leonard called upon him. Quite the contrary. He went to see what manner of man this alien would appear to him, seen in the light of extended experience. And he avoided all reference to Celia. It was in the forenoon that he went. The German was sitting at his piano playing snatches of sentimental ditties and students' songs with a pipe in his lips, which he occasionally put down to warble something in French or German about Mariette remembering Lindor, and all the rest of it, or "How Love survives Absence," "How Hard it is for Friends to Part." His love for music never carried him beyond the ballad stage, and all the things he played were reminiscences of some time spent among students or young officers at Heidelberg, Vienna, or Paris.

He got up—big, massive, imposing—and greeted his visitor cordially.

"Who comes to see me, drinks with me," he said hospitably, "always excepting Ladislas Pulaski, who drinks with no one. Sit down, Captain Coplestone. I am glad to see you so early. That shows that you are going to talk. So—a cigar—*Liebfraumilch*—and good—so. When Fortune means most kindly to a man, she makes him a soldier. I congratulate you."

"You have served yourself?"

"I have—in Austrian cavalry. I had an accident, and could ride no more. That is why I abandoned my career."

"Ah!" said Leonard thoughtfully, "I knew you had been a soldier. One never quite loses the reminiscences of drill."

They went on talking in idle fashion.

"And you still keep up the same interest in the Poles, Herr Räumer?"

"Poles?" He started. "What interest?"

"When last I saw you, I was learning French at the Polish Barrack, and you used to ask me about them—you remember."

"Ah!—Yes.—So.—Yes. I remember perfectly. The poor Poles. But they are all gone now, except one or two, and I had forgotten them."

"Wassielewski remains. You know him?"

"By name; Ladislas talks about him." This was not true. "He is the irreconcilable Pole—the ideal Pole. A harmless enthusiast."

"Enthusiast, perhaps. Harmless, no."

"There are plenty like him about the world," said the German quietly.

"They seldom do mischief. They are in London, Paris, New York, and Stamboul. They are even in Moscow. Let them conspire."

"No mischief!" Leonard echoed. "The Russians prevent that by their secret service, I suppose." He looked at his friend steadily. "We know by Crimean experience how well that is conducted. Why—they had a Russian spy, disguised as a German, all through the war, in our own London War Office. But that you have heard, of course."

Herr Räumer laughed.

"It was very neatly done. Any other but the English would have foreseen a Russian war, and taken care that some of their officers learned Russian."

"At all events, we get on, somehow."

"Yes; because you have a good geographical position; because you have money; and because you have the most wonderful luck. Wait till Russia gets Stamboul."

"When will that be?"

"And commands the Valley of the Euphrates. It is very clever of you to make of Moldavia and Wallachia an independent state; but who is to guard it? Suppose a time were to come when Austria—she is always Austria the Unready—was fettered with diplomatic chains, when France either would not or could not interfere in the Eastern Question, what is to prevent Russia from marching across the frontier of your Roumania? Treaties? Why the whole history of the world is the history of broken treaties. Sooner or later she will try for Asia, from the Levant to Pekin. Of course that will include Afghanistan. Then she will try for India, and win it by force of numbers. Where will your greatness be then?"

"We have fought her before, and we will fight her again."

"Oh yes; you can fight, you English. Perhaps you can fight better than any other people. That is to say, you can do with a hundred soldiers what Russia wants a hundred and twenty to accomplish. But you have only that hundred, and Russia has behind her hundred and twenty ten times a hundred and twenty more. You are commercially great because London has taken the place which the Constantinople of the future will hold, the commercial centre of the world. You have a great fleet. You will lose your great empire because you will not have a great army. England will become less formidable as armies grow greater. If you wish to preserve the power of England, make every Englishman a soldier."

"That will never be," said Leonard.

"Then the days of England's supremacy are done."

He knocked out the ashes of his pipe, refilled it slowly, and lit up again.

"It is by her secret service which you despise that Russia defends herself, and steadily advances. She throws out her secret agents to watch, report, and, if necessary, make mischief. They are the irregular cavalry of politics. Sometimes they are called merchants or scientific explorers, sometimes they are disguised as missionaries, sometimes they are the ministers and rulers of the country, corrupted by Russian gold or flattered with Russian skill. Russia makes no move till she has felt her way. Persia will be hers when the last relic of British influence has been bought out or wheedled out, or when Russian counsels have been able, unmolested, to bring the country into a fit condition for Russian occupation."

"I suppose that Russian influences are already at work in England itself?"

"Not yet," said Herr Räumer, laughing. "The conquest of England would cost too much. But Russian influences are already at work against British interests, wherever they can be met and injured. You have no enemy in the world except Russia. Not France, which changes her policy as she changes her Government, once in every generation. Not America, which is a peaceful country, and more afraid of war than England. The enemy of England, the persistent and ever watchful enemy of England, is Russia, because it is England alone, at present, that can keep Russia from Constantinople."

"Well, you have forewarned us, at all events."

"Forewarned is nothing. You may forewarn a consumptive man that he will suffer in the lungs. That will not prevent the disease. You will go on in England, as you always do, learning nothing, preparing for nothing, acting always as if you had to do with men who tell the truth. Could any country be more stupid?"

"Why," asked Leonard, " should not nations be as honest as men?"

"So they are," he replied, "only you Englishmen will persist in supposing that men are not liars. An English gentleman, I will admit, always speaks the truth. At least, he has been taught to do so, and it comes natural to him. But a common Englishman does not. The man who sells things to you lies habitually, in order to make his profit— lies like a Syrian, goes to church on Sundays, and thinks he is a Christian. An American, I suppose, is pretty nearly the same thing as an Englishman, unless he happens to be an Irish Catholic. I believe that Dutchmen, Danes, Swedes, and Norwegians—small nations without ambition—have a singular preference for the truth. But all other nations lie. I am a German, and I state that unblushingly. Those get on best who lie hardest."

"Suppose that one here and there were to speak the truth?"

"It would do him no good, because he would not be believed, unless he were an Englishman. Diplomacy is a game in which no one believes any one else. The truth lies behind the words—somewhere. It is our business—I mean the business of diplomatists—to find it out. First, you have the actual assurance of the Czar, we will say, conveyed by his ambassador. Of course no one, except, perhaps, an English newspaper, pretends for a moment to believe a pacific assurance. You receive it, and you try to find out what Russia is actually doing, which is a great deal more important. If you find that out, and are able to watch the movements of other Powers, you have a chance of understanding the truth.

"Everything stated openly is stated with intention to deceive. That is the first rule in diplomacy. All friendly assurances must be received with suspicion. That is the second rule. The statement of disinterested action which is always made is, of course, received with derision. No nation is disinterested, except, sometimes, England. There has not been a disinterested action done by any single nation since the world began, save only one or two done by England. I grant you that. Statesmanship means lying for the good of your country, and there is a regular method which is known and adopted everywhere. Except to the ignorant people, it means nothing, and imposes on no one."

"Why not start fair again all round, and speak the truth?"

"What? and spoil the game? Heaven forbid! We have our little fictions in society, why not in diplomacy also? I do not want, as I once told Ladislas Pulaski, to live in a world gone good. It would be tedious to me, that kind of world. And, at my age, I cannot unlearn things. Let us go on as we have always gone on—one nation trying to cheat every other—ambassadors lying—secret service reduced to one of the fine arts—and let us watch the splendid spectacle, unequalled in history, of a nation following a line of policy from generation to generation, beaten at one point and carrying it forward at another—always advancing, always aided everywhere by a swarm of secret agents."

Afterwards repeating the conversation to me,—

"The man," said Leonard, "is a Russian agent himself. I am certain of it. No German ever talked English so well: he has the best Russian manner: he is *rusé*, polished, and utterly cynically frank, unscrupulous, like all the people connected with the Russian Government. He has an important mission here, no doubt, and must have picked up a good deal of information during all these years. I wonder what his name is, and what his real rank in the police."

"You are only guessing, Leonard."

"Perhaps, but I am sure, all the same. My dear boy, I know them. There were Russian papers on the table, too. I saw the *Golos*, of Moscow, among others. He is no more a German than you or I. 'Served in the Austrian cavalry.' 'Fudge and flap-doodle!' as Mrs. Pontifex says. Curious, to see the patronising way in which he talked. I am only a young officer of that stupid nation where diplomatists speak the truth. I should like to checkmate our friend on his own ground."

"But— Celia?"

"Do you think I am going to let Celia be handed over to a Russian spy?" he asked grandly. "A Russian officer would be a different thing. There are splendid fellows among them. But a spy? Pah! The thought makes me ill. Besides, Laddy," he laughed, "I don't think we will let Celia go out of England at all. She is too good for any but an Englishman."

CHAPTER XXXVI.
THE FOURTH ESTATE.

I WAS sitting in Leonard's quarters two days afterwards, idling the time with him, when I became aware of a familiar figure walking slowly across the barrack yard. It was that of Mr. Ferdinand Brambler. I had not seen any of the family for some time, having been entirely occupied with Celia, Leonard, and my Polish schemes. He bore himself with quite his old solemnity, but there was something in his manner which showed change and decay— a kind of mouldiness. As he drew nearer it became too evident that his outer garments were much the worse for wear, his boots down at heel, and his whole appearance pinched and hungry. Things must have been going badly with the children. My heart smote me for neglecting the Bramblers. Were all of them, including my poor little bright-eyed Forty-four, in the same hungry and dilapidated condition?

He made straight for Leonard's quarters, and, coming in out of the broad sunlight, did not at first see me.

"Captain Copleston?" he asked timidly.

"I am Captain Copleston," said Leonard. "What can I do for you?"

"Sir," said the great Ferdinand, drawing himself up, "I introduce myself as representing the Fourth Estate. I am the Printing Press."

"You don't look like one," replied Leonard flippantly. "But go on."

"Don't you know me, Mr. Ferdinand?" I asked, jumping up and shaking hands with him."Leonard, this is my old friend, Mr. Ferdinand Brambler, the brother of Augustus Brambler, whom you recollect, I am sure."

"Of course I do," said Leonard. "How do you do, Mr. Brambler? Your brother was a little man, with a comical face that looked as if he was too jolly for his work. I remember now. Is he in the Legal now, in the Clerical, or in the Scholastic? And will you take a glass of wine or a brandy and soda?"

"My brother Augustus devotes his whole energies now to the Legal," said Ferdinand slowly. "I will take a brandy and soda, thank you. With a biscuit or a sandwich, if I may ask for one."

"Send for some sandwiches, Leonard," I said. "And how are you all in Castle Street?"

"But poorly, Mr. Pulaski. Very poorly. The children are—not to disguise the truth—ahem— breaking out again, in a way dreadful to look at. Forty-six is nothing but an Object—an Object—from insufficiency of diet. Too much bread and too little meat. Ah! the good old days are gone when things were going on—things worthy of an historic pen—all around us, and money flowed in—literally flowed in, Captain Copleston. What with a prize ship here, an embarkation of troops there, the return of the wounded, an inspection of militia, and all the launches, I used to think nothing of writing up to a leg of mutton in three or four hours, turning off a pair of boots as if it was nothing, putting a greatcoat into shape in a single evening, throwing in a gown for Mrs. Augustus and a new frock for Forty-four, or going out in the morning, and polishing off a day's run into the country for the whole family out of a visit from the Commander-in-Chief. I used to laugh at that as only a good day's work. Happy time! You remember how fat and well-fed the children were once, Mr. Pulaski. But those days are gone. I despised then what I used to call the butter and eggs. Alas! the butter and eggs are nearly all we have to live upon now."

"You mean—"

"I mean, gentlemen, the short paragraphs poorly remunerated at one penny for each line of copy. One penny! And at least half of the sum goes in wear and tear of shoe leather worn out in picking up items about the town. I am a *chiffonier*, gentlemen, as we say in the French. I pick up rags and tatters of information as I peregrinate the streets. Nothing is too trifling for my degraded pen. I find myself even, in the children's interests, praying for a fire, or a murder, or a neat case of robbery. Here, for instance, is a specimen of how low in the literary scale we can go." He pulled a little bundle of papers out of his pocket.

"'SINGULAR ACCIDENT.

"'As our esteemed townsman, Alderman Cherrystone, was walking along the pavement of High Street on the morning of Monday last, he stepped upon a piece of orange peel, and falling heavily, dislocated his arm. The unfortunate gentleman, who has been removed to the hospital, is now doing well.'

"Mr. Pulaski," he asked in withering sarcasm, "that is a pleasant thing to come to after all my grandeur, is it not? Think of it, you who actually remember my papers on the arrival and departure of troops. But it is sixpence," he added with a sigh. "Here is another of the same sort. I call it," he added in a sepulchral voice,

"'A LIKELY STORY.

"'On Thursday, before His Worship the Mayor, a young man of dissipated appearance, who gave the name of Moses Copleston'—"

"What?" cried Leonard, "Moses Copleston?"

"Yes, sir, your own name was that given by that individual."

"Go on," said Leonard, looking at me.

"'And said he was the son of a general in the army, was charged with being drunk and disorderly in the streets. The police knew him well, and various committals made in another name were reported of him. He was fined 40S. and costs, or a fortnight. The money was instantly paid, and the prisoner left the court laughing, and saying there was plenty more to be got where that came from.

"'The Mayor recalled him—'"

"Will you give me that paragraph?" Leonard interrupted, and with an excited air. "Will you allow me to keep that out of the paper? I have a reason—it is my own name, you see."

"Certainly, sir," said Ferdinand. "I have no wish to put it in the paper, except that it is worth fourteenpence. And that goes some way towards the children's dinner, poor things."

"I will give you more than fourteenpence for it, my good friend," said Leonard. "Where is this prisoner—this Moses —do you know?"

Of course I perceived the suspicion that had entered his mind. He was jumping at conclusions, as usual, but it was hard not to believe that he was right. I began to think what we knew of our old enemy Moses, and could remember nothing except what Jem Hex—Boatswain Hex—told me —that he was not a credit to his education. This was but a small clue. But some shots in the dark go straight to the bull's eye. Leonard's eye met mine, and there was certainty in it.

I saw he wanted to talk about it, and so I got rid of Ferdinand by proposing to bring Leonard to his house in the evening, when he should pump him, and extract materials for a dozen papers.

"It is very kind of you, sir," he said. "You will enable me to confer on the children next week—ahem—a sense of repletion that they have not experienced for many months."

"I will tell you anything you want," said Leonard. "But you must ask me, because I cannot know beforehand, what you would most like to have."

"Sir," said Ferdinand fervently, "I will pump you to good purpose if you will allow me. Your own exploits, ahem—"

"No—no," said Leonard, laughing. "I must make conditions. You must keep my name out of your story."

Ferdinand's countenance fell.

"If you insist upon it—of course. But personalities are the soul of successful journalism"—it will be seen that Ferdinand Brambler was in advance of his age—"and if I could be permitted to describe these modest quarters in detail—camp-bed, two chairs, absence of ornament—ah!—'The Hero's Retreat;' your personal appearance, tall, with curling brown hair, square shoulders, manly and assured carriage, eagle eye—ah!—'The Hero at Home;' your conversation—' with difficulty can he be induced to speak of those hairbreadth escapes, those feats of more than British pluck, those audacious sorties'—'The Hero in Modesty;' your dress when not on duty, a plain suit of tweed, without personal decoration of any kind, simple, severe, and in good taste—'The Hero in Mufti;' and your early life, a native of this town, educated partly by Mr. Hezekiah Ryler, B.A., at the time when Mr. Augustus Brambler formed part of his competent and efficient staff, and partly by the learned Perpetual Curate of St. Faith's —'The Hero's Education;' your entrance into the Army, ' The Hero takes his First Step—'"

"Stop—stop—for Heaven's sake," cried the Hero. "Do you believe I am going to consent to that kind of thing?"

Ferdinand collapsed.

"If you really will not allow it," he said, "there is nothing more to be done. Just as I am warming into the subject, too. Well, Captain Copleston, if you will not let me describe your own exploits by name, I shall be grateful for any particulars you may be kind enough to give me."

"Yes—on those conditions, that my name is kept out—I shall be glad to help you."

"Sir," said Ferdinand, "you are very good. I will pump you like—like—an organ-blower. I will play on you like—like a Handel. At what time, sir, will you honour our humble abode?"

"We will be with you about eight," I said. "And—and —Mr. Ferdinand, will you give my compliments to Mrs. Augustus, and my love to Forty-four, and say that we hope to have the pleasure of supper with them. Early supper, so as to suit Forty-six and the rest."

Ferdinand sighed, and then smiled, and then with a deep bow to the Hero, retired.

"What about Moses?" cried Leonard.

"How do you know it is the real Moses?"

"There can be but one Moses," said Leonard; " and how should any other get hold of my name? Do you think he is in the town now?"

I began to make inquiries that very afternoon, bethinking me that Mrs. Hex, Jem the Bo's'n's wife, might know something about it. Jem had been married some time now, and was the father of a young family, who lived in one of the streets near Victory Row, in a highly respectable manner. Mrs. Hex had been a young lady connected on both sides with the service, so that it was quite natural that she should marry a sailor, and it was an advantageous match on both sides. She remembered Moses perfectly well; he was always going and coming, she said; would be seen about for a day or two, and would then disappear for a long time; he had been in prison once for something or other; then he disappeared for some years; then he came back in rags; and then—-just a short time ago—he suddenly blossomed out into new and magnificent toggery, with a gold watch-chain and a real watch, with rings on his fingers and money in his pocket, and he got drunk every night. Also, he called himself Copleston, which Mrs. Hex thought should not be allowed. Most likely we might find him at the "Blue Anchor" in the evening, where there was a nightly free-and-easy for soldiers and sailors, at which he often appeared, standing drinks all round in a free and affable manner.

"Quite the Moses we used to love," said Leonard in a great rage. "We will go to the 'Blue Anchor,' and wring the truth out of him."

For that day we had, however, our engagement at the Bramblers', which we duly kept, and were ushered into the front room, Ferdinand's "study." He was sitting at the table in expectation of us, with paper and pencil before him. He was hungering and thirsting for information. Beside him stood Augustus, as cheerful and smiling as though the children were not breaking out. Except that he was shabbier than usual, there was no mark of poverty or failure upon him.

"This, Captain Copleston," he said, "is a real honour. I take it as a recognition of my brother Ferdinand's genius. My brother Ferdinand, sir, is a Gem."

"Brother Augustus," murmured the author bashfully, "nay—nay."

"A Gem—I repeat it—a Gem. And of the first water. What says the poet?—

'Full many a time, this Gem of ray serene,
Outside the Journal Office may be seen.'

He will do you justice, sir. Mr. Pulaski," he sank his voice to a whisper, "shall we leave these two alone? Shall we retire to the domestic circle, not to disturb History and Heroism? At what time shall we name supper, Captain Copleston? Pray, fix your own time. Think of your convenience first. We are nothing—nothing."

"I never take supper, thank you," said Leonard, who was beginning to be a little bored with the whole business.

"Don't speak of supper to me," said Ferdinand. "This is my supper," he patted the paper affectionately. "This my evening beer." He pointed to the inkstand. "This is my pillow," indicating the blotting-pad. "And for me there will be no night's rest. Now, sir, if you will sit there—so—with the light upon the face—we can converse. Affluence is about to return, brother Augustus."

Augustus and I stole out of the room on tip-toe. In the back room the table was laid, and the children were crowded in the window, looking at the cloth with longing eyes. Poor little children! They were grown pale and thin during these hard times, and their clothes were desperately shabby. Forty-four, a tall girl now of fourteen, angular and bony, as is common at that age, preserved some show of cheerfulness, as became the eldest of the family. It was hers to set an example. But the rest were very sad in countenance, save for a sort of hungry joy raised by the prospect of supper.

"Always something kind from the Captain,'' murmured the poor wife.

"It was lucky," I said, "that we had that cold round of beef in the larder. Cannot we have supper immediately? I am sure the children would like it."

The poor children gave a cry, and Forty-six burst into loud weeping.

"Things have not gone very well, latterly," said Augustus, looking uncomfortable. "Sometimes I even think that we don't get enough meat. We had some on Sunday, I remember"—and this was Friday—"because Ferdinand said it was the first real meal he had enjoyed for a week. That was while we were sitting over our wine after dinner."

Nothing, not even actual starvation, would have prevented the two brothers from enjoying their Sunday pretence of sitting, one each side a little table, at the front window, with a decanter and two glasses before them. I do not know what the decanter contained. Perhaps what had once been Marsala. Ferdinand cherished the custom as a mark of true gentility, and was exceedingly angry if the children came in and interrupted. He said grandly that a gentleman "ought not to be disturbed over his wine." I think Augustus cared less about the ceremony.

Meantime the mother, assisted by Forty-four and Forty-five, brought in the supper—cold beef and hot potatoes— with real beer—no toast and water.

I pass over the details of the meal. Even Augustus was too hungry to talk, and Forty-six surpassed himself. I sat next to Forty-four, who squeezed my hand furtively, to show that she was grateful to the Captain. She was always a tender-hearted little thing, and devoted to her brothers and sisters. The pangs of hunger appeased, we talked.

"You now have an opportunity," said Augustus, leaning back in his chair after the fatigues of eating; "you now have an opportunity of boasting, my children, that a Crimean hero has actually come to this house, in order to tell the history of the war to your uncle Ferdinand, the well-known writer."

The boys and girls murmured. This was indeed grandeur.

"We will drink," said Augustus, filling his glass, and handing me the jug. "We will drink a toast. I give you, children, coupled, the names of Captain Copleston, the Hero, and Ferdinand Brambler—your uncle, my dears—the Historian. It is my firm belief that this night has commenced what I may in military language call an Alliance, or—speaking as a lawyer, one may say that this night has witnessed the tacit execution of a Deed of Partnership"—he relished his words so much that he was fain to repeat them—"between the Hero and the Historian, which will result in their being known together, and indissolubly connected by the generations, yet to come, of posterity. For myself, I have, as you know, little other ambition than to be remembered, if remembered I am at all, as Augustus Brambler—your father, my dears—formerly an ornament to the Legal."

We drank the toast with enthusiasm. There were nowhere to be found children more ready to drink or eat toasts than the Bramblers.

"By our own family connections, Mr. Pulaski," Augustus continued, "we have more sympathy with the Navy than with the Army. Mrs. Brambler—your mother, my dears— is highly connected as regards that service; and it is, I confess, my favourite. Sometimes I think of putting Forty-six into it, though if they were wrecked on a desert island, and provisions run short, he would come off badly. Forty-eight, of course, is out of the question where discipline and obedience are concerned. It would, however, have been just the service for poor little Fifty-one, my dears, had that interesting child been born."

He looked critically at Forty-six, sadly at Forty-eight, and shook his head. All hung their heads sorrowfully, as was customary at mention of the Great and Gifted Fifty-one—unborn.

"Two members of my wife's family—she was a Tollerwinch —were members of that gallant service, Mr. Pulaski. One of them, her uncle, held the rank of Master's Mate, and if he had not had the misfortune to knock down his superior officer on the quarter-deck, would now, one may be justified in supposing, have been Rear-Admiral Sir Samuel Tollerwinch, K.C.B.—of the White. I drink to the health and memory—in solemn silence —of the late Admiral."

Such was Augustus's enthusiasm, that we all believed at the moment the deceased officer to have died in that rank.

"The Admiral," Augustus sighed. "You must not be proud, my dears, of these accidents—mere accidents—of distinguished family connections. Your mother's first cousin, James Elderberry, entered the service also. He was a purser's clerk. I think I am right, my dear, in stating to Mr. Pulaski that James was a most gallant and deserving officer."

"He was, indeed," said Mrs. Brambler. "Poor Jem! And sang a most beautiful song when sober."

"Universally esteemed, my children, from the yardarm—to speak nautically—and the maintop mizenmast, wherever that or any other portion of the rigging is lashed taut to the shrouds, down to the orlop deck. His service was not long—only three weeks in all—and it was cut short by a court-martial on a charge of—of—in fact, of inebriation while on duty. He might have done well, perhaps, in some other Walk—or shall we say, Sail of Life?—if he had not, in fact, continued so. He succumbed—remember this, Forty-six— to the effects of thirst. Well, we must all die. To every brave rover comes his day." Augustus rolled his head and tried to look like a buccaneer. "Your mother's cousin, my children, must be regarded as one who fell—in action."

CHAPTER XXXVII.
LOVE'S VICTORY.

I SHALL premise that my story now becomes the journal of three days—every hour of which is graven on my memory. And I must tell the events which crowd that brief period as if I was actually present at all of them.

Our rejoicings and dinner parties were all over outwardly, at least, we had all dropped back to our old habits. I had no lessons to give, because we were in holiday time, and divided my day between Celia and Leonard, unless we were all three together. But Celia was anxious; I was waiting with a sinking at the heart for Wassielewski's signal; and every day the face of Mr. Tyrrell grew more cloudy and overcast with care. He was mayor for the year, as I think I have said before, and had the municipal work in addition to the business of his own office.

The first of these three days was June the 28th—a week after Leonard's return. He had met Celia every day—sometimes twice in the same day; as yet he had said nothing.

"Suppose," he said, "suppose, Laddy, that—I only put a case, you know—that I were to meet you and Celia in the Queen's Bastion; suppose there should be no one else in the place—"

"Well?" I asked.

"Would it, I say, in such a contingency, occur to you to have an appointment elsewhere?"

I forget whether Perseus had fallen in love with Andromeda before the slaying of the dragon; if so, the agitation in the breast of the warrior must have been greatly intensified, especially when he found he had only just arrived in time.

I told him that it was a clear breach of trust; that Celia was allowed to come out with me in a tacit understanding that there should be no lovemaking; that I was a male duenna; that I should be ever after haunted by the knowledge of the crime; that I should be afraid to face her father; that Herr Räumer—but, after all, it mattered nothing what Herr Räumer thought; and—finally, I acceded, promised to efface myself, and wished him success.

I do not know how it was that on the morning of that 28th day of June, Celia looked happier and brighter than she had done for weeks. She was dressed, I remember, in some light silver-grey muslin dress, which became her tall and graceful figure, and the sweet calm face above it. I knew every shade of her face; I had seen it change from childhood to womanhood; I had watched the clouds grow upon it during the trouble of the last few weeks; I had seen the sunshine come back to it when Leonard came home again, to bring us new hope. The dreariness was gone out of her eyes, with the strange sad look of fixed speculation and the dreamy gloom.

"Yes, Laddy," she said, catching my look and understanding it. "Yes, Laddy, I am more hopeful now Leonard has come home again. I do not know how, but I am certain that he will help us."

On this morning there was a Function of some kind—a Launch—a reception—a Royal Visit—going on in the Dockyard. From Celia's Arbour we could see the ships gay with bunting; there were occasional bursts of music; it must have been a Launch, because the garrison bands were playing while the people assembled in the shed, the naval and military officers in full uniform; the civil servants in the uniform of the Dockyard Volunteers—not those of 1860, but an earlier regiment, not so efficient, and with a much more gorgeous uniform; ladies in full war-paint, each in her own uniform, prepared to distract the male eye from contemplation too prolonged of naval architecture; the Mayor and Aldermen in gown and gold chain, splendid to look upon, in official seats, ready with an address; and no doubt, though one could only see him, as well as the Corporation, with the eyes of imagination, there would be among them all Ferdinand Brambler, note-book in hand, jerking his head up at the sky and making a note; looking at his watch and making a note; gazing for a few moments thoughtfully at the crowd and making a note—all in the Grand Historical Style—and not at all as if he was calculating the while what items of domestic consumption this Ceremony would "run to."

Presently, turning from the contemplation of the flags and discussion of hidden splendours, we saw, mounting the grass slope, with the most hypocritical face in the world, as if his coming was by the merest accident, Leonard himself.

"You here, Leonard?"

"Yes, Celia." Now that I looked again, I saw that his face had a grave and thoughtful expression. It was that of a man, I thought, who has a thing to say. She read that look in his eye, I believe, because she grew confused, and held me more tightly by the arm.

It did not seem to me that there was any occasion here for beating about the bush, and pretending to have appointments. Why should I make up a story about leaving something behind? So I put the case openly. "Leonard has asked me to leave you with him, Cis, for half an hour. I shall walk as far as the Hospital and sit down. In half an hour I will come back."

She made no reply, and I left them there—alone. There was no one but themselves in the Queen's Bastion, and I thought, as I walked away, that if Heaven had thought fit to make me a lover like the rest of mankind, there was no place in the world where I would sooner declare my love than Celia's Arbour—provided I could whisper the tale into Celia's own ear.

Half an hour to wait. At the end of the long straight curtain, in the middle of which was the Lion's Gate, with its little octagonal stone watch-tower, and where the wooden railings fenced off the exercise-ground of the Convalescent Hospital, I found the little Brambler children playing, and stood watching them. They took up fully ten minutes. Three tall, gaunt soldiers, thin and pale from recent sickness, were on the other side of the fence watching them too. One of them, bore on his cap the number of Leonard's regiment.

I asked him if he knew Captain Copleston.

He laughed. "Gentleman Jack?" he asked. "Why, who doesn't know Gentleman Jack? I was in the ranks with him. Always a gentleman, though, and the smartest man in the regiment. It was him as took the Rifle Pit. That was the making of him. And no one grudged him the luck. Some sense making *him* an officer."

From which I gathered that there were other officers in the regiment who had not commended themselves to this good fellow's admiration.

The Bramblers, headed by Forty-six, now a sturdy lad of twelve, were celebrating an imaginary banquet, in imitation of last night's tremendous and unexpected feed. The eldest boy occupied the chair, and ably sustained the outward forms of carving, inviting to titbits, a little more of the gravy, the addition of a piece of fat, a slice of the silver side, another helping, pressing at the same time a cordial invitation on all to drink, with a choice of liquors which did infinite credit to his information and his inventive faculty, and sending about invisible plates and imaginary goblets with an alacrity and hospitality worthy of a One-eyed Calendar at the feast of a Barmecide or a super at a theatrical banquet. It was an idyllic scene, and one enjoyed it all the more because the children—their breakings-out were better already—entered into the spirit of the thing with such keen delight, because one knew that at home there was awaiting them the goodly remnant of that noble round of beef; and because the historio-graphically gifted Ferdinand had found fresh and worthy subjects for his pen, which might result, if judiciously handled, in many legs of mutton.

By a combination of circumstances needless here to explain, Forty-six subsequently became, and is still, a shorthand reporter. He does not go into the Gallery of the House, because he prefers reporting public dinners, breakfasts, and all those Functions where eating and drinking come into play. You may recognise his hand, if you remember to think of it, when you read the reports of such meetings in the accuracy, the fulness, and the feeling which are shown in his notice of the viands and the drinks. It is unnecessary to say that he has never parted with the twist which characterised him as a boy, and was due to the year of his birth, and he may be seen at that Paradise of Reporters, the Cheshire Cheese, taking two steaks to his neighbour's one; after the steaks, ordering a couple of kidneys on toast, being twice as much as anybody else, and taking cheese on a like liberal scale. He is said, also, to have views of great breadth in the matter of stout, and to be always thirsty on the exhibition of Scotch whiskey.

When I was tired of watching the boys and girls, I strolled part of the way back, and sat down on the grassy bank in the shade, while the thoughts flew across my brain like the swallows flitting backwards and forwards before me, in the shade of the trees and in the sunshine.

Leonard and Celia on the Queen's Bastion together. I, apart and alone. Of two, one is taken and the other left. They would go together, hand in hand, along the flowery lane, and I should be left to make my lonely pilgrimage without them. Who could face this thing without some sadness? All around were the sights and sounds which would weave themselves for ever in my brain with recollections of Celia and of Leonard and the brave days of old. How many times had she and I leaned over the breastwork watching the little buglers on the grassy ravelin beyond the moat practising the calls, all the summer afternoon? How many times had we laughed to see the little drummer boys marching backwards and forwards, each with his drum and pair of sticks, beating the tattoo for practice with unceasing ruba-dub? Down in the meadows at my feet, where the buttercup stood tall and splendid, we had wandered knee-deep among the flowers, when Celia was a tiny little girl. The great and splendid harbour behind me, across which we loved to sail in and out among the brave old ships lying motionless and dismasted on the smooth surface, like the aged one-legged tars sitting on their bench in the sunshine, quiet and silent, would for ever bear in its glassy surface a reflection of Celia's sweet face. Listen: there is the booming of guns from the Blockhouse Fort; a great ship has come home from a long cruise. Is every salute in future to remind me of Celia? Or again—do you hear it? The muffled drum; the fife; the dull echo of the big drum at intervals. It is the Dead March, and they are burying a soldier, perhaps one of the men from India, in the churchyard below the walls. Backwards with a rush goes the memory to that day when Leonard stood with me watching such a sight, and refusing to believe that such a man, poor private that he was, had failed. No doubt 'twas a brave and honest soldier—there is the roll of musketry over his grave—God rest his soul! Down below, creeping sluggishly along, go the gangs of convicts armed with pick and spade. No funeral march for them when their course is run; only the chaplain to read the appointed service; only an ignoble and forgotten grave in the mud of Rat Island; and perhaps in some far-off place a broken-hearted woman to thank God that her unfortunate, weak-willed son has been taken from a world whose temptations were too much for his strength of brain. Why, even the convicts will make me think of Celia, with whom I have so many times watched them come and go.

All the life of the garrison and seaport town is in these things. The great man-o'-war coming home after her three years' cruise; the launch in the Dockyard; the boys practising the drum and bugle; the burial of the private soldier; the gang of prisoners—everything is there except Wassielewski and the Poles.

All our petty provincial life. Only that? Why, there is in it all the comedy of humanity, its splendour, its pride, its hopes, its misery, its death.

I could look at none of these things—nor can I now—without associating them with the days and the companions of my youth.

Sad were the thoughts of those few minutes—a veritable *mauvais quart d'heure*—for I saw that I should speedily lose her who was the sunshine of my life. I did not think of the many visits we should pay each other, the happy greetings, after days of separation, in the future. I thought only of the barren hours dragging themselves wearily along, without Celia. The rose of love that had sprung up unbidden in my heart was plucked indeed, but the pricking of its thorns in my soul made me feel that the plant was still alive. Was, then, Celia anything more to me than a sister? I never had a sister, and cannot tell. But she was all the world to me, my light, my life—although I knew that she would never marry me. What, I said to myself, for the half-hour was almost up—what can it matter so long as Celia finds happiness, if I do not? What selfishness is this that would repine because her road lies along the lilies while mine seems all among the thorns? After all, to him who goes cheerfully among the appointed thorns, a thousand pretty blossoms spring up presently beneath his foot. And among the briars, to lighten the labours of the march, there climbs and twines the honeysuckle.

While I was sitting with these thoughts in my brain, this is what was going on at the Queen's Bastion.

Leonard and Celia face to face, the faces of both downcast, the one because she was a girl, and knew beforehand what would be said; the other because he reverenced and feared the girl before him, and because this was the fatal moment on which hung the fulfilment of his life. Above them the great leafy branches of the giant elm, prodigal in shade.

Leonard broke the silence.

"I have been looking for this hour," he began, stammering and uncertain, "for five long years. I began to hope for it when I first left the town. The hope was well-nigh dead, as a child's cry for the moon ceases when he finds it is too far off, while I fought my way up from the ranks. But it awoke again the day I received the colours, and it has been a living hope ever since, until, as time went on, I began to think that some day I might have the opportunity of telling you—what I am trying to tell you now. The time has come, Celia, and I do not know how to frame the words."

She did not reply, but she trembled. She trembled the more when he took her hand, and held it in his own.

"My dear," he whispered, "my dear, I have no fitting words. I want to tell you that I love you. Answer me, Celia,"

"What am I to say, Leonard?"

"Tell me what is in your heart. Oh, my darling, tell me if you can love me a little in return?"

"Leonard—Leonard!" She said no more. And he caught her to his heart, and kissed her, in that open spot, in broad daylight, on the forehead, cheeks, and lips, till she drew herself away, shamefaced, frightened.

"My dear," it was nearly all he could say—and they sat down presently, side by side upon the grass, and he held both her hands together in his. "My dear, my love, what has become of all the fine speeches I would have made about my humble origin, and devotion? They all went out of my head directly I felt the touch of your hand. I could think of nothing, but—I love you—I love you. I have always loved you since you were a little child: and now that you are so beautiful—so sweet, so good—my queen of womanhood —I love you ten times as much as I ever thought I could, even when I lay awake at night in the trenches, trying to picture such a moment as this. My love, you are too high for me. I am not worthy of you."

"Not worthy? O Leonard!—do not say that. You have made me proud and happy. What can you find in me, or think that there is in me, that you could love me so—for five long years? Are you sure that you are not setting up an ideal that you will tire of, and be disappointed when you find the reality?"

Disappointed? He—and with Celia?

He released her hands, and laid his arm round her waist.

"What a mistake to make! To be in love with a woman and to find her an angel. My dear, I am a man of very small imagination—not like Laddy, who peoples his Heaven with angels like yourself and lives there in fancy always— and I am only certain of what I see for myself. What I see is that you are a pearl beyond all price, and that I love you—and, Celia, I am humble before you. You shall teach me, and lead me upwards to your own level, if you can."

When I came back, the half-hour expired, they were sitting side by side on that slope of tall grass still. But they were changed, transformed. Celia's face was glowing with a new light of happiness; it was like the water in the harbour that we had once seen touched by the light of the rising sun; her cheeks were flushed, her eyes were glistening with tears; one hand lay in Leonard's, and round her waist was Leonard's arm.

As for her lover, he was triumphant; it was nothing to him that he was making demonstrative love in this public place, actually a bastion on the ramparts of Her Majesty's most important naval station and dockyard. To be sure there was no one to see them but the swallows, and these birds, whose pairing time was over for the season, had too much to do fly-catching—the serious business of life being well set in for swallows in the month of June—to pay much regard to a pair of foolish mortals.

"Come, Laddy," he cried, springing to his feet and seizing her by the hand, while Celia rose all as blushing as Venus Anadyomene, "be the first to wish that Celia may be happy. She has been so foolish, this dear Celia of ours, this dainty little Cis, that we love so much, as to say that she will take me just as I am, for better and for worse." He took her hand again with that proud and happy look of triumphant love, as if he could not bear to let her go for a moment, and she nestled close to him as if it was her place, and she loved to be near him. "There is a foolish maiden for you. There is an indiscreet and imprudent angel who comes down from the heavens to live with us on earth. Congratulate me, Laddy, my dear old dreamer. I am so happy."

Celia shyly drew her hand away, and came over to me as if for protection. I saw how her proud and queenly manner was in some way humbled, and that she was subdued, as if she had found her master.

She laid her hand upon my shoulder, in her caressing way, which showed me that she was happy, and then I began to congratulate them both. After that I made them sit down on the grass, while I sat on the wheel of the gun-carriage, and I talked sense and reason to them. I told them that this kind of engagement was one greatly to be deprecated, that it was highly irregular not to go first to head-quarters, and to ask permission of parents. That to confess to each other, in this impetuous way, of love, and to make promises of marriage, were things which even Mr. Pontifex, when the passions of his youth were so strong as to make him curse the Goose, had not to repent of; that Mrs. Pontifex had always recommended Celia to follow her own example, and wait till she was of ripe and mature years before marrying any one, and then to marry a man some years younger than herself; that they ought to consider how a soldier's life was a wandering one, and a captain's pay not more than enough for the simple necessaries; that they might have to wait till Leonard was a field-marshal before consent could be obtained; that the Captain would be greatly astonished; that neither he nor I intended to allow Leonard to carry Cis away with him for a long time to come; nor had we dreamed that such a thing would follow when we welcomed him home. Many more things I added in the same strain, while Leonard laughed, and Cis listened, half laughing and half crying; and then, because the occasion was really a solemn one, I spoke a little of my mind. They were good, and bore with me, as I leaned over the old gun and talked, looking through the embrasure across the harbour.

I reminded Leonard how, five years ago, he had left us, with the resolution to advance himself, and the hope of returning and of finding Celia free. Never any man, I told him, had such great good fortune as had fallen on him, in getting all he hoped and prayed for. And then I tried to tell him how for five years the girl whose hand he had won had been growing in grace as well as beauty, feeding her mind with holy thoughts, and living in forgetfulness of herself; how it had been an education to me to be with her, to watch her, to learn from her, and to love and cherish her—and then Celia sprang up and interrupted me, and fell upon my neck, crying, and kissing me. Oh! happy day! oh! day of tears and sunshine! Oh! day fruitful of blessed memories, when for once we could bare our hearts to each other, and show what lay there hid. No need any more to pretend. I loved her, and I always had loved her. She loved me too; if not in the same way, what matter?

Well, it was all over, Celia was promised to Leonard. And yet it seemed as if it was only all begun. Because, after a little while, Cis turned to me with a cry, as one who remembers something forgotten.

"Laddy, what about Herr Räumer?"

She and I looked at each other in dismay. Leonard laughed.

"There is Perseus," I said, pointing to him." He is strong and brave. He is come to rescue Andromeda. What did I tell you, Cis, the day before he kept his promise?"

She had not forgotten one word about the loathly monster and the distressful maiden.

"Now it has all come true," I said. "Meantime, the first thing is to tell the Captain. And that I shall go and do this minute. You two will come on when you please—when you are tired of each other."

Leaving them behind me hand in hand was like plunging at once into the loneliness which loomed before me when they two should be gone. One had no right to be sad. I had enjoyed the companionship of Celia for five years, all to myself; it could not be expected that I was to have her exclusive society for all my life. Besides, there was Poland—it really was hard to keep one's thoughts in that dark groove of revenge; I constantly forgot my wrongs and my responsibilities. Nor did I even, I fear, thoroughly realise the delights of battle and the field of patriotic glory.

At the bottom of the slope there came to meet me the very man—old Wassielewski himself. He was radiant.

Without a word of preface, he cried out, as he seized me by the hand:

"You are in luck. To-morrow they will call upon you."

"Who?"

"The deputies from Basle, Geneva, London, and Paris. They will call upon you at three, with me. Be at home to meet them."

"And when, Wassielewski?"

"When do we begin? At once; next week we must start. Courage, boy; you go to avenge the blood of your father. To-morrow—to-morrow—at three."

He waved his arms like the sails of a windmill.

Just then the bands in the yard, amid a deafening shout, because the ship was launched, struck up a splendid march.

"Listen," he cried. "That is an omen. Hear the music which welcomes the news of another Polish rebellion. A good omen. A good omen."

He sped swiftly away.

But it was a wedding-march, and I thought of Leonard and Celia.

CHAPTER XXXVIII.
THE KEY OF THE SAFE.

I WAS walking along the street after leaving this pair of lovers, full of thought, with my eyes on the ground, when I was aware of a voice calling my name. It was Augustus Brambler tearing along the pavement without a hat, a quill—Augustus would never descend to the meanness of a steel pen while in the Legal—still behind one ear, his coat-tails flying behind him, enthusiastically anxious to execute an order for the Chief. It was a simple message, asking me to step in and see Mr. Tyrrell. I complied, and turned back.

"And the children?" I asked.

"Better, Mr. Pulaski. The Breakings-out have almost disappeared, thanks to an increase of Affluence. My brother Ferdinand is hard at work on his new series of papers. He calls them 'Reminiscences of the Crimea,' compiled from Captain Copleston's private information combined with the back numbers of the *Illustrated London News*, and the morning's Launch will be new boots all round. I don't think," he added in a whisper, "that the Chief is very well. Herr Räumer was with him this morning before he went into the Yard, and when he sent for me just now he was pale, and shivered. No one knows what we lawyers go through: no one can guess the wear and tear of brain. Dear me! On Saturday night I often tell Mrs. Brambler that I feel as if another day would finish me off. But then Sunday comes, when Ferdinand and I can sit over our wine like gentlemen, and rest. Here we are, Mr. Pulaski,"sinking his voice to a whisper. "I must return to a most important Case. Talk of intricacy! Ah!"

Mr. Tyrrell was leaning against the mantle-shelf, looking, as Augustus said, anything but well. The Mayor's robes lay in his arm-chair, and round his neck still hung the great gold chain of office. Usually a high-coloured, florid man, with a confident carriage, he was now pale and trembling. His hands trembled; his lips trembled; his shoulders stooped. What was it that had placed him in another man's power?

"Ladislas," he groaned, "I wish I were dead!"

That seems, certainly, the simplest solution of difficulties. I suppose every man, at some crisis in his fortune, has wished the same. At such times, when it seems as though everything was slipping under one's feet, and the solid foundation of wealth, honour, name, all the fabric of years, was tumbling to pieces like a pack of cards, even the uncertainty of the dread Future seems easier to face than the changes of the Present. Here was a man who mounted steadily, swiftly, without a single check, up the ladder of Fortune. He had saved money, bought houses, owned lands, possessed the best practice in the town, held municipal distinctions, was the envy of younger men and the admiration of his own contemporaries; and now, from some real or fancied power which this German possessed over him, he was stricken with a mortal terror and sickness of brain.

"I wish I were dead! " he repeated.

"Tell me what has happened, Mr. Tyrrell."

"He has been here again. That is nothing—he always is here. But he came with a special purpose last night. He came to say that he wanted an answer."

"Wants an answer?"

"Celia must give him her decision."

"I am very—*very* glad, Mr. Tyrrell," I said, "that he did not want it yesterday morning. I will tell you why presently."

"He is jealous of young Copleston. Says Celia sat up all night with him and you when he came home. Is that true?"

"Quite. We had so much to say that we did not separate till five in the morning."

"To be sure, you were all then children together. Why, you used to play in the garden and on the walls—"

"And so Herr Räumer is jealous?" I asked, interrupting.

"He is mad with jealousy. He accuses me of fostering an attachment—as if I know anything about attachments!—he declares that he must have an answer to-morrow morning, and if it is not favourable—"

"My dear friend and benefactor," I said, "suppose it is not favourable. Can he take away your daughter? Can he rob you of your money? What can he do to you?"

"I dare not tell—even you, Laddy," he replied. "Money? No. He cannot touch my possessions. My daughter? No; he cannot carry her off. But he can almost do as bad. He can—he can—lower me in the eyes of the world; he can proclaim—if he will—a thing that men who do not know the whole truth will judge harshly. And he will disgrace me in the eyes of my daughter."

I was silent, thinking what to say.

Presently I ventured to ask him whether it would not disgrace him more in the eyes of Celia for him to lend his favour to a suit so preposterous.

He groaned in reply.

"You do not know, Laddy," he said, "the trouble I have had to build up a name in this place, where I began as a boy who swept the office, the son of a common labourer. My brothers are labourers still, and content with their position. My sisters are labourers' wives, and content as well. I am the great man of the family. I had much to contend with, want of education, poverty, everything but ability. I am sure I had that because I surmounted all, and became—what I am. Then I married into a good family, and took their level. And the old low levels were forgotten. Why, if all the world were to remind each other aloud that I once swept out an office, it would not matter."

"Of course not, sir. Pray go on."

"It is fifteen years ago, when Herr Räumer first came to the town. He had a plausible tongue and wheedled himself into the confidence of all whom he cared to know. He wanted to know me. He made me his lawyer—sent round that great safe, where it has been ever since, and used to sit with me in the evening talking affairs. There was nothing in the town too small for him to inquire into; he wanted the secret history of everything: and he got it from me; I violated no confidence of clients, but told him all I knew."

"Did he talk much about the Poles?"

"He was at first very inquisitive about the Poles. Said he sympathised with them—I did not, so I had little to tell him. Then came the time when they made the railway on our side of the harbour—"

He paused for a moment.

"—that was the fatal time. I yielded to his instigations and, together, we—never mind what it was, Laddy. It was nothing that could bring me within the power of the Law, but it was an action which, stated in a certain way, would ruin me for ever in the town."

Successful men, I think, are apt to over-estimate the opinion which men have formed of them. They know that they are envied for their success, which is real; and they easily persuade themselves that they are admired for their virtues, which are imaginary. I do not believe that the town at large would have cared twopence if Herr Räumer had gone to the balcony of the old Town Hall, and after sticking up a glove in the old fashion of the burgesses when a town Function was about to begin, such as the opening of the fair, had there in clear and ringing tones denounced the great Mr. Tyrrell of such and such a meanness. They would have lifted their eyebrows, talked to each other for a day, reflected in the morning that he was rich and powerful, and then would have gone on as if nothing had happened. Because I do not think that any man in the place, however unsuccessful, believed in his heart that Mr. Tyrrell was a bit more virtuous than himself. But that the lawyer would not understand.

I think that one of Rochefoucauld's maxims is omitted in all the editions. It has somehow slipped out. And it is this—

"Every man believes himself more virtuous than any other man. If the other man is found out, that proves the fact."

I was thinking out this moral problem, and beginning to test its truth by personal application to my own case, when I was roused by the consciousness that Mr. Tyrrell was talking still.

"—Terrible and long labour in building a name as a Christian as well as a lawyer—good opinion of the clergy—"

It was very wonderful, but the theory did seem to fit marvellously well. I really did believe myself quite as good as any of my neighbours—except Celia and the Captain—and better than most! much better than the Reverend John Pontifex.

"Tell me what you think, Laddy."

"I think, sir," I replied, "that I would lay the case before the Captain, and ask his opinion. I know what it will be."

"You think—"

"I know that he will say, 'Laugh at him, and tell him to do the worst. Let him tell a miserable old story to all the town, but let Celia follow her own heart.' And another thing, Mr. Tyrrell—Celia's heart is no longer free."

"What? Was he right?"

"Quite right. Herr Räumer is a very clever man, and he seldom makes a mistake. Half an hour ago Celia listened to Leonard Copleston, and they are now engaged."

"It only wanted that," he replied with a groan.

This looked as if things were going to be made cheerful for the lovers.

"Will you see the Captain if he comes to you? Or, better still, will you go yourself and talk things over with him? It is half-past twelve, and he will be home by this time. And tell him all."

"I must have advice," he murmured. "I feel like a sinking ship. The Captain will stand by me whatever happens—Yes, Laddy—yes. I will go at once—at once "

He rose, and with trembling hands began to search for his hat.

It was standing on the safe—the closed safe—with the name of "Herr Räumer" upon it in fat white letters.

Mr. Tyrrell shook his fist at the door.

"You are always here," he cried, "with your silent menace. If you were open for five minutes—if I had the key in my hands for only half a minute —I should know what answer to give your master."

He left me, and went out into the street, I after him. But he forgot my presence, and went on without me, murmuring as he went in the misery and agitation of his heart.

I suppose it was the pondering over this successful man as over a curious moral problem, and a certain uplifting of heart as I reflected that there was nothing at all for me to be ashamed of, even if I was found out, that laid me more than commonly open to temptation.

At all events, it was then that I committed the meanest action in my life—a thing which, whenever I meet my accomplice, even after all these years, makes me blush for shame.

My innocent accomplice was no other than little Forty-four.

As I was passing the Bramblers' house in Castle Street, Mr. Tyrrell being some twenty yards ahead of me, and going straight away to consult with the Captain, I not being wanted at all, I thought I would call upon my friends. No one was at home except Forty-four, who was sitting before the open kitchen window sewing and crooning some simple ditty to herself. Her mother was gone a-marketing—that was good news. Uncle Ferdinand, who had received an advance upon his series of papers called "Personal Recollections of the War"—everybody remembers what a sensation those articles caused—was gone out with his note-book to attend the Launch. Augustus Brambler was at his post, no doubt engaged on his labyrinthian case. The children were all on the walls where I had left them playing their little game of Feasting. And Forty-four was in charge of the family pot, which was cheerfully boiling on the fire.

She looked up with her bright laugh.

"Come into the kitchen, Mr. Pulaski, if you don't mind. I've something to tell you."

"What is it?" I asked. "Are things looking better?"

"Oh! yes. Thanks to you know who. We had a dreadful time, though. The man the people call Tenderart—do you know him?"

I knew him and his satellite of old.

"He is our landlord, and he came to take the things to make up the rent. There he stood and began to pick out the things to put in a cart. Uncle Ferdinand asked for time, and the man only laughed. Then Uncle Ferdinand banged his head against the wall and said this was the final Crusher, and we all cried. Then papa ran to get an advance from Mr. Tyrrell."

"Did you ask Herr Räumer?"

"Yes; I went up to ask him—and he said politely, that he never helped anybody on principle. Well, papa got the advance, but it was stopped out of his salary, and so—you see—we have had very little to eat ever since. But Tenderart was paid, and he went away."

"I see; and now things are better?"

"Yes. Because Uncle Ferdinand has found something to write about. And papa has got the most beautiful idea for making all our fortunes. See."

She opened a paper which lay upon the table, and showed it to me. It was written in a clerkly hand, partly couched in legal English, and referred to a scholastic project. So that in this document the threefold genius of Augustus was manifest.

"ROYAL COLLEGIATE ESTABLISHMENT
"For the Education of both Sexes,
"Conducted by the Brothers BRAMBLER.

"The object of this Institution is to impart to the young an education to fit them for the Learned Professions, for Commerce, for the Legal, the Scholastic, or the Clerical. Pupils will be received from the age of eight to fifteen. The College will be divided into two divisions, that for the ladies under the management of Mrs. Brambler, a lady highly connected with the Royal Naval Service, and Miss Lucretia Brambler."

"That's me," said Forty-four ungrammatically.

"I thought you had no name," I said.

"Mr. Ferdinand Brambler, the well-known Author, will undertake the courses of History, Geography, Political Economy, and English Composition. Mr. Augustus Brambler will superintend the classes of Latin, Euclid, Arithmetic, and Caligraphy—"

"My dear, when is the college to be started?"

"Oh! not yet," cried Forty-four. "When we are a little older, and all able to take a part in the curriculum. Fancy the greatness!"

"Yes. It is almost too much, is it not? Don't set your heart too much on things, Forty-four." I did not finish the document, and returned it. The poorer Augustus grew, the more brilliant were his schemes. So Hogarth's starving poet sits beneath a plan of the mines of Potosi. "Is Herr Räumer at home?"

"I think he is gone out. Shall I run up to see?"

We went up together. I had nothing to say, and no reason for calling, but I was excited and restless.

He was not in his rooms. The table was littered and strewn with foreign papers, German, French, and Russian. The piano was littered with his songs—those little sentimentalities of student life of which he was never tired. There was the usual strong smell of recent tobacco in the place, and—it caught my eye as I was going away—there lay in an inkstand on the table—a temptation.

It was the key of the safe.

I turned twice to go, twice I came back, drawn by the irresistible force of that temptation. It riveted my eyes, it made my knees tremble beneath me, it seemed to drag my hand from my side, to force the fingers to close over it, to convey itself, by some secret life of its own, to my pocket, and, once there, to urge me on to further action.

"Mr. Pulaski," cried Forty-four, "why are you so red in the face? What is the matter?"

"Hush!" I whispered; "stay here for five minutes, Forty-four—if Herr Räumer comes home, bustle about and prevent his touching the table. And say nothing—promise to say nothing."

She promised, understanding no word.

I furtively descended the stairs, I crept swiftly, in the shade of the wall, though it was of course broad daylight, looking backwards and forwards, though there were only the usual people in the street, with beating heart and flushed face, towards Mr. Tyrrell's office. The outer door was open, that was usual; I pushed into the hall, and silently turned the handle of the chief's own office. It was not locked—they did not know he was out—there was, of course, no one in the room. Like some burglar in the dead of night I crept noiselessly over the carpet to open the safe.

It was done.

I was back in the street, the key in my hand; I was back at the Bramblers' house, I was upstairs again, the key was restored to its place. I seized Forty-four by the hand, and hurried her downstairs.

"What is it?" she asked again.

"Remember, Forty-four, you have promised to tell no one. It was the key of Herr Räumer's safe. I borrowed it for five minutes—for Celia Tyrrell's sake."

She promised again—nothing, she said, would make her tell any one. No one should know that I had been in the room: she entered as zealously into the conspiracy as if she was a grown woman married to a St. Petersburg diplomatist, and engaged in throwing dust into the eyes of an English plenipotentiary.

CHAPTER XXXIX.
BORROWED PLUMES.

MEANTIME, we had not forgotten our old friend Moses. The "Blue Anchor" was a music hall before that kind of entertainment was supposed to be invented. That is to say, long before the name of music was debased, and song dragged in the dust before London audiences of shop-boys and flashy gents, the thing was already flourishing in our seaport towns for the benefit of soldiers and sailors. The "Anchor," as it was lovingly called, stood in a crowded street, where every second house was a beershop, and the house between a pawnbroker's. It had a parterre, or pit, the entrance to which was free, where Jack the Sailor, Joe the Marine, and the Boiled Lobster could sit in comfort and dignity, each man with his pipe in his mouth and his pot before him. It was a long, high, and narrow room. At the end stood a platform, where the performances took place, and under the platform, just as you may see in the present London houses, was a table where the proprietor, acting as Chairman, announced the songs and dances, called order, and superintended the comfort of his guests. A small and select band of admirers rallied round the Chairman, and were privileged not only to call for drinks to assuage the great man's thirst, but also from time to time to take the hammer of authority. At the other end of the hall was a small gallery, where young naval officers and subalterns sometimes honoured the representations by their appearance. It was to this gallery that we repaired, Leonard and I, accompanied by a second lieutenant of the Navy. He was a cheerful youth, of smiling demeanour, whose chief merit in my eyes was his unbounded admiration for Leonard. He met us by accident, and volunteered to join us, not knowing the nature of our quest; on being informed that there might be a row, he became the more eager to come with us. The fervent prayer of every young naval officer, on every possible occasion, that there may be a row, is surely a healthy distinguishing characteristic of the Navy. Certainly the members of no other service or profession with which I am acquainted are desirous of a fight on any possible occasion.

We went, therefore, into the gallery, where there were a dozen of noisy middies and young naval fellows, who had been dining not wisely, but too well.

There was an interval in the performance, and a buzz of conversation going on. Now and then one of the audience would lift up his voice with a snatch of a chorus, to be taken up by his neighbours, or, if it was a favourite, by the whole audience.

We looked about the room. No Moses had arrived yet. That was quite certain, because from our gallery we could see everybody in the hall, and there was no doubt about our recognising Moses—so old a friend.

We sat down in the front row and looked on.

Down came the hammer, with some inaudible remarks from the Chair. There was silence for a moment, and then a shout, not of applause, but of derision, as a man, dressed in sailor rig, bounded on the stage, and began to dance a hornpipe.

"Where was you shipped, mate?" "When was you last paid off?" There was no denying the dance, which was faithfully executed, but in consequence of the absence of some professional detail, probably in the dancer's get-up, the sailors with one consent refused to recognise him as a brother. The row grew tremendous as the performer went on, resolutely refusing to recognise any objection raised to his personal appearance. At last a stalwart young fellow bounded from a table in the auditorium to the platform, coolly hustled the professional with a hitch or two of his shoulder off the stage, and proceeded to execute the hornpipe himself, amid the exclamations of his comrades and brethren of the sister services. The band, consisting of two fiddles, a harp, and a cornet, went on playing steadily, whatever happened in the house. It was like Wassielewski, fiddling while the sailors sang, drank, and danced—himself unregarding.

The dance over, and the applause subsided, the young fellow jumped back to his place, and down came the Chairman's knocker again. Sam Trolloper, he announced, this time—without any prefix or handle to the name, as if one would say Charles Dickens, or Julius Cæsar—was about to sing the Song of the Day.

The illustrious Sam, who was a popular favourite, and received the vociferous applause as something due to real merit, appeared in a suit of shore-going togs. He wore a coat all tails, with a hat all brim, and trousers of which one leg was gone, and the other going. Boots without socks, a ragged shirt and a red kerchief tied around his neck, completed a garb which, coupled with the fellow's face of low cunning and inextinguishable drollery, made him up into as complete an habitual criminal as you are likely to meet outside of Short's Gardens. He brandished a short stick, with a short preliminary walk across the stage, and then began the following:—

""Tis oh! for a gay and a gallant bark,
A brisk and a lively breeze,
A bully crew and a captain too,
To carry me o'er the seas.
To carry me o'er the seas, my boys,
To my own true love so gay,
For she's taking of a trip
In a Government ship,
Ten thousand miles away.
Then blow, ye winds, heigho!
For a roaming we will go,
I'll stay no more on England's shore,
Then let the music play;
For I'm off by the morning train
Across the raging main,
I'm on the rove to my own true love,
Ten thousand miles away.

"My true love she was beautiful,
My true love she was fair,
Her eyes were blue as the violets true,
And crimson was her hair.
And crimson was her hair, my boys,
But while I sing this lay
She's doing of the grand
In a distant land,
Ten thousand miles away.

"The sun may shine through a London fog,
The Thames run bright and clear,
The ocean brine may turn to wine
Ere I forget my dear.
Ere I forget my dear, my boys,
The landlord his quarter day,
For I never can forget
My own dear pet,
Ten thousand miles away.

"Oh! dark and dismal was the day
When last I saw my Meg,
She'd a Government band around each hand,
Another one round each leg.

Another one round each leg, my boys,
Dressed all in a suit of grey,
'My love,' said she,
'Remember me,
Ten thousand miles away.'

"Oh I would I were a bo's'n tight,
Or e'en a bombardier;
I'd hurry afloat in an open boat,
And to my true love steer.
And to my true love steer, my boys,
Where the dancing dolphins play,
And the shrimps and the sharks
Are a having of their larks
Ten thousand miles away.
Then blow, ye winds, heigho!
For a roaming we will go,
I'll stay no more on England's shore,
Then let the music play;
For I'm off by the morning train
Across the raging main,
I'm on the rove to my own true love,
Ten thousand miles away."

This ditty, which the singer gave with a rich rollicking baritone, and in a rolling tune, was accompanied by a chorus from a couple of hundred throats, which made the windows rattle and the glasses vibrate. Such a chorus, all bawling in unison, I never heard before. When the last bars, affectionately clung to by voices loth to let them go, died away, the illustrious Sam had disappeared, only to emerge again in a new disguise and sing another song. But, as the hammer fell to announce his return, Leonard touched my arm, and I saw our old friend Moses walking grandly among the chairs in the direction of the President.

I had not seen him for more than twelve years, but there was no mistaking his identity. It was the same dear old Moses. There was no real change in him; only a development of the well-known boyish graces. The blotches upon his fat and bloated face; the swagger with which he swung along the room; the hat cocked on one side of his head; the short stick carried half in the side pocket of his coat; the flashy rings upon his fingers; the gaudy necktie; and the loud pattern of his trousers—all seemed part and parcel of the original Moses. He was only the infant Moses grown up; Mrs. Jeram's Moses expanded, according to the immutable laws of Nature, which allow of no sudden break, but only a wavy line of continuity. Selfish, greedy, and unscrupulous he had been as a child, just such he appeared now. Was it education alone, I thought, which made the difference between him and Leonard? It could hardly be that, because there was Jem Hex, himself as good a fellow as ever piped all hands, to set on the other side. Leonard! For a moment he stood irresolute, his hands clenched, just as he used to look in the days of old before he "went for" Moses. He waited till he saw his enemy seated by the Chairman. Then he touched my arm, and strode across the benches of the gallery to the door. I followed, and so did our friend the Navy man. We got downstairs and followed Leonard closely as he marched, head erect and with flashing eyes, straight up the hall.

There was a little commotion among the soldiers at sight of him.

"Gentleman Jack," the men whispered to each other.

Leonard took no notice. One or two of them stood up to salute him. "Three cheers for Gentleman Jack and the Rifle-pit," shouted an enthusiastic private of his regiment. Everybody knew about the Rifle-pit, and the cheering was taken up with a will. Leonard stopped for a moment and looked round. When the cheers ceased he held up his hand and nodded. Three times three. The music, meantime, went on, and the singer made no pause. It was the illustrious Sam again—this time in the disguise of a soldier— supposed to be in liquor, and suffering from the melancholy of a love disappointment, as appeared from the only two lines of the song which I heard:—

"There I see the faithless she,
A cooking sausages for he."

But the attention of the audience was at this point wholly distracted from the singer. The Chairman and the band alone paid attention to him: these were of course professionally engrossed in admiration of the performance. For two circumstances, besides the cheering for Leonard, and both of an agreeable and pleasing character, happened at this juncture to call away the thoughts of the men from imaginary sorrows. The first was that the middies in the gallery, having succeeded in hooking up a soldier's cap by means of a string and a pin, were now hauling away at their line, while the owner vainly imprecated wrath below. To join common cause with a comrade is the first duty of a soldier. A dozen men instantly jumped upon the tables, and a brief parley, in which strong words were answered with gentle chaff, was followed by a storm of pewter pots, whose battered sides indicated that they had before this hurtled through the air on a similar occasion. The middies instantly ducked, and the shower of projectiles passed as harmlessly over their heads as a cannonade at a modern siege. The storm having ceased, one middy, cautiously peeping over the gallery, seized the moment of comparative calm and hurled a pewter back. Instantly another and a fiercer hail of pint-pots. These having ceased, the middies swiftly creep over the seats and skedaddle, heaving over a spare half-dozen ere they reach the portals and fly down the stairs. When the brave redcoats have swarmed up the eight feet pillars and stormed the gallery, they found it like another Malakoff—empty. Then they shout. Who can withstand the bravery of the British soldier? All this takes time and attracts attention. Meantime another scene is enacted at our end of the hall.

Leonard stalking up the room, the red-jackets shouting for "Gentleman Jack," the curiosity of those who do not know him, draw upon us the eyes of our old enemy, Moses. He knows us instantly, and with a hasty gesture to the Chairman, whose glass he has just filled, he rises, to effect a retreat by the way of the orchestra and under the stage-door. Not so fast, friend Moses. Leonard makes for him; there is a cry, and the pretender to the name of Copleston is dragged back to the table by the coat-collar. "Now—you—whatever you call yourself," cries Leonard. "What do you mean by taking my name?"

"Let me go." Moses wriggles under the grasp which held him by the coat-collar like a vice, and drags him backwards upon the table among the glasses, where he lies like a turned turtle, feet up and hands sprawling, a very pitiable spectacle.

"Let me go, I say."

"Presently. Tell me your name."

"Moses Copleston," he replied, with an attempt at defiance.

"Liar!"

"Moses Copleston, oh! Won't any one help a fellow?"

"Liar again! "

"Let me get up, then."

Leonard let him rise, his friend the Lieutenant being at the other side of the table, and a few of his own men having gathered round, so that there was little chance of the man's escape.

"What have I done to you now?" whined Moses. "What have I done to you, I should like to know? See here, Mr. Chairman of this respectable Free-and-Easy Harmonic Meeting, what did I say to him? What did I do to him? Here's a pretty go for a peaceable man to be set upon for nothing."

"Why have you dared to take my name," cried Leonard, "to drag into police courts and prisons?"

"Your name? O Lord! His name! What a thing to take! Which he was born in Victory Row, and his mother—"

Here a straight one from the left floored Moses, and he fell supine among the chairs, not daring to arise.

The Lieutenant picked him up, and placed him—because he declined to stand: and, indeed, the claret was flowing freely—in the President's arm-chair.

"Yar—yar!" he moaned. "Hit a man when he is down. Hit your own brother. Yar—Cain—Cain—Cain and Abel! Hit you own twin brother."

"Liar, again," said Leonard calmly. "Do you see any likeness, Grif,"—Grif was the sobriquet of the young sailor—"between me and this—this cur and cad?"

"Can't say I do, old man."

"He has taken my name; he has traded on it; by representing himself to be—my mother's son—he has obtained from some one money to spend in drink. I do not know who that person is. But I mean to know."

"Ho! ho!" laughed Moses, mopping up the blood. "Can't hit a man when he's down. Yaw! Shan't get up. Wouldn't he like to know, then? Ho! ho!"

"Get a policeman," said Grif. "Follow him up and down."

"Beg pardon, sir," said one of the men, saluting Leonard, "best search his pockets."

Moses turned pale and buttoned up his coat.

"That seems sound advice, Leonard," I said. "Sit down, and let the men do it for you."

Well—it was a strange performance in an Harmonic meeting, but it attracted considerable attention, much more than the ditty which it interrupted; as much as the flight of pewters backwards and forwards in the lower end of the gallery.

They told off four, under a corporal, and then they seized the unhappy Moses. First the Chairman said he would turn down the lights, but was persuaded by Grif, not without a gentle violence, to sit down comfortably, and see fair play. Then the orchestra left off playing to see this novelty in rows, a thing they hadn't done, except in the daytime and on Sundays, for twenty years. Then the Illustrious Baritone, Sam, himself came down from the stage to witness the scene. And, but for the kicks, the struggles, the many unrighteous words used by the victim, one might have thought that it was the unrolling by a group of *savans* of an Egyptian mummy.

First they took off his coat. It contained, in his pockets, the following articles :—

1. A "twopenny smoke," as described by the Corporal.
2. A pipe constructed of sham meerschaum.
3. A box of fusees.
4. The portrait of a young lady (daguerreotype) in dégagée costume.

5. A penknife.
6. Three pawnbrokers' tickets.
7. A small instrument which, the Corporal suggested, was probably intended to pick locks with.
8. Another " twopenny smoke."
9. A sixpenny song book, containing one hundred sprightly ballads.

There was nothing else in the coat, but I was certain something else would follow, because I had noticed the man's sudden pallor when the operation was suggested.

They next removed his waistcoat.

In the pockets were:—

1. A pipe poker.
2. A quantity of loose tobacco.
3. Another "twopenny smoke," a little broken in the back.
4. Another box of fusees.
5. More pawnbrokers' tickets.
6. The sum of six shillings and twopence.

That was all, but on my taking the garment I felt something rustle.

There was an inside pocket to the waistcoat. And in this—Moses made a frantic plunge—I found two letters. One, in a lady's handwriting, was addressed to Mr. Copleston, Post Office, to be called for; the other, in what may be best described as not a lady's hand, addressed to "Miss Rutherford, Fareham." Now, Fareham is a small town at the upper end of the harbour. These letters I handed to Leonard. He read the address and put them in his pocket.

"Miss Rutherford," he repeated, with a strange light in his eyes.

Moses had recourse to violent language.

"Beg your pardon, sir," said the Corporal. "What to do next?"

"Let him go," said Leonard. "Or—stay—put him outside the place—but gently."

"Ah !—Yah!" Moses bellowed, bursting into what seemed a real fit of weeping." This is the way that a twin brother behaves—this is getting up in the world."

"He is no brother of mine," said Leonard. "Come, Laddy—come, Grif."

The soldiers, when the weeping Moses had resumed his coat and waistcoat, ran him down the hall in quick and soldier-like fashion. As he was being run out, the orchestra played half-a-dozen bars of the Rogue's March, which was, under the circumstances, really a kindness, as it confirmed the minds of any possible waverers as to the iniquity of the culprit.

All was quiet again; the pewter pots were being collected by a barman in the gallery; the noisy middies were gone; the soldiers were sitting down again, and Moses received undivided attention as he was escorted to the doors.

Down went the Chairman's hammer.

"Gentlemen! Sam Trolloper will again oblige."

Twang, fiddle; blow, horn; strike up, harp.

We went away as the orchestra played the opening to the accompaniment, and as the Illustrious Sam began a ballad of which we only heard the first two lines:—

> "As I sat by the side of the bubbling water
> Toasting a herring red for tea."

CHAPTER XL.
MORE UNPLEASANTNESS FOR PERKIN WARBECK.

GRIF, greatly marvelling, went his own way, and Leonard, seizing my arm, hurried me home.

The Captain was gone to bed; we lit the lamp in the little parlour, and Leonard tore open the two letters with impatience.

That from Moses, ill-spelt, ill-conditioned, in a tone half bullying, half crawling, asked, as might be expected, for money. It was evidently not the first of such letters. It referred to his previous communications and interviews, appealed to his correspondent's close relationship, and went on to threaten, in case the money was not forthcoming, to do something vague, but dreadful, which would bring him within the power of the law, in which case, he hinted, he should, from his commanding position in the dock, let all the world know that he had been driven to perpetrate the desperate deed by the obdurate and unrelenting heart of his own mother's sister, who rolled in gold and would give him none of it.

"There's a pretty villain for you," said Leonard, reading the last words with a clenched fist.

"I wish to go Strate," wrote Moses, in conclusion, "as I have always gone Strate. If I am drove to go kruked there shan't be no one as shan't know it was Misery and your kruelty as done it. I must have a tenner to-morrow or the Day after if you've got to pawn your best black silk dress. Take and pawn it. Isn't that your Dooty? You in silk and me in rags and tatters. Why it makes a cove sick to think of it. There. And specially a cove as is innercent, and one as is only got his karakter behind his back to depend upon—which the Lord He knows is a good one. So no more for the present from your affeckshunate nevew, Moses. P.S. Mind I want the money right down. P.S. I know a most respectible pawnbroker and will call for the gownd myself. P.S. I am thinkin if it would be pleasant for you to have me at home always with you. Aunts and nevews oughter not to be sepperated."

"There's a precious villain for you," repeated Leonard, banging the table with his fist.

The other letter, to which this delightful epistle was apparently in reply, was written in expostulation of the man's extravagance and profligate habits. Evidently the writer was a lady. She spoke of her own small income: of the poverty in which she had to live in order to meet the demands which this fellow was perpetually making upon her; she had reminded him that he had drawn a hundred and fifty pounds out of her already; from which we inferred that the claims were comparatively recent; that she lived in daily terror of great demands; that she implored him to endeavour in some honourable way to get his own livelihood; and that his conduct and extravagance were causing her daily wretchedness—a letter which ought to have melted the heart even of a Moses. One thought, however, of the way in which that boy used to walk up all the jam, and felt sure that nothing would melt his granite heart.

"Laddy," cried Leonard. "Think! That fellow may be even now on his way to make a final attempt upon this poor lady—my mother's sister—my poor mother's sister."

His eyes filled with tears for a moment and his voice choked.

"On the very day," he went on, "that Celia has promised to be my wife, I am restored to my own people. I cannot wait till to-morrow. Come with me, Laddy, if you will—or I will go alone—I cannot rest. I shall go over to Fareham now, to-night—if only to protect her from that fellow. Good heavens! And he has got half-an-hour's start."

"He will walk," I said. " We will go into the town. It is only half-past nine. Get a dog-cart, and drive over. We can easily get there before him."

"He had a few shillings," Leonard reflected. "It is not likely that he will spend them in driving. And yet he knows it is his only chance to see her to-night. If you cross the harbour first it is only six miles to walk. Of course he will walk. By road it is eleven miles. We can do it in an hour and a half. Come, Laddy. Quick! "

It was easy enough to get a dog-cart, and in ten minutes we were bowling along the road, Leonard driving something like Jehu.

He did not speak one word all the journey until we saw the lights of the little town in the distance. Then he turned his head to me and said quietly—

"I wonder what she will be like?"

We clattered over the rough stones of the street, and stopped at the inn, where we had the horse taken out. The ostler undertook to guide us to Miss Rutherford's cottage.

It was nearly eleven o'clock, and most of the lights in the town were put out. For economy's sake the gas in the streets was not lit at all during this time of the year. We followed our guide down the street and beyond the houses, where began that fringe of small villa residences which is common to our English country towns, and distinguishes them especially from all Continental towns. Stopping in front of one of these, our friendly ostler pointed to the garden gate.

"That's Miss Rutherford's, gentlemen. But you'll have to ring her up if you want to see the lady very particular, and to-night, because they're all gone to bed."

It was true. The house was dark, and its occupants probably asleep.

The ostler retraced his steps. We looked at each other in dismay.

"I feel rather foolish," said Leonard. We can't very well knock at the door and wake up the poor lady."

"Moses will probably have fewer scruples if he arrives to-night on his private and very urgent business."

"Yes; that is true. Look here, Laddy, you go back to the inn, and get a bed there. I will stay outside, and watch here all night till the fellow comes."

I would not consent to that. It seemed to me fair that we should each do our turn of watching.

All this time we were standing outside the garden gate. Within—one could see everything perfectly in the midsummer twilight—was a trim and neat lawn, set with standard roses and dainty flower-beds. Behind, a small house with a gable, round whose front there climbed Westeria and passion-flower. The air was heavy with the scent of the former. A lilac was in full blossom among the shrubs, and added its fresh spring-like perfume to the heavy odour of the creeper.

"It is all very peaceful," whispered Leonard. "Let us go inside and sit down."

We opened the gate, and stepped in as softly as a pair of burglars. On the right was a garden seat, over which drooped the branches of a laburnum. There we sat, expectant of Moses.

"I wonder what she is like," Leonard said again. "How shall we tell her? You must tell her, Laddy. And what will she tell me?

"It will be something more for Celia," he went on, "that her husband will have relations and belongings. It is too absurd to marry a man without even a cousin to his back. I have been ashamed all my life, not so much that I was born—as I was—as that I had no belongings at all. I used to envy, when I was a boy, the family life that we saw so little of—the mothers and sisters, the home-comings and the rejoicings—all the things one reads of in novels. We had none of these—except at second-hand, through Cis. You were better off than I, Laddy, because no one could take away your ancestry, though the compassionate Czar relieved you of the burden of your wealth. But I had nothing. And now—what am I going to have?

"She was good, my poor mother. So much Mrs. Jeram knows of her. But her mind wandered, and she could not, if she wished, have told her who or what she was. She was good, of that I am quite certain. But what about my father?"

I made no reply. Within the sleeping house lay the secret. We had to pass the night before we could get at it. Perhaps, when it was found, poor Leonard would be no happier.

Twelve o'clock struck from some church tower near at hand. I thought of the night but a few weeks ago, when Celia and I sat whispering through the twilight hours in the stern of the boat. Well, he had come, of whom we talked that night; he was with us; he had told Celia that he loved her. It was quite certain what answer she would give her elderly suitor. Celia's father, besides, had got the key of the safe, the thing by which he declared he would rid himself at once of his persecutor. I had done that with Forty-four. Oh! guilty pair. Was little Forty-four lying sleepless and remorseful on a conscience-stricken pillow? I, for my own part, felt small and rather mean thinking over what I had done—and how I had done it—but perhaps the "small" feeling was due rather to the knowledge how pitiably small we should look if we were found out. I believe that repentance generally does mean fear of being found out, when it does not mean the keener pang of intense disgust at having been actually exposed, in which case we call it Remorse. Borrowing that key for those few minutes, and setting the door of the safe open, was, as Mr. John Pontifex would have said, shaking his head and forefinger, a Wrong Thing, a thing to lament, as awful an event as his own profane language over the tough goose when in the full vigour and animal passion of his youth. And yet—and yet—one could not but chuckle over the thought of Herr Räumer's astonishment when he found the safe open and his victim free.

There was too much to think about as we sat beneath the laburnum in that quiet garden. Behind the forms of Celia and Leonard, behind the orange blossoms and flowers, rose a gaunt and weird figure, with a look of hungry longing in its eyes, which were yet like the eyes of Wassielewski. It reached out long arms and great bony hands dripping with blood to seize me. And a mocking voice cried, "Revenge thy father! revenge thy father! "My brain reeled as thin shadows of things, real and unreal, flitted across my closed eyes. I awoke with a start.

One o'clock.

And just then we heard in the distance the crunch of slow steps over the gravel of the road.

"Moses," Leonard whispered, springing into attention.

The steps came nearer; they were a hundred yards off; they were on the other side of the hedge; they stopped at the garden wall

"Moses," whispered Leonard again.

It was Moses. And Moses in very bad temper. He swore aloud at the garden-gate because he could not at first find the handle. Then he swore aloud in general terms, then he swore at the people of the house because he would have to ring them up, and then he came in banging the door after him, and tramped heavily upon the grass—the brute—crunching straight through the flower-bed, setting his great heavy feet as if by deliberate choice on the delicate flowers. We were invisible beneath the laburnum tree.

Leonard rose noiselessly, and stepped after him.

See, another step, and he will be at the door, ringing the bell, terrifying out of their wits the women sleeping within. Already, as his scowling face shows in the twilight, he has formulated his requisition in his own mind, and is going to back it with threats of violence. The demands will never be made. The threats will never be uttered. Leonard's hand falls upon his shoulder, and Moses, turning with a start and a cry, finds himself face to face again with his old enemy.

"Come out of this garden," said Leonard. "Dare to say one word above your breath, and—"

Moses trembled, but obeyed. It was like Neptune's *"Quos ego—"*

Leonard dragged him, unresisting, into the road, and led him along the silent way, beyond earshot of the house, saying nothing.

"What shall we do to him?" he asked me.

"Oh! Mr. Ladislas," whimpered Moses, "don't let him murder me. You're witness that I never done nothing to him. Always hard on a poor innocent cove, he was, when we were all boys together."

"You came out to-night," said Leonard, "thinking you were going to find an unprotected woman asleep in the dead of the night; you were persuading yourself that you would frighten her into giving you more money, knowing that it was your last chance."

"No, sir," whined Moses abjectly. "No, Captain Copleston, sir. Not that. What I said to myself, as I came along, was this: 'Moses,' I says, says I, 'the plant's found out. All is up. That's where it is.' So I says to myself—if you don't mind, sir, takin' your fingers from off o' my coat-collar, which they have a throttlesome feel"—Leonard released him. "Thank you, sir. I says to myself, then, 'I'll up and go to Miss Rutherford—which she is a generous-'earted lady, and tell her—tell her—Hall.' That's wot I meant to do, Cap'en Copleston, sir. Hall I was a-goin' to tell her."

"A likely story, indeed," said Leonard.

"Very likely, sir," Moses echoed. "Yes, and I should have said—"

"Now—you—drunken blackguard and liar," said Leonard. "You have come here to make a final attempt. You have failed. Henceforth you will be watched. I give you fair warning that if you are ever seen by me about this place, or in any other place, I will instantly give you into custody on a charge of obtaining money on false pretences. You understand so much. Then go—get out of my sight."

He accompanied his words with a gesture so threatening that our prisoner instantly set off running as hard as he could down the road. If fear ever lent wings to a fugitive, those wings were produced for Moses on this occasion.

"I was in such a rage," said Leonard, as the steps died away in the distance, "such a boiling rage with the creature that I think I should have killed him had I not let him go. It is too bad, because he richly deserved the best cow-hiding one could give him. Odd! All the old feeling came back upon me, too. I used to hate him in the old days when we fought night and morning. And I hate him now."

"What is to be done next?" I asked. "Are we to go back to the friendly laburnum? There is no fear about Moses any more."

"No; I don't care what we do. I am restless and excited. I cannot sleep. Perhaps she gets up early. Let us go for a walk."

Half-past one in the morning was rather late for an evening walk, but I complied, and we went along the deserted road. Presently I began to feel tired, and was fain to rest in the hedge under a tree. And there I fell fast asleep. When I woke it was broad daylight. Leonard was walking backwards and forwards along the road. What a handsome man he was as he came swiftly towards me, bathed in the early sunshine which played in his curly hair, and lay in his eyes!

"Awake already, Laddy?" he cried. "It is only four o'clock. I am less sleepy than ever. And there are two long hours to wait. She can't get up before six. Perhaps she will not be up before nine."

I confess that those two hours were long ones. Leonard's restless excitement increased. I made him walk. I made him bathe. I tried to make him talk, and yet the minutes crawled. At last, however, it was half-past six, and we retraced our steps to the cottage.

CHAPTER XLI.
MISS RUTHERFORD.

MISS RUTHERFORD was already up. At least a lady about five-and-forty, small, fragile, and dainty, with delicate features and an air of perfect ladyhood; she wore a morning dress of muslin, with garden gloves and a straw hat. And she was gazing with dismay at the footprints—that brute Moses!—on her flower-beds.

We looked at her for a few moments, and then Leonard opened the garden-gate, and we presented ourselves.

At least I presented both of us.

"Miss Rutherford,"—she looked surprised. "I am speaking to Miss Rutherford, am I not?"

"Yes. I am Miss Rutherford."

"We have something to tell you of importance. Will you take us into your house?"

She looked from one to the other.

"It is very early," she said. "My servants are not down yet—but come—you appear to be gentlemen."

She led the way to a little drawing-room, which was a mere bower of daintiness, the pleasant and pretty room of a refined and cultivated lady, with books and pictures, and all sorts of pretty things—fancy the hulking Moses in such an apartment!—and offered us chairs. There was nothing in the room which pointed to the presence of the sterner and heavier sex. Even the chairs seemed only calculated for ladies of her own slender dimensions. Leonard's creaked ominously when he sat down.

"Let me go back twenty-three years," I began. "But first I must tell you that my name is Ladislas Pulaski—here is my card—and that we do not come here from any idle motives. This gentleman—but you will see presently who he is."

"Three-and-twenty years ago?" Miss Rutherford began to tremble. "That was when I lost my sister—and my nephew was born. You come about him, I am sure. He has done something terrible at last, that boy, I am afraid. Gentlemen, remember under what bad influences my nephew's early life was spent. If you have to accuse him of anything wrong—remember that."

"Pray do not be alarmed," I went on. "Your nephew's early influences were not so bad as you think, and you will very likely see reason to be proud of him."

She shook her head as if that was a thing quite beyond the reach of hope.

Leonard was looking at her with curious eyes that grew softer as they rested on this gentlewoman's sweet face.

"Twenty-three years ago, your sister died. Would it pain you too much, Miss Rutherford, if you would tell us something about her?"

"The pain is in the recollection, rather than the telling," she replied. "My poor sister married an officer."

"His name was Leonard Copleston," I said.

"Yes—you knew him, perhaps? She was only eighteen —three years younger than myself—and she knew nothing of the world—how should she, living as she had done all her short life in our quiet country vicarage? She thought the man she married was as good as he was handsome. She admired him for his bravery, for the stories he could tell, for the skill with which he rode, shot, and did everything, and for the winning way he had. My father liked him for his manly character, and because he was clever, and had read as well as travelled and fought. And I believe I liked him as much as my father did. There was never any opposition made, and my poor dear was married to him in our own church, and went away with him on her eighteenth birthday."

She paused for a moment.

"He was not a good man," she went on; "he was a very, very bad man. I hope God has forgiven him all the trouble and misery he brought upon us, but I find it very hard to forgive. My sister's letters were happy and bright at first; gradually—I thought it was my own fancy—they seemed to lose the old joyous ring; and then they grew quite sad. In those days we did not travel about as we can now, and all we could do was to wait at home and hope. Six months after her marriage she came back to us. Oh! my poor dear, so changed, so altered. She who had been the happiest of girls and the blithest of creatures was wan and pale, with a scared and frightened look"—Leonard rose, and went to the window, where he remained, half hidden by the curtain—"such a look as an animal might have who had been ill-treated. She came unexpectedly and suddenly, without any letter or warning—on a cold and snowy December afternoon: she burst into passionate weeping when she fell upon my neck; and she would never tell me why she left her husband. Nor would she tell my father.

"He began to write to her. She grew faint and sick when the first letter came; she even refused at first to read it; but she yielded, and he kept on writing; and one day, she told me that she had forgiven her husband, and was going back to him.

"She went. She went away from us with sad forebodings, I knew; she wrote one or two letters to us; and then—then we heard no more."

"Heard no more?"

"No; we heard nothing more of her from that day. My father made inquiries, and learned that Captain Copleston had left the army, sold out, and was gone away from the country—no one knew whither. His own family, we learned for the first time, had entirely given him up as irreclaimable, and could tell us no more. We heard nothing further, and could only conjecture that the ship in which they sailed had gone down with all on board. But why did she not write to tell us that she was going?

"We waited and waited, hoping against hope. And then we resigned ourselves to the conviction that she was dead. The years passed on; my father died, full of years, and I was left alone in the world. And then, one day last year, a letter came to me from America. It was a letter dictated by my sister's husband on his deathbed—"

"He is dead then? Thank GOD!" Was that the voice of Leonard, so hoarse, so thick with trouble?

"He implored my forgiveness, and that of his wife if she still lived. He confessed that he had let her go away—driven her away by his conduct, he said—when she was actually expecting to be confined, and that in order to begin life again without any ties he had emigrated. The letter was unfinished, because Death took him while he was still dictating it. Yet it brought me the comfort of knowing that he had repented."

"And then," I asked, because she stopped.

"Then I began again to think of my poor sister, and I advertised in our two papers, asking if any one could give me tidings of her. For a long time I received no reply, but an answer came at last; it was from my nephew, that unhappy boy, who seems to have inherited all his father's vices and none of his graces."

Poor Leonard! What a heritage !

"It was from him that I learned how his mother—poor thing, poor thing!—died in giving birth to him: he told me that he had been brought up in a rough way, among soldiers and sailors; that he knew nothing about any of his relations, that, as his letter would show me, he had little education, that he was a plumber and joiner by trade; and that by my help, if I would help him, he hoped to do well. In answer to his letter I made an appointment, and came down to meet him. I can hardly tell you what a disappointment it was to find my poor dear sister's son so rough and coarse. However, it was my duty to do what I could, and I moved down here in order to be near him, and help him to the best purpose."

She stopped and wiped away a tear.

"I have not been able to help him much as yet," she went on. "He is, indeed, the great trouble of my life. He has deceived me in everything; I find that he has no trade, or, at least, that he will not work at it; he said he had a wife and young family, and I have found that he is unmarried; he said he was a total abstainer—and—oh! dear me, he has been frequently here in a dreadful state of intoxication; he said he was a church-goer and a communicant.—But these things cannot interest you."

She said this a little wistfully, as if she hoped they might.

"They do interest us very much," I said.

"After all, he is my nephew," as if she could say much more, but refrained from the respect due to kinship.

"You have been deceived," I told her. "You have been very grossly deceived."

"I have," she said. "But I must bear with it."

"You have been deceived, madam, in a much more important way than you think. Listen to a little story that I have to tell you.

"There were once four boys living together in the house he showed you, all under the charge of an excellent and charitable woman named Mrs. Jeram, to whom we shall take you. One of these boys, the best of them all, was your nephew."

"The best of them all!" she repeated bitterly. "Then what were the others like?"

"One of them, to whom I can also take you, was named James Hex. He is now a boatswain in the Royal Navy, a very good boatswain, too, I believe, and a credit to the service. Another was—myself."

"You?"

"I, Miss Rutherford. I was placed there by my countrymen, the Poles, with this Mrs. Jeram, and maintained by them out of their poverty. When one of these boys, your nephew, was eight or nine, and I a year or two younger, we were taken away from the good woman with whom we lived by a gentleman whom you shall very soon know. He adopted us, and had us properly educated."

"Properly educated? But my nephew can hardly write."

"Your nephew writes as well as any other gentleman in England."

"Gentleman in England?"

"My dear lady, the man who calls himself Moses Copleston is not your nephew at all. He was the fourth of those boys of whom I told you. He is the one among them who has turned out badly. He knew, no doubt from Mrs. Jeram, all about your nephew's birth. What he told you, so far, was true.

All the rest was pure invention. Did you ever, for instance, see any resemblance in him to your late sister?"

"To Lucy? Most certainly not."

"To his father?"

"Not in face. But he has his father's vices."

"So have, unfortunately, a good many men."

"But I cannot understand. He is not my nephew at all? Not my nephew? Can any man dare to be so wicked?"

It really was, as we reflected afterwards, a claim of great daring, quite worthy to be admitted among those of historical pretenders. Moses was another Perkin Warbeck.

"Most certainly not your nephew. He is an impudent pretender. I do not ask you to accept my word only. I will give you proof that will satisfy any lawyer, if you please. He must have seen your advertisement, and knowing that the real nephew was gone away, devised the excellent scheme of lies and robbery of which you have been the victim. Last night we wrung the truth from him; last night he came here, to this house, intending to make a last attempt at extortion, but we were here before him. Your house was guarded for you all night—by your real nephew."

She was trembling violently. She had forgotten the presence of Leonard, who stood in the window, silent.

"My nephew? My nephew? But where is he? And oh! is he like that other? Is there more shame and wickedness?"

"No! No shame at all. Only pride and joy. He is here, Miss Rutherford. See! This is Leonard Copleston, your sister's son."

Leonard stepped before her.

"I am, indeed," he said. "I am your sister's son."

What was it, in his voice, in his manner, in his attitude, that carried my thoughts backward with a rush to the day when he stood amid the snow in the old churchyard, and cried aloud to the spirit of his dead mother lying in the pauper's corner?

And was she like her dead sister, this delicate and fragile lady who must once have been beautiful, and who now stood with hands tightly clasped, gazing with trembling wonder on the gallant young fellow before her?

"My nephew?" she cried. "Leonard—it was your father's name—you have his hair and his eyes, but you have your mother's voice. Leonard, shall you love me?"

He took her two hands in his, and drew her towards him like a lover.

I thought they would be best left alone, and disappeared.

After meditation for a space among the flowers I went back again. They were still standing by the table, her hands in his. He held a miniature—I guessed of whom— and was looking on it with tearful eyes.

"Leonard," I said, "I shall take the dog-cart into town, and leave you with your aunt to tell your own story. Bring her with you this very afternoon, and introduce her to the Captain. Miss Rutherford, you are pleased with this new nephew of yours?"

"Pleased?" she cried with a sob of happiness. "Pleased?"

"He is an improvement upon the old one. Moses, indeed! As if you could have a nephew named Moses, with a drink-sodden face and a passion for pipes and beer!"

She laughed. The situation had all the elements of tears, and I wanted to stave them off.

"And then there is Celia," I added.

"Celia? Who is Celia?" she asked, with a little apprehension in her voice. "Are you married, my nephew, Leonard?"

"No," he said. "But I am in love."

"Oh!"

"And you will like her, Aunt."

They were strange to each other, and Leonard handled the title of relationship with awkwardness at first. It was actually the very first of those titles—there are a good many of them when you come to think of them—that he had ever been able to use.

"Miss Rutherford must be prepared to fall in love with her," I said, to reassure her;" everybody is in love with Celia."

Then I left them, and went back to the tavern, where I had breakfast—nothing gives a man such an appetite as these domestic emotions—and drove back to town.

CHAPTER XLII.
A FAMILY COUNCIL.

LEONARD'S promotion to family connections was a thing so startling that it almost drove away from my mind the recollection of the crisis through which all our fortunes were to pass that very day—Celia's refusal of Herr Räumer and my Polish deputation. In the breathless rush of those two days, in which were concentrated the destinies of three lives at least, one had to think of one thing at a time. Fortunately, I could give the morning to Celia. She was agitated, but not on her own account. Her father, she said, had given her his unqualified approval of what she was going to do.

"He has behaved," she said, "in the kindest way possible. He knows all about—about Leonard."

"I told him."

"And he says he is very glad. I am to meet Herr Räumer at twelve in his office and give him my answer. But there is something behind all this which troubles me. Why is my father so sad?"

"It is nothing at all, I believe. He fancies that the German can injure his reputation in some way. Be of good heart, Cis. All will go right now."

And then I fell to telling her how Leonard had at last come into the patrimony of a family, and was no longer a foundling. This diverted her thoughts, and carried us on until twelve o'clock, when I went to the family conference which was called at that hour in Mr. Tyrrell's office. Celia remained in her own room until she was wanted.

It was a complete assemblage, gathered together to hear Celia's answer to her suitor. Nothing but the gravity of the situation warranted this publicity, so to speak, of her decision. It was an acknowledgment, on the part of her father, that more was at stake than the mere refusal of a girl to marry a man old enough to be her grandfather. Mr. Pontifex was there also with his wife. He wore the garb which he assumed on occasions of ceremony. It consisted simply of a dress-coat, with perhaps an additional fold to the very large white neckcloth which he wore about his long neck. That dress-coat, which he certainly never associated especially with the evening, bore an air of battle about it, although the wearer's face was much meeker than usual, and his upper lip longer, and therefore sadder to look at. They sat each bolt upright in two chairs side by side against the wall. The lady was present under protest. As I heard afterwards, she consented to come on the express understanding that her carriage should be kept waiting, so that at any moment, if she were offended, she might go; also, that the maintenance of her will on its present terms depended on Celia's behaviour. Her husband, the principal sufferer in their family disturbances, had, I suppose, received orders to be on distant terms with everybody, as if we were all on our trial. I gathered this from the way in which he acknowledged my presence, with that sort of dignified movement of the head which the clergy reserve for pew-openers, sextons, national schoolmasters, and the like. He was present at the meeting, perhaps to represent the virtue of Christian resignation, while his wife preferred that Christian wrath the exhibition of which is not a sin.

Mrs. Tyrrell sat on the other side of the room in a state of profound bewilderment. Things were beyond her comprehension. But she seemed to feel my arrival as a kind of relief, and immediately proposed, as a measure of conciliation, wine and cake. No one took any notice of the offer except Mr. Pontifex, who sighed and shook his head as if he should have liked some under happier circumstances.

It was very evident that Aunt Jane thought she had been invited to witness the acceptance of the enemy's offer. There was in the carriage of her head, the setting of her lips, the rustle of her silks, the horizontality of her curls, a wrathful and combative look. And if her eyes seemed to wander, as they sometimes did, into space, it was, one instinctively felt, only the absorption of her spirit in the effort to find fitting words to express her indignation when the time should arrive.

I looked at the safe. Yes, the door was slightly open; I had left it wide open. There could be no doubt that Mr. Tyrrell had found it open. Presumably, therefore, he had—what had he done? Abstracted papers? The thought was an ugly one; and yet, for what reason had I committed an ugly act and borrowed the key? Abstracted papers; made things safe; robbed his enemy of his weapons; that did not ring musically—as every musician knows, evil is discord. And yet Mr. Tyrrell did not look like—one shrinks from calling things by their right names. He bore, on the other hand, a quiet look of dignity which contrasted strangely with the restless nervousness of the last few weeks.

With him was the Captain, standing with his back to the fireplace, the favourite British position, summer or winter.

All these observations were made in a moment, for, as if he had been waiting for me, Mr. Tyrrell began to address us, fidgeting his fingers among the papers on the table.

"I have asked you to come here this morning," he said. "I have asked you, Aunt Jane and Mr. Pontifex, as Celia's nearest relations, and you, Captain, as an old friend, and you, Ladislas, as her closest friend, to witness her own decision in a matter which concerns her own happiness, whatever we may have thought or said about it—and which must be left entirely to herself."

Mrs. Pontifex snorted.

"I keep my own opinion, George Tyrrell," she said, "and I mean to keep it."

"You all know that this offer took us entirely by surprise—none more so than myself—and especially for the reason that its rejection by Celia will most likely result in the enmity of a man who has for many years been my friend and my client."

Here Mrs. Pontifex murmured in an undertone, so that her husband and I were the only persons who heard it—

"Fudge and flapdoodle."

"There is nothing against Herr Räumer. He has lived among us an irreproachable life, so far as we know."

"Old enough to be her grandfather; a foreigner; and, for all you know, a Roman Catholic."

John Pontifex lifted his head at the last word, and made a remark—

"That we should innocently connive at the marriage of an unfortunate Papist would be—ahem—in fact—a shocking state of things!"

"Of coarse he is not a Catholic," said Mr. Tyrrell impatiently. "And as for his age, many girls marry elderly men and are perfectly happy. It so happens that eight or ten years ago I laid myself under an obligation—a very great obligation—to Herr Räumer. I cannot allow myself to forget the debt I owe him. At the time when I expressed my gratitude and asked in what way I could best show it, he laughed, and said that I could give him—my little daughter. I acceded, laughing, and thought no more about the matter until he himself reminded me of it. It seems that he had not forgotten it. At the same time, he offered to take his chance; if I would give him such good offices as I could, in the way of paternal influence; if I would give him opportunities of frequently seeing my daughter; if Mrs. Tyrrell could also be got to approve—"

"Nothing could be more regular, I must say," sighed Mrs Tyrrell, "or more becoming."

Mrs. Pontifex pulled out her pocket-handkerchief and coughed.

I distinctly heard the last syllables, drowned by the kerchief —"doodle."

Her husband, terrified beyond measure by this repetition of his wife's very strongest expression, shook his head slowly, and ejaculated, Heaven knows why, "Alas!"

"I say," Mr. Tyrrell went on mildly, disregarding these interruptions, "that he very properly left the decision to Celia herself. At first I considered the situation favourably for my old friend. Here was an establishment, a certainty, an assured position. I brought pressure—not cruel or unkind pressure—but still a certain amount of pressure—to bear upon Celia in his behalf. I am sorry now that I did exercise that influence, because it has offended some here, and because I find it has made my daughter unhappy, and that"—his voice broke down a little—"is a thing I cannot bear to think of.

"Yesterday, however," he went on, after a pause, during which Mrs. Pontifex did not say, "Fudge and flapdoodle," nor did her husband say " Alas!" but looked straight before him—"Yesterday I saw Herr Räumer again; he came to tell me that he had waited two months, that Celia was now exposed to the attention of a far younger and more attractive man in the shape of Leonard Copleston, and that he would ask Celia himself for her decision. I have this morning talked with her upon the subject. I have told her that I withdraw altogether every word that I said before in favour of his pretensions; I have asked her to be guided in the matter entirely by her own heart. And I invited you here, with her consent, in order that, before you all, she might tell Herr Räumer what answer she has decided to give."

"So far, George Tyrrell," said Mrs. Pontifex, "you have acted worthily, and like yourself."

Then, the Captain lifted up his voice.

"Our friend, George Tyrrell," he began, "told me yesterday a thing which has been hitherto known only to himself and to this Mr.—Herr Räumer. It is a matter which may, or may not, do harm if generally known. And it appears that yesterday, probably in the heat of jealousy or disappointment—because we all know Celia Tyrrell's sentiments on the matter—this gentleman held out a kind of threat against Celia's father of spreading the business abroad. We can afford to laugh at such menaces; we stick to our guns, and we let the enemy blaze away. He cannot do us any real harm."

"Menaces? Threats?" cried Aunt Jane, springing to her feet, and shaking her skirts so that they "went off" in rustlings like a whole box of lucifer matches at once. "Threats against you, George Tyrrell? Against a member of my family? Threats? I'll let him know, if he begins that kind of thing. He shall see that I can be resolute on occasion, meek though I may be habitually and on Christian principle."

"Certainly, my dear," said John Pontifex sadly. "You can be resolute on proper occasion."

George Tyrrell smiled—rather a wan smile.

"It is never pleasant to have one's peace and ease disturbed by threats and misrepresentations."

"We've got you in convoy," said the Captain heartily; "and will see you safe into port. There's eight bells. Now, then."

I was still thinking about the open safe. Could a man who had spoken as Tyrrell spoke, with so much genuine feeling, so much dignity, actually have in his pockets abstracted papers? Then why the undertone of melancholy? If he had nothing to fear, why did he speak or allow the Captain to speak of possible attacks? In any case, I was the real culprit, the cause and origin of the crime.

CHAPTER XLIII.
CELIA GIVES HER ANSWER.

WE had not long to wait. Almost as the last clock finished its last stroke of noon we heard outside the firm and heavy step of Celia's suitor, and I am ready to confess that the heart of one guilty person in the room—if there were more than one—began to beat the faster. Mr. Tyrrell turned pale, I thought, and Mrs. Pontifex stiffened her back against the chair, and looked her most resolute. I do not know why, but John Pontifex began to tremble at the knees, the most sensitive part apparently of his organisation.

Herr Räumer stood before us in some surprise.

"I did not expect," he said, "to find a *conseil de famille.*"

Then, drawing from the solemn aspect of Mrs. Pontifex, the dejection depicted in Mrs. Tyrrell's face, and the terror of John Pontifex, a conclusion that the meeting was not favourable to his cause, he assumed an expression which meant fighting.

"I hope that Mrs. Pontifex is quite well," he said blandly, "and the Rev. Mr. Pontifex, whom I have not heard for several Sundays."

Then he took a chair, and sat at the table.

"Now," he said to Mr. Tyrrell, with a certain brutality, "let us get to business at once."

Beside him was the Captain, leaning his hand on his stick, and looking as if he were ready with the loaded artillery of a hundred-gun man-o'-war.

Mr. Tyrrell rang the bell.

"Ask Miss Celia to be good enough to step down," he said. Whatever was before him he looked ready to face.

The German, as if master of the situation, sat easily and quietly. He looked as if he were a mere spectator, and the business was one which concerned him not at all. And yet he must have known, from the fact of the family gathering, that his chances were small indeed. But he said nothing, only removed his blue spectacles, and gently stroked his heavy moustache with the palm of his left hand. He was dressed, I remember, in a white waistcoat, only the upper part being visible above his tightly-buttoned frock-coat. He wore a flower in one button-hole, which was then not so common as it is now, and a tiny piece of red ribbon in another. Also he wore lavender kid gloves and patent-leather boots. In fact, he was dressed for the occasion. With his heavy face, his large and massive head, his full moustache, and his upright carriage, he looked far younger in spite of his white hair, than the man who sat expectant before him. Celia entered in her quiet, unobtrusive way, kissed her great-aunt, and, refusing a chair which Herr Räumer offered, took mine, which was next Aunt Jane.

"Now, Celia," said that lady, "we are all here, waiting for your decision, and as that may possibly—mind, child, I do not expect it—but it may possibly be such as John Pontifex and I cannot approve, the sooner we get it the better."

"One moment," said Herr Räumer, rising, and pushing back his chair. "I am also deeply concerned in Miss Tyrrell's answer. May I speak first?"

He considered a moment, and then went on.

"I am now a man advanced in years. I have for twelve years and more watched the growth of a child so carefully that I have at last, perhaps prematurely, come to look upon that child as, in a sense, my own. You would laugh, Mrs. Pontifex, if I were to say that I have fallen in love with that child."

"Fudge and flapdoodle!" said the lady for a third time, so that her husband's teeth began to chatter.

"Quite so. But it is the truth. I hope—I still venture to hope—that my declining years may be cheered by the care of a young lady, who, in becoming my wife, would not cease to be my much-loved and cherished daughter."

"Man," said Aunt Jane, "talk Christian sense, not heathen rubbish. You can't marry your daughter nor your granddaughter either. Not even in Germany, far less in this Protestant and Evangelical country."

"I went to my old friend, George Tyrrell," Herr Räumer proceeded, regardless of the interruption, "I put the case before him. You know the rest. Celia, I have not pressed my attentions upon you. I have said no word of love to you. I know that it might be ridiculous in me to say much of what I feel in this respect. You know me well enough to trust me, I think. It was enough for me that you should know what I hoped, and it was right that you should take time to reflect. Will you be my wife?"

She clasped my hand, and held it tight. And she looked at her father with a little fear and doubt, while she answered—

"I cannot, Herr Räumer."

His face clouded over.

"Think," he pleaded. " I have watched over you, looking for this moment, for ten years. You shall have all that a woman can ask for. I can give you position—a far higher position than you dream of. You shall be rich, you shall be a guest of Courts, you shall lead and command—what can a woman want that I cannot give you?"

She shook her head.

"I am very sorry; you have been very kind to me always."

"His attentions have been most marked," said her mother.

"Clara," said Aunt Jane sharply, "hold your tongue! "

"You have been so kind to me always that I venture to ask one more kindness of you. It is that you forget this passage of your life altogether, and—and—do not suffer my refusal to alter the friendly relations between my father and yourself."

"Is this scene preconcerted?" he turned to Mr. Tyrrell. "Am I invited here to make one in a dramatic representation? Are these excellent friends gathered together to laugh at the refusal of my offer?"

"No—no," cried Celia. "There is no dramatic representation. There is no preconcerted scene. Come, Aunt Jane, come, mamma; let us go; we have nothing more to do here. Herr Räumer"—she held out her hand —"will you forgive me? I—I alone am to blame—if any one is to blame—in this matter. I ought to have told you three weeks ago that it was impossible. I hoped that you would see for yourself that it was impossible. I thought that you would of your own accord withdraw your offer. Will you forgive me?"

He did not take the proffered hand.

"You refuse my hand," he said, "and you ask me to take yours! Pardon me, Miss Tyrrell. We do not fight with ladies. I have now to do with your father."

Mrs. Pontifex—I think I have said that she was not a tall woman, being perhaps about five feet two—stepped to the table, and rapped it smartly with her knuckles.

"You have to do with Jane Pontifex," she said, "as well as with George Tyrrell. Take care, John Pontifex!"

"My dear!"

"Remain here. Watch the proceedings, and report them to me, exactly. Now, Clara and Celia, go on upstairs. You are under my protection now, my dear. And as for you, sir"—she shook her finger impressively at Herr Räumer—"if it were not for your age and infirmities, I would take you by the collar and give you as good a shaking as you ever had. John Pontifex! "

"My—my—my—dear?"

"I charge you— not to shake him by the collar."

"No, my dear, I will not," he promised firmly.

"In moments of indignation," Aunt Jane explained to her niece, "John Pontifex is like a lion."

She stood at the door to see Celia safely out of her suitor's clutches, and then followed, closing it with a slam.

John Pontifex, the Lion-hearted, resumed his seat against the wall, and sat bolt upright with more meekness than might have been expected of one so disposed to Christian wrath.

"Now, sir," said Herr Räumer to Mr. Tyrrell, "the she-dragon is gone, and we can talk—"

"I have promised, Johnny," whispered Mr. Pontifex to me, "not to shake him. By the she-dragon, I presume, he—actually—means—Mrs. Pontifex. This wickedness is, indeed, lamentable!"

"—and we can talk. Is this bravado, or is it defiance?"

"It is neither," said the Captain. "I know all the particulars of this business. It means that we are doing our duty, and are prepared for the consequences."

"Ah!" said Herr Räumer. " It is very noble of you to recommend this line of action, seeing that the consequences will not fall upon your head. You are one of the people who go about enjoining everybody, like Nelson, to do his duty because England expects it. England is a great and fortunate country."

"You may sneer, sir," said the Captain with dignity. "I have told you what we propose to do."

"Are you aware what the consequences may be if I act upon certain information contained in that safe, that you so boldly recommend the path of duty?"

"I believe the consequences may be unpleasant. But they will be made quite as unpleasant to yourself; they cannot produce the important effects you anticipate; and— in any case—we shall abide the consequences."

"I give you another chance, Tyrrell. Let the girl give me a favourable answer in a week—a fortnight—even a month. Send young Copleston away—use your paternal pressure, and all may yet be well."

He had quite put off the bland politeness of his manner with Celia, and stood before us angry, flushed and revengeful. It was pretty clear that he would get what revenge he could, and I began to hope that, after all, Mr. Tyrrell had possessed himself of those papers.

"Come, Tyrrell," he said, "you know what will follow. Think of your own interests. I have never yet been beaten, and I never will. Those who stand in my path are trampled on without mercy."

"No," said the Worshipful the Mayor, "I will not be under any man's power. Do what you like, say what you like; and as you please. I would rather see Celia dead than married to you."

"Then you declare war?" He took a little key—ah! how well I remembered that instrument of temptation—from his waistcoat-pocket. "You declare war? This is refreshing. Some people say that nothing will induce an Englishman to declare war again. And here we have an example to the contrary. But I must crush you, my friend. I really must crush you."

"Gad!" cried the Captain. "Can't you open fire without so much parley? We are waiting for your shot."

"Tyrrell"—Herr Räumer turned upon him once more—"I am almost sorry for you, and I have never been sorry for any one yet. Such a pity! The Worshipful the Mayor! The rich and prosperous lawyer! The close relative of the great Pontifex family! With so large a balance at the bank, and so many shares, and such an excellent business! And all to come to such a sudden and disagreeable end. It does seem a pity."

"Pluck up, Tyrrell! this is all bounce."

I wondered if it was. At that moment Mr. Tyrrell quietly went to the safe.

"I will not trouble you to open the safe. It is already open."

Herr Räumer sat down and looked at him.

"This is a stroke of genius," said he. "I did not think you had it in you. Were you, too, Captain, an accomplice? He finds my safe open, or he gets a key, or in some way opens it; he takes the compromising papers, and then, you see, in full family gathering he defies me. It is an excellent situation, well led up to and well contrived, and executed admirably. Tyrrell, you are a dramatist lost to your country."

He did not appear the least disconcerted; he took it as quite natural that he should be defeated by deceit, craft, and cunning; they were weapons which he held to be universal and legitimate; he had, as he might cynically say, used them himself all his life. Now, in an unexpected manner, he was actually met and defeated by his own methods.

"This is really refreshing. Who is the best man in all the town, Ladislas Pulaski? Is it George Tyrrell? Why, he is better than the best, because he is the cleverest."

"Perhaps not," said Mr. Tyrrell, as he took a bundle of papers tied in red tape out of the safe. "I found this open last night. I suppose you left it open. There are all your papers—untouched."

The German snatched them from his hands, and began to turn them over.

"All? All?" He untied the tape, and opened paper after paper. "All? Impossible." He looked carefully through the whole bundle. As he got to the end his face changed, and he looked bewildered. "They are all here," he said, looking at us with a sort of dismay. "What is the meaning of this?"

He sat down with the papers in his hands, as if he were facing a great and astonishing problem.

"You are a theologian, Mr. Pontifex, and have presumably studied some of the leading cases in what they call sin. Did you ever read of such a case as this?"

"When I was a young man at Oxford (where—ahem—I greatly distinguished myself), I certainly did—ahem—study a science called Logic, which my reckless companions— "

"A man," interrupted Herr Räumer, and addressing his remarks to me, "a man gets possession of a bundle of papers which contain facts the suppression of which is all-important. He may destroy them without fear; no one knows about them except a single person who has no other proof; he deliberately adopts a line of conduct towards that person—who is a hard man with no sentimentality about him, and who has never once forgiven anybody any single wrong, however small—which that person is bound to resent. And while he does this he hands back to that hard and revengeful person the very papers which alone give him the power of revenge. That is the most extraordinary line of action I have ever seen pursued, or ever read of. What am I to think of it? Is it part of a deeper plot?"

"Rubbish," said the Captain. "Can't a man avoid a dishonourable thing without having a plot? Do you suppose we are all schemers and conspirators?"

"The English are, indeed, a wonderful race," said Herr Räumer.

"Can you not believe in a common act of honesty? Man —man!" said the Captain, "what sort of life has yours been?"

"I have seen a good deal of the world," Herr Räumer went on, meditatively. "I was in Vienna and in Paris in 1848. You got a considerable amount of treachery there. But I never before saw a case of a man who had ruin—yes —ruin staring him in the face—who was too honest to prevent it. Too honest."

He sat down and resumed his blue spectacles, and then took his hat, still holding the papers in his hands.

At last he said with an effort—

"I honour the first piece of genuine honesty that I have ever, in the whole course of my life, actually witnessed. 'All men,' I said at my leisure, 'are liars.' George Tyrrell, I give you back these papers. Take them and use them as you please. Best burn them. I give you the key of my safe; you can paint my name out to-morrow, if you please. Gentlemen, you will all three, I am sure, wish to keep this secret of our friend's life, as far as you know it, locked up and forgotten. Mr. Pontifex, you will say nothing about it to—to the she-dragon."

"I promised not to shake him, Johnny," Mr. Pontifex said, as if that engagement was sacred, and the only thing which prevented him from committing an act of violence.

"*Allons*" said the philosopher gaily, "let us be friends, Tyrrell; shake hands. I am going to leave this town, where I have spent ten years of my life, and shall return to-morrow or next day—to—to the Continent. I shall see you again, Ladislas. Perhaps this afternoon."

He stopped at the door.

"Tell Celia," he said, "that she is free, and that I shall always regret that I could not take her away with me."

He laughed and went away.

Then we all looked at each other as if we had been in a dream. There was actually a weak spot in the whole armour of cynicism with which Herr Räumer had clad himself, and we had found it.

Celia rescued. Andromeda free; the loathly dragon driven away; Andromeda's papa delivered from personal and private terror on his own account; and by the strangest chance, the whole brought about, though not continued by me. I, who borrowed the key; I, who did a mean and treacherous thing, which gave the opportunity of an honourable and fearless action. After all, as Herr Räumer once said, the world would be but a dull place without its wickedness. It was as if Perseus, instead of flying through the air with winged feet and a sword swift to slay, conscious that the eyes of the Olympians were upon him, had crouched behind the rock when the Ægean wave lapped the white feet of the damsel, and from that safe retreat astonished the monster with a Whitehead torpedo. Nothing at all to be proud of. And yet no dragon assailed with a torpedo could be more astonished than our foreign friend at the exhibition of an undoubted act of pluck and honesty. No doubt the admonitions of the Captain spurred on the hero, out of which I came, myself, as I felt, rather badly.

Let me say, once for all, that I do not know what the papers contained. Whether my old friend had committed a crime—whether it was forgery, or burglary, or anything else of which his conscience might have reproached him, and the opinion of the world looked askance upon, I do not know. Nothing more was ever said on the subject. The four actors in that little drama, including John Pontifex, maintained total silence. Even the safe disappeared. And neither then, nor at any subsequent period, was the leading lawyer of the town, its Mayor, its most eminent Freemason, subjected to the slightest suspicion, attack, or misrepresentation.

I asked to see Celia, but she had gone to her own room. I wrote a short note to her, sent it up, and went into the drawing-room, where Mrs. Pontifex and Mrs. Tyrrell, newly reconciled, were sitting in great state and friendliness. Cake and wine were on the table, not that the ladies wished to sustain nature, but that their production, like the pomegranate in the mysteries of Ceres, was a symbolical act. It meant reconciliation, and Mrs. Pontifex, who liked that the family should agree in the way she thought fit, contemplated the glass of sherry before her with an eye of peculiar satisfaction. I briefly narrated what had passed, glossing over the part that related to the papers, and dwelling chiefly on Herr Räumer's disinterested and generous conduct.

"And what were the threats?" asked Mrs. Pontifex.

"There hardly appeared to be any threats," I replied. "Herr Räumer made some allusion to papers in the safe, but as he left papers and all with Mr. Tyrrell, I presume they were unimportant, and referred to private transactions."

"I must say, Clara," said Mrs. Pontifex, "that George's behaviour was very good throughout. I am much pleased. In a moment of weakness, no doubt, he listened to the proposals of this foreigner, who is, I admit, a clever and plausible person. Both George and Celia said quite the right thing in the right way, and I am greatly pleased. You say the man is gone, Ladislas?"

"Yes; he is going to leave the town, and return to the Continent."

"So much the better. He and his church on Sunday mornings, where he hoped to catch Celia! Fudge! I can forgive most things, Clara,"—she did not look as if there was much she would forgive, but I am giving her own words—"hypocrisy I cannot forgive. I watched him once actually pretending to listen to one of John Pontifex's best sermons —that on Capernaum, which has, you remember, an application to the present condition of thoughtless mirth which has possessed our young people."

It was pleasant to feel that peace was restored between the two Houses of Pontifex and Tyrrell. More pleasant still to feel that a great danger had been averted.

Let me hasten with the story of this day big with fate. Imagine, if you please, the newly-born pride of Leonard as he introduced Celia to "My aunt, Miss Rutherford." Imagine the satisfaction and joy of that excellent lady on being quite certain that Moses—Moses with the spotty face and the passion for beer—was exchanged for this gallant and chivalrous young fellow—"he has got his father's graces," she whispered to me, "and his mother's sweetness."

Pass over the little tender scene where Miss Rutherford thanked the Captain solemnly for his care and bounty to "her boy"—we cannot describe everything; there are some things which are better left unrecorded. It was a time of great joy. We had an early dinner at home—the Captain, as usual on great occasions, produced champagne. There was Celia and Miss Rutherford, both shy and a little frightened of each other, but hopeful that each would turn out as delightful as she looked. There was Leonard, of course, and the Captain, and myself. And be sure that Mrs. Jeram had not been forgotten, before dinner—else why those tearful eyes with which Miss Rutherford left our old housekeeper, and which spoke of talk over the poor creature who staggered three-and-twenty years before into Mrs. Jeram's arms, to die after giving birth to a man-child? There was nothing noisy or mirthful in our party—nothing to illustrate Aunt Jane's "present condition of thoughtless mirth among young people." And but for the disquiet of the morning deputation, I should have been perfectly happy—as happy as Leonard and Celia. And Leonard's face was like the sun in June for beaminess and warmth.

We fell to talking over old times. The Captain discoursed on the boys and their admirable qualities; Leonard told stories of Mrs. Jeram's *ménage* and the fights he used to have with Moses; Miss Rutherford listened with delight. She was in a new atmosphere—this retired and secluded lady who knew nothing of the world—the atmosphere of the fighting world; the old Captain who had fought; the young officer who had fought; I even belonged to a fighting stock. And it was half-past two when Celia took the elder lady away to introduce her to her mother—and we began to clear the decks for our deputation.

"You will let me be present," said the Captain. "I have something to say to them. Rebellion, indeed! What sort of a rebellion is that got up by half-a-dozen exiles in foreign lands? No, my boy, I don't deny the right of the Poles to rebel—but you shall not throw away your life till the whole nation rises. Then, if you like, you may go."

CHAPTER XLIV.
THE DEPUTATION.

FIVE minutes for rest and reflection. What would this deputation of Poles say to me, and what was I to say to them? How to receive them? Was I to feign an ardour I did not possess; to put on the zeal of passionate Wassielewski, and clamour for the revenge which my English training made me hold to be impotent and barbaric; to throw in my lot with a knot of hopeless enthusiasts, and for the gratitude and respect I bore to one man to throw away my life in mad enterprise?

Or—the other line—was I to stand before them and say, like another Edgar Atheling—"I have no thought or care about the Fatherland; I am a Pole in name only; I will not fight myself, nor lend you my name, nor join your ranks. Go your own way. Let the dead past be buried, and for the future the cause of Polish freedom shall have no aid from me." Or—lastly—could I say, "I am an Englishman, and not a Pole; I have an Englishman's sympathy with an oppressed people; but I see no sense in obscure risings, and I hate conspiracies"?

And yet that was the truth. Wassielewski, a son of the soil, preserved all the prejudices and most of the ignorance of his country. His ideas of revenge were barbaric, but he did not know that; to shoot down Russians because, twenty years before, Russians had been made to commit unheard-of atrocities—as if we should suddenly resolve on murdering Hindoos in memory of Cawnpore—was in his mind a great, a noble, a patriotic act—more—an act which was pleasing in the eyes of his dead mistress, my mother, the Lady Claudia.

It is true that there were moments when the old conspirator's projects and plots had appeared to me admirable and worthy of emulation; when the thought of my father's cruel march through winter snows and summer heats on his weary way to be slowly done to death among the commonest and vilest criminals maddened me; or when I looked at the wooden cross he carved in the gloom of the Siberian mine for me, his little child, whom he was never to see again; or when I pictured him as he had been seen a year or two before he died, white-haired at thirty, aged and bent; or when I remembered—the anguish of that memory has never left me—the convoy of carts filled with children dragged from their mothers, the despairing women who ran behind crying, shrieking for their little ones—my own poor mother among them. Then, indeed, as now, I should be less than human did not the blood boil in my veins, did not the pulses quicken within me, did not a passionate desire for some kind of wild justice well up in my heart. Revenge is insatiable—had one killed with the vigour of a Nero, the spilling of blood could never quench the righteous wrath, or deaden the pangs of sorrow and pain which would rise again in thinking of that great suffering, that most terrible crime. My mother, without doubt, has long since, in the land where all tears are wiped away, forgiven. I cannot forgive, for her sake. Perhaps I understand how sins against oneself may be forgiven, but not sins against those we love. Lastly, against this conflict of opposing forces I had to place the calm good sense of the man whom most I had to consider—the Captain; the entreaties of the girl whom most I had to love; the firm decision of Leonard, that, happen what might, I should not be dragged into the plot.

I hope I have not tried to depict myself in any false colours. I was not a hero; in calm moments I saw the madness of the projected insurrection. I knew that such revenge as the old conspirator proposed was wild and useless; and yet, in his presence, by the enthusiasm of his ardour I was carried away, so to speak, out of myself, and was ready to dare and to do. But since Leonard's arrival this infection of enthusiasm had been checked. By his help I saw things in their true light.

"You, Laddy?" said Leonard, laughing. "You to go out a-rebellirig, with your face and your eyes? Go tell the Russians who and what you are; announce your intention of raising the standard of insurrection; they will laugh at you; they will take you in and make much of you, give you a piano, and refuse to let you come home again because you play so well. We are no longer in the days of the terrible Nicholas. Alexander has begun a new era for Russia, which Wassielewski and his friends cannot understand."

"I am too obscure," I said, bitterly, "even to do any mischief!"

"Any man," said the Captain, "can do mischief. I was aboard a frigate once that was set on fire by a powder-monkey. If you want to do mischief, Laddy, in Poland or anywhere else, you can do it."

I have mentioned once before little Dr. Roy, the neatest and most dapper of tiny men. He, too, must needs join in the general cry.

"I hear," he said, one day meeting me in the street, "I hear a whisper that the Poles are stirring, and they want to make use of you and your name."

I made no answer.

"Don't," he said impressively. "Believe a man who once risked his neck in rebellion that it is a most miserable line to take up. It was in Canada—I daresay you have heard something about it. We had grievances; we made a clamour about them; the Government would not give in; so we rose, and we did a little fighting. It wasn't very much, but it brought out pretty clearly all the miseries of revolt. We were put down. Everything that we rebelled to gain was granted by the British Government; everything, properly represented, would have been granted without rebellion. We had our revolt, our fighting, our loss of life; our destruction of property; our jealousies and personal squabbles; our treacheries and our treasons; our trials and our escapes—just all for nothing. No one got any good out of it at all, not even the half-dozen who went across to the States to gas about their bravery. Even the grandeur of being a rebel—" I thought of Herr Räumer's remarks on the rebel's enjoyment of being shot—"does not compensate for the trouble. And then to find out that you have no real grievances, after all. My own reward for the Canada rising was that I lost a capital practice in a very delightful Canadian town; that I was very nearly caught; that if they had caught me I should have been hanged; and that I am here on sufferance, because—which I am not afraid of—they might arrest and hang me to-morrow on the old account. For Heaven's sake, Pulaski, keep out of rebellions. They won't give you back your father's lands."

All in the same tale; Herr Räumer's sneers and contempt were on the same side as Celia's prayers. Little Dr. Roy with his experiences was on the same side as the Captain.

And, against all these, I had to consider especially poor old Wassielewski. The old man, crazed with inextinguishable rage, looked on me as an instrument, ready to his hand, given him by Providence. For my part, I had to regard him as my saviour, the protector of my infancy, the faithful friend of my father, the devoted servant of my mother. Could I inflict upon him the cruel pain, the bitter humiliation, of seeing a Pulaski refuse to fight for Poland? Every Pole, he used to say, owed his life absolutely to his country. When he cannot fight to defend his rights, he ought to die in order that his people may not forget them.

I venture on a suggestion to rulers and despots. There are two or three ways of treating unsuccessful rebels. To shoot them publicly, transport them, torture their wives, and issue arbitrary laws of repression—all this is simply to give the Cause immortality. That is what the Russians have always done. The best way, surely, would be to forgive them, simply, and take away their arms, and to say, "My friends, you have now neither guns nor powder. We are not going to give you any. Sit down and grow your crops." Then such hot-headed irreconcilables as my old friend would be impossible. Or if they must be punished with death, then let it be done, as with Jugurtha and Catiline's conspirators, in the secrecy of some dark dungeon where newspaper correspondents cannot penetrate.

"Where are they, these heroes of Poland?" asked Leonard, laughing.

He was determined that the thing should not be treated seriously. "Let us push the table back to the window—so. Now, Laddy, if you stand there on the hearthrug to receive them, it will be like holding a Levée. The Captain shall be your Court—I will be your *aide-de-camp*. And here they are."

Five men, headed by Wassielewski, came solemnly into the room, nearly filling it up. The last of the five shut the door carefully as if he was shutting out the world. But it opened again, and to my boundless astonishment admitted Herr Räumer, in his blue spectacles. He came in as if invited to take part in the ceremony, walked across the room, and stood in the window, his back to the light, beside the Captain. We formed two groups, I on the hearthrug, with Leonard at my right hand; and on the left the Captain, who contemplated the strangers with eyes of no favour, and beside him our German friend, to whom, since his magnanimous conduct in the matter of Celia, one felt an access of friendliness. And before us, the five men of my father's nation.

It was, as Leonard said, something like a Levée, only there was a certain incongruity about it which made one feel rather ashamed.

It was curious to consider that the men who stood before us were, so to speak, pledged to fall for their country. One thought of the prisoners brought out to fight their last battle with each other; every man resolute to make a brave show and please the thousands; every one hopeless of any escape; every one looking forward with a certain fearful expectation to the down-turning of the thumb; one or two perhaps, the more aged men, not sorry to escape the miseries of captivity in the glorious rush and shout of vivid battle; some whose thoughts turned back—then Leonard touched my shoulder, and I gave my attention to things present. Wassielewski was there to introduce; not, he said, to speak. He wore a satisfied and even a glad expression. The long-wished for moment had arrived. He had brushed his black coat and buttoned it tightly round his long lean figure; his white hair was combed back and fell behind his head, leaving his face standing out keen and eager with bright and deep-set eyes, and full white beard. His nervousness and restless manner was gone. You might think of him thus calm and collected charging his rifle for one more shot in a hailstorm from the advancing grey-coats.

The first of the four who came with him, and the most important, was a Pole about forty years of age; a tall, upright, and strong man, looking like a Frenchman in dress and the cut of his hair. His eyes had something of the wild look which characterised Wassielewski.

Wassielewski was about to introduce him to me, when he broke away and advanced, speaking in French, with a certain gaiety of manner, and held out his hand—to Leonard.

"Count Pulaski," he said, " we are indeed rejoiced to find you like your father, among the friends of Poland. Wassielewski had not prepared us for such an accession to our ranks."

I was hardened by this time to any reference to my deformity, but I must own that it was not without a pang that I witnessed disappointment in his face, as Leonard bowed and indicated myself, the hunchback.

"Pardon, M. le Comte," he said. "This is my friend, Ladislas Pulaski."

The Pole's face fell, in spite of a polite attempt to disguise his disappointment. To be sure, there was some difference between a tall and handsome young man, whose very face commanded trust, and proclaimed him a natural leader, and myself, short, round-backed, and dreamy-eyed. We shook hands, and he said nothing, but stepped aside to make room for the other three. I received the greetings of all in turn. One of them was a short and thick-set man, apparently an artisan, a man of fifty or so, in ragged and threadbare blouse, whose face was decorated like Wassielewski's with a sabre cut. Another was a much older man in spectacles and black cloth clothes. This was a Professor in some American College, who had come across the Atlantic in vacation to see his compatriots, and learn the chances. The third was, I believe, an importation from Warsaw direct, who spoke nothing but Polish, and was pained to find that I could not understand him. It seems strange that Wassieleski should have allowed me to grow up in ignorance of so important a thing. As they stood before me I was struck with a resemblance which they all seemed to bear to each other. It was only for a moment, and was due, I suppose, to the Slavonic type of face. And oddly enough, Herr Räumer's face bore this same characteristic. I thought of Leonard's suspicions. Could he, too, be a Slav? But it was absurd to harbour suspicions against one who had actually been converted—that very morning—to the conviction that there may be honest men in the world.

"We are all friends of Poland, I suppose?" said the leader of the deputies, looking suspiciously around. It was odd that no one, not even Wassielewski, took the least notice of Herr Räumer.

"I am an old friend of Ladislas," said Leonard. "I am almost his brother, as Wassielewski knows. But we will withdraw if you wish."

"He is an officer in the British army. He has fought the Muscovite," said the old man. " He may stay."

The first speaker, the Gallicised Pole, drew out a paper.

"This is little more," he said, "than a meeting to make the acquaintance of a young Pole of illustrious descent, great misfortunes, and undoubted talents."

I bowed.

"Whose pursuits, we learn, have hitherto been peaceful. We hear, however, with pleasure, that we may confidently look for his adhesion, whenever we find it possible—"

"That is, immediately," said Wassielewski.

"To take practical steps in the desired direction."

"To call Poland once more to arms," explained Wassielewski. "Speak, Ladislas Pulaski."

"Gentlemen," I said, speaking in French, "you see me as I am; deformed from my childhood, bearing a name that can never be made glorious by any achievement of my own. You know my story, and the fate of my father. Wassielewski has urged upon me to join you."

"And I," said Leonard, also in French, "have urged upon him the madness and folly of joining in your plans. Gentlemen—you, M. le Comte"—he addressed the chief of them—"are not wild enthusiasts. If you concert any plan of rebellion, draw it up without consulting my friend, Ladislas Pulaski. He is not a soldier, nor is he of the stuff which makes soldiers. He is a poet and a musician. If you must pit the feeble resources of a province—I beg your pardon—a nation like Poland against the armies of a mighty empire which has been able to resist for two years the combined forces of England, France, and Turkey, do not add to your numbers a man who in the field will be useless to you, whose death can do you no good, and whose life may do others much good."

The leader hesitated. Then he whispered to Wassielewski.

And then the old Captain had his say.

"I do not," he said, stepping forward, and laying his hand upon my shoulder—"I do not unfortunately understand any language but my own. I have never regretted the fact till the present moment. Gentlemen, this boy is my son. I have adopted him, I have educated him, I refuse to let him go."

"The name of Poland—" began my old conspirator.

"In the name of Poland," said the Captain, "I would let him go if I thought he would be of any use. But this is not in the name of Poland. It is —pardon me if I am rough—in the name of a conspiracy. Assure me, if you can, that the nation is with you, and Ladislas shall go."

"No, no," cried poor old Wassielewski. "He comes of his own accord, he cannot be kept back, he fights for his mother's wrongs. Tell me, Ladislas, tell me, is not that the case?"

His voice trembled, his eyes were so pathetic that I could not resist their appeal. I took his hand, and pressed it, but I had no word to say.

The man they called the Count looked disappointed and uneasy.

"This is not," he said to Leonard, "quite the reception which we expected. Still no doubt there is truth in what you urge, and besides—besides—nothing is quite certain. Be assured, M. le Capitaine," he addressed the Captain,"that we shall spare Count Pulaski if possible. If his name will help us, and if we can satisfy you that we obey the voice of the nation, we may call upon him "

"If—if?" repeated Wassielewski. "Why, are the Poles gone mad to forget the glorious name of Pulaski?"

"Not mad, my friend," said the Count. "But twenty years have passed. In Polish villages, where there are no books and no papers, much is forgotten in twenty years."

I understood his look as he said these words. I was not to go. Of what use could I be, and who after all these years would be stirred for a moment by the intelligence that a Pulaski had joined the insurgents? Was my first feeling one of relief or of humiliation?

But the conference was brought to a sudden and unexpected end. The Count, looking round, perceived Herr Räumer standing modestly in the shade of the curtain.

"And who is this gentleman?" he asked. "Is he also a friend of yours, Count Pulaski?"

Before I could answer, Herr Räumer replied for me. It was in his most mocking tone, which brought out the curious rasp in his voice. It was a voice which somehow haunted one—you could never forget it. I hear it still, sometimes, in dreams.

"A friend of Ladislas Pulaski, and a friend to Poland. Perhaps a closer friend than any of you. Pray proceed with your papers, M. le Comte."

It was the ragged workman, the man in the blue blouse, who sprang forward as if he had been shot, and pushing everybody aside, began gazing in the German's face, gesticulating and gasping.

"I know that voice," he cried. "I have heard that voice—many times. When? In Warsaw. From whom? From an agent of the police—the police—the Russian police."

His voice rose to a shriek. Herr Räumer did not move or answer. His massive face seemed to be of marble as he stood there returning the other's gaze. And when the workman removed his blue spectacles he made no resistance, nor any sign.

"Who is this man, Wassielewski?" asked the Count.

"I do not know," he replied, carelessly. "I did not see him come in. I have seen him walking with Ladislas. He belongs to the town."

"Man! " cried the *ouvrier*,"do you not know his voice? Are you deaf then? Have you forgotten? Speak again— you. Speak, spy!"

But Herr Räumer did not speak. He folded his arms, looking down upon the little *ouvrier* with an expression of great contempt. But he did not speak.

The workman shrieked in a kind of rage.

"*Mais oui,*" he cried, "mais oui. I am not mistaken. Wassielewski, M. le Cornte, look at this man, I say again. Look at him. Here is treachery, here is a spy of the Muscov. We are invited to meet a Pole—bah! a Pole who cannot speak his own tongue—and we find our enemy in the middle of us. *Mes fréres,*" he looked round him with a face which revenge and hatred made a curious and hideous caricature, "*mes fréres*, shall we let this man leave the house alive?"

"*Enfin,*" cried the Count. "Who is he? Is it any use, Count Pulaski, asking you who he is?"

"It is Herr Räumer," I said, "a German gentleman, who has lived in the town for many years."

"Who brought him here?" asked the chief.

"He came in with you," I replied. "I thought Wassielewski brought him." The old man, puzzled and uneasy, shook his head. He was so eager to begin the fighting, this veteran rebel, that this preliminary talk, even talk of traitors and spies, worried him. No: he had not brought in this stranger, he said.

Then Herr Räumer laughed and spoke.

"I came," he said, in that deep bass voice which jarred upon our nerves like a violoncello out of tune, "I came uninvited. Let that be understood. I was not asked to come by any one. I wished to make one in this gathering of Polish conspirators. It is a movement in which I take so deep an interest that I may be excused for wishing to know all that goes on."

Of course he was sneering, and, equally of course, he did not expect to be believed.

The Parisian Pole shrieked and danced with rage, ejaculating, cursing, pouring out imprecations with a volubility almost incredible.

"Here!" he cried, a little exhausted, "here! In the very presence of the young Count Pulaski. You. Wassielewski, look at him. Do you not know him?"

He lifted himself on his toes and hissed a name in Wassielewski's ear.

The old man staggered.

"Here—in the same town—all these years—and I not to know it"—he cried. "Not to know it " Then he advanced upon Herr Räumer, tall, threatening, wild-eyed, waving his arms like the sails of a windmill.

"Oh! men—men—shall we kill him?"

He was hungry for the blood of the spy. Had he possessed a weapon, I think there would have been an end of him at once. Two of the others, the Professor and the Count, placed themselves before the door, and the man in the blouse danced round and round, loudly crying that he should be killed and that at once.

"He is a spy—O Ladislas!—hope of my heart—the son of my dear mistress whom this man murdered, what have you told him about us—about our plans?"

"Nothing, Wassielewski. Remember—I know nothing."

"He has told the spy nothing," Wassielewski repeated. "Have you eaten his bread, Ladislas? Have you entered his house? Have you taken his hand?"

"I have done all those things," I replied.

Herr Räumer laughed.

"He has done all those things. Why not, conspirator and rebel?"

Wassielewski pointed to the man in the blouse.

"Tell him," he said, "tell Ladislas Pulaski why he should not have done those things."

"He should not have eaten his bread, or entered his house, or taken his hand, because the bread is paid for by Russia, because the house is the house of a Russian spy, and because the hand is red with Polish blood."

"And more—and more," said Wassielewski.

"Much more. That hand was the hand which arrested Roman Pulaski on his way to the Austrian frontier. It is the hand of the man who led the Cossacks when they robbed the Polish mothers of their children. Count Ladislas Pulaski, there stands the man who murdered your mother, and made you what you are."

"More," said Wassielewski. "More."

"It is the hand of the man who drove Roman Pulaski along the road from Warsaw to Siberia."

Leonard laid his hand upon my shoulder.

"Steady, Laddy—quiet, dear boy, patience."

Then the Count spoke.

"It is unfortunate. We might have known that Russian spies would be in this place somewhere. We did not expect to find one in our very midst."

"Among us all these years, and I never knew him," groaned poor Wassielewski. "Poles! What shall we do with this man?"

"Meantime," said the Count, "we have to face the fact that he has been here to-day, that he knew of our coming, and the reason of it, and that all our proceedings will be reported immediately to St. Petersburg. This, at least, changes our plans."

"Not to-day's proceedings. For he shall die—he shall die! " cried the workman.

And then there was a dead silence. The men looked at each other, as if asking who would strike the blow.

The Captain interfered.

"Gentlemen," he said, "do not forget that whatever this man is, or has been, he is in my house, and in England, and must be allowed to go unhurt. You cannot, as you might in Poland, kill him as a spy. That is impossible. You must let him go."

"Let him go?" cried the Parisian, springing to the front. "Never!"

I will do the man justice. He never flinched or showed the slightest fear. But the Count drew him back gently.

"Let him go in peace," he said. "In England we cannot shoot him. Go! all that we can do, Monsieur le Mouchard, is to parade your name, to describe your person, to make your calling impossible unless you can disguise yourself, and therefore to ruin you with the Secret Service Department. Go, loathed and accursed among men! Go, canaille! "

He turned from him with such a gesture as Peter might have made to Judas. Leonard, to my astonishment, took Herr Räumer by the arm, and led him to the door, going out with him, as the Poles fell back right and left. Wassielewski and the man in the blouse whispered together for a moment, and then followed together. That boded ill for the spy, and I was relieved, on the whole, to think that Leonard was with him.

I was left alone with the three Poles and the Captain.

"Count Pulaski," said the leader, "I greatly deplore this accident. I hoped that we should have been able to lay before you all our plans, to enlist you in the cause, and to hold out hopes of an immediate insurrection."

"And now?"

"Now, we have no plan. We must first find out how far our secrets have been made known by that man."

"Can I not help you?" I asked. "I am—what you see me—but I might do something yet for Poland."

"You shall live for Poland," he went on, with a sad but kindly smile." No; we shall not, as your friend said, add murder to revolt in dragging you away from your peaceful life. Think, if you can, sometimes, of those who have personal sufferings and degradations burning in their souls. You have none. My back has felt the Russian stick; my cheek yet burns with the Russian blow. Still, you have the memory of your father's death, and you cannot love the Russian cause. Forget us as soon as you can. I shall take Wassielewski away, and leave you free. We shall have meetings, I suppose, but you will not be asked to join. Everything is uncertain, because in London, Paris, everywhere the *mouchards* throng. And of all *mouchards*, the most crafty, the most difficult to detect, is the Russian. I wish you farewell, Count Pulaski."

He took my hand and was gone, followed by his three friends, and I was left alone.

This was the end of my grand deputation.

I was free! my promise would never be fulfilled; I was relieved of my pledge. And I was profoundly humiliated. For I was allowed to go as one who could be of no use to the Cause. I saw the disappointment on the chief's face when he turned from Leonard to me; I saw the readiness with which he acquiesced in Leonard's expostulation; I was of no use to him or to his party. The last of my race was another Edgar Atheling.

And would they think—no—they could not—that I had revealed the plot to this Russo-German spy? Or that I was a foolish creature who could not hold his tongue?

CHAPTER XLV.
HERR RÄUMER'S INTENTIONS.

IN the street Leonard released his hold of Herr Räumer's arm.

"You are free," he said. "Go your own way."

The spy laughed.

"Of course I knew there was no danger. The danger begins now. Come with me to my lodgings. I have something to say to you." Leonard followed him.

In his own place the man opened a bottle of hock, and after offering a glass to Leonard, who refused, drank glass after glass without stopping.

"Nothing," he said, "steadies the nerves like hock. So you will not drink with a member of the Russian Secret Service? No. You will not sit down in his room? No. You will not take his hand? No. You think it a disgrace to belong to that service? Good. That is not a disgrace, but it is disgraceful to be found out, and I do not disguise from you that it will not do me good at headquarters to have been discovered. After all, they will remember that I have had a good long run.

"Our friend in the blue blouse"—he sat down and crossed his legs—" was quite right, though he put things roughly. The Poles cannot see the other side of the question. That is why I wanted to explain to you one or two little things."

He paused, as if trying to find words.

"I cannot hope," he said, "to make you understand that the execution of orders in the Police is no more disgraceful than in the Army. I did arrest Roman Pulaski. I tracked him down, and caught him just upon the frontier. That was my duty. I did escort him part of the way to Siberia, whither he walked on foot. That was my duty. The sentence was the Czar's. I was his servant. Do you blame me? No; you cannot. As regards the other charge about the children, that is also partly true. I was not in charge of the carts—but I rode part of the way with them. I am in no mood for lying, or for defending myself with you, but I ask you to let young Pulaski know that this is the first I have heard about his connection with that day. I did not know, when I first made his acquaintance, that he was one of the victims of that—that—excess of zeal on the part of our Cossack friends. I knew nothing about his mother. You may believe me or not when I tell you that when I made his acquaintance —when I found him to be a poet and a dreamer —I resolved to prevent him if possible from being led to death by a madman. Do you blame me for that?"

"Yes," Leonard replied. "I blame you for ever speaking to him or knowing him. I blame you—because you are a spy."

"A servant in the Secret Service Department. Yes, and in that capacity I have been of use to my country."

"I dare say you have," said Leonard. " I do not care to hear about that., I have only one more thing to say. Did you happen, when you came away, to catch the expression in old Wassielewski's eyes?"

"I did. I watched all the eyes. Shall I tell you what they said as plainly as eyes can speak? That boy looked at me with a sort of wonder, as if it was not possible; the Professor with curiosity; the Count with disappointment, but no surprise. I know the Count, he is a clever man, and, if he does not get shot in Poland, will rise in Paris. The old Captain would have liked to hang me up at the yard-arm, and the other two, Wassielewski and our Parisian, looked murder."

"I came with you, to warn you."

"Thank you very much; I need no warning."

"What are you going to do?"

"Murder and revenge," he repeated."That sounds ugly. But I have seen the look of murder in a good many eyes before now. The look does not kill. I shall do nothing."

"You will remain here?"

"Yes, here—in this town—in this house. They may come up here to murder me. I have pistols. I sleep with the door locked. I shall not be frightened away by any pair of Polish patriots."

"That will not do at all," said Leonard."You must go away."

"Must? and why?"

He explained that there were other reasons besides the fear of those two. These Poles would spread it abroad that he was a Russian spy; the town was full of sailors only a year or so from the Crimean War, and that an English mob were generally rough.

Lastly, Leonard assured him that so far as lay in his power he should take care that he should enter no respectable person's house, that his profession should be told everybody, and that a highly coloured description of the deputation scene should be forwarded to the local and to the London papers.

Then Herr Räumer gave way.

"You are a pertinacious man," he said, "and you want to see me go. Well. I will go to-day. Will that satisfy you?"

"I want, for the sake of poor old Wassielewski, to avoid a scandal.

See,"—Leonard pointed to the window—"the little man in the blouse is watching you in the street."

This was indeed the case. He was marching backwards and forwards, gesticulating and incessantly casting an eye at the door of the enemy's house.

"Go in the daytime," said Leonard. "There is a train to London at five—go by that."

"Perhaps," said the spy. "Perhaps by a later train. But I shall go to-day. That I promise you, for Wassielewski's sake.

"All this," he went on, after more hock, "all this, I confess, is horribly annoying to me. I had formed a pleasant plan for the future which has been entirely disarranged. At sixty-two one does not like to have one's plans upset. I pictured to myself ten years of ease and retirement from active work, giving my advice and experience to the Department, going on those special missions reserved for the higher officers of the service, decorated, pensioned, and living at St. Petersburg with a young and beautiful wife. I confess I am disappointed. Now, I dare say, I shall never marry at all. After all, he who expects nothing from life gets the most. I am content."

"I came away after that," said Leonard. "What a man it is! He has no shame, he glories in his trade. I hope he will go, as he promised, but I am not easy about it. I should like to watch old Wassielewski, or lock him up. And it seems too much to think that he will go away in broad daylight like a man who isn't a spy. Most likely he will steal away in the dark by cross-cuts and lanes, and on tiptoe, after the manner of a stage spy."

CHAPTER XLVI.
A FAMILY GATHERING.

SO all seemed settled, and there was nothing at all left for us but to rejoice and be glad together. All is well that ends well. Leonard and Celia were to be married, the Captain and I were to go on together as of old, there was to be no more threatening of insurrections, life would resume the same calm which is so dull to look back upon, and yet so happy while it lasts. We celebrated the event of Celia's engagement immediately by a family gathering that evening at Mr. Tyrrell's. It was also an entertainment in commemoration of the reconciliation of Aunt Jane with her niece, and, if on that account alone, the best tea things were produced, and there was a lavish expenditure in the matter of muffins and tea-cakes.

Nothing shows the march of civilisation more than the decay in the consumption of muffins and tea-cakes. Nobody has tea at all now, except at five o'clock, because those who remember what a tea-party used to be cannot call handing tea round in trays having tea. Nobody sits down now to a table covered with cake in various forms, but it was in those days the commonest form of entertainment. I suppose everybody of the middle classes looked upon a tea-party as the chief instrument of social intercourse, and Mrs. Tyrrell was by no means singular in attaching a symbolic importance to her best tea-service.

Nothing could have been finer than the manner of Aunt Jane. She kept Celia beside her. She offered no objection whatever when her husband, presuming on the unusually fine weather, ventured to ask for more sugar. She made no allusion to any Christian privileges, either by way of example or admonition, and having found out that Miss Rutherford's father had been a distinguished writer and preacher of the same school as herself, that is, of the severest Calvinistic type, she received her with marked cordiality. Calvinism in that gentle lady, however, was so tempered with native kindness that it lost all its terrors.

As for Mr. Tyrrell, the removal of the weight upon him almost restored him to his youth. He made jokes; he laughed; he was attentive to his wife, he was not only happy again, but he had recovered his old confidence and importance.

In the evening we played, Celia and I, then we sang duets, then Celia sang by herself, but only one song, because everybody wanted a little confidential talk with her in turn.

First it was Aunt Jane.

"Well, my dear," she said, with an inclination of the head in the direction of Leonard, "as you have made your choice I suppose there is nothing more to say."

"But, dear Aunt,"—well-brought-up young people in those days did not venture on such a respectful endearment as "Auntie"—I should like to have seen any one address Mrs. Pontifex as "Auntie"—"you have no objection to Leonard, have you?"

"No—no," she replied critically. "He is, I am told, though not yet a Professing Believer, not without hopes. A husband, my dear, is what a wife makes him. You would hardly believe, perhaps, the trouble which my husband, John Pontifex, has given me by the violence of his natural inclinations. All men, in the matter of eating and drinking, require strong and constant discipline. That you will have to administer with constant searchings into your own conscience. Mere worldliness I need hardly warn you against. You must not encourage your husband's tendency to over-estimate the value of earthly distinctions, though I am glad to learn from his aunt that he comes of a County Family. We who have been blessed, by Providence, with County connections would be blind to our privileges did we not remember that fact. You will never forget your own maternal connections. I refer rather to military distinction. And, above all, my dear, guard against inordinate affection. I need hardly warn you that before marriage any demonstration of—of—of what I suppose you call Love, is highly improper. No girl who values herself or calls herself a Christian gentlewoman, would allow her lover to kiss her on the lips. My first husband, it is true, once surprised me by kissing what he called my marble brow. I never allowed John Pontifex more than the tip of my fingers. After marriage you will find they are not so anxious for kissing. Remember that, my dear.

"He is what the world calls handsome, I fear,"—as if it were a blot upon his moral character—"and he has been successful so far." Here she sighed, as if that was another moral blot."But he is young. I could have wished you to remain, as I did, single to the age of thirty, or even forty; you then might have chosen a man some years your junior, and enjoyed the privileges which age and maturity add to marriage. That has been the case with John Pontifex."

Then it was the Captain.

"Come to me, Cis, my pretty," the old man called her to sit beside him. "Come and tell me all about it. And so you have accepted my boy Leonard, have you? Happy man! I believe I am jealous of him. You must not forget the old house by the Milldam."

"No," said Cis. "I shall not forget the old house, or its owner."

"When is Leonard going to take you away? Don't let him hurry you, Celia. We shall be dull when you are gone."

They protested to each other like a pair of lovers, the old Captain and the girl. I believe she loved the old man as well as any one, after Leonard.

She looked shyly happy, and was as radiant as a moss-rose half-blown, with the sunshine on it. Her eyes kept lifting to Leonard as if she could not bear that he should be out of her sight for a moment, and they were full of a new, strange, and wonderful light. A change had fallen upon her all in a day. A man loved her, and she could give him love for love. It was no mushroom passion, the growth of a ballroom, brought into being by a pair of bright eyes, an intoxicating waltz, the whirl of white arms, and the glamour of music; it was a life-long affection, suddenly ripened into love by the touch and words of Leonard the magician. I have watched other maidens since then, and have seen that look in some of their eyes, but not in all. "She loves him; loves him not," I say, according to the light of her eyes.

"And not a word for me, Cis, for my own private ear?"

"What shall I say, Laddy?"

"Are you perfectly content and happy, my dear?"

"Yes, Laddy, quite, quite happy. There is nothing that Heaven can give me more. I am more happy than I can say. And you? There is no more danger about this Polish business?"

"Happily, none; I am free. My poor old Wassielewski exaggerated the certainty of his insurrection. He saw what he wished to see. The Poles are not ready yet, and, so far as I am concerned, they would not have me if I wanted to go. Of that I am certain."

"I am glad. I could not bear to think of you breathing revenge and bloodshed. You will stay at home and make the world happier with music, Laddy. You must be a great composer."

And then Mr. Pontifex claimed her.

"I have, I believe," he began, "to offer my—ahem—my congratulations on so auspicious an event as your—in fact— your engagement. Marriage is an honourable, condition, although not, as the Papists ignorantly make it, one of the Sacraments of the Church. We have known the young man your—your—in fact, your betrothed—for many years, and we rejoice to find that he has not only distinguished himself as greatly in—ahem—in action—as others," meaning himself —"sometimes distinguish themselves at Oxford in examination, but he has also been enabled under Providence to recover what some would consider an indispensable condition of acceptance with a family of respectability—I mean respectable connections of his own."

Celia laughed.

"At all events, we liked Leonard before he had found Miss Rutherford."

"That is most true. You will, however, Celia, be rejoiced to learn that Miss Rutherford herself belongs to a County family, and that Leonard, both on his father's side and his mother's, is of an excellent stock."

"I am glad if Leonard is glad."

"Your Aunt—in fact, Mrs. Pontifex—thinks that steps should be taken to put Leonard in communication with his father's family, a subject on which she proposes to speak at another occasion. For the present, Celia, my dear, she will probably do no more than invite you to dinner. Mrs. Pontifex has resolved, I may say, upon having a dinner. I do not myself, I confess, greatly admire our own, or rather her style—ahem—of entertainment. I have, on one or two such occasions, arisen from the meal with an unsatisfied appetite. But we think too much on carnal things."

And all the time Leonard was talking with his newly-found Aunt. It seems a prosaic ending for one who never had a father. Leonard was a foundling, or next door to it; he attained to the three-and-twenty without knowing where he came from, and he then, having just occasion to thank Heaven that his father was no more, found—an Aunt. No lordly lineage, no rich and childless father brooding over the irretrievable past, no accession to wealth and fortune, only a widow Aunt, with a small income, only a confirmation of the fact stated by the poor dying mother that he was a gentleman by birth. Yet the confirmation pleased Leonard as much as if he had been proved an earl by birth, and was declared the missing heir to boundless acres and a genealogy going beyond Noah.

It was a quiet evening, with no general conversation, but always these sub-divisions and sections of two and three. It was not late when we separated, and Leonard, leaving Miss Rutherford to the care of Cis, came with the Captain and myself.

The Captain had his pipe and glass of grog, and went upstairs, to turn in. We, left alone, sat silent, looking into space, at the open window, wrapped in our thoughts.

Surely, I considered, Leonard is the spoiled child, whom nothing can spoil, of Fortune. He has fought his way through the briars and brambles of poverty and obscurity, the friendly hand of Fate warding off bullets, bayonets, and the breath of disease. He has come back to us, bearing the Queen's Commission, a successful hero, where so many equally heroic, only less successful, had fallen by the way, and now lay dead on the plains of India or in the Cemeteries of Scutari and the Crimea—he had the gift of Good Luck—*la main heureuse*. Whatever he tries to do, he does well. To be sure, he does it with all his might. What we call Luck, a small and degraded word, the ancients called Fate, because to them success and failure meant much more than they mean now. To lose your high estate; to be a slave who was once Queen of Troy with gallant sons foremost in the fight—that was Fate. To return in triumph, leading the captive Kings at the chariot-wheel—or to be one of the captive kings, shorn of all your former magnificence—Louis Quatorze with the wig off—that was Fate.

To sit in obscurity, to go on living upon a small income, to be unknown, when you know yourself as good a man as he whose name is in every paper, whose voice is heard at every gateway, whom the Lord Mayor delighteth to honour—that is Luck. It seems at first to be a thing quite independent of personal virtues, except that you ought not to be conspicuously vicious; Luck was with Leonard. And yet he was conspicuously, like all successful men, one who deserved his Luck.

"What are you thinking of, Laddy?"

"I am thinking that of all men on earth you are at this moment the happiest."

"I think I am, indeed," he said softly. "I have Celia; I have my Commission and my medals: and now I am no longer a waif and stray in the world, come from nobody knows where, but I have my place with the rest, and can talk of my forefathers like any Howard."

CHAPTER XLVII. THE POLE'S VENGEANCE.

IT was past eleven o'clock, but the day had been exciting and we could not think of sleep. It was a hot night, too, with a little wind, but a full bright moon shining in the placid waters of the Milldam. The town was very quiet; in the kitchen, a cricket chirped loudly; in a neighbouring garden was baying a foolish dog, driven nervous by the moonlight, which, as everybody knows, makes wandering spectres, if there are any about, visible to dogs. Frightened at length by the sound of his own voice, perhaps awed by a more than commonly dreadful ghost, he left off barking and retreated to his kennel. Then we were quite quiet, and sat face to face in silence.

My nerves that night were strung to the point at which whatever happens brings relief. I felt as if something was going to happen.

So did Leonard.

"Come," he said, "we must either talk or go off to bed. I feel as if something oppressive was in the air. Is it thunder? No; it is a clear and beautiful night. Let us go into the garden."

We went to the end of the garden, and stood on the stone coping, looking over the broad sheet of water.

"You are content, Laddy, with the turn things took this afternoon?"

"Yes," I said, "content and yet humiliated. Why did I ever learn the story of my people?"

"Poland has no claim upon you," said Leonard. "Your education—your disposition—everything makes you a man of peace. Stay at home and make the name of Pulaski glorious in art."

"Who is that, Leonard? Listen."

An uneven step in the quiet street. That was nothing, but the step seemed familiar. And it stopped at our door.

And then there was rapping, a low rapping, as if the late caller wanted to come in confidentially.

There was a light burning, in the hall, and Leonard, snatching it up, opened the door.

It was Wassielewski. And then I knew, without being told, that some dreadful thing had happened.

"Let me come in," he said. "I have a thing to say. Are you two alone?"

"Alone," echoed Leonard. "Come in."

"The soldier," murmured the old Pole. "Good; he will understand."

As he stood in the light of the candles I was conscious of a curious change that had fallen upon him. His eyes had lost their wild and hungry brilliancy; they were soft and gentle; but his cheeks were flushed, and though he held himself upright, his hands trembled.

"I am here to tell you, Ladislas Pulaski, that you are avenged upon the murderer of your mother."

"Wassielewski! You have killed him!"

I knew it without another word from him. The spy was dead, and the hand of my poor old friend was red with his blood.

"Yes I have killed him," he said gently.

"Tell us all," said Leonard. "Courage, Laddy, courage. And speak low."

"It was in fair fight," said Wassielewski. "I am no murderer. Do not think that I murdered him. We watched him, that good and true man from Paris and I, all day. We knew that he would escape by train if he could, and so we drew lots. One was to go to the station and watch there. He was to take a ticket for the same station as the spy, he was to telegraph for friends to meet him in London, he was to get out with him, he was to follow him, and he was to find out where he went. Because, you see, we meant that this man should do no more mischief to Poland. The other one was to watch the house, and follow the spy whenever he came out.

"The lot fell to me to watch the house. The other man went to the railway station. But the spy will send no more intelligence to St. Petersburg. He lies dead in a meadow beneath the town walls. I killed him there."

He spoke quite calmly, and as if he was merely stating a fact which we had every reason to expect. There was, however, no trace of bravado in his tone.

"I watched outside, from a window in a house opposite where they know me, from four o'clock till ten. Six hours. But I was not impatient, because I knew that the Lord had delivered him into my hands. After I thought things over, I perceived clearly that it was I, and not you, Ladislas, who was to avenge your mother. So I waited with patience, and, as one must guard against every accident, I even ate and drank.

"It is light, now, till nine, and there is light enough to see across the street till past ten. Soon after sunset I saw that he had lit a lamp, and was destroying papers. When he had gone through all the papers, he began to pack a trunk. I saw him put up his clothes; I saw him write an address on a card; and then—a quarter before ten was striking from St. John's Church—he took that long cloak of his which you know, and put out the gas. There is a night train at half-past ten. He was going to take it, and to send for his boxes afterwards. So I went out after him.

"When he saw me, which he did at once, because he turned at the sound of footsteps, he stopped and waited for me. 'You propose murdering me,' he said. I told him that he was quite mistaken, and that, if he had used his opportunities of knowing the Poles better, he would understand that Poles never murder people at all—having contracted a horror of murder from the contemplation of such murders as those of Roman and Claudia Pulaski.

"'What do you want with me, then?' he asked.

"'I want to fight you,' I said. 'I intend to fight you.'

"He laughed at first, and asked me if I thought him such a fool as to fight with a mad Polish exile—he, a Russian official.

"Then I told him that he should not escape a duel; that if he were to call the police, it would be of no use, because others were waiting for him; that if he escaped the town, the telegraph had sent messages to London, and he would meet the Poles on arriving there; and if he tried to fly anywhere else, he would be watched, traced, and made to fight then.

"'Madman!' he said, 'what are we to fight with?'

"Then I showed him two long knives, which I have had for years, never thinking what a use I should put them to. Knives like short swords, only without the hilt. And I told him he should have his choice. But fight he must.

"He hesitated, considering. He saw very well that what I offered him was his best chance. Man for man. If he killed me, he would probably get away somehow. My comrade was at the station, and might be eluded. Then he was younger and stronger than I.

"'You understand,' I said, 'the duel is to be *à outrance*. I shall kill you, unless you kill me first.'

"'Where are we to fight, madman?' he asked.

"I told him of a place I knew of, a meadow surrounded with trees, beneath the town wall. He knew it, too, and nodded.

"'You are younger,' I said. ' You have that advantage; on the other hand, you have a bad cause, and I a good one. You will fight your best, but you have to fight two, not one—Roman Pulaski as well as Wassielewski. One is dead, and it is hard to fight a dead man.' He laughed; he was no coward, that man. No, no; I never said that the Muscovites are cowards; but it is not well to laugh at dead men. The dead arm may still strike. He was no coward; he was brave, like all his countrymen. But he laughed at the dead; he said he was ready to fight a dozen dead Poles. 'But as for you, a mad old patriot and fool, I will not fight you. Stand out of my path.' ' Do you wish to fight in the street?' I asked him. 'Here is your knife; here is mine. For fight you shall.' I suppose he saw that it was of no use to refuse, for he took the knife and cursed me. He could curse very well, that man. I said nothing, because the Lord had delivered him into my hand, and it is not good to begin a fight with cursing. So I walked beside him, feeling the point of my knife—at his left hand, because the Muscovite spies are treacherous, and he might have tried to stab me had I been on the other side. One has to be careful with such men as that."

"I think, Wassielewski," said Leonard, "that you had better sit down and rest. This talk is too much for you."

The old man was swaying backwards and forwards, flinging about his arms, acting the scene, imitating his enemy's voice and gestures, so that one could picture the big, ponderous-looking spy staring straight in the Pole's face in his insolent, cynical, and contemptuous way. But his voice grew shaky, and his lips were parched.

Leonard poured out a glass of spirits and water, which he drank greedily.

"Aha!" he cried, "I forgot that I was thirsty. Now I can go on."

"Laddy," said Leonard, "don't stare at him with that scared face. Courage, dear boy. Wait till we come to the end. Keep your imagination quiet now, above all times. If you are ready, Wassielewski, to go on—"

"Yes, I am ready. Oh! yes. Quite ready.

"It is a beautiful moonlight night. Almost like a moonlight night in Poland. I thought of the night marches we used to have in 1833, singing as we went through the woods—those were the times for the Poles, when we met the enemy in the morning, and cut him off before he was awake. And then I thought of the moonlight nights—ah! how many years ago—fifty years and more, when Napoleon promised to free Poland, and all of us flocked to his army—and the merry days when we danced all night long with the Polish girls, long before the Muscovite forbade them to wear their own dress, and stopped their dancing altogether. The more I thought of these things, the more happy I felt to be walking side by side with the spy. Because I knew—oh! yes, I knew very well indeed—that I was going to kill him.

"And as I was back in Poland I thought of other things. It is a good thing that one can think so quickly. I was with the rebels again. I had in my hands the very gun which the Lady Claudia gave me. I was creeping in the underwood towards a Russian outpost; I was sentinel all night in the insurgents' camp; I was fighting behind a barricade; I was following Roman Pulaski in a charge; I was running after the carts in which the children were being carried away; I was crying over the dead body of Claudia, with little Ladislas in my arms—I saw it all—all my past life, as well as I see you, Ladislas, and you, Leonard Copleston, before me at this minute. It was a sign to me that I was to gain some signal and great honour. And no honour could be so great to me as the killing of that spy. Because I knew very well indeed that I was certain to kill him.

"Then a strange thing happened. I saw that on the other side of the spy, marching silently, was your dead father, Roman Pulaski. His face was stern and hard, not like the happy face he wore when he married his wife, when he tossed his child, and when he set off to fight the Russians, but stern and hard. He meant that justice should be done. There was the memory of his long march to Siberia in his look, and the years of misery in the mine. He was worn and haggard, and his hair was grey, though his step was firm. Roman Pulaski was going to fight for me. It seemed unfair for the man between us, but it was justice.

"At my right was Lady Claudia. She took no notice of the spy who was going to be killed, not the least notice, because he was beneath her contempt. But she whispered in my ears gracious words, 'Faithful Wassielewski! brave old servant! this one battle over, and your work is done. Courage and patience. You shall see me again before long, when this man is killed.'

"We marched in silence, we four, with the steps of two, side by side along the deserted streets. No one met us, the patrols were all gone back to their barracks, and no policeman passed us. It would have astonished a policeman to see four persons walking together, and two of them dead. When we got to the place where we were to fight—you know it well, Ladislas. It is where you and the lady walk sometimes, and sit among the flowers—we got over the gate side by side, and walked across the grass."

Good Heavens! The man, then, was lying dead among the buttercups in our own meadow under Celia's Arbour, the place where we had talked, played, and sauntered so many, many times, so many years.

"He said nothing, but kept his eyes on me—he did not seem to take any notice of Roman Pulaski—while he threw off his cloak and hat. It is a full moon, and the meadow was as light almost as day. He chose his own position, where the moonshine fell full upon my face, so that it might blind my eyes. Fool! As if it mattered while Roman Pulaski was by my side. I laughed at his madness, and took the place he left for me. The Lady Claudia remained behind. It was not for her to watch the fight. She stood beneath the trees, where I saw her white robes fluttering in the breeze. You cannot expect a saint in Heaven to look at the punishment of a spy.

"Foot to foot, and in each right hand a knife. He fought well, he sprang upon me like a lion, he struck at me here, there, everywhere, but he struck at me in vain, because all his blows were warded off. He was a brave man, but he fought against the dead. All the time he cursed and swore at me for a madman, a mad old Pole, a mad old lunatic, everything that was mad. But I never answered, watching his knife, and waiting my chance. And close beside me stood Roman Pulaski, tall and strong as in life, but his face was hard and stern.

"And then the chance came, and he fell. My knife was plunged to the handle in his heart. I had no scratch upon me, no hurt or wound of any kind. And when he fell I thought of Lady Claudia's words, 'Only this one battle left, and your work is done.' I am past seventy years of age. I fear I shall kill no more spies.

"I looked at him as he lay on the grass. There was a pool of blood, the knife was in his heart, and he was quite dead. And then I came away.

"Before me strode Roman Pulaski, and presently he joined the Lady Claudia. She waved her hand to me, and they both went out of sight hand in hand.

"Then I thought I would come here and tell you, Ladislas, that your enemy is dead. He can do you no more harm and Poland no more harm. The Czar has one spy the less."

He ended his story which he told throughout with a quiet and suppressed vehemence, and with the exultation of one who has done a noble and a brilliant action. Much brooding and a solitary life had driven him mad. He could see no cause for regret or repentance; he had slain his enemy in fair fight, he was the instrument of Providential retribution, he obeyed the behests of his dead mistress, and he had no doubt whatever that the phantoms of his disordered brain were real visitants from the realms of the upper world.

Real visitants! They were real to me while I listened, with trembling lips, to his story. I felt the great horror which, as they tell, falls always upon those who see, or think that they see, the spirits of the dead. It was as if in the room with Wassielewski were those sacred shades whom I longed but dreaded to look upon. And for the moment the horror of the murder, the image of the dead man lying on his back in the long grass, were lost in the eagerness of that desire that they would show themselves to me as they showed themselves to their old servant, and speak to me as they spoke to him. They never came, they never spoke, no voice or whisper from the grave has come to me, nor will come. And yet I doubt not that some time I shall see them both in earthly beauty glorified, and with earthly love transformed into heavenly love.

"That will be best. She said my work was done. In Poland I shall find a grave near hers. I know where she lies beside the road, because I buried her. I will seek out the spot and die there too. My work is done."

Leonard listened gravely. He had not interrupted him, except to ask for the knife. Now he looked at me with a pitying despair on his face. He could do nothing. The poor old man would be tried for murder. And he was quite mad.

Meantime Wassielewski sat down and rested. The exultation was dying out in his brain, and he looked wearied.

And as we asked each other in despairing looks, Leonard and I, what to do next, we were startled by a step outside.

"Good Heavens!" I cried. "Who is that?"

Wassielewski had left the door open. The steps came into the hall; then we heard the street door closed gently. And then our own door opened slowly, and a muffled voice, hoarse and thick, whispered through the opening—

"All friends here?"

CHAPTER XLVIII.
AN UNEXPECTED FRIEND.

"ALL friends here?"

Leonard sprang to the door and threw it open. In the doorway stood—good Heavens! was it Herr Räumer himself, wrapped in his long cloak which fell to his heels, and was thrown over his left shoulder?—a figure the same height as the spy, and having a black felt hat pulled forward over his face.

"The spy's cloak," said Wassielewski quietly, and without the least symptom of alarm or discomposure, "and his hat. But I killed him."

The figure cautiously removed the hat.

That action disclosed a head covered with short, thick, and stubbly red hair, a face whose expression was one of cunning, impudence, and anxiety all combined: such a face as you may meet on the tramp along country roads, one that glances upwards at you as you pass the owner supine in the shade, or that you may see sitting outside a village beershop, or where the more adventurous class of tramps, vagrants, and gipsies most resort. Not the thin hatchet face, with receding forehead and protruding lips, which belongs to the lowest class of London habitual criminals, the face of a class whose children will be cretins, the face which is the result of many generations of neglect, overcrowding, and vice. This was the face of a strong and healthy man, and yet the face of a sturdy rogue. And in removing the hat, the fellow looked round with assurance and nodded cheerfully to Wassielewski.

"His cloak," said Wassielewski, pointing to the garment, "and his hat. But it was I who killed him."

"Right you are, guv'nor," responded our new visitor cheerfully. "His cloak it is. Likewise, his hat it is. And I see you a-killing of him. But don't you be frightened, mate. All friends here?"

He turned his impudent face to us, as if we were a pair of accomplices.

"About the putting of that chap"—he jerked his finger over his shoulder—"out o' the way, I don't want to say nothink disagreeable. There's lots as ought to be put out o' the way, only there's the scraggin' after it—an' I do hope, guv'nor, as you won't be scragged. Bless you, there's a many gets off, on'y the papers don't say nothink about it. And don't you frighten yourselves, young gents both. I've got a word to say as'll please all parties, give me time to say it. Lord help you, I feel like a pal a'ready to this old guv'nor here—and do you think I'd split upon a pal? Gar!"—he made a gesture indicative of contempt for those who split on pals—"and if you could oblige me with a drop o' somethink to drink an' a bite of supper, and p'r'aps a mouthful o' baccy, I could say that word in a more friendly way. Lord! let's all be friends."

He sat down at the table, and, throwing off the cloak, disclosed the uniform of a convict.

"Things are getting mighty pleasant," said Leonard. "Pray, are there any more of you outside? Who is going to turn up next?"

"No one, noble Cap'en. No one—I'm by myself, and I wish to remain as such. There ain't no more of us—and we don't want no more. As you see, a convict I am and a convict I've been for the best part of a twelvemonth, working in that blamed Dockyard of yours. Is that rum in the decanter?"—the Captain's spirit-case, in fact, stood on the sideboard, with a ham placed there for his supper, and not removed. "Give me a drop, my noble Cap'en, I haven't tasted rum for—not too much water—Lord! it's delicious," he gasped, as he drank off half a tumblerful, which Leonard gave him. "Another glass! And is that ham? I've really got somethink important to tell—jest a morsel of that ham. There's no ham to be got in quod. Ham— and rum— Moses! what a chance!"

We gave him the ham and a plate, and contained our impatience while he sat down and made a supper. He devoured hurriedly, and yet took a long time, because he devoured an immense quantity. Either Nature had gifted him with a profound appetite, or the diet of the hulks was meagre. In either case, I never saw a man put away such an enormous quantity of provisions at one time. He wolfed the meat as if he had never tasted meat before, and drank as much rum-and-water as Leonard would give him. It was like a horrible nightmare to see that man calmly devouring his food while we waited his completion of his meal, as if a homicide was a matter that could wait to be talked about till things of greater importance, such a supper, were first discussed. But his appearance served one purpose. It helped to calm one's nerves after the first shock of Wassielewski's story. The old man sat silent and steady, looking at the stranger with a little curiosity. He finished at length, and then, taking one of the Captain's pipes without asking leave, filled it with tobacco, lit it, and began to smoke and talk in an easy, companionable way.

"Yes," he said complacently, "I'm a convict. One-and-twenty years I got. And if I'm caught, it will be a life sentence, I dessay—with a flogging. I've had nearly a year, and might have got out six months ago, but it was a pity not to let the Chaplain have a chance. Pro-fesh burglar. Cracker of cribs. That's what I am. Bagger of swag. That is my calling—it hath bin." I think he persuaded himself that he was quoting from the poets, because he repeated the line, 'That is my calling—it hath bin.' "I was lagged last summer for a little business in the country, and came down here with a few other gentlemen, also in misfortune, to work out the one-and-twenty years.

"One-and-twenty years! What do they think of it, them Beaks and the Wigs? One-and-twenty years! It drops out as glib as—as—this here rum and water. Home they goes to their port wine and their sherry wine, and off we goes to the skilly and water. One-and-twenty years! Why don't they take and hang a man at once? Well—see here, now, there ain't a crib, not one solitary crib you can pint to in this blessed world, that I can't crack. And so I've cracked even that convict crib that they thought to make so precious tight. Cracked it, I did, like—like—a egg; and here I am. First, aboard a hulk. That's poor work, because you've got to swim ashore when you do get out, and when you are ashore what's a man worth in wet clothes? Besides, I can't swim. If everybody knew what was comin' in the future, everybody' ud learn to swim. As long as I was aboard that hulk I was sad. Seemed as if a fellow hadn't got a chance. When we come ashore, I began to pick up my spirits, looked all about, and I made up my little plan at wunst, and after a month or two—picking up a nail here and a nail there, and havin' the use of my fingers, as one may say, and not being altogether a bloomin' idiot—why—here I am."

"Yes," said Leonard, "you certainly are here. But as we don't care about the society of burglars and escaped convicts, perhaps you will go on to say what you have to say, and relieve us of your company."

"Quite right, my noble lord," replied the burglarious professor cheerfully. "Quite right, and just what I should have expected of such an out-an'-out tip-top swell as you. It ain't the society you're accustomed to, is it? And yet you can't, I should say, as a general rule, be fond of entertainin' slaughterers and killerers, can you? Now what I've got to say is just this here. I see the whole fight from the beginnin' to the end. Where was I? Curled up in the shade I was, behind a tree, wishing that there rnoon"—here he used a strong adjective, which, with other strong adjectives, I suppress even though their absence detracts from the fidelity of the story and the splendour of the style—"would hide her face behind a cloud. Then a fellow might ha' had a chance. There is a 'ouse in this town which I knows of, where I'd a bin taken in and kep' secret and comfortable for a bit, perhaps—naturally I wanted to get to that 'ouse. A moonlight night and the month o' June, without a atom of real dark. Ah! give me a good December night, as black as your hat, and a sweet crib to crack in the country, with on'y a woman Or two in the place. Dear me!—Well, gents both, as I was a-lying there, wishin', as I said—I see a brace o' men get over the gate and make for the middle of the field."

"Three men," said Wassielewski, "and a lady. Two were spirits."

"Now, don't you interrupt, mate. I know nothink about spirits. I ses to myself, 'What's up? ' I ses. 'Cause some-think was bound to be up when two men gets into a field a' midnight and stand face to face in the moonlight. 'It can't be,' I ses, 'that they're looking after Stepney Bob'—that's me, gents both, 'cos he ain't missed yet, and won't be missed before five o'clock in the morning. So I concluded to keep quiet and see. Next moment, one of 'em chucks his hat and cloak—this hat and this cloak—on the grass, and then I see the two knives flash in the moonlight, and the fight began. One was a tall thin man with long white hair—that was you, mate—and t' other was a tall stout man with short white hair. That's the dead un—him as owned this cloak and this hat.

"I *have* seen 'em fight at the Whitechapel Theayter—one, two, three, give and take, while the music plays—and I don't suppose there's a properer way of getting through a long evening than the gallery of that 'ouse when there's a good fightin' piece on. But such a fight as this here I never see before on no boards whatsumever. For one, he began to cuss and swear, and danced about flourishing his knife, making lunges—like that"—the gentleman illustrated his narrative with a supper knife—"and never managed to hit the t'other at all. Reg'lar wild he looked. Couldn't fight proper for rage. Lor'! put such a chap as that before Ben Gaunt, and where'd he be in a pig's whisper? Never done no mischief with his knife. The t'other, this here old cove—there now, it was a real treat to see him. The moon was in his face so as I should have thought it blinded him; but he took no notice; only looked his man straight in the eyes—that's the trick that does it—never said ne'er a word, and kept on parry in' them lunges quiet and beautiful—like this"—more illustration with the knife.

"A matter of six minutes it might have lasted, that fight, or perhaps ten, because you don't count the time when you're lookin' at a fight. And then all of a sudden like, I see this same old cove put out his fist with the knife in it—and the t'other falls back upon the grass. That was all, wasn't it, mate? He got up once on his arm, but he fell back again. And he was dead, wasn't he, mate?"

He stopped to take breath and another pull of the rum-and-water.

"Another dollop o' that cold ham on the sideboard, little gunner, would be very grateful, it would indeed, after the patter. Thank ye kindly. Now I'm better."

He actually devoured another plateful of ham before he would go on again.

"Well, what I came for to say is this here. After the t'other un rolled over I see the old cock here walk up and down the meadow slow, as if he was thinkin' what to do next. 'Why don't he bolt?' I ses. 'Why don't he clear his pockets?'"

"I was walking to the gate with Roman Pulaski," explained Wassielewski.

"No—not a bit—never went near his pockets. He goes on walkin' up and walkin' down mutterin' with his lips. Presently he makes for the palin's. I instantly begins to crawl through the grass. When he got over the rails and walked away I was free to look after the t'other. Quite dead he was, dead as a door-nail."

"The Lord delivered him into my hands," said Wassielewski.

"And then I saw what a blessed Providential go it was for me," the convict went on. "First I picked up his cloak, this most beautiful cloak, which you see goes right down to my heels, and covers up the uniform lovely. Then I picked up this here hat, which is a tile as good as new, and fits me like as if it was made for my head and not for his'n. A better tile I never swagged. Then I remembered that, if I had a little money, it wouldn't be a bad thing. So I searched his pockets. There was a purse and there was a lot of letters and papers. I left the letters and I opened the purse. Twelve golden sovereigns and some notes—for I won't deceive you, gents both. What d'ye think I did? I ses to myself, 'If they bring it in murder ag'in the old un, they shan t bring it in robbery too, 'cos robbery is one thing and murder's another. These two things ought never to be combined.' I ought to know, 'cos I've cracked cribs since I was big enough to walk, and might ha' murdered dozens of innocent and confiding women asleep in their beds. But I never did. No, never. So I takes all the sovereigns in the purse, and in his waistcoat pocket I leaves three or four shillin's, and I leaves all the rest, the flimsies, a lovely gold watch, a sweet chain, and a diamond ring. It went to my 'art not to have 'em but I thought of this jolly old game rooster, and I left 'em."

"Chivalry," said Leonard, "is always a pleasant thing to meet with, even—go on, most excellent burglar."

"The knife was in him, and his own knife was in his hand. What do you think I done next? I takes the knife out of the wound, and sticks it in his hand, 'stead of his own. And I've brought along his own, and here it is.

He laid the knife upon the table—it was a long pointed knife, like a stiletto—of foreign shape and make. I did not ask Wassielewski if it was his, but gave it to Leonard. "One more thing," this philanthropist went on,"one more thing I done. There were marks of feet, and the grass was trampled. So I dragged him away, and laid him under the trees at the side of the field. They'll never think of looking in the middle and finding marks of a fight. After all that, I shouldn't wonder—I rally shouldn't—if they brought in a Fellar D. C. But my advice to you, a game old cock as deserves to get off and die in the sheets, a laughin' at 'em all, is this: Whatever the werdect, you up and leg it, and then bring in a alibi. You ain't the sort to get off in a hurry; you walked so precious slow down the street that I had time to do all that and catch you up before ever you got out o' sight. I dodged yer all the way here, and sneaked in after you. 'Cos, I ses, I'd like to let him sleep comfortable if I could, ses I."

After all, one could not but feel grateful to this enthusiastic lover of a fight, in spite of the horrible circumstances of the case, and the tragedy which had just taken place. Somehow its outlines looked less horrible told by this gaolbird than when Wassielewski related the story.

"And now I'll go," he said, getting up and wrapping his cloak about him; "I can tramp it up to London, and hide all day somewheres. No one won't suspect Stepney Bob beneath this milingtary cloak and this out-an-out tile. Once back in Whitechapel, I know a place or two where they won't nab me for a spell I don't think, and p'r'aps I'll step it altogether. And then you'll maybe hear of me cracking cribs for the Americans. Good-night, gents both. Goodnight, matey. Don't ye be down on your luck. But take my advice and leg it."

"Stay," said Leonard. "It's a delicate thing interfering with your arrangements, and one's actions might be misunderstood, but if I might advise "

"Go on, guv'ner."

"I would suggest that if you are not missed you will not be suspected, and a first-class traveller to London by the mail train at one-thirty, disguised, as you say, in that excellent cloak, would have a better chance of reaching Whitechapel safely than a tramp."

Stepney Bob was struck with the suggestion.

"That's true," he said thoughtfully. "The train 'ud be in by four, and I shan't be missed till five. And in case o' accidents, I suppose"—he looked hard at Wassielewski—"I suppose that there ain't no one here who'd be so generous and so werry thoughtful as to step half a mile out o' the town and take a pair o' shears, and nip they (strong adjectived) telegraph wires. Now, that 'ud be a job worth braggin' about. Come, now, they'd make a song out o' that job, I'd bet a trifle, and you'd be sung up and down the streets; all Whitechapel should ring with it, and the Dials too, and Ratcliffe Highway. Think o' that, mate."

No one volunteered to cut the telegraph wires, and after a little more rum-and-water, Stepney Bob decided on going, and disappeared after a cautious inspection of the street.

"It would read sweetly in the paper, wouldn't it," said Leonard, "how Captain Copleston and Ladislas Pulaski spent the night in assisting the escape of a convicted burglar, known in the profession as Stepney Bob—however—"

"And what will you do, Wassielewski?"

"I shall do nothing. My work is over. I shall start for Poland—to-morrow. Ladislas Pulaski, if you marry and have children, teach them always that they are Poles. I was wrong in trying to get you with us. I see now that I was wrong. You will never fight for Poland. Another life is yours. God bless it for you—for the dear memory of your mother."

He laid his hand upon my head, rested it there for a few moments, and then went away, walking slowly and heavily, as if wearied with the weight of his life's work.

"Bear up, Laddy," said Leonard. "Come —be a man— poor old Wassielewski is not responsible for his actions. Go to bed, and to-morrow we will act."

"I feel somehow as if the blood of that man was on my head, Leonard. It is through me that he was detected."

"Some people would say that the finger of Fate was in it, Laddy—I say that it is a fitting end to a life of spying, watching, and informing. I wish all secret service agents could be got rid of in a similar way. Meantime, we must wait for to-morrow—I must think what we had better do."

"I cannot go upstairs, Leonard. I feel as if that dead body were lying in my room, waiting for me. Do not leave me to-night."

I could not bear to be alone. My nerves were like cords tingling and vibrating. I was in the presence of death and the other world. My brain was reeling.

Leonard carried me upstairs, I think, and laid me on the bed, when presently, while he sat beside me, as if I was a sick girl, I fell into a deep sleep, and dreamed that Wassielewski and I were trudging together along a road which I knew to be in Poland, and that before us stood our home—a stately mansion—and on the steps were Roman and Claudia Pulaski, holding out arms of welcome. And as I looked, Wassielewski suddenly left me, and I was alone. But he had joined the other two, and now all three were standing together waiting for me. Whenever, now, I dream of the past or of that fatal day, it is to see those three waiting still for me to join them.

CHAPTER XLIX.
A CORONER'S INQUEST.

IT is a shame for a man to have to confess his own weakness; but the truth has to be told. I broke down at this point, and lay on the bed to which Leonard carried me for three weeks, in delirium. I suppose the great horror and shock of the evening, following on the nervous agitation of the preceding three days, was more than my brain could bear. At any rate, I had a bad time for the next fortnight or so, during which things went on without my being interested in them. Could one remember what delirium means, a chapter might be written—but one would need to be De Quincey to write it. First the chest seems to expand, and then the head to swell out and become of gigantic size. Then you lay your hands upon the forehead to make sure that it has not been carried somewhere else. Then you grow big all over, hands and feet and limbs. Then you lose all sense of weight, and seem to be flying in the air. And then, just as you are beginning to feel uncomfortable, your mind runs away from your control: things grotesque, things splendid, things absurd, things of the past, things from books, wild imaginations crowd the brain, and move before the eyes like a real pageant of living creatures. Nothing astonishes, nothing seems strange; there is no sense of incongruity; and when you recover, all is forgotten but the genera] impression of grotesque unreality. They told me afterwards what had happened.

They discovered, early in the morning, two things. First, that a convict had escaped, and secondly, that a dead man was lying in the meadow beneath the walls.

At first they connected the two things, but subsequent inquiry led them to believe that the convict had nothing to do with the homicide.

As soon as Leonard could leave me with the Captain he sought the old Pole. Wassielewski's single room was on the second floor in one of the crowded streets near Victory Row. The sailors' wives were all gathered about their doors, though the rain was falling heavily, talking of the discovery of the dead body, and wondering whether it was a murder or only a suicide. Most of them knew Leonard as an old inhabitant of the quartier, and saluted him kindly as Gentleman Jack, a name which they learned from their husbands' friends, the soldiers.

Leonard asked if the old man had been seen that morning. He had not, it was too early in the morning. It was his custom to remain in his room until noon, unless he was engaged to play for a paid-off crew. At twelve he descended, and would seldom return home till the evening. Leonard would find him in his room.

He mounted the stairs, and knocked. There was no answer. He knocked again. Again there was no answer. Could he have gone off already, on his way to Poland, acting on the burglar's advice?

Leonard went down the stairs again, and asked the mistress of the house. No, he had not gone out. He came home late, she said, perhaps as late as twelve, because she must have been in bed some time, and his footsteps woke her; but she had been up since six, and he certainly had not come down stairs.

She came up with Leonard this time, and they both knocked.

Then they called him by his name.

All was still and silent.

Leonard leaned his shoulder against the door and pushed. The bolt came away from the rotten wood, and the door fell open.

Wassielewski was kneeling- by the bedside. In his hands was the miniature of my mother, and his lips were pressed closely to it. But the lips were as hard and as cold as the hands that held the cross, for the poor old man was dead.

He was not undressed. He died in his devotions, perhaps immediately after he came home. Redhanded with the blood of the spy, he went unrepentant to the after world. The two souls, side by side, departed almost together.

This event, as Leonard said, simplified matters amazingly. It was no longer necessary for him to consider how the old man ought to give himself up to justice. It seemed pretty clear that the convict would hold his tongue, even if he got caught, while if he got away he would certainly tell nothing. On the other hand, if he did tell, it would be time enough to reveal the real truth. There was excuse, at any rate, in the plea that, the old Pole being dead, nothing could be gained by letting the world know that, like Lamech, he had slain a man.

The inquest on Wassielewski was very short. He had been found dead, he was an aged man, the doctor certified that the cause of death was disease of the heart, the verdict was given in accordance with the evidence, and the poor old man was buried with the rites of his own Church.

By common consent of the few Poles who remained in the town, Leonard took possession for me of the few effects which the old. man left. There were two or three weapons, relics of the last struggle, and his violin. We looked through the drawers and cupboard, but there were only a few papers containing lists of names and plans of campaigns. These were burnt to prevent accidents. Also there was a bag full of sovereigns—

seventy or eighty—which he had put together in readiness for a start at a moment's notice. With the Captain's consent, and by his advice, I subsequently distributed the legacy among his fellow-countrymen, who all came to the funeral of the most determined patriot that ever Poland produced.

A most important inquest was that held on the same day upon the body of Herr Räumer.

Ferdinand Brambler was, of course, present, taking notes with the air of one who has got hold of a good thing and means to make the most of it. Also he was himself conscious of an accession of importance, for was not the deceased a lodger in his brother Augustus's house?

They first called the policeman who had found the body.

He deposed that early in the morning, at half-past four, he took the walk under the walls in the course of his beat, that he saw lying on the grass just within the meadow the body of a man. The man was dressed, but without a hat. Money was in his pocket—somehow the statement of Stepney Bob and that of the policeman did not exactly tally, and either the burglar helped himself to more than he confessed, or the policeman took advantage of the situation and took two notes, at least, on his own account—that the deceased had upon him also a watch and chain and a diamond ring, those, namely, that lay on the table.

A suspicious juror—there is always, I believe, a suspicious juror—here requested to see the watch and chain, which he inspected minutely. The deceased lay, the policeman went on, as if he had fallen backwards after the blow was inflicted, and never moved again. The knife, which was that lying on the table, was of foreign make, such as a German gentleman might have carried. Being asked if he thought it was a murder, he said that there were no marks of violence or trampling in the grass, that, as he had not been robbed, he did not see why it should have been a murder. That from the knife being held tight in the right hand he thought it was suicide.

Then the doctor was called, the same doctor who gave evidence in the case of Wassielewski. He stated that the death had been caused by a deep wound which punctured right through the heart, that the death must have been instantaneous; that although such a wound would require the greatest determination, it was quite possible for a man to inflict it upon himself; that the right hand tightly held a knife covered with blood, and that the wound, in his opinion, was undoubtedly inflicted by that knife, the one before the jury.

The next witness was Mr. George Tyrrell, the Mayor of the Borough. He deposed that Herr Carl Räumer and himself were on friendly and intimate terms: that he had the management of his affairs; that he knew nothing whatever of his family connections in Germany; that a short time previously the Herr had instructed him to realise certain investments, which had been done as he requested; that he had last seen the deceased on the morning of his death, when nothing whatever passed which could warrant a belief that he was about to commit suicide; that, on the contrary, he stated he was about to go away to the Continent, there to take up his permanent residence. But, on the other hand, he had received a note in the evening which struck him as singular. This note he would read. It was short, and was as follows:—

"DEAR TYRRELL, —I find that my departure will take place earlier than I intended. I wished to see you again; I shall, however, go this night and for ever. My affairs are all settled. I wish, as you will never see me again, that you will take care of Ladislas Pulaski. Do not let the boy be persuaded ever to go to Poland. That is my solemn advice to him.—Yours, C. R."

He said that on the receipt of the letter he thought at first of going round, but as the hour was late he refrained, to his present great regret. The letter was brought by a child, daughter of his clerk, Augustus Brambler, in whose house Herr Räumer lodged.

The Coroner asked if any of the jury wished to put any questions to His Worship the Mayor. The suspicious juror wished to ask the Mayor if he was quite certain about the handwriting. The Mayor had no doubt whatever of the letter being in his old friend's writing.

Then Charlotte Brambler was called. The report in the paper of the following Saturday, with which, of course, Ferdinand Brambler had nothing to do, spoke of her as a most intelligent, straightforward witness, who gave her evidence clearly and to the point. "Her face," the report went on, "is singularly attractive, and her appearance and demeanour elicted universal respect and admiration. She is, we understand, the eldest, not the second daughter, as reported, of Mr. Augustus Brambler, long and honourably connected with the Legal interests of the Borough."

Little Forty-four did give her evidence very well. She had to say that she attended to Herr Räumer, and that at nine o'clock in the evening he called her up, and sent her with a letter to Mr. Tyrrell. There was no answer, and she returned immediately after delivering the note. Then he rang the bell again and told her that he was going away that night—going on a long journey.

An intelligent juror here interposed. He said that a long journey might mean anything, and he asked the witness why she did not ask him how long it was?

Forty-four replied that she never asked Herr Räumer anything, but answered his questions, and as he did not say where he was going, it was not for her to inquire. She went on to depose that he added that he should not return any more; that instead of a month's notice he paid down a month's rent; that as she had attended him for some years he gave her a five-pound note, which he advised her to keep for herself, and not waste it in buying things for her brothers and sisters—this was a touch entirely Räumeresque. Then he looked about the room, and said that the furniture could go to Mrs. Brambler, and she might have his old piano if she liked. Then she asked him what they were to do with the books which are in French, with yellow paper covers, in fact, French novels. He laughed, and said that if she pleased she might keep them till her brothers grew up, and then give them the books, which would certainly teach them a good deal about life previously unsuspected by them; but that, if she preferred, she might sell them for what they would fetch as waste paper. At all events, he would never want any of the books or any of the things any more.

The Coroner here interposed, and asked her if she was quite sure that those were the very words the lodger used.

The witness was perfectly certain that those were his exact words.

"He would never want the books or any of the things any more."

The jury whispered together.

Then the Coroner asked the girl about the knife.

She knew nothing about the knife; she had never seen such a knife in his room; but could not swear that he had no such knife, because he kept everything locked up. Perhaps the knife had been lying among Herr Räumer's things in one of the drawers. Had never tried to look into the drawers, would not be so mean as to pry into things.

Here the suspicious juror remarked plaintively that he should like to see the five-pound note which the deceased had given her. She produced the note, which was handed round among the jury, who examined it as carefully as if it had been an important *pièce de conviction*. Then they all shook their heads at one another, and gave it back to the Coroner, who restored it to Forty-four.

There being no other evidence to call, the Coroner proceeded to sum up.

The jury must consider, he said, all the circumstances. The deceased informed an old friend in the morning that he intended to go away shortly; in the evening he sent a very extraordinary epistle, stating that he was going away "for ever "—the jury would make a note of that expression. At the same time he tells the little girl who was accustomed to attend upon him—and he was constrained to express his admiration at the very straightforward way in which that little girl's evidence was given—that he was going away, and was not coming back again. Let the jury mark, at this point, the suddenness of resolution. He took nothing with him; he abandoned the piano, his books, everything; and even made the very important remark that he should not want any of them any more. Why not? If a man goes on the Continent he does not give up reading; if a man changes his residence he does not throw away, so to speak, all his furniture, but carries it with him, or sells it; but Herr Räumer was not, as he told the girl, Charlotte Brambler, going on the Continent; he was going—let the jury mark this very earnestly, he was going—on a long journey. Very good: but consider another point. The doctor was of opinion that the blow, if that of a suicide, must have required great determination. Possibly, perhaps, Herr Räumer had not the requisite amount of resolution, but the jury all remembered him—a stout, stern, and determined-looking person. As to courage, no man could tell when any other man's courage came to an end. And there were the facts that the knife was found in his hand, covered with blood; that there was no sign of any struggle on the ground, and that the knife was of foreign manufacture. If it was not suicide, what was it? Could the jury believe that a man of singularly quiet, regular, and reserved habits, should go out in the dead of the night, after making those remarkable statements and writing that remarkable letter, for a stroll, without his hat, on the walls? That he should then, still with the intention of taking a purposeless stroll, have climbed over the wooden railings into the field, and then presented his breast, offering no resistance, to the murderer? Then it was whispered that a convict, escaped that morning from the prison close by, might have done the deed. First of all, he must say that it appeared to him disgraceful that any convict should escape, but it was absurd to connect the convict with the death of a man he could not have known and whom he did not rob. Also, how did that convict get hold of a foreign knife? Let the police catch and produce the fugitive, and it would then be time to consider the absurd suggestion. There, in fact, was the evidence, all before the jury. They were a body of educated and intelligent men; they had sat at Coroners' inquests before, and he, the Coroner, was glad to say that a more trustworthy body of men to weigh evidence impartially he did not hope or desire to find. He therefore dismissed them in the confident hope that they would shortly return with a verdict.

In five minutes the jury came back. Their finding was unanimous. It was that the deceased committed suicide while suffering from temporary insanity.

This verdict, never disputed, was the end of the whole business. The deceased was buried at the expense of the Mayor, who acted as chief mourner. Our Polish friends made not the slightest sign of any knowledge of the deed; no one in the town knew anything, and our only accomplice was Stepney Bob. I never heard that he was recaptured, and I have every reason to believe that he managed to escape altogether and get to America or some other part of the world, where his possible good private qualities had not been obscured by his public reputation as a cracker of cribs. Nor did it appear that any inquiry was made into the matter by the Russians. They did not acknowledge the *mouchard* who died fighting for his life with one of the people whom he was paid to watch. If he had friends or relations, none of them ever turned up. No doubt his was an assumed name, under which no one of his own people would be likely to recognise him.

When I recovered, and was able to be told everything, I confess to a feeling that fortune for once had found a fitting death for a man.

We never told the Captain, Leonard and I. But once, when Mr. Tyrrell had been lamenting in public over his great private loss, while he was perfectly oblivious of the little facts which preceded the death of his friend, I ventured to tell him privately the whole history. After that we never mentioned him again. The behaviour of Leonard in suppressing the real facts was, like his conduct when first he introduced himself to the Captain—what Mr. John Pontifex called a Wrong Thing.

CHAPTER L.
"LEONARD AND CIS."

I GOT well again and strong, but I was forbidden to do any teaching work for two or three months, and had to give up all engagements for that space.

A holiday of three months, with Celia to come every day, till I was strong enough to go out, and read to me; the Captain to fidget about what was best for me to eat and drink; Leonard to tell stories, and sometimes the Rev. John Pontifex to come and sit with me, making profound remarks on the wickedness of man in general, his own fearful backslidings in his youth, and the incredible amount of repentance which they involved, the ignorance of the Papists, and the strength of will possessed by his remarkable wife. Or Mr. Broughton, who would come round, and, by way of giving me a fillip, read a little Greek with me and then send round a few bottles of choice old port. Mrs. Pontifex sent strawberries and tracts; she also told me that my fever was no doubt intended to bring me more directly under the influence of her husband's ministrations. Augustus Brambler would come bursting in between the intervals of writ-serving and message-running, to tell me joyfully of the great business done by the House. And little Forty-four would come as often as she could; if no one else was with me she sat down, beaming with smiles, the tenderest of little nurses, and told me how they were all getting on,—Forty-six developing into a real genius over his books—he was the son who subsequently became a Reporter and Journalist; Forty-eight, who had been caned at school for insubordination, and so on. I learned, too, from her that the famous five-pound note had been, contrary to the donor's intention, distributed in new clothes, as far as it would go among the whole family. A new lodger had been found who was at least more considerate than the former, did not dine at home, and talked to the children.

But, of course, Celia was the most regular visitor, and with her, Leonard. They came together and went away together; and in my presence he made shameless love till sometimes the light of answering love flashed for a moment in her eyes, and then she drew herself from him, blushing, and fell to busying about my pillows. Miss Rutherford drove over from Fareham, too. She turned out to be exactly what she looked at first sight—for that matter, people always do; a gentle, quiet, and careful old lady, who ought to belong to some planet where there are no such things as temptations, follies, or worldliness. She was always prettily and daintily dressed, and as became an elderly lady, behind the fashion.

She had a sweet and pleasant face, with an expression on it which reminded one of Leonard, and when she spoke it was in a clear and precise way, like the ripple of a stream over stones. And when she looked at her nephew it was with an ever-growing wonder that there should be in the world such a boy as that to call her Aunt.

Imagine all the sentimental and tender things that these two women, Miss Rutherford and Cis, would say to each other and to me as they sat beside my arm-chair while I was recovering. Think, if you can, how they were bound together by their common love for one man, and how they would read, as women always try to do, in each other's soul, dissatisfied until they succeed in finding, as in a mirror, each her own image in the heart of the other. Some women can have no half measures; they must love wholly and trust altogether; and they must receive back as much as they give.

I tried to write down some of these tender scenes, but I have torn them up; words that are altogether sweet and precious when spoken sometimes look sentimental and meaningless when they are written down. What they came to was this, that two women tried to spoil one man by attention and thoughtfulness, and did their best to make another man vain by their exceeding love for him. I do not think either was much injured.

In September we all four, Miss Rutherford acting chaperon, went to the Lakes together in order to complete my recovery.

I have been in many places since the year 1858, and enjoyed many holidays. I have learned to know this beautiful garden set with all manner of delights, with mountain, stream, lakes, and forests, with all kinds of sweet flowers and singing birds to raise the heart of man, which we call England. I have dreamed away the hours in the pleasant land of France, among old castles by the stately Loire, or where the white cliffs of Normandy face their sisters of Albion. I have sat among the students of Germany and wandered among the sweet-scented pines round mountain feet, but I have had no holiday such as that. A dreamy time, when one was still weak enough to allow the sentiment of the situation to dwell in the mind, with a clinging for the last time to the robe of Celia, while all sorts of sweet phrases and cadences gathered themselves together and took shape in my heart, to be expressed in music when I might find time to set them down, with a new interest in listening to the talk, so truthful and so old-fashioned, of the lady whom chance had joined to our party, who ought to have been set in a bower full of flowers and fruit, with pictures about her of angels—not Churchy angels—ladies could be pious twenty years ago without ecclesiastical rubbish—and faces of holy women full of trustful thought. With this, the old admiration for Leonard, the strong, the brave, the handsome Leonard.

One evening, after sunset, we were in a boat on Derwent-water, Leonard, Cis, and I. Leonard was rowing us gently, letting the oars dip slowly in the smooth water, and then resting, while the boat made slow way among the wooded islets. Cis and I sat side by side in the stern, she was steering. The dark foliage was black now, and the lighter leaves were changed into a dark green. The lake was still and quiet, now and then a fish came to the surface with an impatient splash as if it really was getting too dull down below; or a wild fowl flew over our heads with a whirr; or a noise of voices, mellowed by distance, came across the water from the hotel, and far off somewhere a man was blowing a horn, and the echoes flew from hill to hill.

"Blow, bugles, blow, set the wild echoes flying."

Celia quoted softly.

And then we were all silent again.

It was Leonard who spoke next. Deeper darkness had fallen upon us now, clouds were coming up in the west, and the breeze began to rise. The boat was quite motionless, on either hand an islet, before us in the distance the lights of the hotel reflected in the water. And again the sweet rolling echoes of the horn.

Said Leonard, speaking softly—

"There is a thing I should like to tell you, Cis, if Laddy will let me. It is a thing which he told me in his delirium, a thing I ought to have suspected before, but did not, so dull and selfish as I was. Can you guess what it is?"

I could guess very well. There was nothing else that I could have told unknown to Cis already.

"I thought I was the only one who knew," Leonard continued. "But I was not; the Captain knows."

"He knew before," I murmured. "Tell Cis, if you please, Leonard, if you think well. But remember, it is all a thing of the past—forgotten—torn up by the roots."

"When I went away, Cis, dear," Leonard began, "I left you in the charge of Ladislas. You were, I told him, in my conceited way, to be his peculiar trust, he was to look after yon, to watch you, and to anticipate everything that you could want."

"And so he has done," said Cis."Haven't you, Laddy?"

"The reason I gave him was that I loved you, my Queen, and that if things went well—all looks easy to a boy—I proposed coming back, and telling you myself—in five years' time. Observe, please, the extraordinary selfishness of a boy of eighteen. At that age one cannot possibly think of anything but oneself. Well—I went away— I came back. Fortune had been kinder to me—far kinder than I ever deserved. I am loaded with the gifts of Heaven. Don't think me ungrateful, because I talk little about these things. I can only talk of them to you two. But that is nothing. While I was away, Cis, you grew from a child into a woman."

"Yes, Leonard."

"What I did not think of was that Laddy was growing too from a boy to a man—what I forgot was that there would be one girl and two men—that both men might love the same girl."

"Laddy! " Cis cried with surprise and pain.

"Forgive me, Cis," I said,"Leonard has told you the truth. For a time—it was early this year, I think—what he hinted at was the case. I fought with it, and I beat it down, because it was hopeless, and because of the promise I gave to Leonard. But it is true that there was a time when I gave way, and—ventured to love you, otherwise than a brother may. Why did you tell her, Leonard?"

"Because I want her and myself to feel more what we owe to you, Laddy, to your unselfish labour, your watchfulness, and the sacrifice of your own interests. He loved you, and he gave you up, Cis. I wonder if any words of mine could make you understand what that meant to him."

"It could never have been, Leonard," I said. "How could it? Celia was my sister, always."

She laid her hand in mine and one arm upon my shoulder.

"Always your sister, Laddy dear. And henceforth more and more. There is now nothing that we have not told each other."

Henceforth, more and more. Yes, as the time has gone by, nothing has dimmed the steady trust and affection which Celia has showered upon me. I can see now, too, how different her life would have been, how wanting in fulness, had things been different, and had she married me. Some women are happiest with a man of action; how could the life of a dreamer like me satisfy the aspirations of a girl who worthily fills the place of Leonard's wife, and has stepped gracefully into the rank to which his success has raised her?

About that one thing we never spoke any more.

Leonard rowed us quietly back to the hotel, the lawn of which ran down to the water's edge. The garden was full of the visitors, for the evening was warm. They looked at us as we passed them, Celia with her hand on my shoulder in the old familiar fashion, staring with that half-impudent, furtive way in which English people at hotels look at each other and at strangers. In the salon was nobody but Miss Rutherford, quietly waiting our return.

She asked Leonard to take her into the garden for a walk, and left Celia and me alone.

Then I sat down to the piano, and collected my thoughts—all those musical thoughts of which I have spoken,—and began to play them.

It was no improvisation, because the ideas had been long in my head, and many of them had been already noted down and tried over, but it was the first time I played the piece as a whole.

"What is it, Laddy?" Celia asked, as she saw me striving to talk to her in the old fashion with my fingers on the keys, a language unknown to the outer world. "What is it? I cannot understand it yet."

"Listen, Cis. It is a love poem of two young people—we will call them 'Leonard and Cis.' It tells how one went away, and how after five years he came back again, not a prodigal son, but covered with honour; how they fell in love at once, and how after many difficulties, which were got over in a most surprising and extraordinary manner, quite as if these two lovers belonged to a novel, which, of course, they did not, they were finally married, and lived happily for ever and ever. Now listen."

The symphony came forth from my brain clear and distinct, and, after a few bars of prelude, flowed straight on to the end. I have written plenty of music since, though I am not, as Celia affects to think me, a great composer, but I have written none that has pleased me so much, that dwells so constantly in my mind, and where I have found such fulness of expression. It is, I am sure, by some such masterful wave of passion that the highest expression and the noblest conceptions are brought together in the brain, and great works are produced.

I could see in my own music—and Celia could see it as well—first a rippling movement showing the peace and sunshine of early maidenhood; then the yearnings and unconscious reaching out of hands in thought for a fuller and richer life; then the awakening of Love the glorious, like the awakening of Adam in the garden, to look about with wonder, to walk with uncertainty, to feel his way in broad daylight, to fear lest it should be a dream, and that the vision should pass away, and all be nothingness again. Presently followed the growth of passion till it became a great river for strength. And lastly, the Wedding Hymn of triumph.

"Do you understand it, Cis?" I asked. "It is meant for you, and written for you. I shall copy it all out, and give you a copy, as my wedding present."

"I think I understand—some of it," she replied. "How can your pupil understand it all at first? O Laddy! you have made me very humble to-night. How can men love women as they do? What are we, and what can we do, compared with them, that they should lavish such affection upon us?"

"Ask Leonard," I replied, laughing.

And outside the people were all listening in the garden. When I finished there was a general applause, as if I had been playing for them.

That night, an hour later, I heard below in the garden the voices of those who sat up still.

"Who was it playing?" asked a girl's voice. "He has a sweet face; it is a pity he is deformed."

"It is a certain Pulaski—Pole, I suppose. Patriot most likely. Count, of course, or Baron, or Duke"—this agreeable person was a man, perhaps the young lady's husband—"some adventurer, most likely, who goes about trying to pick up a rich English wife by his tale of misfortunes and his pianoforte-playing. To-night's performance was an exhibition. No doubt he wants to fascinate that extremely pretty girl, almost as pretty as some one else I could name."

"Nonsense, sir, a great deal prettier; and, besides, she's engaged to the tall young man, who is a Captain Copleston and a Crimean officer. The old lady with them is a Miss Rutherford. She is his aunt, and plays propriety. I do not know anything about the pianoforte-player."

"Well, I'm glad she is not going to marry a hunchback, pianoforte-playing Pole."

Listeners, as has been frequently observed, never here any good of themselves. But I played no more at the Derwentwater hotel, because next day we returned southwards, and began all of us to prepare diligently for Celia's wedding.

CHAPTER LI.
"RING, WEDDING BELLS!"

I HAVE come to the end of my story, the only story I have to tell from my own experience. How should it end but with a wedding? There is no romance where there is no love; there is no pleasure in the contemplation of love unless it ends happily, and is crowned with orange blossoms; love is the chief happiness of life, as everybody knows—except, perhaps, John Pontifex—and has ever been completed by the wedding-bells.

Ring, wedding bells, then; shake out the clashing music of your joy over all the fields, startle the farmer at his work, rouse the student at his desk, strike on the ear of the sailor out at sea, echo along the shore, mingle with the roar of the saluting guns to greet the ship's crew when they come home, so that they may know that during their three years' cruise the world's happiness has not altogether died away. Bring back to the old a memory of a day long gone by. Lift up the heart of the young with hope. Put ambitious thoughts of such a day of victory into the mind of the maidens who would like nothing better than to hear the bells ring for themselves on such a wedding morning, and walk in such a procession, decked with such white robes and such orange wreaths. May they ring for every one of our girls, so that not one shall miss the love of a man but those who are unworthy.

They were married in the old church, the parish church, a mile from the town.

It is a day at the end of October, a breezy day of autumn; the clouds are driving across the sky, light clouds which leave plenty of clear blue sky and sunshine; the leaves are lying all about the old churchyard, drifting in heaps against the headstones and whirling round and round like unquiet spirits within the iron railings of the vaults; at the edge of the paupers' corner is a small new cross, quite simple, which I have not seen before. It is "In memory of Lucy, wife of Captain Richard Copleston, late of Her Majesty's Tenth Regiment of Dragoons, who died in this town in childbirth, in her twenty-first year." Poor Lucy! Poor hapless victim of a selfish and cold-hearted villain! I knew that Leonard would put up some monument to his mother's memory, but he had not told me that it was done already. Doubtless he wished it to be there before his marriage.

The churchyard is full of people waiting to see the wedding; the honest folk from Victory Row are there. I shake hands with Jem Hex and his wife and half a dozen more, who knew me in the old days of Mrs. Jeram's guardianship. They care less for the bride than for the bridegroom, these denizens of Victory Row. That a boy, so to speak, who used to run ragged about the logs on the Hard, who played on their own doorsteps, who was accustomed to fight Moses daily, and on small provocation, before the sight of all; who actually, only the other day, did not disdain to remember the old time, and cowhided Moses again at the Blue Anchor; that such a boy should have become such a man was not, of course, unexpected, because out of Victory Row have come plenty of distinguished men—though not down in books—Nelson's bulldogs, mind you, and a few of Wellington's veterans. But that he should have developed to that height of greatness as to be a real Captain in the army, and come home to marry nothing short of the daughter of the Mayor, and her a lady as beautiful as the day—that was, if you please, something quite out of the common.

Here is the Captain, marching up the walk in uniform and epaulettes, as becomes a great occasion. Fall back, good people, don't crowd the Captain. God bless the Captain! Is the Captain looking well to-day? And a happy day for him, too, if all's true that's said. Which if any credit is due to anybody for that boy turning out so well, it's due to the Captain. There was only one Captain for these people. Other persons held equal rank in the Navy, it is true; there were, for instance, Captain Luff, Captain Hardaport, Captain Bobstay—who was only a retired master with Captain's title—all living not far from Victory Row; but they had their names assigned to them as well as their titles—ours had not. The old man, pleased to see so many people gather together to do honour to him and his, stops and has a word to say to every one, and then goes on to the church, where he stands by the altar, and waits.

The Rev. John Pontifex and Mrs. Pontifex his wife. The sailor-folk know nothing of them except as residents. So they pass in the silence of respect, John Pontifex with his long-tail coat on, and a very voluminous white muffler round his neck.

The Rev. Verney Broughton. He it is who is going to marry them. Ah! quoth John Hex, and a right sort, too, as he has heard, either for a glass of wine, or for a marriage, or for a sermon. From Oxford College, he is, and once taught Master Leonard a mort o' learning which, no doubt, helped him agin them Rooshans.

Among the people, bustling here and there with importance, is the historiographer, Ferdinand Brambler, note-book in hand. He goes into the church; comes out and dashes down observations in his note-book on a tombstone; listens to the people and jots down more observations, and then, absorbed in meditations, is seen standing motionless, as if grappling for the mastery of language. This is a great day for Ferdinand.

Round the church door are all the younger members of the Brambler family, told off to strew flowers at the feet of the bride. Augustus is with them, bearing in his hands a pair of new white cotton gloves, and an air of immense dignity. These crowds, this ringing of bells, strewing of flowers, and general excitement, all attest in his eyes to the greatness and glory of the Legal. Nothing in the Scholastic, not even a prize-giving, ever came near it. All the children are dressed in new clothes, presented by the Captain, so that they may do fitting honour to the occasion.

Leonard had pressed me to be his best man, which, indeed, was my proper place. But I wanted to play the organ for Celia's marriage, and I had promised myself to play my own Love Symphony, which she alone knew. It was a fancy of mine. Forty-four, my faithful little ally and friend, begged to come with me to the organ loft.

It is after eleven, and time to go up the stairs. What are those heavy heels tramping in the aisle? They are Leonard's company, with, I believe, half the regiment, come to see Gentleman Jack married. I remembered the faces of the rogues; they were at the "Blue Anchor " that night when he thrashed Moses, and made him give me up the papers. Jem the organ-blower is in his place; Forty-four is by me to turn over the leaves. Stay one moment, Forty-four, let us look through the curtains again. There is Leonard going up the aisle. He is in uniform, as are his best men as officers of the Garrison—the young naval officer whom they call Grif, and a man of his own regiment. A brave show of scarlet and gold. His brother officers are mostly in the church, and the Colonel among them.

"There comes Uncle Ferdinand," says Forty-four. "Oh! how beautifully he will describe it! "

All are there but the bride. She is coming. Now, Forty-four, for Celia's Symphony.

The music rolls and echoes among the rafters in the roof. As I play I am a prophet, and see before me the happy years unfold their golden wings. All is as it ought to be; let those who have to sit during their lives outside the halls of human joy take pleasure in the prospect of others' happiness, and be thankful that they can at least look on.

"There is the bride," whispered Forty-four. "Oh! how lovely—oh! how sweet she looks!"

My Wedding Hymn of Prayer and Praise—listen to it, Celia—I know that you are listening—as you stand for a moment before the altar beside your lover waiting for the words to be spoken. Listen! There is no joy, says the music, given to men and women like the holy joy of love; there can be no praise too full and deep for the gift of love; there can be no prayer too eloquent for the continuance of love. Listen! it is the voice of your heart speaking in the music which rings and rolls about the pillars of the old church—I learned it reading in your heart itself—it is singing aloud to God in gratitude and praise, singing in the music where I have enshrined it and preserved it for you.

I finish my symphony, and the service begins. The words are faint and low as they mount to the organ-loft. I have pulled the curtains aside, and we watch, we three, Forty-four, Jem the organ-blower, and I, from our gallery, while Leonard holds Celia's hands in his, and they take the vow which binds them for ever to each other. You are crying, Forty-four? Foolish child.

All is over, and they have gone into the vestry. Come, we have played Celia's Symphony before the wedding, with her Hymn. Now for the March. Mendelssohn alone has reached the true triumphal rapture. His music is the exultation of the bridegroom; it is a man's song; the song of a man who bears his bride away; the song of the young men who clap their hands; the jubilant blare of cannons and trumpets which throw their music abroad to the winds that envious men may hear; and though the women cry, like foolish little Forty-four, we drown their tears with song and shout. A bridegroom's song of triumph this.

But the bride is gone, and the bridal company with her; the children have strewn their flowers upon the ground; the carriages have driven off; only the people are left; they, too, are leaving the church; in a few moments we shall be alone in the loft.

Consummatum est. Leonard has come home; Leonard has won his bride: Celia has gone from us. Shut up the organ, Forty-four; let us go down and join the wedding guests. Somehow I do not feel much like feasting.

Mr. Tyrrell was by no means the kind of man to make a mean show on this auspicious occasion. He had a marquee erected in his garden, where two tables were laid; he invited to the breakfast his whole staff of clerks with their families, including all who bore the name of Brambler—they had the second table; he would have invited all the regiment if Leonard had allowed him. As it was, there appeared a great gathering of his brother officers. No nobler wedding breakfast, Ferdinand Brambler reported, had ever before been witnessed in the town, and it reflected, he said, the greatest credit on Mr. Honeybun, the eminent local confectioner and pastrycook, who evinced on this occasion talents of an order inferior to none, not even Fortnum and Mason, the purveyors to princes. It may be mentioned that the occasion was one of which Ferdinand made four columns and a half. The wedding report ran to the butcher's bill for three whole weeks, and included a small outstanding account with the greengrocer, as Augustus himself told me. It was headed, "Wedding of the

Mayor's only Daughter," in large type, and was divided into headed sections. Thus: "The Churchyard," "Decorations of the Church," "The Organist," of whom he spoke with some reticence, for Ferdinand had feeling for my long friendship with bride and bridegroom; "The Bridegroom and his Gallant Supporters," "The Arrival of the Bride," "The Wedding," in which he gave the rein to religious feelings, and spoke of the impressive reading of Mr. Broughton, the reverent attention of those war-stained heroes, the officers of the regiment, and the tears of the bridesmaids; "The Departure," in which my own rendering of the "Wedding March" was gracefully alluded to; and, finally, "The Wedding Breakfast," in the description of which he surpassed himself, so that those who read of that magnificent feed felt hungry immediately. I do not know what reward he received of Mr. Honeybun, the confectioner, but he ought to have had free run among the tarts for life. It was not at all a solemn or a tearful meal. Mr. John Pontifex, seated well out of his wife's sight, was between two young officers, to whom he communicated recollections of his early life at Oxford, and the reckless profligacy which he had witnessed, and even—"Oh!" I heard him say, "it is a most awful event to look back upon"—participated in and encouraged. He told them the Goose story, he told how he had once fallen in love with a young person—in fact, of the opposite sex— in Oxford, and how, excepting that single experience, "Love," as he said, "has never yet, I regret to say, reached this poor—cold—heart of mine." All this was very delightful to his two hearers, and I observed the rapture with which they plied him with champagne, of which he drank immense quantities, becoming frightfully pale, and listened to his reminiscences. No doubt Mrs. Pontifex would have been greatly pleased had she been present that evening in the mess-room, and heard the reproduction of these anecdotes. It was in the ponderous manner peculiar to clergymen of his standing and scholarship, that Mr. Broughton proposed the health of the bride and bridegroom. He had known them both, he said, from infancy. There were no words at his command strong enough to express his affection for the bride, or, if he might say so as a Christian man, his envy of the bridegroom. On the other hand, for such a bride, there was none fitter than such a bridegroom. This young Achilles, having obtained from the gods a better fate than the hero to whom he likened him, had returned victorious from the wars, and won the fairest prize. They all knew Leonard Copleston's history, how the young gentleman, the son of a long line of gallant gentlemen, met adverse fortune with a resolute front, and conquered her, not with a sword, but with a bayonet; what they did not know, perhaps, was what he could tell them, as Leonard's tutor, that he had always as a boy looked on the gallant soldier as the noblest type of manhood. "We all," said Mr.

Broughton,"envy the man who fights; even the most popular priest is the priest militant: the glory of a poet or a painter is pale compared with the glory of a general; let us wish for Leonard Copleston a long career of honour and distinction, and for them both, my friends, for Leonard and Celia Copleston, let us wish that their love may endure beyond the brief moon of passion, and grow in depth as the years run on; that in fact, like the finest port, age may only develop its colour, bring out its bouquet, and mature its character."

The old Captain would not speak, though they drank his health. He had been sitting opposite to Celia, and when they said kind things about him—it was Leonard's Colonel who said them—he only got up, and with a breaking voice said that he thanked God for the happiest day in all his life.

CHAPTER LII.
CONCLUSION.

"DRAW the curtains, Mrs. Jeram; we will shut out the night, I will light the candles."

It is nearly twenty years later than Celia's wedding. Mrs. Jeram is an old woman now, and blind, but it pleases her to do little things, and to fancy that she is still housekeeper.

Everything is changed in the town. They have pulled down the old walls and levelled the moats; the Dockyard has spread itself over the place where from Celia's Arbour we looked across the harbour. All the romance went out of the place when they swept away the walls and filled up the moats; it was a cruel thing to do, but no one seemed to remonstrate, and it is done now. The Government wanted the ground, they said. There was plenty of other ground lying about, which they might have had. The Milldam is filled up, and a soldier's hospital has been built upon it; of course, the King's Mill has gone too. All the old guardhouses have been taken down; the gates are no longer shut at night; in fact, there are no more gates to shut. The harbour, too, is not what it was; they have wantonly broken up and destroyed nearly all the old historic ships, save the one where Nelson died, and she is as naked and as empty as when she first came out of dock; only a few of the venerable hulks remain, and I daresay, while I am writing these very lines, some economic Lord of the Admiralty is issuing orders for the destruction of the rest. The veterans with their wooden legs have all left the bench upon the Hard, and gone to the churchyard. The very bench is gone; steam launches run about the harbour to the detriment and loss of the boatmen; and a railway runs down to the edge of the water. No doubt the improvements were wanted, but still one regrets the past. Of course, the sailor of the present is not like the sailor of the past; that we all know, and there is little room for sorrow on that score. A new suburb has grown up behind our old wild and desolate sea-shore; it is a fine place, and we are proud of it. We are all changed together with our surroundings, and the *vie de province* is no longer what it was in the days of Mr. Broughton and the Captain. As for me, I have not changed. I am still a music-master. As I said at the beginning, you may read on my brass plate the name of "L. Pulaski, Teacher of Music and Singing." And people have quite left off the little confidential whisper, "a Pole of illustrious family—might enjoy a title if he wished." I have made a little name, not much, by certain things

I have written, especially the Symphony I wrote for Celia—the best piece I have ever done. Mrs. Jeram, as I have said, lives with me still, and talks about the old, old days. She is sitting before me now as I write. See—I leave the table, and open the piano. The tears come into her darkened eyes.

"It is the tune the Captain liked," she says.

"To be sure it is."

"'The wind that blows, and the ship that goes, And the lass that loves a sailor.'"

Almost needless to say that the old actors in the drama of my life are all dead.

The first to go was Mrs. Pontifex. She was, in her way, fond of me, and I should have been guilty of ingratitude if, in return, I had not conceived a respect for her. As I think of her, so gaunt, so unbending in principles and shoulders, so upright in morals and in backbone, so unyielding in doctrine and in muffins, I wonder if I am already only forty, since she has left no one like her, and her race is extinct. She died of a cold caught through her adherence to one of her Christian privileges—never to light a fire in her sitting-rooms till November.

It was in 1860, a year about which I remember nothing except that it rained from June to October without stopping, and a wag announced in Punch that there would be no summer that year because the Zodiac was taken up for repairs. We all laughed at that, and then some of us began to reflect with shame, and especially those who had been educated by the Rev. Verney Broughton, that very likely it was true, and that certainly we had no sort of idea what the Zodiac was.

At the end of that continuous rain, then, Mrs. Pontifex died, and was gathered to her forefathers. A fortnight after I called on her husband. He was gardening, looking, as he stooped with his long thin figure over the plants, very much like a letter of the Hebrew Alphabet.

He was weeding the strawberry bed—the strawberries that year, by reason of the long rains, had been like turnips for size and taste. He rose when he heard my footsteps, and shook his head solemnly. In either hand he held an apple. It struck me that this was the first proof of recovered liberty, as in his wife's time he had never been allowed to eat any fruit at all. The prohibition, based on hygienic reasons, always appeared to me to have been issued because John Pontifex was particularly fond of fruit.

"I mourn not, Johnnie," he said, taking a bite out of the right-hand apple; "I mourn not for her who is departed. Rather," he added, with emphasis, biting into the left-hand apple, "I rejoice— ahem—with exceeding great joy." Whether he rejoiced because she was gone, or because of an assurance of her future, did not appear on the face of his statement. What he added was more obscure still. "Next year," he said, with a noise which might have been a sob and might have been a chuckle, "next year I shall have all those—ahem—those apples and strawberries to myself, Johnnie."

Shortly after this conversation he entertained at dinner the Rev. Mr. Broughton, the Captain, and myself. It is noteworthy that the "beverage " of which his wife would never allow him to partake was on this occasion, and many subsequent occasions, freely produced. In fact, I should say, from recollection only, that he and his brother clergyman despatched a bottle and a half each. It was orthodox Port, but indubitably inferior to that possessed by the Perpetual Curate of St. Faith's.

One thing pleased Mr. Pontifex mightily to relate at that dinner. An unfortunate curate, enthusiastic, but young, had the Sunday before preached a discourse in which his rev. senior fancied he saw glimpses of Tractarianism. So he waited till the misguided youth came out of the vestry, and then said to him, before the church-wardens and a small gathering of friends.

"Well, that was—ahem—a most infamous sermon of yours."

And then he walked away, leaving the poor young man to seek such explanations and apologies as he pleased.

"The Tractarians," he said to-night, after the first bottle had brought up the natural pallor of his cheek to a ghastly whiteness, "the Tractarians may use their arguments as they please, but to me they fall off as water from the back of the—ahem—the proverbial duck, though I have never yet, I confess, poured anything but gravy upon the back of that— ahem— toothsome delicacy, and therefore am not in a position to assert that water actually does run off their backs."

"The Tractarians," said the Perpetual Curate, whose face was quite purple, "are the Actarians. They are up and doing. They will make a clear sweep of pastors like me and idle shepherds like you, Brother Pontifex."

And now they are both gone, and the Perpetual Curate's prophecy has come true, and the Church has been reformed, with, of course, a small gathering of the foolish who want to go on beyond the bounds of reason. Such a service as I knew at St. Faith's would be impossible now even in the sleepiest City church. The duet between the Parson and the Clerk has ceased, the choir is trained, the hymns are improved, and the people are attentive. Speaking as a musician, I do not find the change altogether for the best. I miss the old melancholy hymns of Wesleyan origin which we used to sing. It seems to me that life is sad; the note of rapture at which we strike so many of the new hymns is strained and unreal. We are still too much like the poor little charity children of my youth, when, after the three long services of the day, through which they had been cuffed and caned into attention, they had to sing as a concluding or parting hymn—

"Oh! may our earthly Sabbaths prove A foretaste of our joys above."

I find, but then I am only a humble organist in a country town, and never go about in the world, but for myself I find too much elation, too much joy, to suit the grey tints and sombre colours of the working and sorrowing world.

Mr. Pontifex, the type of the old high-and-dry Calvinist, whose life was as strait-laced as his doctrine, with whom laughter was a sin, and every innocent recreation an occasion for repentance, is gone, and his place knows him no more.

Mr. Broughton, the jolly old parson of the high-and-dry Church type, who enjoyed all that can be enjoyed by a scholar and a Christian in the world, strong in his firm and undoubting belief that the doctrines of the Church, faithfully held, avail unto justification, has gone too. We have none like him now. I am not a theologian, and, in Church matters, doubtless a fool. Nevertheless, I venture to say that I regret and mourn his loss. He was not only a gentleman—there are plenty of gentlemen still in the Church—he was not only a man of pure life and benevolent conduct, but he was a scholar. And I look in vain for scholars—*rari nantes in gurgite vasto*—in these later days. Here one, there one; but, ah! the old Greek scholar, massive and critical, is no longer to be found even among the sleeves of lawn; such scholars as we have mostly run to history—a study which Mr. Broughton held to be vain and illusory, except when it was the History of the Chosen People—and as regards all but modern history, fruitless, because history, he thought, repeats itself, and everything new has all been done before.

"We have Hume," he used to say; "we have Gibbon; we have Robertson; and we have the grand histories in Greek and Latin of the days when men were great. What more can one want? Let us sit down and read them; let us teach the boys to read them; and let us leave to restless witlings the task of labouring in a worn-out field."

Restless witlings! Dear me! Suppose Mr. Broughton had lived to the present day!

Others have passed away who twenty years ago took part in the drama that I have tried, with pen unpractised, to relate. The two brothers Brambler sleep side by side in the new cemetery, cut off in their vigour, Ferdinand from a cold caught while in the excess of his zeal noting the incidents of a review during a hail-storm; Augustus from a sort of grief consumption which seized him at the death of his brother. He "never joyed after;" and though on Sunday afternoons he still maintained the imaginary state and splendour of a "gentleman sitting over his wine" at the front window, it was a performance which brought him no pleasure but that of mournful reminiscence. And so he drooped and died, trusting that he would be remembered by posterity for his services in the Legal.

Friends there were who took charge of the little ones, from Forty-four to Fifty-three. And they all did well. My especial friend, Forty-four, is married, and has a row of children like herself, as apple-faced, as cheery, and as sanguine. I hope they will do better than their grandfather. She is good enough to maintain her old friendship towards myself, undiminished by the love she bears her husband and her offspring, and confides to me all her joys and sorrows.

Let me pass to the last scene of my story.

After Celia married, and the regiment went away, the good old Captain began to droop. He was nearly seventy years of age, it is true, but I thought he was hale and hearty—good for ten years more.

That was not so. Age crept upon him with stealth, but with swiftness. He still went out every morning, but his afternoon walks were gradually shortened, and finally had to be dropped altogether.

Then his friends began to call in the evening to talk to, and cheer up, the old man. Mr. Broughton would come with a story and anecdote of bygone days; one or two old naval men, chums of his youth, would drop in for a glass of grog and a yarn; we became hospitable, and kept open house. And all went well, in spite of increasing weakness, until one day it became apparent that the old man could not go out to make his morning round.

Then, for the first time, I learned from him, though I had long known it, what the morning round had been, for more than twenty years.

He sat feebly in his arm-chair, patient under the inevitable. Nothing was wrong with him, but the weakness of extreme old age. His mind was bright and clear, as the last runnings of a cask of some noble vintage; but on this morning he realised that he must not think of going out any more, as he had been wont, in fair weather and foul. A cold east wind blew down the street, and a bright sun shone without warmth from a steel-blue sky.

"The end is growing near, Laddy," he said. "They will miss me when I am gone."

"Who, sir?" I asked.

He was silent for a space, thinking.

"To all of us," he said, "the Lord giveth His gifts in trust. To me He gave, besides Her Majesty's pension of two hundred pounds a-year, a private fortune. No need to talk about it to you, Laddy, or to Leonard. It was not a great fortune, only this house and a hundred pounds a-year, which my father saved up out of his pay. It was in the old prize days."

I began to understand.

"So long as you and Leonard were boys," the Captain went on, "we had the pension to live upon. Plenty for us all. And there was the hundred a-year for which I was a trustee, you know. When you began to make an income the pension became part of the trust—"

"Of course, sir, I quite see that."

"That made three hundred a-year. A good deal ought to be done with such a sum. I doubt whether I have done the best—but I have tried—I have tried. If a man tries to do his duty—he may be stupid—but if he tries, the Chief knows. You will find out, when I am gone, how far I have done the best, Laddy. It will be yours, the hundred a-year and the house; you will use it, my boy, as you think best—not to follow up my lines, unless you think that the best way, but as a trust from the Lord, unless your income fails, when it will keep you from want. No, Laddy, no need to promise. We have not lived together for five-and-twenty years for me to begin distrusting. But, if you can, look after them, my boy. They are ignorant; they have no friends; they are degraded; you will meet at first with all sorts of insult and disappointment: but go on, never leave them; and you will end, as I have done, by winning their confidence."

I did not ask him who "they" were, partly because I guessed. The old seaport town had dens of wickedness in it of which I have said nothing. Indeed, as children, though we went daily through the streets which reeked with every abominable thing, we saw and knew nothing—how should we? It is the blessed prerogative of innocence that it plays unhurt in the den of wild beasts, rides upon the lion, and walks scatheless among the rabble rout of Comus.

All that morning the Captain sat in disquiet. The current of his daily thoughts was interrupted. After our mid-day dinner, he refused his pipe of tobacco and sat in the window, gazing silently upon the Milldam pool, crisped by the cold east wind. His work was over; nothing more for him to do but to sit in the chair and wait for the end. That must be a solemn moment in a man's life, when he realises that everything is finished. The record complete, the book of work shut up, and after all attempted and achieved, the inevitable feeling of unprofitable service.

Two days passed; the east wind continued, and grew colder; there was no hint at any possibility of going out; and on the third day there came, creeping stealthily, a deputation consisting of two women, to ask after the Captain. They stood shame-faced at the door, and when I asked them to enter and see him, they hesitated and looked at each other. Then they came in, looking strange and abashed. I took them to the Captain, where he sat in his arm-chair, and left them with him. Presently, sitting in the other room, I heard sobs and cries.

Afterwards others came, not always outcasts: old greybeards who had been sailors, some of the wooden-legged veterans whom I remembered as a boy, aged women, their wives and widows, even young fellows, sailors themselves, their sons and grandsons. Among them all, one woman who came oftenest and stayed the longest. I remembered her as the black-haired fury who, as Leonard had reminded me, came one evening and made the night air horrible with imprecations. Now she was subdued, now she sat as long as we would let her, silent and gazing with her black and deep-set eyes in the old man's face. It matters nothing about her history, which may be guessed—there is a dreadful similarity about these stories: an emotional, impulsive woman who loved and hated, sinned and repented, with the same ardour and vehemence; who believed in the Captain, whose patience she had sorely tried, as one believes a Gospel. He was her Gospel.

The end came more quickly than we expected. One morning I saw a change, and telegraphed for Leonard and Celia to come quickly. The Captain knew, I think, that his last day had dawned, for he asked me when we had dressed him if I would send for "the boy" and Celia.

They could not arrive before the afternoon. We allowed no one to see him except the one who would not be denied, and she sat crouched in a corner of the room, her arms round her knees, looking at the feeble figure in the arm-chair.

The Captain spoke little, he suffered no pain, he was perfectly cheerful.

"Do you think they will come in time, Laddy?" he asked. "I should like to see them before I go."

Presently he slept, and so passed away the morning unconsciously, the black eyes of the woman watching him from the corner. Outside there were gathered knots of twos and threes, the women, the old salts, the outcasts, waiting sadly for news.

Leonard and Celia came at last. The old man woke as he heard "the boy's" voice, and eagerly held out his hand.

"Don't cry, my pretty. Don't cry, Celia, my dear," he whispered. "To every man his turn, and then we separate for a while—a little while, Celia, and then we shall all be together—you and Leonard and Laddy and I—all together, dear. Never to part again."

He was growing weaker every moment. I gave him a little wine. As Celia knelt at his feet and laid her head upon his right hand, the other woman, as if jealous, crept stealthily from her corner and seized the left. The Captain looked down on both, turned from one to the other, and then, disengaging his hands, laid one on either head, as if with a solemn blessing, equal alike for Martha or for Magdalene.

"Laddy," he murmured," put on my uniform, coat, and cap, and give me my sword."

It was his fancy that he would die in the uniform of which he was so proud. We dressed him in the coat and epaulettes; we pinned on his medals, we laid his sword across his knees, and we placed his undress cap upon his head. And then we stood round him in tearful silence.

Presently a shiver ran through his limbs.

"Leonard"—his voice was very low now—"take the sword. It is all I leave you. God bless you, Leonard—Laddy—Celia—and you—" His hand felt out as if for the poor woman, who threw herself forward with sobs and passionate crying.

And then a strange thing happened. His voice, which had been sinking to a faint murmur, suddenly grew full again and strong. He lifted his figure and sat upright. His eyes flashed with a sudden light as he raised his voice and looked upwards. He lifted his right hand to the peak of his cap—the old familiar salute of a sailor—as he reported himself—

"Come aboard, sir!"

Then his hand dropped and his head fell forward. The Captain was dead.

. . . .

We buried him in the old parish churchyard, a mile from the town. Leonard's mother lay there, somewhere among the paupers; Wassielewski slept there in peace, Poland at last forgotten: Wassielewski's victim lay there too. The brand-new cemetery, which they opened a year or so later, would have been no fitting place for the remains of one who in death, as well as in life, should be among his fellow-men. And in that great heap of bones, coffins and human dust, piled five feet above the level of the road, we laid the Captain. It was not without a certain fitness that his grave lay next to the Paupers' Acre. When the great Resurrection shall take place the Captain shall lift his head with the ignoble and unknown herd for whom he gave his substance, and march along with them to that merciful Judge who knows the secret of every heart.

While we were yet half a mile from the church the funeral procession was stopped. There was a crowd of old sailors and people of every degree, but chiefly of the lowest; some of them stopped the hearse, and others, opening the doors of the carriages, invited the occupants to descend. We complied wondering. They quickly formed themselves into procession. First went the old tars, two and two, stumping on wooden legs; then came a band, then the coffin borne on the shoulders of sailors, sons of those who marched first; on the pall were the Captain's cocked hat and his sword, and then we, the mourners, fell in.

The big drum, muffled, gives the signal—boum—boum!

How many times before had that March from Saul awakened my soul to the glory and mystery of death; the knell of warning, the wail of sorrow, the upward cry of yearning faith—and now I can never hear it without my thoughts flying back to the old man before whose honoured remains a grateful and lamenting folk did this reverence.

Boum—boum—boum! A man who loved his fellow-men is dead. He will bring no more words of counsel, no more exhortations to duty—no more comfort for the afflicted, no more solace for the outcast. Boum—boum—boum! Wail and weep, clarions, with us whose hearts are sore. Boum—boum—boum! And yet it is but for a season. Change, oh music inspired of God, the souls of those who mourn till they become the souls of those who trust.

We are at the lych-gate. Mr. Broughton—none other—waits to read the service.

"I am the Resurrection and the Life "

From every lane and court, from every ship in harbour, from every street, the mourners are gathered together: in the presence of Death, in the graveyard, in the hopes of immortality, we are all equal; all brothers and sisters. The women weep aloud; there is not one who is unrepentant now; the tears run down the faces of the grizzled men who are standing by the grave of their brave and single-hearted old officer; none in all the world to harbour an evil thought, to raise an accusing word, against the man of seventy summers who lies in yon black coffin. Throw flowers upon him; pile the lid with flowers, with every flower a tear. The flowers will be crushed and killed by the cold clay, but the memory of the Captain shall be green.

And of all the mourners around that grave there were none—there could be none—who mourned the Captain more deeply, who loved him better, who owed him more than the two boys whom he had picked from the very gutter, to bring them up in the fear of God and the sense of duty.

When Mr. Broughton came to certain words in the service his voice fell, and his speech was choked for a moment. Then he cleared his throat, and looking round upon the folk, read out in clear and triumphant tones, as if the words should at once bring admonition, as well as joy and consolation and hope for us all—

"In sure and certain hope of the Resurrection to Eternal Life."

THE END.

Lightning Source UK Ltd.
Milton Keynes UK
UKHW022133280421
382787UK00010B/2328

9 780957 241374